D1174836

"The last word of Mary E. Mitchell's *Starting Out Sideways* is 'delicious,' and for good reason. Her novel is delectable from start to finish."
—Susan Quinn, author of *A Mind of Her Own*, *Marie Curie*, and *Human Trials*

"I don't know when I've read a book whose protagonist is as beset by heartache and worries as Rosie Plow, and yet manages to deliver such mirth and comfort. Mary E. Mitchell knows how to laugh at problems without minimizing them, and how to honor hard times without losing sight of a brighter picture. She has written a novel that is a rollicking pleasure, jam-packed with twists, and, above all, brimming with warmth."
—Leah Hager Cohen, author of *Heart, You Bully, You Punk*, and *House Lights*

starting out sideways

mary e. mitchell

starting out sideways

Thomas Dunne Books
St. Martin's Press
New York

≈

THOMAS DUNNE BOOKS.
An imprint of St. Martin's Press.

www.thomasdunnebooks.com
www.stmartins.com

Book design by Stephanie Huntwork

Library of Congress Cataloging-in-Publication Data

Mitchell, Mary E., 1951–
    Starting out sideways / Mary E. Mitchell.—1st ed.
        p. cm.
    ISBN-13: 978-0-312-36821-0
    ISBN-10: 0-312-36821-6
    1. Self-realization in women—Fiction.   2. Marriage—Fiction.
3. Family—Fiction.   I. Title.

PS3613.I8596 S73 2007
813'.54—dc22

                                                        2007008925

First Edition: May 2007

10 9 8 7 6 5 4 3 2 1

For Ross

Starting Out Sideways is a work of fiction. All of the characters in the book are products of my imagination and not based on any person, living or dead. Any resemblance to real people, therefore, is entirely coincidental. The SaveWay supermarket, where much of the story takes place, is also not based on any store with a similar or even matching name, and no store has been involved with or endorsed this book. Finally, while I found *Cosmopolitan* to be the perfect magazine for my character to devour, I have fictionalized the content of the magazine as well as my character's reaction to it. There is no relationship between *Cosmo* and me or my publisher, but I did have fun reading it.

ACKNOWLEDGMENTS

I would like to thank my agent, Sally Ryder Brady, for her endless encouragement and relentless belief in me and my work. I am honored to work with Erin Brown, my editor, who has taught me so much and infused me with her unique brand of passion for the written word. I am most grateful to Angela Gerst and Mike Scott, who have read every word of this novel and guided me along with their wisdom and suggestions. Thank you, Donna and Martin Moore-Ede, for fueling me with your confidence. To my brilliant writer friends at Two Bridges Writers' Group, you have my gratitude for your support and encouragement. I thank Melissa Mitchell and Elena Gonzalez for their careful reading and spot-on editing of the book's first draft. It is nice to think of a world with these young adults in it.

Thank you to my cousin Ellen Powers, who offered to dress me for my readings long before an editor ever saw this novel, and to my cousin Marie Hautigan, a fine writer herself, whose enthusiasm for my work has kept me afloat for years. Thanks also to Judi DeCew for reading my manuscripts over and over again with the pride of a big sister. Hugs to my sisters, Betty Barker and Josie Muccio, who make me so proud of Long Island girls. Bless you, Elayne King, for being my best friend, and thank you to my two moms, Dot Fussa and Anita Berman, for always knowing your daughter could write a novel.

I would be nowhere in life, on or off a page, without my wonderful, loving family. Joe, Melissa, and Ross, you will never know how much I love you.

who's a putz?

my name is Roseanna Plow, and I came down the birth canal sideways. All my life, this is the way my mother has introduced me to strangers. She's never described my birth with malice, only with wonder. It is the wonder of my mother's life that when I left her womb, some thirty-two years ago, I made the decision to enter this world broadside, oblivious of the discomfort this might cause her, my benevolent baker, my main sponsor. My mother would hug me hard to her curvy side as she explained my arrival once more for new ears.

"She came down the canal sideways," she'd tell the surprised listener, and I'd feel the pokey bone of her hip against my cheek and imagine myself arriving on Long Island on some sort of gondola, no one at the helm, the boat floating sideways, smashing into everything else in the narrow channel. Always there was a beat of silence when my mother finished describing the event, as if she were waiting for the school nurse, the new neighbor, my first grade teacher to offer some reason why I might have chosen to do this.

Sideways down the canal. It is an apt metaphor for the many collisions I've had in my life—the constant clashing of horns with my mother, my now-deteriorating marriage to my husband, Teddy, which my mother had anticipated ("Marry someone respectable," she had said, when she showed me the navy blue pantsuit she planned to wear at my wedding, "and I'll consider wearing a dress to the church."), the way I'd upset my father during college by shortening my name from Pulkowski to Plow. Last week, my husband sat me down at our kitchen table and told me in a calm voice that he was in love with another woman. Not just any woman, he explained, but my best friend, Inga. Then, as if in compliance with my mother's prediction of his worthlessness, he packed a bag and walked out.

My mother is coming across town for dinner tonight, my first guest since Teddy's departure. She is coming alone, leaving my father at home with his pot roast and his beer. She is planning, I suppose, one of those woman-to-woman talks I've gotten used to now. On the stove in my small apartment's kitchen, I'm simmering a nice spaghetti sauce. It's my mother-in-law's recipe, of which my mother will undoubtedly disapprove.

Just the same, I'm glad for her company. It's been eight days and three hours since Teddy packed the small Champion gym bag—tenderly tucking his iPod in last—and left our apartment. In that time I've imagined him in the arms of my best friend, Inga. I've imagined them in her bed, in her bedroom, which I've seen a thousand times. The patchwork quilt made by her grandmother. The white wicker shade on the bedside lamp. The prim smell of lavender emanating from her drawers and closet. There is a little wooden plaque, which hangs between her closet doors. I gave it to Inga on her thirtieth birthday. THE *F* IN FRIEND MEANS FOREVER, it says. Now at night, when my wine bottle is almost empty, when the last chocolate chip cookie is eaten, when I've cried as much as my body allows, the plaque seems funny to me. Inga, my F'in-friend.

"I never liked that lantern jaw," my mother grumbled on the phone, when she'd gotten the gist of how it was that Teddy had left me. I could feel her fidgeting on the other end, one hand buried deep in the pocket of her pleated brown slacks, the other squeezing the receiver. "That broad needs a good shot in the head," she said. So rough my mother can be, like a moll in the Rat Pack. I wondered what my father was thinking as she said this.

After I'd shaved all those letters off my last name, my father stopped talking to me for a while. My mother never had the same problem.

"Plow," she sniffed the day I first breathed my new name into the dormitory phone. "Why not Steamroller instead of Plow, for the way you've run over your father's heart?"

"Ma," I pleaded, but a cold silence whistled back at me through the wire. I could read her thoughts. Sideways, she was thinking. Everything half-assed and sideways.

She has a mouth like a sailor, my mother. She's tough, despite her slender body and pixieish face. She's Donna Reed on drugs, Shirley Partridge with an attitude. She was forty-two when I was born. She's seventy-four now and she still smokes. While my friends were having their nice seventies and eighties childhoods, I grew up in a fifties nightmare, with tuna casseroles and Jell-O molds where suspended things floated, with a mother who believed that Kraft Miracle Whip could be used in anything. Back in the fifties, according to my Aunt Sophie, my mother used to open doors for men. Heavy glass bank doors, reception hall doors, the doors to the train station. She would swing them open violently with one thin arm, staring down boxy men in their thick-lapelled suits and ordering them through with a little half smile. "Go 'head through," she'd tell the men, and they went. They felt her eyes on their backs as they walked ahead of her. We all do.

My mother stopped sending me care packages after I changed my name to Plow. No more home-baked cookies and Tetley tea bags. No more crackers with orange cheese that squirted like shaving cream from a can. She was outraged when the college sent home word of Roseanna Plow's making dean's list. My 3.8 grade point average meant nothing to her. She saw only the missing vowels and consonants. The next time I went home, I found my dean's list certificate tacked up over my father's workbench. Someone had put little carets between the letters of my truncated name, adding the *u* and the *k* and the *ski*.

I knew it was my mother. I was eighteen at the time and a little chubby and I stood in the garage and saw how I hadn't worked out for her, how she'd wanted me to be everything she wasn't—better educated and yet submissive. It was a puzzling paradox, considering how I'd been raised by this strong, proud woman, a woman men didn't fuck with, even back in the fifties.

My mother calls my father Pulkowski, as in: "Pulkowski, crack me open a beer," and "Come over here and light my cigarette, Pulkowski," and "Pulkowski! Put the kid to bed and watch the ball game with me." Never an ounce of Cinderella in her, ever. How I wish I'd been a bit more like her this past terrible year of my marriage, where Teddy's back has been a cold marble wall dividing our bed in two.

Even when my parents dressed up for a party, my mother smothering us in her cloud of Evening in Paris, wearing her wide, full-skirted bowling dance dress and her string of pearls and her red lipstick, even then, she'd wink at my father in his good suit and say, "Nice threads, Pulkowski. Now help me with this goddamn zipper." How I wish I could have ordered Teddy around with the same confidence! *Hold me in your arms, Stracuzza! Kiss me, goddamn you!*

The way my mother talks to my father dazzles me still and makes me jealous. The way he responds is the main reason I changed my name from Pulkowski to Plow. When I left home and heard my name aloud in other people's mouths, I felt like my father being pushed around by Helen Pulkowski. I'd hear someone say "Pulkowski" and there was my mother, cigarette dangling between her thin red lips, eyes twinkling seductively at her man. No article in *Cosmo* has ever, remotely, suggested my mother's techniques for seducing a man.

At ten to seven, as I'm seasoning my sauce, I listen for the sounds of my mother's arrival. First the click of my unlocked door opening, then the soft flopping of her jacket over the back of the couch. She's arrived early, as she tends to do when she deems an event formal. She sighs, clears her throat, and finally calls her greeting.

"Good evening, Madame Butterfly."

"I'm in the kitchen," I call from my steamy little corner, but my mother's footsteps recede instead of moving closer. She's heading for my bedroom. She'll peek through there, open a few closets, maybe go through the medicine chest, searching for confirmation of Teddy's departure.

Soon enough she's standing beside me with her thin wrists crossed, a cigarette caught between the fingers of one hand. She's wearing a crisply ironed oxford shirt and blue polyester slacks. She's studying me, looking for signs of damage.

"Hi, Ma," I say, looking up from the sauce. She nods once, like a store clerk. I feel her heated thoughts. That bastard better not have damaged her little girl. She'll give him such a lump. I swirl my spoon around and around in the sauce, my wrist moving like I'm rowing a boat.

"What's the matter? You nervous?" she says. "Give me the spoon, before you scrape a hole in the bottom of the pot."

She slips her cigarette into one side of her mouth before she pulls the wooden spoon away from me.

"Move," she says, knocking me lightly with her hip from my spot in front of the stove. Her Salem Light dangles over our dinner.

"Ma, your ashes . . . ," I warn.

"Yeah, yeah, my ashes." She stares into the sauce. "Let me just tell you something, Miss Ashes. There's no shame in your husband leaving if he was a nudnik to begin with."

"Ma!" I say, grabbing the spoon back from her. We can only talk if we're stirring. "You never gave him a chance," I tell the sauce.

My mother snorts a little, stretches her open hands in front of her. "Teddy's a putz," she explains calmly. "And now he's left you. Case closed."

I squeeze the spoon so tight my knuckles crack. Something about my Yiddish-speaking Catholic mother decreeing my husband a putz reminds me of another time. When I was a kid, she used to load me into the Plymouth station wagon and drag me off to Bascome Brothers Photographic Studio for an annual portrait. Mr. Bascome would seat me on a little mound of beige carpeting and then pull down screens behind me that looked like window shades with pictures on them. One moment, I was posed beneath the boughs of a cherry blossom tree. Then—a tug again—and there was a Christmas tree over my shoulder, a fireplace to my left. One last pull and I was floating in azure blue clouds, as if I'd died and Mr. Bascome was photographing me now up in heaven. I'd feel goose bumps each time his hairy wrist reached above my head and changed my world. This is what my mother did with her short, snitty proclamations, spelling out my life in her singular opinions.

"Ma," I say, still stirring wildly, sauce spilling over the sides of the pan, sizzling onto the range. "You don't understand anything."

"I understand this," she says, grabbing the spoon and pointing it at some imaginary chart that hangs above us. "Even Oprah doesn't bother wasting an hour on 'My husband left me for my best friend' anymore. It's that predictable! It's that uninteresting! It's so"—my mother is pointing the spoon at me now—"*beneath* you, Rosie! You went to college! You were on the dean's list!" The sauce plops on my white tile floor like perfect drops of blood. "Your problems should be more *educated* than some putz leaving you for a bottle blonde."

"Ma! Put the spoon down!" I shriek, wrestling the spoon

from her, using hold techniques I've learned in my work for keeping the autistic safe. I take a deep breath, try to restore calm in the room. "Everything isn't about TV!" I cry. "I'm sorry my problems aren't trendier, but did it ever occur to you that this separation might just be temporary?"

"Please!" my mother snorts, and a cloud of smoke, or maybe steam, exits her mouth.

"Ma!" I yell, waving the dripping sauce spoon like a baton. "The point is you don't know *enough*! You can't call Teddy a putz if you don't know enough! He's *my* husband. It's *my* marriage. *I* decide who the putzes are. *I* decide."

I drop the spoon, reach above the stove into the cupboard, and start pulling out dishes. My mother is uncharacteristically silent beside me. I'm pulling out the salad bowl when I feel her fingers gently pinching the exposed flesh at my waist. "Hmm," she muses, "most women *lose* weight when their husbands leave."

"Ma!" I whirl around, slamming the bowl down too hard on the countertop.

"Hey," she says. "Hey, hey, hey." She pats me gently on my cheek. "It's only a few pounds." She runs her fingers through a thick tangle of my long hair.

"You're a beautiful girl, my Rosie," she croons. "Look at you, with your father's gorgeous chestnut hair." She flicks her cigarette into the sink. I take a step back from her, give her my chilliest look.

"I can't believe you are evaluating my life on an Oprah scale."

"It's not on the Jerry Springer scale, that's for sure, since you've never hauled off and walloped the putz. Which I have wanted to do about a hundred times . . ."

"Enough!" I announce, running cold water over her cigarette butt. "We're eating dinner now."

Something about my proclamation silences her. "May I set the salad bowls?" my mother asks sweetly.

We eat my mother-in-law's spaghetti sauce in silence. After dinner, when my mother finally leaves for her 10.29-mile drive back to Commack, down the Veterans Highway, then a little ways west on Jericho Turnpike, I sit at the table and stare at the salt shaker. My mother is right, of course. Teddy *is* a putz. But he is the putz I married, four and half years ago. And marriage is a sacred thing. Even my mother believes this. I head for the refrigerator and uncork a half-full bottle of Pinot Noir. Is it really so wrong to try to work things out with my own husband? I pour myself a nightcap, then pull out the Chips Ahoy! from the cupboard. Helen Pulkowski, of all people, should appreciate the sanctity of marriage.

I'm scrubbing sauce off the range when I discover the wine bottle is empty. I double bolt the door and settle myself on the couch. I plump up the cushions before moving into the corner, shoes off, feet tucked beneath me like a sunbathing cat. I hum a little—the way I do when I'm sort of loaded. I lift the phone receiver: white, lightweight, shaped like a bar of soap. I inhale deeply, exhale, and punch in the number. Eleven merry tones. The phone rings once, twice, and when I hear someone picking up, I almost slam down the receiver. But then I don't. Why should I? Who would wish to hurt me? My best friend? My husband? Of course not. A second later, a female voice is speaking.

"Hello?"

It's Inga. I recognize her slightly whiny voice, the Olive Oyl tones that used to make Teddy and me laugh. *Oh! Popeye!* we'd whisper, behind Inga's back, then zip our lips again when she turned around. I hear myself giggling.

"Hi. This is Roseanna," I say, trying to control myself.

There is not a sound from the other end.

"Roseanna Plow," I say.

Now Inga gives a little sigh.

"Formerly Pulkowski," I go on. "Now Mrs. Stracuzza," I hiss. "Are there any other Stracuzzas around I might actually speak to?" I laugh merrily, like all of this is just good fun. I do this for Inga, my last little gift to her.

"Roseanna," she says, "it's ten o'clock."

"Thank you," I tell her, "for that update."

"Roseanna," she says, "it's *late*."

I squeeze the phone as if to throttle it.

"Get him."

The phone clunks down like it's been thrown. I rub my arm as though I've been bruised. Someone's put a hand over the receiver, so that they can talk about me without my listening. This is what they did the last time I called. This is how they treat me. So why have I called again? What is the *pretense*, I mean. I know I've called because my mother has planted this image in my mind of Teddy as putz, and I'm anxious to be rid of it. But how could a phone call help? Teddy *is* a putz. I slap my face lightly with my free hand. Focus! What was the *bogus* reason for this call? Teddy picks up the phone just as I remember.

"Yes?" he says, his voice so formal that I glance down at myself to see if I'm completely dressed. "It's ten o'clock," he continues.

"Your adulteress has pointed this out to me."

Coldness billows out of the little holes in my earpiece. I squeeze a mauve couch cushion, try again.

"I'm just calling to let you know that our Visa bill's come in." (I love using this word *our* when I know she's standing beside him, maybe even listening with her ear pressed to the phone and her cheek brushing his.) I continue: "You know those sheets we bought for our bed at Macy's last month?"

"Sheets *you* bought," he corrects.

"For *our* bed," I point out.

"Roseanna," he sighs, "you'd better start paying off the credit card expenses that are yours. Because I must inform you, I'm closing those accounts. Visa, American Express, Discover . . . there's another one, isn't there?" He's silent for a second. "Yeah. First Bank MasterCard."

"You're *closing* them?" I say. "What do you mean, you're closing them? You can't just *close* things . . ."

"Roseanna, those are my cards. You can get your own cards. You have your own income."

He is referring to my work as a job counselor for the developmentally challenged and other handicapped workers. I'm surprised. He's never thought of my work as much of an income, not to mention a career, in the past. Moron management is what he'd called it during one awful fight. Still, the money's been steady, and Teddy hasn't turned away a cent of it. And we've always shared the cards, all of them in his name, all of them half-paid off by me.

"Teddy," I say. "Be reasonable." My heart is squeezing like a sponge. "We're married," I say. "We've got stuff together. Bank accounts. Cars. Sheets." I'm reciting the meat of our married life as though it's a shopping list. "Now, I know you and Inga are having this . . . *thing* . . . right now, but we can't start dividing up our lives all of a sudden. We have to *talk*. . . . "

I hear what I have just said and it stops me momentarily. Even through the haze of grapes, I realize how pathetic I sound. I am drunk-dialing a man who's left me for my best friend. I sit up straighter, determined to end this unfortunate phone call immediately.

"Roseanna," Teddy says before I can do this. "There's something I think you ought to know. Inga and I are buying a house."

Little bursts of light, like popping flashcubes, dance before my eyes. A house? Has he gone mad? He *has* a house, which I am sitting in right now. *This* is our house, or, at least our apartment. It's the one we'll move out of when we buy our own house, after Teddy makes partner at his law firm and I get pregnant. He's promised me this, he's *promised* me.

"A house?" I manage. Teddy is silent. I gaze around the empty living room, where everything is suddenly pink. The window, the door, everything. The inside of my brain is pink.

"A house!" I scream. "You can't buy a house with Inga! You live *here*, in this apartment. You have a wife . . ."

"Roseanna," he says firmly. "I will speak to you again when you can be civil."

Clunk! goes the phone, and I yell, "Goddamn you, Stracuzza!" I yell it so loud, I think I see the individual fibers of my carpet shaking. But he doesn't hear me; he's hung up. Just like a putz.

slightly beautiful

my dear girl," my mother says the next morning on the phone. "My life hasn't been all violin music and veal Parmesan, either." This is either my mother's idea of a pep talk or she is trying to make up with me, after calling my marriage sub-Jerry Springer. I have often wondered why she never had a second child, someone else whose life she could ruin.

"No news from the prodigal son, then?"

I picture her sitting in her antiseptically neat living room where everything's beige—beige walls, beige carpeting, beige slipcovers—her coffee cup and ashtray beside her on the pinewood TV tray. Beige is the best base, my mother often offers. Nothing is loud in its presence; nothing clashes against it. I cannot to this day wear normal shades of pantyhose.

As a child, I used to dream in primary colors to ward off all the beigeness that surrounded me. Even now, when I find myself in someone else's home where the decor moves me, I pull out the memo pad I hide in my purse and list the attributes that keep the house from beigeness. *Black kitchen appliances,* I write, *make a bolder statement! Fruit in bowl: add tomatoes for color. Coffee table book: magenta.* More than once when I've gotten home, I've adjusted my rooms according to these lists. Sometimes Teddy notices and is pleased, as with the time I replaced our shower curtain with a plastic map of the world. Now I could see him as he showered, scrubbing his armpits with Canada across his chest, the continent of South America tactfully covering his genitals. I was happy when my husband commented on my little touches. It made me feel like his good wife. There are so many things a woman must do to be successful in the home. My mother has told me this all my life.

I hear her television going. Her mind is half on *Good Morning America* and half on me, her unhappy daughter, who is waking up again in an empty bed, getting herself ready to go and teach the "retards," as she calls them, to bag groceries at the Ronkonkoma SaveWay.

"Dinner was lovely last night," my mother sings. "Pulkowski was sorry he didn't join us."

I don't respond to this, because I don't really think my father wanted to come to dinner. If he'd come to dinner, he would have had to speak. My father probably hasn't spoken a full sentence since the Great Depression. It's embarrassing, really. My parents are a piece of living history and I'm their last-minute New Deal. I'm the only person I know whose father actually fought in World War II. Sure, he was seventeen when he enlisted in 1944, lying to the recruiter about his age, but that still makes him old today.

"Rosie? Are you there?"

I'm half-dressed for work. I'm tired and unprepared and due at an appointment on the progress of my favorite client, Milton Beyer.

"I have to run," I tell my mother. "I have a meeting at the SaveWay."

"One of the retarded baggers?" she asks sweetly.

"Ma, my clients are *developmentally challenged*."

"Hmm," she sniffs. "Next week you'll call them something else. Your clients will still wake up retarded in the morning."

"Yes, well, it's not *nice* to call a productive human being with a job *retarded*."

"Right. Just like it's not nice to call you and me *girls*. What else could women be? Boys?"

"I'm late," I tell her. I'm holding the phone to my ear with my chin, pulling my skirt up. "I've got to get going."

"Are you heading over to the Ronkonkoma SaveWay? The one where that nice new manager works? I love that manager, Rosie. He is worth skipping the Pathmark and driving the extra few miles. Plus his produce is nice."

She is referring to Mickey Hamilton, Milton's boss. She seems to have a crush on him. This means she thinks that I should marry him. My mother has always been into vicarious romance.

"I have to go to work," I tell her again.

"Yes, well I suppose *someone* needs to pay for that monstrous television set your husband purchased."

Now she is referring to the wide-screen TV that makes our small living room look like an over-lit sports bar. I knew she hadn't missed it last night. I hadn't wanted Teddy to buy it, either. It's loud and vulgar and larger than life. How huge does the "before" face on *Extreme Makeover* have to be, I'd asked him when he first plugged it in, for us to understand that this person is going to need lots of expensive cosmetic surgery? He'd just stared at me blankly, his head already filled with cleavage and Viagra and Lexuses.

"Look," I tell my mother, "I feel bad enough about Teddy without your rubbing it in."

"I'm sorry, Miss Muffet. It's not you I'm cross with. It's your husband."

"Well, try to remember he *is* my husband."

My mother is silent. She knows what I have said is ridiculous. Teddy is no more my husband now than she is.

"Some people are just not good at choosing mates, Rosie," my mother says softly. "Perfectly sane people sometimes have a problem with this."

I shove my foot hard into my shoe. "Enough," I say.

"There'll be a man, someday, who loves you the way you should be loved—"

"Enough!" I shout. And then, I do it. I hang up, although I'll pay for this later.

I take a deep breath, try to focus on Milton. His meeting starts in twenty minutes, and I'm the one who's been pounding Punctuality on the Job Site into the boy's head these past few months. He's been collecting shopping carts for three weeks now, picking up his check faithfully three Fridays in a row. He's planning to wear his bow tie and his suit jacket to his evaluation, and the sight of Milton dressed this way—soft brown hair at the back of his neck curling around his white collar—could break your heart. I find my other shoe and my purse and head for the door.

Inching along my flat Long Island streets, my thoughts wander back to Teddy and Inga. Despite how common it may appear on television, I try to make it real that *my* best friend could actually be screwing my husband. What kind of house are Teddy and she planning to buy? A new one? A big one? One of those houses on "the hill," in the fancy part of Ronkonkoma? In a way, I feel more betrayed by Teddy's leaving me for another house than I do about his leaving me for Inga. I gaze out my side window. The August heat has brought the babies out like flowers. Along the sidewalks, I see them gripping the metal bars of their Japanese strollers with little round fists and wide eyes and taffy smooth brows. Watching them, I feel an ache so wrenching in my empty womb that my brain says Midol, but my heart knows better. Oh yes, Roseanna Plow wants a baby. It was only Teddy who stopped me from ripping down the bookshelves holding all of those unused law books of his and long ago turning the second bedroom into a nursery. But Teddy wanted to wait. Until he was with a good law firm. Until he was at least junior partner somewhere. He was thirty-six years old the day he walked out of our apartment and no one had asked him if he'd like to be junior partner yet. Still, our trade-off was implicit. You want me, you hold off on the baby. I guess I must have agreed to this, even though I didn't see exactly how the deal would work. When I started wanting a baby, did it mean that I would have to relinquish wanting Teddy? And what if we really did get the big house and his big job first, before the baby? Then how would it be, with him working seventy hours a week, up at five, out by six, back in bed by seven, making love to me once a week, and maybe even then with his beeper on?

I can see Milton Beyer as I pull into the parking lot of the SaveWay. He's wearing his bow tie and jacket all right, but being out of uniform hasn't stopped him from automatically gathering up any shopping carts that have wandered away from the nice neat rows lining the supermarket's doors. His polished leather shoes glint in the sun as he moves his captured carts closer toward the curb. His broad twenty-two-year-old back is bent over the front of the head cart. He'd be such a knockout with thirty more points on his I.Q. Women would fall in love with him and he would be arrogant. He wouldn't hang around with the likes of me. I honk once and he turns his brown eyes, his surprised child's face toward me.

"Miss Plow!" he smiles, and I smile back. Forever I am a maiden to him, for I have found it impossible to teach Milton that I am married. It's this way with many of my clients, most of whom are twenty-two-year-old men and women, finally on their own, now that the state is no longer required to pay for them. Most have come out of back-hall classrooms where burned-out teachers taught them to sort screws and nuts into buckets, and called it vocational education. My job is to transition them into a productive independent life. I wonder if my mother thinks her job with me is the same.

Milton is hurrying over to my car now in unbridled delight. I look at his lovely face and imagine the hopes his parents had for him when they named him Milton. I think about how I've been greeted by Teddy all these years of our marriage, the way in which he's met me at airports, at parties, at my office, with his face struggling to close off his pleasure, as though it would be so bad for his wife to know that she brings him joy. Teddy could learn a lot from Milton that wasn't taught in law school. Such as the way Milton opens my car door now and escorts me to the SaveWay.

"You look very nice, Milton," I tell him, admiring his shirt and jacket as he blushes deeply.

"You do, too," he says, being careful not to touch me as he has been taught, his fingers curling at his sides. "You're beautiful, Miss Plow. You're a beautiful lady. I could kiss your . . ."

"Now Milton," I chide him gently. "Remember the way we speak at the workplace."

"Yeah," he says dolefully. His smooth brow furrows as we walk the rest of the distance through the parking lot, Milton feeling slightly admonished, me feeling slightly beautiful.

They call this store manager "Ham" because he was once a butcher. This was years ago, but the taint of meat remains. Not to say Mickey Hamilton isn't likeable. My mother is in love with him. He treats Milton well. He enjoys watching the wide swath my pelvis cuts when I enter a room, much as Teddy once did before he discovered the allure of half-starved girls such as Inga. Those men are out there, the ones who love women with a little flesh on them, despite what you read in the magazines. But even Ham's fondness for my form won't guarantee that Milton keeps his job. To do this, Milton must refrain from fraternizing with customers or fooling around with the empty two-liter soda bottles, juggling them and such. No kissing babies. No sitting in the florist department, either, plunked down in the middle of the bouquets of roses. These are the behaviors Milton must learn if he is to keep his job. Sometimes I feel guilty about training the pleasure out of his life, just so the rest of us will feel more comfortable.

"The electric eye sees us!" Milton informs me excitedly and, sure enough, the glass door slides open just as he says it. We walk side by side down the dairy aisle, past tubs of sour cream and gallons of milk and, Milton's favorite, little red bunches of Laughing Cow cheese.

"I love the way they look at me," Milton confesses as I swing open Mickey Hamilton's office door.

"Remember," I whisper, my mouth close to his brown curls, "your interview manners."

Our eyes adjust to the relative darkness of the windowless space behind the cheeses. We find Mr. Hamilton sitting at his desk, which is really a scarred wooden table. He is so tall, the table looks too small for him. He's a nice manager, late thirties, with a pleasant, uninteresting face. He's a graduate of my father's School of Silent Men, one of those males who doesn't speak much. A curtain of his sandy hair often falls over his gray eyes when he speaks to you—almost as if he is hiding under there. He does, to his credit, have a nice butt.

The rustle of my skirt lining makes him look up now, and Milton, modeling his best interview behavior, extends a hand, which Mr. Hamilton grasps and shakes firmly.

"How are you, Milton?" he asks politely.

"I'm fine," Milton says. Then his face crumbles a little. "But I have to pee."

"You know where the restroom is," Ham tells him, avoiding

eye contact with me. We're both silent as Milton lumbers away. No one knows where to look.

I open my notepad to ease the awkwardness. I write the date. I start a grocery list, so long as I am here. *Skim milk. Fat-free cottage cheese. Chocolate.* I glance at my watch, wondering how long this meeting will take. *A new life,* I add to the list. We can hear the toilet flushing as Milton comes striding from the restroom.

"I washed my hands," he tells us proudly.

"Way to go, my man," says Ham.

We pull out our folders and get to work.

red rags

marcie slaps down a folder on my desktop and brazenly studies me from behind her horn-rimmed glasses. "What's up with you?" she asks.

Marcie is administrative assistant at our offices at EPT (Employment Partnership and Training, same acronym as the pregnancy test), but really, she runs the whole show. She is amazingly powerful for a woman of twenty-five. She sleeps with Sean Zambuto, our boss, which, in actuality, makes her the boss and Zambuto the sex slave. Our developmentally challenged clients, who tend to become confused and frightened in the office setting, all are in love with her. Social workers, myself included, crawl to Marcie ten times a day for directions. This entitles her to know all of our personal business.

"You look like hell," Marcie says. "And it's only Tuesday." She shoves a hunk of ruthlessly chopped black hair (it used to be naturally blond and beautiful) behind one ear. Her glasses, which look like the kind that come with attached noses and moustaches, hide eyes that are shrewdly focused on me. I will never understand what the deal is with her. Born with a Reese Witherspoon face and Jessica Simpson body, she has been battling back her good looks for as long as I've known her.

"He hasn't come home yet?" she demands.

Marcie can ask me questions like this because she is my friend. What bothers me is that she is my mother's friend, also. They talk on the phone at least once a week. It's my own fault for bringing Marcie home to dinner once, one lonely Sunday afternoon when Teddy didn't want to go. My mother could not have cared less if Teddy came. She and Marcie bonded over the vintage clothes in my mother's closet and that week's *Star Magazine,* and the rest is history.

"He's buying a house with her," I say.

"He's *what*?"

Sean Zambuto suddenly appears at the open door, studying us with his sad sack eyes. He is sixteen years older than Marcie, and has never been married. His prematurely baggy cheeks make him look like the dwarf Sleepy. The thought of them sleeping together is more disturbing than Marcie's new glasses. But he's a nice guy, as he now illustrates, nodding at us politely. "May I have a word with you, Marcie, on this Fallon case?" he asks.

"In your office," Marcie barks. "I'll be with you in a minute."

Sean flashes me a pathetic smile before slinking away like a bad dog. I'm sure he's heard everything about my sorry little life. It's office buzz these days, the unofficial open case that spices up lunches and prolongs time lolled away at the copier. Everyone feels sorry for me except Marcie, who just seems angry. She's tapping her foot like a metronome. She doesn't like Teddy, never has. She finds Inga despicable. You've got to love her for that alone.

"Forget that ass monkey," she orders. "He's never coming home."

"*Ass* monkey?" I repeat. I don't even feign offense.

"Okay. Loser. Sorry."

"That loser is my husband!" I retort, perhaps too shrilly.

Marcie hoots. It occurs to me that I'm having the same conversation with her that I had with my mother. Only the insult has changed. Teddy has moved from a putz to an ass monkey.

"He's been gone for less than two weeks," I say. "Do you think I might enjoy a little denial here, please?"

She looks at me with tremendous pity, as though perhaps I am an old woman who has spilled creamed carrots on her blouse. "Your marriage has been in the toilet from day one," she pronounces. "Denial won't help you now."

She's tough, this Marcie.

"You sound like my mother," I accuse her.

"I like your mother," Marcie replies.

"I hate your haircut," I retort, but she just laughs and hugs me, enveloping us both in the expensive scent of her ridiculous Baby Phat Goddess perfume.

"You've had a bad break, Rosie," she says, patting my back. "If your husband's not an ass monkey, then Inga certainly is."

I hate the way tears just roll off my bottom eyelids when I'm trying to have a simple discussion. Marcie sees them, despite my efforts to quickly swipe them away. She's *caused* them, for God's sake, by bringing up Inga, a woman who helped me pick out Teddy's and my bedroom set, the friend who always said I was beautiful, just the way I was. Thirteen years we were friends, since she sat beside me in Psych class in college. We've supported each other through the worst of times and the best of diets—not that she ever needed to go on one. She has baked me zucchini mushroom casseroles, using Smart Beat margarine instead of butter, and I have told her honestly if I thought her boyfriends were worthy of her. I was the one who would cheer her up when she was lonely, or after she had been dumped herself.

Marcie gently taps the folder she's placed on my desktop, bringing me back. "Eleanor Scudder," she says softly. "You got a call at eight thirty from the Mineola Professional Dental Suites." She pushes her heavy glasses up her perfect nose. "We'll continue this other conversation later, okay? And you know why?"

"Why?"

"Because I love you, you big dope."

This is Marcie's idea of a compliment. Her black nail polish flashes as she pats my hand and leaves. I sit fuming in my white cubbyhole of an office, an overpriced double latte growing cold on my desktop. What does Marcie know of my marriage being bad from day one? I can remember lovely mornings in bed with my new groom, daring lovemaking on a North Shore beach (sand in all our crevasses), the way Teddy's face looked when he lifted my wedding veil at the altar. How had it looked? Nervous. Scared. Like he hoped he could make me happy. Or he hoped he wasn't making a mistake.

I try to pace, but really, there's no room. Five days a week I am trapped in this tiny office in this bland brick county office building, cornered like a gerbil in a cheap, one-tube Habitrail. EPT's first-floor offices have walls so thin that you can eavesdrop on every wrong number Marcie has to process. *No,* I hear her saying, at least once a day, *this isn't the pregnancy test answering service. Look on your box for an eight hundred number, hon.* She is surprisingly gentle with these errant callers, most of whom, I imagine, are young and confused and scared to death— not unlike a lot of our clients.

I sip cold coffee, steeling myself for the dreaded call I must make to Eleanor's boss. Hearing from Dr. Sharpe's office can mean only one thing. Eleanor has seen a red rag. Eleanor is my client with Down syndrome who has been cleaning the Mineola Dental Suites for five months. She's been a boon for everyone involved, mainly because of her unusual love of vacuum cleaners. Once the engine is switched on, Eleanor feels tactilely stimulated by the hum and vibration of a Bissell and loves to roll it back and forth, back and forth endlessly over the carpets. (Teddy used to feel the same way about the Magic Fingers beds we'd find in cheap motel rooms. You never really know a man until you've been to a cheap motel with him. There you see the man's id in its natural playground.) Anyway, the dentists have told me that they hadn't known the true meaning of *clean* until they'd met Eleanor. This only left the issue of red rags for us to work with. Eleanor weeps over them. No one knows what it stems from, but give Eleanor a scarlet cloth to dust with and she sobs inconsolably until you remove her from the job site. The dentists have been warned about checking her cleaning bucket from time to time, but who knows, maybe someone slipped up anyway.

I'm reaching for the phone to dial Mineola when it begins to ring. I knew Teddy would call. I *knew* it.

"Roseanna Plow. EPT," I say, in my most professional voice.

"Ham here. Mickey Hamilton, down at the SaveWay."

My heart sinks. Milton. More baby kissing.

"How're things over there, Mr. Hamilton?" I ask.

"Please," he says. "Mr. Hamilton is my father."

"Mickey," I say.

"Ham," he corrects me.

I just can't do Ham.

"Well," he says, after a few seconds of silence, "things are terrific down here."

"Great!" I exclaim, puzzled. "And Milton . . ."

"Milton's doing fine."

"Good!"

"I, uh, was just wondering something. Are you married?"

"Excuse me?"

"Are you married?"

I am shocked. This, from a man who usually doesn't speak.

"Well, yes, sort of," I respond.

"I won't ask you to explain."

"Good."

"But would you like to go out to dinner sometime?"

I stare out my little office window. A red car passes, then a black one. A tiny spider crawls up the glass.

"Do you think that would be a good idea?"

"Yes, I do," he says.

The spider swings gently from an invisible line of web. Inga, I'm suddenly thinking. Stupid rotten Inga. What kind of friend is she?

"Are *you* married?" I ask.

"No, I'm not."

I wait.

"Divorced," he says.

I don't say it, but I'm thinking that probably the divorce is his fault. I can't imagine that a divorce isn't the man's fault. Who wants to go out with a man like this?

"Let me get back to you," I tell Mickey Hamilton.

"Okay," he says. "Please do."

I hang up, and for a few minutes I can't pick up the phone again. I walk around my teeny office, shifting my suit jacket from the chair back to the wall hook, straightening out a few files on a shelf. I try to imagine something I've said or done that has caused a former butcher to ask me on a date. Has my mother put him up to it? I wouldn't put it past her. How could it work, anyway? After our Long Island iced teas and surf 'n' turf dinner, if I told him that no, I didn't think I'd like to see him again, or kiss him, or cuddle with him in his hamburger-shaped water bed, would Milton be fired? Picked on? Written up? I sigh, flick a dead fly off the file case. It would be nice to make Teddy jealous, anyway.

I pick up the phone and dial Mineola. Dr. Sharpe's receptionist is in a tremendous dither over the condition of the office there. Mops and buckets are everywhere. The vacuum cleaner was still humming when she arrived in the morning.

"It was my jacket," the receptionist confesses. "It's red. I left it in the office when I went home. It must have fallen to the floor. The place looks ransacked!"

"And Eleanor?"

"She was here when we came in."

"She was there all night?"

"She had a lot of wrecking to do."

"The counselor from Cooperative Living didn't look for her? No one tried to find her?"

"Apparently not. They're sending a counselor over this morning. Eleanor was asleep in the office restroom when I got here."

I'm already grabbing my jacket off the hook as I hang up. My mind is shooting arrows through the heart of the night supervisor at Eleanor's group home. How could you forget that someone was missing in your own home? I'm pulling my door shut when the phone rings again, and I almost don't pick it up. I succumb on the fifth ring.

"I've been trying to get through all morning," my mother says.

"Yes, well I work for a living."

"You ought to get that callus-interruptus the phone company offers."

"That *what*?"

"You know, that thing where you're speaking to one party, and then you get a beep . . ."

"Trust me, that's the last thing I want."

"Hmm," my mother observes. "You're in a fine snit this morning."

"Ma, I'm running out the door. Emergency in Mineola."

"Is Teddy back?"

When I don't answer, she says, "Go 'head to Mineola. Just call me back tonight."

Driving down the sluggish expressway, I am irritated and agitated. My mother knows damn well Teddy isn't back. And it's not funny anymore. If he doesn't return today, it will be ten days since he left. Ten. Double digits. Close enough to the two-week mark. Very close to the three-week mark, when he will officially become an ass monkey, even by my own standards.

I jam on my brakes, cursing softly. Sweet Eleanor with her half-moon smile. What must it have been like, all night alone in that dental suite? Poor Mrs. Scudder, who struggled with the decision to allow her daughter to leave her childhood home, who wanted only what every mother wants (what *my* mother wants, I begrudgingly must acknowledge), only that her daughter joyfully embrace the next milestone in life (in my case, divorce; in Eleanor's, independence). Here is Eleanor's opportunity to live with others, to cook her own meals and shop for her own socks. And what happens while she is on my watch? They leave her out, like a bike on a curb.

At the dentist's office, signs of last night are everywhere. A vertical blind is crumpled to the floor, slats splayed open like a giant fan. A stain the shape of Texas darkens the taupe carpeting. Beside it rests an upturned bottle of Murphy Oil Soap. A single male patient in a chrome chair nervously flips through a *Martha Stewart Living* magazine, pretending all is well. The receptionist leads me to the door of the office restroom and knocks.

"Eleanor?" she calls. She tries the doorknob. The brass knob turns easily. "I think Dr. Sharpe wants to talk to you later," she whispers to me before departing, giving me that see-me-after-class look.

I open the restroom door wide. Beneath a pedestal sink with beautiful gold fixtures are the bare flat heels of Eleanor's feet. She's sitting flush against the wall in her white cleaning lady's uniform. Her crumpled socks and nurse shoes surround her in an arc, like a little garden.

"Eleanor," I say.

Her eyes are as vacant as a rubber doll's. I crouch down beside her and take her hand. "Hey, sweetie," I whisper. She turns her head away and I wonder if I'll ever see her half-moon smile again. "Your counselor's coming and you're going home now."

"I can wait here," she says. Her hair is sticking up like porcupine quills, a look Marcie would probably try to emulate if she saw it.

"Eleanor," I say again, squeezing her short, thick-fingered hand. She throws her arms around my neck, almost throttling me.

"It's okay," I tell her, though it really isn't. She's shaking like an earthquake survivor. "It's okay," I say again. After a while she allows me to guide her to her feet. We're holding hands as we walk past the man with the Martha Stewart magazine. He looks alarmed, one of those people shocked by a human gesture he hasn't seen on a television show. *It's only a barefooted woman with Down syndrome*, I want to tell him, *holding hands with a slightly overweight vocational counselor.*

After I've settled Eleanor in an inner office to wait for her counselor, I return to the reception area to await her myself. I hate her already, this unknown bitch, this abandoner of Eleanor, and I yearn to give her a piece of my mind. Eventually, a pale blonde in rimless glasses comes through the door. She bustles toward me with an air of importance and a *Sports Illustrated* swimsuit model physique, as though she knows having a killer body trumps everything. She takes one look at me, then slinks over and shakes my hand firmly.

"Ms. Plow? Chelsea Hannigan from Cooperative Living." Her voice is like Inga's, all high-pitched and piping. "Where is Eleanor?" she asks.

"Where is she *now*? Or where did she spend her night?"

A cloud of confusion, like a swarm of fruit flies, passes in front of her eyes. I hate the way she makes wearing glasses look attractive. When she opens her mouth to speak, the man with the magazine looks up.

"Ms. Plow," she says, "I am not the person who was responsible for Eleanor last night—"

"Ms. Hannigan," I interrupt, "that is not the point. The point is that she was left. Abandoned. Do you know what it's like to believe someone's looking out for you, only to discover that they're *not*? That you've been totally forgotten? That you're on your own?"

Chelsea Hannigan stares at me. Apparently I am yelling. She has *just told* me that she was not in charge last night. My speech seems a bit melodramatic even to the man in the chrome chair. He glances up, then down again at his magazine. Perhaps neither of them, in their sheltered little lives, realizes that I am talking from experience, that I am *living* the experience of abandonment, I am the *poster child* for abandonment, and I am not in the mood to play pass the buck about Eleanor's abandonment. Tears fill my bottom eyelids. I'm ready to lay into Chelsea Hannigan some more when my cell phone begins chirping the theme song from *Chariots of Fire*.

Teddy. His stupid choice for his personal ring signal. A man who buys a hundred pairs of fancy running shoes, then takes the car to the corner for a newspaper. Still. My hand flies into my purse like a thief's. "Just a second," I tell Chelsea Hannigan, and she looks relieved when I step out of the reception area and into the restroom that Eleanor has vacated. I lock the door behind me and settle onto the toilet lid.

"Roseanna," Teddy says in his prim, cold, scolding voice. "I am calling to insist that you stop making these constant calls to me and Inga."

Oh, this makes me steamed. "And how am I supposed to reach you?" I snap.

"Reach me for what? I am trying to conduct the practice of law over here and do not appreciate—"

"Over where?" I interrupt, brushing down the front of my skirt.

"Excuse me?"

"Over where are you trying to conduct the practice of law? At my best friend's house? In her bed? Because I SURE AS HELL HAVEN'T SEEN YOU AT HOME FOR MORE THAN A WEEK!"

It occurs to me I have escalated from yelling. I am now screaming. Screaming from the seat of a toilet. I'm glad my mother isn't in the other room to hear this. If Milton were here, he wouldn't think I was beautiful anymore. He'd think I was crazy. *Remember how we speak in the workplace.* But Teddy has been missing from the *home* place, and I can't stand it anymore. I want him to know what he has done to me is awful. I want him to know he is an ass monkey, just as Marcie says. I need to know *why* he's left, and if somewhere, deep in the recesses of his little brain, he is still carrying a crinkle of love for me. Then, suddenly I have an inspired idea.

"Teddy," I say, in my most threatening voice. "You'd better come by this Sunday and pick up that stupid television. I don't want it, and I do not plan on paying for it."

I think I hear a little gasp on the other end of the line. Encouraged, I continue: "It's only three weeks old and I have the receipts, and if you don't come and get it, I'll return it myself on Monday."

"You'll *what?*"

Teddy sounds incredulous. I've finally hit him where it hurts. In his plasma screen. Relinquishing his wife is one thing, but his television is quite another matter.

"You heard me," I say. "Come by Sunday and don't bring that Jezebel with you."

"Rosie . . ."

"Come after seven, when I'm home. I don't intend to waste a whole day waiting for you to show up."

I hang up.

Rosie. He called me Rosie. I decide this is enough evidence that what I am doing is the right thing. I will give him one more chance. For the sake of the marriage. Or so I tell myself.

When I return to the waiting room, everybody seems to have

vanished. The man with the magazine is gone. Chelsea Hannigan has made her escape with Eleanor.

"The counselor left with Miss Scudder," Dr. Sharpe's receptionist says, when I go to her desk. "Dr. Sharpe has left, too."

She won't look at me. It's almost as if she's afraid of me.

"Right-o, then," I say, attempting to sound British. I don't know why I think this will help. I gather as much dignity as possible as I turn to leave. There'll be plenty to deal with over here later—the cleaning bill, repairs to the shades, insurance issues, Eleanor's evaluation. I just can't think about it now. Not when Teddy might be coming home again, and the fate of our marriage lies in the balance, glimmering in the light of a plasma TV.

be faithful to your methods

the next night is "MR Night," and I'm brewing the coffee in the EPT conference room, waiting for the parents to arrive. It's a regular monthly meeting for the parents of my mentally retarded clients, and about twenty of them will show with their usual questions and complaints and their usual appetite for butter cookies. I peel Saran Wrap off a freshly baked platter, trying not to get crumbs on my pink skirt. I'm tired and my back hurts from sleeping alone on my too-hard mattress (chosen by Teddy, of course), tossing and turning all night, and wondering if Teddy will turn up Sunday to retrieve his flat-screen TV.

On the white board in front of me, I silently arrange my magnetized banners, which I've extracted in an envelope from my soft leather briefcase. INDEPENDENCE! SELF-ESTEEM! TEAM PLAYING! COMMUNICATION! exclaim the shiny rubber strips. BE FAITHFUL TO YOUR METHODS falls from my manila envelope to the floor. I stoop to pick it up, laughing at the irony of finding myself teaching such a load of nonsense. There's certainly been no sense of team playing in my four-year marriage. Communication is abysmal. Self-esteem is plummeting. As for being faithful to one's methods, only Teddy has succeeded in this. He has figured out how to get everything he wants from our union, including a television and my best friend.

The door opens and Mrs. Beyer strides in wearing a Caribbean blue suit, walking with that high-shouldered posture of a woman who kicks ass in a man's world. Her smooth knee-length skirt shines like it's backlit against her lean, shapely frame. I can see why she sells the big houses, out in the Hamptons, so handily. She probably makes more money in one commission than I make in a year, training her son to dust shelves of soup and dog food.

"I'm glad you could make it," I tell her.

She smiles a beautiful smile, then frowns a beautiful frown. "Milton is here," she says. Her auburn hair swings. "He's sitting outside your office. He insisted on coming, said he'd take a bus if I didn't drive him."

"It's fine," I tell her, assuming this is her son carrying his torch for me a little too far. "It's great that he's comfortable taking the bus," I add hopefully.

The conference room has begun to fill up, with a small cluster of parents and group home counselors hovering around the butter cookies, laughing softly and eating. Soon the usual gang is assembled in their seats: Milton's mother, Linda. The group home counselors who look like junior high students, all of them fresh out of college. Mr. Schieb, still wearing his Jiffy Lube shirt, here for his son Nicky. Mr. and Mrs. McCabe with their look-alike wire-rimmed glasses. Mrs. Scudder, here for Eleanor. Arlene Horton, with her massive leatherette purse sitting on her lap like a small dog. Not a bad crowd. People are beginning to peel the backs off their adhesive name tags, a sign for me to begin.

"Welcome," I tell them. "Maybe we could start by giving you all a chance to share."

After a few awkward seconds of silence, Mrs. McCabe clears her throat and begins. "Well," she says, "Susan's having a little trouble."

I smile encouragingly. Susan works in the laundry at the Babylon Terrace Motel.

"She's been stealing washcloths," Mrs. McCabe says. The overhead lighting glints on her lenses. "She stuffs them into her bra and athletic socks before she leaves."

Heads nod gravely. "It's the temptation, you know," Mr. Schieb contributes, making me wonder what kinds of things he's lifted from the lube shop. Again heads nod.

"My husband and I, we're not going to be around forever," Mrs. McCabe says, a proclamation you hear a lot of at this type of meeting, "and then who's going to smooth things out with these motel people?"

All eyes turn to me, as if I know the answer, as if they believe I'll be there for their children when they're dead. Suddenly, we all seem sad in the small room. I feel the parents waiting for me to say something that will make them sleep better tonight.

"Well!" I exclaim, clapping my hands. "Here is why we're all in this together. I can speak to Susan's manager and you can communicate directly with Susan."

They look at me dully. I begin pointing at one of the magnetic signs, the COMMUNICATION! one, my arm extended and my suit jacket rising over the hump of my hip. "Be faithful to your methods, Mom and Dad," I encourage, moving along to the next strip. "*Tell* your children when they are doing something wrong. Don't tell them one time, and then the next—"

I am interrupted by the door swinging open and Milton Beyer bursting in, marching past the rows of chairs and up to the front, where I stand. He is moving with an urgency that shows in his lowered head, his swinging shoulders, his clenched fists. The normal sweet expression is gone from his handsome face. He looks bad, his hair all mussed up and the waist of his jeans a little high and uncomfortably twisted to one side. His blue sweatshirt has a picture of the Road Runner on front. BEEP BEEP!! it reads, beneath the cartoon feet.

"Miss Plow?" Milton says, as he draws nearer. I see the slightest bit of a five o'clock shadow on his nice, angled jaw.

"Milton," I say.

"Remember my work manners. Remember my work manners."

"Well, yes. But, no. Milton, what I was going to say is that we're in the middle of a parent meeting now . . ."

"Miss Plow, I have *got* to talk to you."

Milton swings around to face the group, his eyes bypassing his mother's and settling on Arlene Horton in the first row.

"I'm a very good worker!" he tells her. "I'm a very good person!"

"I'm sure you are, dear," Mrs. Horton says, squeezing her massive purse.

"I'm an asset. Mr. Hamilton says I'm an asset."

"Yes, you are, Milton," I tell him, leading him gently by the elbow to the back of the room. "And I promise we will talk later. After the meeting, okay?"

I feel Milton's resistance as I guide him back toward the door. But it's a parent meeting and I must be faithful to my methods. No clients at the parent meetings.

"I just wanted to tell you you're beautiful," Milton says. "And I love you."

The room settles in a silence that you don't find many other places. No snickering, no uncomfortable shifting around in chairs. These parents don't laugh at proclamations of love.

"We'll talk later," I tell Milton again. Then I pour him a cup of Amaretto coffee and hand it to him. He sips it and smiles. "Mmm," he says. "Armadillo."

I open the door for him. We all watch Milton shuffle out with his coffee and his cookies. Mr. Schieb breaks the silence after a minute, scratching his arm and sighing. "Jeez," he says. "It's always something."

secrets to irresistible sex

i try not to get my hopes high that Teddy will show up on Sunday, but oh, how I would love to hear the jingle jangle of keys on the other side of the door, and then see his adorable face at the threshold. His smooth olive skin. The broad shoulders. The thick brown hair, more a pelt than a hairdo. Teddy, as in bear. My teddy bear, my errant husband, come home to mama again!

I shake off the thought, try to come to my senses. Teddy has another home now, with Inga. It is no longer rational to love him, realistic to believe he is coming back, or even permissible for me to be in denial, according to Marcie. And yet a part of my heart sits at the door like the family pet, waiting for Teddy to walk in. One more chance. That's all I'll give him. That, and possibly the TV.

By seven o'clock, nothing has happened. I bring a *Cosmo* to bed with me. I have no idea why I own a stack of them. I think they're stupid, but I almost never miss an issue, even pay retail each month, snatching up the newest half-exposed cover girl at the SaveWay register, as though my fingers have a will of their own. I try not to let Milton or Ham see me buying them.

This month's issue is all about love. Well, sex, really, but according to *Cosmo*, sex and love are pretty much the same thing. SPRINKLE FRESH MOVES ON A BED OF LOVE! the cover blares, its red print running across the model's crotch. The model looks a little like Chelsea Hannigan, which makes me hate her. I read on. GETTING IT ON AT THE TANNING SALON: LEARN HOW TO BAKE AND SHAKE, a second headline suggests. This only makes me hungry for chicken. I move to the headline covering one breast. URGES YOU SHOULD *NOT* CONTROL! reads the provocative panel, its block letters bold and smoky purple. I have to laugh at this one. My whole professional life has been about teaching twenty-two-year-olds to control their urges. Do not kiss the babies in shopping carts. Do not have a tantrum if you see a red rag. Maybe I've been so busy training the urges out of others that I have trained them out of myself. Maybe this is why Teddy left. Maybe I don't have enough urges.

It's only seven thirty when I'm through reflecting on *Cosmo*'s sage cover advice. The sun hasn't really set yet, but still, officially, it is evening. It makes *sense* that I am in bed, holding a phone in my hand. All sorts of normal, nondepressed people go to bed in the evening, holding phones in their hands. It looks pretty certain Teddy is not coming over for his TV. He probably doesn't believe I'll return it anyway. The truth is, I don't have the receipt. I don't even know where he bought it. He just rolled it in on a dolly one day, as if he had found a stray dog.

I suppose my stunned silence was tantamount to telling him he could keep it.

I sip my Less Stress tea, avoiding the untouched devil's food cake my mother baked and left for me on my doorstep this morning. A *friendly enemy*, they call my mother's type at Overeaters Anonymous meetings. Someone who sympathizes with you on the one hand and passes you a three-million-calorie cake with the other. I flip idly through the ten-pound sex manual on my lap, until I come to an article called "Secrets to Irresistible Sex." I gaze at the photo of a blond toothpick woman with obvious breast implants, draped in the arms of a stud. Quotes abound, advice from generous readers whose names have been changed to protect their privacy. I begin reading them, masochist that I am. *My baby and I create bedroom bedlam, first by stroking each other's ego in the buff and then by stroking each other's . . . well, you know!—Jenna P.*

I do know, Jenna, though I haven't done much stroking lately. I move on. *Mama mia! We have found eating spaghetti in bed on Friday nights really "sauces up" our lovemaking!—Rita S.*

This one makes me cringe. All I can see are the stains on the sheets. Tomato sauce is the worst to get out, regardless of what the detergent ads tell you. I'm ready to close the magazine when another comment, Kristi M.'s, jumps out and catches my eye. *Let's play ball!* it says. I read on. *My man gets so excited by baseball games on television. I decided to cash in on that excitement by watching the games with him—wearing only a thong with his team's name on front. Once the game ends, we're ready for some curve balls between the sheets!*

"Hah!" I laugh, pulling up the comforter. I know just what

Kristi M.'s man is like. Teddy gets apoplectic about baseball games, too. I'd never thought to watch them with him in my underwear, though.

This gives me an idea.

On our first anniversary, Teddy bought me some fire-engine-red lingerie from Victoria's Secret, which I quietly tucked in the back of a drawer, where it has lived, unmolested, for three years. I remember feeling *so fat* when I pulled them out of the pretty pink tissue paper and held them up. The bra was okay—Teddy knew my size—but the panties wouldn't have fit a nine-year-old gymnast. Had Teddy been trying to tell me something? That I should have been thinner, like Inga, even back then?

I throw the comforter back, jump out of bed, and begin furrowing through my top drawer. I find them in the back, still in the tissue, crumpled but whole. I drop my flannel sweatpants to my ankles, rip off my WE ALL HAVE CHALLENGES T-shirt (a freebie from our last staff picnic), and wriggle into the panties.

Well, thong, as it turns out. Who wears these things? Aren't wedgies something people try to avoid? I move on. I pretend the thong is not violating me as I clip on the bra. My breasts flow like lava over padded half crescents of lace. I step in front of my pedestal mirror to take a look.

I look like a torture victim. Amnesty International should place some calls and help me. My behind looks like a rump roast in butcher string. My breasts, which are too large to begin with, might as well have arrows painted on top saying, "Look at me! Look at me!" Still. I suppose I look sexy, in a zaftig kind of way. And my man does love baseball on television. And I do miss those curve balls between the sheets.

I go into the living room and turn on the giant television set. A huge commercial materializes. A man with a shit-eating grin is driving a truck the size of a ranch house up the side of a mountain. I find the remote and click around. Lawyers. Cops. Doctors. More cops. Finally, oh yes, there *is* a God, *finally*, I hear the static of a ballpark crowd and then see the face of a ballplayer, standing at home plate, swinging his bat and spitting in the dirt. A spitting *Yankee*, no less!

Yes! I yell to no one, jumping up and down and causing the thong string to injure some hidden part of me permanently. Teddy's Yankees are on his giant television! I pull the string out, but it just snaps back into place again. No matter. I watch the sun plunge toward the horizon in my window, strengthening the bluish glow of the TV, casting the living room in velvety shadows. I turn down the volume and curl up on the couch.

Then I hear the sound I've waited all day to hear. The jingle jangle of keys. The turning of the doorknob. The slight whoosh of the opening door. I glance over the back of the couch and there he is. His adorable face and his swarthy skin, his broad shoulders and his mouth agape. Teddy. I have willed his existence once more in our home with my thong and my lacy bra and his beloved big screen appliance. My husband is here to reclaim his television and maybe, just possibly, if he's really, really sorry, to reclaim me. I rise from the couch to greet him. *Let's play ball!*

curve balls

O**h my god!**" Teddy cries.

It matters deeply to me what he says next. As he gazes at his wife, prone on the couch in a couple of strings and a Miss Piggy pose, what does he really think? Glancing quickly down at myself, I note with pleasure the ample swell of my hips, the undulating flow of my profile from shoulder to calf to toes. Glancing back at Teddy, I see his mouth fallen open like a little cave entrance, his eyes as round and bewildered as Eleanor's. He could *be* Eleanor, gaping at a fallen red rag.

I hope this isn't the case.

"The Yankees are on," I say in a sure and sultry tone, feeling suddenly confident and full of high self-esteem, despite the thong still pinching me. Whether I look seriously hot or not, this outfit is doing the job. I feel in total control of the situation. Teddy hasn't looked at the television screen once.

"Remember you bought me these? On our first anniversary?" I run my fingers over a lacy half crescent of the bra.

"Oh my God," Teddy says again.

I rise then and walk toward him with the same stride Chelsea Hannigan used at the dentist office. I feel sexier than Chelsea Hannigan. There are more curves approaching Teddy than Chelsea and Inga put together. Chelsea is nothing but elasticized angles, Inga all twigs. Whereas I am roundness and swelling. Roundness and swelling are good. I can tell from the way Teddy's keys drop to the floor, his hands falling limp and open at his sides.

"The Yankees are on," I say again.

"Who are they playing against?" Teddy asks in a small frightened voice.

Damn. I'd forgotten these teams don't just stand around home plate, spitting for their own teammates. "Why don't you sit down and find out?" I purr, tentatively taking his hand, gently pulling him toward the couch.

He follows, and I move a mauve couch cushion to make more room. I feel Teddy's eyes on my derriere as I bend to arrange things. I don't know why I feel like such a slut when this happens. The man is, after all, my husband. He theoretically knows every inch of my body. I've just never trussed it in strings before. What a difference a thong makes. Now I am beginning to understand why so many women suffer, wearing them everywhere—to the supermarket and the gym and their eye doctor appointments. You never really know when you'll have an opportunity to take everything else off, and it's worth it to be prepared.

I straighten up again and gently push Teddy down onto the couch. His eyes are glazed and I'm betting now that it's me and not the Yankees. "Do you like my outfit?" I ask him coyly.

"Jesus, Roseanna," he says.

"You can call me Rosie," I say, sliding down next to him. "I *am* your wife, after all."

Teddy bolts to his feet and buries his hands in the pockets of his two-hundred-dollar jeans. I see that I shouldn't have used the *wife* word. He's sweating slightly. It looks like he's worried. About cheating on my best friend with his wife. I reach out a hand from my reclined position and run it slowly down his pant leg. "Shh," I say. "Everything's fine now, Teddy. You're home. Relax. What could be wrong with you being in your own home?"

I think it is my cleavage, more than my words, that appeals to him. His eyes seem to be glued there. It is possible he hears no words at all. But with his gaze firmly set upon my breasts, he sits again, sighing like a prisoner as the cuffs are snapped on. *Take that, you pathetic 32 A's,* I think, feeling proud that Teddy is staring at one hundred percent flesh, no silicone, no saline. Maybe even one hundred fifty percent flesh, from the way his eyes widen. *Take that, you skinny Inga girls.*

Men are so simple. Feed them. Take care of them. Flash them some cleavage and they'll follow you around like Rover. I rack my mind to think which one of these I wasn't doing enough of. Which deficit caused Teddy to leave?

It doesn't matter now. He is so completely under my spell. The Red Undies Spell. I go for the kill, leaping across his lap and finding his lips and kissing him hard. He does not back away. I push my breasts into his chest, push my tongue into his mouth and simultaneously (and a little roughly) strip him of his shirt.

"Rosie," he gasps. "Rosie. I am in a relationship."

"You certainly are," I breathe into his ear. "It's called marriage."

"No, *another* relationship," he says, stiffening slightly.

"There *are* no other relationships when you're married," I correct him, pulling at his belt loop. "And there is nothing wrong with making love to your wife."

"Well," he says, relaxing a little, "if it means that much to you, Rosie."

"It does," I assure him. "It really does."

We have never made love with a crowd roaring behind us before. But it seems a Yankee double play is paralleling our own exercise, and the effect is surreal but glorious. It is like old times again with Teddy. I am enveloped once more in the feel and scent of him, the steam of his breath, the sting and brush of his five o'clock shadow. It is wonderful. Only, it is really quick. Too quick, actually.

Too, too quick. Teddy is up in a flash, buckling and buttoning his dragging designer garments on his way to the bathroom. He stays in there a long time. Long enough for me to feel slightly foolish in my twisted thong and unanchored bra. With a heavy heart I rise from our mauve couch. I find a robe in the bedroom and put it on. I hear the faucet going in the bathroom. I stand outside the door listening to the tumble of water, feeling my own emotions tumble through me in a similar flush of steamy heat. He got up too quickly. He's hiding in our bathroom now, washing all traces of me away.

The stupid involuntary tears start up. I wipe them away, take a deep breath and walk back to the couch. When Teddy finally emerges from the bathroom, he is completely buckled and buttoned. His hair is combed. His hands are back in his jeans pockets. "Sit awhile," I say, trying not to sound too imploring, but Teddy just shakes his head firmly.

"I think it's best if I come back for the TV later," he says. "And I'd also like to take my leather desk chair."

"Teddy, can't we talk?"

His face softens a little, then he looks away. "Roseanna, I told you. I'm buying a house with Inga." His voice gentles, perhaps because he see the effect his words have on me. "I have told you this," he repeats. "Nothing has changed."

"Nothing has *changed*?" I pull my robe tighter around, feel it struggle against my lacy red bra. "Didn't you just make love to me?"

He looks away, a little sheepishly. "You seemed to have wanted that."

A slap in the face couldn't feel worse. "So it was a favor?" I ask.

The crowd in the ballpark is going crazy again. With all that big screen noise, it's a fine time to start crying.

Teddy takes a few steps toward me, then moves away once more. "Look, Roseanna, I feel bad about this, but I can't help it. I *love* her." He sighs as my heart cracks down the middle. "I didn't think it would harm you to give you something you wanted . . ."

". . . on your way out."

Teddy sighs. "Yeah, I guess so."

I look up at him, flushed and puffy-eyed. "Well, thanks tons. I hope it wasn't too much trouble."

"Not at all," he says, like some kind of insensitive putz.

So here's my mother, I think. As usual, being right.

sometimes life sucks

i spend monday morning with an emotionally disturbed Dairy Barn worker and a dyslexic plumber's assistant. It seems a suitable punishment for a woman desperate enough to try to win her husband back with a thong and an appliance. After lunch I'm at the SaveWay, teaching Milton to sweep the parking lot with a big, wide wooden broom. He's pushing paper cups and deli wrappers toward the curbs and islands, then depositing them into the outdoor trash bins. I show Milton how to remove the lids of the bins, take out the full heavy sacks and re-line them again with fresh plastic bags. Huge black clouds hang ominously over us as I wrap up our training session. "Let's hurry up and line this barrel," I tell Milton.

"Yes!" he exclaims, standing at my back like a shadow, bending over me as I bend over the can. I can feel his breath on my hair.

"My mother says sex is a sacred thing," Milton whispers into the back of my head. All I can smell is the plastic.

I remove my head from the Glad bag, straightening up to see his anxious face. A good next thing to say escapes me.

Milton carries the broom over his shoulder like a rifle as we move along to the next trash bin. I'm cradling the roll of garbage bags in my arms like a baby. Then I think of what to say.

"Milton." I am sure to make eye contact. "I hope you don't talk about sex with any of the SaveWay customers."

I watch his eyes go round and soft: sweet milk chocolate. "Oh, no, no, no," he says. "Only with you."

Lightning flashes, followed by thunder. Milton seems oblivious to it. He is lost in sex thoughts as we head toward the store. His mother says sex is a sacred thing. *Tell Teddy that,* I think. I glance again at Milton and he is smiling at me, beatifically. Drops of rain are glinting on his handsome cheekbones. It's pouring by the time we get inside.

I'm standing in the cheese aisle by Mickey Hamilton's office door, my hair dripping, waiting for Milton to put away his broom. I don't want Ham to see me this way, in jeans instead of a skirt, my head fresh from the interior of a garbage can. What if he asks me out again? It is easier to say no to someone if you're wearing professional attire. This is how presidents and priests have gotten away with so much for so long.

Something's got to give in the infatuation department with Milton. Speaking with his mother at the last MR Night has only seemed to make things worse. I have my own love-life problems to worry about. I am still fuming over the thought of my husband feeling guilty for sleeping with his own wife. Was a mistress's rights bill passed by Congress when I wasn't paying attention? I swipe angrily at my hair with a wet fist, impatient for Mickey Hamilton to come out of his office so we can get Milton's training session over with. The office door opens but it is Milton who emerges, wearing his Kelly green SaveWay rain poncho, all set to resume his cart-collecting responsibilities. His massive hood casts a shadow across his eyes, but still, I see how he's gazing at me, like he's found Miss America in the dairy aisle.

"Oh, Miss Plow!" he suddenly exclaims too loudly. A woman handling string cheese drops the package and turns to stare.

"Milton," I whisper, "remember our inside voices."

"But Miss Plow! I have to *talk* to you!"

"Yes, well, we can do this with our inside voices . . ."

"But, Miss Plow, I *love* you," Milton says, stopping everything in aisle six: the pushing of carts, the buying of sour cream, even the Muzak, which pauses momentarily between insipid songs. "What am I supposed to do if I *love* you?" Milton asks. He spreads his arms wide as he comes sailing toward me. His poncho arcs like eagles' wings. He's ready to gather me into a hug.

I could use a hug, but not from Milton in the cheese aisle. The woman with the string cheese is smiling, but it's a frightened smile, a smile that says, *Oh look at the retarded boy acting up.* It makes me want to smack her. I will never understand why people with mental retardation so terrify the masses. We could put the Miltons of the world on our police forces and homeland security teams and protect our borders with their exclamations of love and good will. People seem that frightened. I unwrap myself gently from Milton's hug, then guide him by the elbow toward the store exit.

"Milton," I tell him calmly as we walk. "I am glad that you love me . . ."

"You *are*?" His face shifts toward me in the hood.

"Yes, of course I am. But, Milton . . ."

He squeezes my hand. " 'Cause if you love me back, Miss Plow, I was thinking. We could get married."

I gaze miserably at his beautiful face.

"We could have a big party," he says. "We could dance, and you could wear a white dress and I . . ."

"Milton!" I have raised my voice and look him full in his handsome face. "We're in the workplace. Remember?"

Milton lowers his eyes.

"Remember what I told you about our work lives and our private lives and how they are separate?" My voice is softer now. "You and I have a *professional* relationship."

Milton turns away. "Yeah," he sighs, not looking at me.

"Good," I say. Then I add: "You're a wonderful worker, Milton."

He doesn't respond. I watch him walk out into the rain, shoulders slumped like he is carrying a heavy load. Shoppers pass. He doesn't look up.

Mr. Hamilton sidles up beside me, approaching out of nowhere. He's got his sports jacket slung over one shoulder, hooked in place there by a fingertip. He's got his seventies sideburns and his plain old face.

"Tough day?" he asks, as we walk together toward his office.

"No, no," I lie, not wanting to explain how every day is a tough day for my clients. We enter Mickey's cave of an office in silence and sit in our usual positions at the scarred pine table.

Mickey loosens his tie, reaches behind him, and pulls down a box of doughnuts from a shelf.

"May I offer you one?" he asks, and I shake my head no, suspecting, of course, a hidden agenda. Offer the fat girl a doughnut. On the other hand, it could be Ham's way of saying that my big boned physique is all right with him. Or, he could just be trying to offer me a doughnut.

"You look upset," he says.

"I'm fine, Mr. Hamilton," I tell him. I open the manila folder with Milton's papers and pretend to study them.

"May I ask you a question?" he says, and my eyes move immediately toward the door. "Why won't you call me Ham?"

At first, I don't answer him, as it seems so obvious. Calling yourself "Ham" because you were once a butcher seems to me a little, well, *ass-monkey-ish*, as Marcie might put it. It's like being the kid at school with the KICK ME sign taped to his back. But how do you explain this to a man who is so irritatingly nice all the time?

I look down at the table top, where Mickey has his big hands clasped, waiting for my answer. I clear my throat, annoyed that we must have this discussion, which has nothing to do with Milton's progress. Mickey rises from his chair and puts the doughnut box back on the shelf, showcasing his very nice butt.

He turns and looks at me, still waiting.

"You're nicknamed for the *meat* department," I finally say.

He sits down again across from me. "I prefer to think I'm nicknamed for what was once my *profession*."

Please, I think.

Mickey stares at me with steady gray eyes. Boring eyes. Eyes that are gray the way my mother's walls are beige. A nice ass isn't everything. I gaze again at his large hands on the tabletop, trying to imagine them holding a meat cleaver. This helps.

"It's nothing new," he says, "people being named for their work. I mean, think about all the Fishers and Goldsmiths in the world."

And Plows, I think, but of course I don't say this. "That's different," I only offer.

"Not really," he insists. "It's the same. I worked in meats and I was good at my work. Ergo, Ham."

Ergo? What kind of person says "ergo"? Time to wrap this up, I think.

"Look," I say. "My error, okay? I'm sure you did a good job in the meat department . . ."

"But you're not sure my calling was as noble as yours. Are you a vegetarian?"

"No."

"Do you eat meat?"

"Now wait a minute," I protest.

"I was as proud of my perfectly halved sides of beef," he sighs, "as you are of Milton's garbage pail lining."

"Enough!" I rise indignantly from my chair.

"In spite of your snobbish ways," he continues, unruffled, "I'm still willing to make good on my dinner offer."

"Yes, well, I'm sorry," I say. "But I've already been proposed to today."

"So I heard."

"And I'm not exactly in the dating market, either. I'm . . . half married."

"I've heard that, as well," he says, rising from the table himself. "But there's something you should know about me," he says, oh so tentatively brushing my hand with his. "I'm a very patient person."

I'm out of his office in a flash. I decide to e-mail him Milton's training report, so I can go straight home. I want my bed badly. I want to be in it, even though it's big enough to hold a tennis team, and I am just one person with a quilt. I want to be under that quilt, where no one can propose to me, or ask me to dinner, or ask for a television, or perhaps even a divorce. I pound through the misty parking lot, Milton's train of shopping carts vibrating loudly behind me. I don't turn around to look. I throw my briefcase across the passenger seat and hurl myself into the car. Milton is standing beside my front window, just as I'm starting the engine. I lower the window and he sticks his wet face in. Rain drips down the sides of his hood and into my car.

"Are you all right?" I ask, but he just stares at me, the edges of his mouth trembling.

"Oh Miss Plow," he finally says, "sometimes life sucks."

I should remind him that *suck* is one of those words we don't use in the workplace. But instead I pat his wet cheek, reaching my hand through the open window.

"You're right, Milton," I tell him. "You're exactly right."

I drive away slowly, creeping past the usual Long Island shoppers—the big-haired housewives, the stout old ladies, the "professionals" with their moussed hair and oversized clunky jewelry—all of them loading their cars with plastic bags and brown bags and huge walls of cello-wrapped toilet paper. Perhaps, with the passage of time, I will become one of the stout old ladies, another big-boned old woman like Teddy's mother, Mrs. Stracuzza, with her Queens Italian accent, her ziti, her thick ankles and Catholic superstitions. The wife of a house painter, she's never understood why Teddy wanted to be so different from them. His fine wines and expensive lawyer suits, in an odd way, have disappointed them. I sometimes think that I am the booby prize Teddy brought home to comfort them—a chubby Long Island girl with working class parents and, if not an Italian last name, well, then, at least a Long Island—sounding one.

The sun is out again by the time I reach home. I see my mother waiting for me in the Ronkonkoma Arms visitors' space, leaning against her car with her arms and legs crossed. She looks like the mother in the Dick and Jane readers, with her full-skirted shirt-dress and her tiny half-jacket, pocked with pink flowers.

"Hello, Dolly," she says, studying me from behind the speckled frames of her sunglasses. "Came to get my cake dish, if you're through with it."

"Ma, you left the cake on my doorstep yesterday. Do you think I ate a whole devil's food cake in twenty-four hours?"

She raises her sunglasses to her forehead. I watch her eyes travel to my hips.

"Cut it out, Ma. It's been a long day."

"At work?"

"Yes."

"Dressed like that?

"Yes," I tell her. "Dressed like this. Okay?"

I turn my back on her and begin walking to the elevator. She's quiet as a ghost, trailing me. She knows she's hurt my feelings. When the elevator dings, she slides in beside me. I look into the mirrored wall and there we are: a small woman in a Donna Reed costume and a large woman in blue jeans. A peanut and a gourd, side by side. My eyes are raw and pink. My mother's lipstick glows red.

I unlock my door and watch my mother precedes me in. Her gaze turns left and right as she inspects my home for tidiness, dust, husbands. I'm relieved I remembered to stuff the red thong and bra back into the bureau drawer. My mother sits primly on the couch in her tea-taking position. I don't offer her tea. It would be nice if she'd take her cake plate and leave. But of course, she isn't here for the cake plate.

I sweep past her into the kitchen, grab the heavy covered dish from the counter.

"Here. Why don't you take this home?" I hold it out in front of her startled, upturned face.

"But there's an untouched cake in there!"

"God knows it'll only make me fatter."

"It's your favorite recipe! From the church cookbook! You think I made that cake for *me*?"

"How do I know who you made this cake for? Weren't you just staring at my hips? Full-figured gals don't need cake, Mom. Remember?"

My mother crosses her legs, brushing imaginary specks of dust from the top knee. Her mouth makes a straight line. Hurt, hurt.

"Rosie, you're . . ."

". . . chubby, Mom. I'm chubby, okay?"

"No! You're bitchy."

"I'm flawed, Ma. Let's just compromise at that. My outfit sucks. My husband's left. Do you think you can live with that, Ma?"

She looks down at her hands. I can't seem to stop.

"These things you say, Ma, believe it or not, they actually hurt people's feelings . . ."

Her head snaps up. "You're not *people*. You're my daughter. I thought I could say things to you that are *true*."

I dismiss her comment with a loud wheeze. I will never use a line like this on my own daughter, providing I ever have one. I walk toward my bedroom, past the spare room that should have been our baby's nursery. My hands squeeze into fists until my nails stab at the soft flesh of my palms. Inga. The betrayal! My heart stings like a road burn. I am panting lightly, feeling my wounds with a new freshness. I know this can't be all my mother's fault. I know she is just a small woman in a big dress. But still.

"I'm a little tired, Ma," I tell her. "I'm going to lie down."

"Your father's passing blood in his urine," she mutters behind me. I turn and look at her.

"I'm a bit worried that he might die," she says. Then she takes her cake and leaves.

• • •

Instead of lying down, I drive to Inga's house. I find her in her garden, carefully adjusting the bushy boughs of her tomato plants to rest on the metal cages. Her bendy back, like Gumby's, is turned to me. She is taller, maybe a little more wiry than my mother, but still, they're the same type. Winsome. Willowy. So damn thin. I find myself wondering if my father would have been attracted to Inga thirty years ago. Perhaps all men are attracted to the same woman, and the rest of us just walk around looking a bit wrong, waiting for the fallout, waiting for the men who will take us in anyway.

Teddy's car is not here. This is how I've made it to the back of Inga's rented Cape, down the brick path that winds about its circumferences, past the carefully planted shrubs that flank the sides. I had a feeling I'd find her out here. She is most at home in her garden. I wait for her to turn around and look at me, wondering what she'll say, how she'll explain this terrible husband mix-up to her oldest, dearest friend. Instead, when she turns, one red garden glove slowly rising to her open mouth, I am the one who speaks.

"My father's got blood in his urine," I say. "They're testing him for prostate cancer."

"Oh, *no*," Inga says softly. She has met my father a hundred times. She has carefully shaken his hand, called him Mr. Pulkowski and not Mr. Plow. She has allowed him to love her in his quiet way. I am hoping this news hurts her, or at least confuses her. But maybe I'm also hoping I can still go to my best friend with a problem, the way I always have.

Now we're both confused. We stand in Inga's yard silently. Wisps of yellow hair fringe her forehead and the back of her long neck. I push my own hair back, feeling its coarseness against my fingers. "Inga," I say. "How could you do this to me?"

She bites her bottom lip. She bends from the knees when she picks up her garden trowel.

"How could you contemplate buying a house with him?"

Carefully, she brushes the trowel off with one gloved hand. "I've got to go," she says, and then she turns and walks away.

The screen door slaps the door frame, leaving me standing between the tomatoes and marigolds, alone. I follow her path to the back door and stand there, my nose pressed against the screen, my hands forming blinders on either side of my face. I peer into her kitchen at the scalloped valance above the sink, at a recorked bottle of open wine on the counter. She's not in there. She's in some other room. I can imagine each one of them, every painting and lamp and towel there. I'm staring at the room where Inga and I have stood at the open freezer, eating Häagen-Dazs from the container, where we have baked cookies, talked about our sex lives, uncorked countless other bottles of wine. Now it has become *Teddy's* kitchen—at least, until the two of them move into a house with *another* kitchen.

After all these years, I can't seem to invite myself in. "Inga?" I call softly through the mesh of the screen. "How could you do this?" It's easier to talk to her when she's not there. "How could you take my husband away? I helped you *hang* that valance. I helped you choose it."

It's as if she's not inside. "How could you do it?" I ask again, but this time I seem to be shouting. "Inga! How? Inga! Answer me!"

Nothing.

"This is Rosie," I remind her. "Your best friend. Don't you think you owe me an answer?"

Nothing again. And then something. The front door opening and closing. In another minute, I hear a car door slamming, then the engine turning, then the hum of it growing fainter and fainter. Inga's gone. I have chased her out of her own house. That's something, anyway.

I unpress my face from the screen. A woman in the yard beside Inga's is standing on the ladder of her aboveground pool, pretending to skim bugs in a net, but really just watching me. She smiles at me in her unfortunate short shorts, the cellulite on her legs glowing. "I think she's gone," she says.

takes my breath away

My father stopped talking after World War II. Of course, as a child, I didn't know this, because as a child, I had no idea when World War II had ended. I thought my father had never talked. For all I knew, he was born sitting up in a La-Z-Boy lounger, that pleasant wisp of a smile on his face, his big hand wrapped around a can of beer. He's a sort of a Stanley Kowalski with none of the malice. He screams *Stella!* at my mother, but only with his immobile eyes.

It seems enough for her, if it wasn't for me. It was only after I'd married Teddy that my mother confided in me, one day in Commack while we were hanging out her wash, when it was that my father had stopped talking.

"Why, he's never had a full conversation with me since after our first date," she said, pinning his shirt into shrugged shoulders on the line.

You could stand by her backyard clothesline and see five or six other backyards in every direction. That is how Commack is.

It is how all of Long Island is, in my experience. Flat housing developments with mothers in the yards. Endless miles of strip malls, real malls, muffler shops, and car dealers. A slight suggestion of the ocean in the air.

"Ma," I asked, "how could you stand it? How could you marry him?"

My mother turned her sharp eyes on me, and in them I read anger at me, not at my father. "Listen, Missy, if you know your new groom half as well in a year as I knew your father after that first date, I'd be surprised." She was pointing at me with a wooden clothespin. "A person doesn't have to talk all the time to tell you he loves you."

This was four years ago, and I remember answering my mother with, among other things, a smirk. I let her see it through the rows of wet wash; I thought I knew so much! Now that Teddy's gone three weeks, I see the truth in her words, of course. During the course of our truncated marriage, Teddy always talked, but mostly about Teddy. That day I stood with my mother hanging out wash, I still believed that marriages were made by Disney. I was a smarty-pants, freshly imbued with the false sense of wisdom that marching down the aisle gives you.

"Ma," I'd said, stretching a long white sheet across the line to separate us, "in social work, we call it verbal abuse when a person uses words as weapons. When someone doesn't speak to you for over forty years, you might call that *non*verbal abuse."

My mother ripped the sheet off the line and let it fall damp to the ground. Her face was hard and unamused. "Don't speak to me about your father like that," she said, "ever again."

I had the good sense to shut up then. I saw who my mother

would pull into the lifeboat first, if her family were going down on the *Titanic*.

My mother's living room is full of noise this morning, even though it's only my father and me sitting here. It's not us making the noise, it's the TV. A Sunday sports program. Recaps of a Yankee–Red Sox game. My mother is still at church, and the announcer is telling us personal things over the din of the crowd about some pitcher on the mound. I have not said a word to my father about his visits to urologists, oncologists, or to our family doctor, Dr. Nash, the one who found the blood in the urine in the first place. Nothing in his distant mood makes me believe that he will discuss his illness with me, even if this is why I have come here today.

I am ignorant of baseball, uncomfortable sitting here alone with my father. The roar of the crowd makes me think of bad sex with Teddy. The backs of my knees chafe on the nubby fabric of my mother's couch. I wish her sofa weren't so stiff, so scratchy, so *fifties*. Why didn't people like to be comfortable on their sofas in the fifties? I'm almost tempted to ask my father, whose eyes have momentarily wandered from the television screen to me, but then we hear the whine of the back door opening, and we breathe a collective sigh of relief.

"Hel-*lo*!" my mother sings. "I'm back from the Mass that never ends!"

"Hi, Ma!" I yell, over a commercial. I get up to greet her, but she's already rounding the corner of the kitchen, click-clacking on high heels into the living room in her good navy Sunday coat, the same coat she probably wore to my christening.

"That goddamn visiting Jesuit again," she mutters, throwing

her clutch bag onto the sofa beside me. A ripple of excitement travels up my spine at the sound of her cursing. "They spoil them at these damn Catholic colleges," she says sourly, "bringing them their tea and brandy, wiping their behinds for them."

My father's eyebrows rise, more amusement than admonishment. *Stella!* his eyes say.

"You were lucky you didn't go today, Pulkowski," my mother tells him, unbuttoning her coat, and again my father raises an eyebrow. He hasn't gone to Mass in thirty-two years, since my aforementioned christening. Still, every Sunday, my mother makes this same comment.

"You should have heard his sermon!" She smacks herself in the forehead. "About how difficult a man's life is. Everything about a *man's* life, a *man's* cross to carry! As if we women were lying around on our backs all week, waiting to get . . ."

"Helen," my father says, smiling at her, or maybe wincing. My mother stops, startled, almost as if she is just waking up. She takes off her coat, smoothes her skirt, flashes me a dignified red lipstick smile.

"H'lo Rosie," she says. "Let me get you and Pulkowski some lunch."

In a flutter of full skirt and upturned heels, my mother disappears into the kitchen. We stare after her, a little stunned. Then, eyes back on the TV, the baseball fans creating the hum of a vacuum cleaner in the background. I listen, reminded of Eleanor running her Bissell back and forth, back and forth over the dentists' carpets.

"Dad," I say, "how are you doing?"

I keep my eyes on the screen. A player on third base catches the ball then pounces on a runner heading there. He falls on top of him with the ball, squashing him like a cartoon mouse. I hear my father rustling around in his chair. I hear the cushions sigh. I glance over at him. "Okay," he says to the flattened baseball player. Then: "Guess I'll be going in for your mother's meal."

He rises like he's been called by a silent bell. On his way past me he bends from his formidable height and squeezes my shoulder. It is very gentle, very quick. His hand is heavy and warm, the fingers fringed with sparse wiry hairs. I look up at his khaki pants, his short-sleeved business shirt, his television glasses. He's a giant, but he's never raised his hand to me. Still, I need more than a squeeze on the shoulder. I need him to talk to me.

My mother has set the table with horrible Melmac plates that no one else's mother would ever own.

"You'll stay for lunch, Rosie."

"Can't do it today," I tell her, floating past the set table and moving toward the back door.

"What do you *mean*?" my mother asks in her most aggrieved voice. She's standing at the stove with one hand on her hip, the other threateningly gripping a soup ladle. There's a speckle of tomato soup on her cheek.

"I'm going home to make my own lunch," I tell her. "I don't want to turn out like those Jesuits."

"I'll give you such a lump," she warns, waving the ladle. But I'm already gone, out the screen door, off to my car. He should have talked to me. I came all this way over.

I drive slowly through my childhood town. I sit at a red light at the Commack Park staring at the swings my mother used to push me on. Now the metal bars are painted in bright stripes of yellow and red, reminding me of Inga, and the cardboard cartons of Vital-Min products, packaged in the same colors, that she carries around in the trunk of her car. She's made her career selling Almost Cookies, some horrid mash of seaweed and grain and molasses created by a crazed vitamin manufacturer in California. Inga represents the whole line of "organic alternatives," as she calls the mulchy snacks, peddling them to health clubs and natural food markets and even to 7-Elevens all over the Northeast. She sells Almost Candy and Almost Doodles, the chips bagged in the shiny reds and yellows of Fritos, and I have secretly attributed Inga's success in unloading the stuff to the fact that she is blond and thin and female. I, myself, have never been tempted to stock up on Almost products, and in the past, when Inga has offered me a bar of this or a bag of that, I have politely demurred. I've had plenty of experience in almost getting what I want. When it comes to food, I put my size nine down. Still, somebody's swallowing what Inga sells. Maybe Teddy's raising a bluish Almost chip to his pink gums now, masticating it tenderly as he watches Inga weed her impatiens.

At home, the red light on the telephone answering machine is winking seductively in Teddy's abandoned study. I pretend I will find a message there from my father, telling me not to worry, that he's fine, that the blood in his urine is nothing. *Remember, Rosie,* he'll add before the beep, *a person doesn't have to talk all the time to tell you he loves you.* When I get to the machine, a glowing number 3 causes my stomach to jump. Three messages while I was out! My finger jabs at the PLAY button.

Hi Roseanna. How are you? Ham here. Or Mickey, if you like.
Uhh . . . everything's fine at work with Milton. I'm calling . . .
ah . . . on that other matter we discussed in my office earlier
this week. Please give me a call if you have a moment.
BEEP!

Yeah, Roseanna. [It's Teddy!] *Listen, ah . . . Inga men-*
tioned to me that you stopped over this week. At the house.
Possibly looking for me. Please do not stop in at Inga's house
unannounced like that, ah . . . in the future. It's very up-
setting to her and it's not fair to her. If you wish to speak
with me, please call first and we will make those arrange-
ments.
Clunk! BEEP!

Miss Plow? Miss Plow? This is Milton calling! Milton Beyer?
Your best worker at the SaveWay? I'm a very good worker,
Miss Plow. But I'm not at work now. I'm home . . . but my
mother's at the SaveWay, buying some food! Isn't that funny?
I'm calling to tell you something. Just wait.

I wait. I hear a phone receiver bumping around, then some
heavy, anxious breathing.

Take my breath AWAAAAY! AAY! AAY! AAY!

The singing mercifully stops. More bumping. More breathing.

It's okay to tell you I love you, right? 'Cause I'm not at work?
Do you know I looked up your number in the phone book?
Just like you taught me! And guess what? This is really
funny! There are lots of plows in the yellow part of the book.
For snow! Snow plows! Isn't that funny? I love you, Miss
Plow . . . I . . .

   BEEP!

I press the STOP button and then let myself fall into Teddy's
leather chair. It is a supersized overstuffed lounger I've always
hated, ego-building furniture for the insecurely endowed,
which we're still paying off. I rest my cheek against the brown
cushion, which faintly smells of him: Speed Stick and musk.
I'm trying to get the lame Jessica Simpson remake out of my
head when the doorbell rings.

My doorbell.

I open the door and Inga is standing there.

It takes my breath away.

like a blood clot

Inga steps into my apartment without being asked. She's wearing short shorts and a teeny teal tank top with a built-in bra. She is pained, and it makes her face look about ten years older. Even in her pain there is something shallow in her expression, like Paris Hilton with the sun in her eyes at a photo shoot. I wonder why I've never noticed this before.

"May I come in, Rosie?" she whispers in a martyred voice.

"I guess you've already handled that," I say, feeling less cocky than I sound—feeling, if the truth be known, scared. She is gripping a small book in her long smooth fingers. She follows my eyes to the paperback in her hands and takes a deep breath.

"Rosie. Rosie," she says, exhaling dramatically.

"Inga. Inga," I retort unkindly. Her presence in my living room is bringing out the worst in me. I don't mean to be cruel, but she has chosen the wrong audience for her melodrama. When I came to her house to talk, she escaped out another door. I am almost tempted to leap from a third floor window to escape her now. I imagine myself lying on the hard cement side of the Ronkonkoma Arms swimming pool, shocked residents circling my broken body like a wagon train, Inga screaming, "No!"

But how would this teach Inga anything? I guess I don't know *how* one acts under these circumstances.

"I wish I could hug you," Inga says.

I take an involuntary step backward. The thought of Inga touching me makes me ill.

"I wish I could just give you a big hug," she says again, tears rising in her eyes. I discover I like this, the tears rising in her eyes. I hope she's suffering terribly. I hope she sees what she's asking of me, just by standing here in my living room, making me feel nervous and foolish with her crumpled face and her ridiculous desire for reconciliation. My thoughts fly to the cake my mother baked for me, then took home again. I wish I had never let her take it. The dark chocolate cake was moist and the icing was swirly and I could be eating it right now, comforting myself. Or I could be throwing it at Inga, hurling chunks of devil's food at her pale face. I have never felt more confused in my life.

I don't ask Inga to sit down. We just stand there, like two gunfighters in front of Miss Kitty's saloon, Inga armed with her paperback, me armed with, well, nothing.

"I brought this book of poems my mother used to read," she tells me. "I know it seems odd, but it was the best way I knew to explain to you what . . . happened . . . between Teddy and me."

I wince at the mention of my husband's name in her mouth. She holds out the book; I read its title: *Love Poems*. Anne Sexton. Her mother used to read love poems, while my mother was competing in the Pillsbury Bake-Off. How could this woman ever have been my friend?

"They're about adultery," Inga continues. "But in the hands of Anne Sexton, adultery becomes"—she looks down—"*spiritually educational.*" She laughs. "Or, so the introduction claims." A moony look crosses her face. I feel like slugging her. She gushes on.

"Oh Rosie! I so much want you to understand how this thing happened! It was not something we planned! It was . . . here." I watch her flip through some pages. She settles on one and begins reading:

Your hand found mine.
Life rushed into my fingers like a blood clot.

I am speechless. On and on she goes in her lilting voice, something about fingers dancing, her voice on fire now as she delivers the mother load lines.

Oh, my carpenter . . .
They dance in the attic and in Vienna.

She stops there and gazes at me.

I am stunned. "He's not a carpenter," is all I can manage. I find myself falling onto the couch. Inga rushes over and sits beside me. I move quickly away from her. The thought of her brushing up against me makes me homicidal.

"When Sylvia Plath's husband committed adultery, she put her head in the oven," I inform her, this bitch sitting on the couch beside me. This fake, this traitor, this hollow intellectual. She used to watch *Survivor* with Teddy and me. She knows more about how to find fresh water on an island than she knows about Anne Sexton.

"And what's the significance of Vienna?" I ask my knees. "Did you bang my husband there, too?"

Again I'm surprised at myself, at how I'm settling so comfortably into being cruel. I gaze at our row of knees, Inga's bare and smooth as piano keys, mine like two navy blue ham hocks, something Mickey Hamilton would be proud to have said he cut away from the rump roast. Suddenly I hear Inga crying beside me, as though she is the aggrieved party, as though she is the one who is big-boned and abandoned, the one whose husband has walked out on her. She once had a married boyfriend who'd offered to leave his wife for her, but Inga had told him to go back to his wife, that their affair wasn't right. What has happened to Inga's sense of morality? How will I ever know if I don't ask her?

I turn to her lovely face, now a little puffy and tear-streaked, and ask her my question. "Inga," I say. "How could you have done this to me?"

"I *didn't* do this to you!" she sobs. "Teddy did this to *me*."

The room starts spinning, and I'm glad I'm sitting down. "What?" I gasp.

"It was Teddy. He started showing up nights at my house. What was I supposed to do? Turn my best friend's husband out?"

I am incredulous. My hands curl into fists. "Did you think you might have *told* your best friend he was showing up?"

Inga's eyes flash. "Why didn't you know he was out?"

This stops me momentarily. I *did* know he was out. I'd watched him put his bomber jacket on night after night. I'd listened to him make his lame announcements about "getting some air." I'd never questioned him about why he wanted twenty-below-zero air on the coldest winter evenings, never raised a finger to stop him. I was all about giving. Inga lets out another sob and I turn. Looks like I gave my husband away.

I clasp my hands together. I know why I let him go out in the cold. It was because of the coldness he brought *with* him when he entered our home each night. How long had I noticed it, hoping it would dissipate and saying nothing?

"Please, Rosie. You've got to forgive me."

"No I don't," I tell Inga, rising. "I don't have to forgive you at all." I stride to the front door and open it.

"You were supposed to be my friend," I say.

"But Rosie, I *want* to be your friend . . ."

I swing open the door. "I hope you don't mind, but I slept with your boyfriend last week. Of course, he *is* my husband."

Inga's mouth falls open in a gasp.

"I couldn't help it. He was like . . . Vienna! Like a Vienna Finger! I just had to lick him. It was so *spiritually educational*."

"Rosie! How could you?"

"It was easy," I tell her, waving her out at the open door. "That's the guy you're supposedly buying a house with," I add.

Inga rises like an uneasy colt from the couch. I look at her from the door and all I see are twigs and bones. "Look at you," I say. "You're a walking dragonfly. A vertical praying mantis. A stick pin."

This is the meanest thing I have ever said to another human

being. It feels like my mother is coming out of my own mouth. It feels good, though. Better than poetry.

"You look like Kirstie Alley before the diet," Inga seethes, storming toward the open door. Now tears rise in my eyes. It's not the insult so much. It's knowing Inga's and my friendship is ending. It's over. No more laughs, drinks, confidences, shopping trips, dinner parties. It's over, and I'm helping it to be over. I *want* it to be over. I don't want a best friend who could do this to me, who could sleep with my husband, then come by with her mother's poetry book to make it all right.

"I'm sorry I was ever your friend," I tell her. "I'm sorry I shared *anything* with you." But Inga doesn't answer. She just drifts past me like a breeze. She's clutching her paperback in her hand, her lips sealed in a thin embalmed line. I am sure there's nothing in her book of love poems to describe the way she is feeling toward me now. Besides, a person doesn't have to talk all the time to tell you she hates you.

goodnight, spongebob

i spoke to your mother this weekend," Marcie tells me on Monday morning.

"Why? Was I misbehaving in the office?" I drop my overstuffed briefcase in front of my desk.

"She's worried about your father and she's worried about you." Marcie sits on the edge of my desk, making the hem of her blouse rise and the Aztec sun tattooed just above her butt crack visible. One wonders what Sean Zambuto thinks of these little works of art—the Aztec sun, the ankle tattoo, the Chinese symbol for peace that rises from her cleavage. I, of course, can never go down Marcie's road of decorative body art—not if I want my mother to ever invite me into her home again. And maybe this is for the best, as I can only imagine myself at fifty, alone and chubby, with the Aztec sun above my butt crack sagging into a runny blue half-moon.

"Don't you ever feel bad about meddling in my life?" I ask Marcie.

"No. And anyway, your mother called me first." She turns to me, unruffled. "Your mother thinks you should go out with that guy from the SaveWay."

This annoys me, as does Marcie's friendship with my mother, and the fact that I cannot sit down at my own desk, with Marcie blocking it.

"Why don't you just move in with Helen?" I ask.

"I don't think Pulkowski would like that," she laughs. But she doesn't leave. She just sits there, staring at me, like she knows something I don't.

I'm waiting for Eleanor to arrive in the little van that brings her to my office for our meetings, the *retardo-van*, as Marcie calls it, not with a lick of cruelty, mind you, but sort of in the way that rappers affectionately call each other the N word. In truth, she admires my clients deeply. In Marcie's eyes, if you're different, if you're *out there* enough, you're the bomb. No one is more out there than Eleanor.

"May I sit down?" I finally ask Marcie. She rises from my desk, offering me her weekly fashion show, this time in the form of a demented Catholic school student. Her white blouse with its prim Peter Pan collar stops inches above the drooping waistband of her pleated skirt. Her flat stomach is exposed and naked, but for the Celtic cross tattoo stretching its arms dramatically beneath her belly button. "You've got a lunch date on Wednesday," she says. "With me."

"Oh really? Where are we going?"

She smiles like a temptress. "Let's just say it's an open house."

I want to ask her more, but she turns and walks toward the door.

"Your client's here," she says. "Looking sunny in yellow."

• • •

Eleanor walks in without making eye contact. She slouches in the plastic office chair, running her hand up and down her knee like she's DustBusting it. Eleanor has shown up at work this past week with a small mysterious gym bag. At about nine o'clock, she disappears into the dental suite restroom, the very one she's just scrubbed and polished, and changes into a SpongeBob SquarePants nightgown and Garfield slippers.

"Eleanor," I say, peeking at her over the edge of her folder, "tell me again what you do when your work is done at the dentist's office."

Eleanor twists the hem of her brightly flowered blouse into little knots. "I don't like you," she says.

"Eleanor, what do you do after you've put away the vacuum and the bucket?"

"I would never bake a cake for you."

This hurts a little. Eleanor is known for her cakes at the Cooperative Living Center. She is not afraid to stick anything— celery, refrigerator magnets, Cracker Jack prizes—into the icing, to jazz them up.

"Eleanor," I say. "You call home. You call until the counselor picks up, and then you tell her you need your ride."

"Not even if you asked." She crosses her arms.

"Let's review. You dial your telephone number, right on Dr. Sharpe's phone . . ."

"No, I don't! No, I don't!" Eleanor lifts the hem of her blouse over her face, exposing soft breasts in a pink bra, the breadbasket of her stomach in blue polyester.

"Eleanor," I say, "please pull down your blouse."

"No!"

"Come on, Eleanor. Please."

With stubby Down syndrome fingers, she lowers her top slowly. First, the brown almond eyes appear, startlingly beautiful. Then, the doughy flesh of the nose, the flat cheeks, the wide, slightly opened mouth. It doesn't seem fair.

"Can you tell me why you're angry?" I ask.

Eleanor shrugs. She scrunches her shoulders up until she looks like a hand puppet, all neckless and bunchy. I know why she's angry. She's angry because her night counselor might be replaced on account of my phone call and report. Eleanor hates change. She would rather have a lousy counselor greet her in the morning than a new one. It's difficult to keep trusting, over and over again. I can understand this.

I review the dress code again. "Why no nightgowns at work?" I ask.

Eleanor's rocking back and forth in her chair.

"Because you don't sleep there, you *work* there," I explain.

She stops rocking, sits up straight. "I slept there!"

"But that was a mistake."

"I slept there! I slept there!" Eleanor insists. "All night."

"It won't happen again," I assure her. But really, how do I know?

When our meeting ends, I walk Eleanor down to the street to where her ride is waiting. She climbs into the minibus and I follow down the aisle, past the impassive driver who is reading a motorcycle magazine, past a man in a wheelchair who smells like vegetable soup. I struggle with the impossible metal clasp of Eleanor's seatbelt, wondering what it would be like to be pregnant for nine months and then give birth to this exotic, lovely, broad-faced girl—a daughter who would never drive a car, who would never go to college, and who now will never bake me a cake.

I drag myself back upstairs, stopping at Marcie's big desk, the heart of operations in the center of EPT's reception area.

"So where are we going Wednesday?" I ask.

"You'll see on Wednesday," she says, studying me shrewdly. "What's the matter with you?"

"Nothing."

I trundle off to my office. Once there, I shut the door, slump in the chair, and rest my head on my desktop. I stay like that until the phone starts ringing and I pick it up.

"Mickey Hamilton," a deep voice says.

I sit up. Before he gets past hello, I decide to cut things short.

"Mr. Hamilton," I say, using my most professional voice. "I guess I haven't been very clear. I'm not really interested in dating at the moment."

"That's fine," he says, "but I'm calling about Milton."

He says this in his distinct Mr. Hamilton Voice, then lets me wallow in my embarrassment for a few seconds.

"Milton's sick," he says. "A 103-degree fever."

"How do you know?"

"I keep a thermometer in my glove compartment."

"You do? Why?"

"For things like this. I keep a blanket, too."

I sit up even straighter. How thoughtful could a man be?

"Ms. Plow," he says.

I should have suspected he was thoughtful by the way he puts his arm around Milton at the store.

"Ms. Plow."

"Yes?"

"Milton," he says. "What do we do about Milton?"

flies in the ointment

I find mickey hamilton hunched over Milton in his small cluttered office, surrounded by tacked-up messages on his pocked bulletin boards, posters that admonish employees to wash their hands on both sides and refrigerate things correctly. He's holding a mug of something in his big mitt, offering it to Milton in the soft tones of a lullaby.

"Good morning," I say, but they don't look up. Not even Milton, who loves me enough to look for my name in the yellow pages. I walk closer to the two of them, until I am standing behind Mr. Hamilton, or Ham, or Mickey, staring down at the wide shoulders of his white shirt. I've never noticed how wide his shoulders are, possibly from hacking meat. In a second he rises.

"Ms. Plow," he says. "I didn't see you."

I smile a little. I have always loved it when a man doesn't see me. "How is Milton?" I ask.

Mickey Hamilton leans his face toward my ear. His breath

warms my cheek as he speaks. It smells of mint Life Savers. "Not good," he confides.

We decide that I should get Milton home. Maybe his mother will be there by now. Mickey Hamilton slings Milton's arm over his shoulder and wraps his own arm around Milton's waist. We usher him to my car and lay him carefully across the backseat. He is so sick that he doesn't even smile for me. His handsome face is closed, the adult drained out of it. His fever frightens him. I catch myself in the act of almost stroking his hair.

"You'll be okay," I tell him soothingly.

"Wait," Mickey says, and I watch him jog to a shiny blue pickup at the end of the lot. He opens the door, extracts a pink blanket, carries it toward us. He tucks it around Milton and gently closes the car door.

"I'd take him home myself," he says, "but my assistant's out sick."

I nod.

"Flu," he says. "Probably what Milton's got, from him."

"Right," I say.

"Better get him home."

We drive in silence. I try not to inhale too much. I follow a map in my mind to Milton's house. I try not to think about what nice shoulders Mickey Hamilton has. Then I remember him lecturing me on all the Fishers in the world. If he weren't such a sanctimonious ass, Ham might be all right.

Then again, it's only his personality that's a problem. And his sideburns. But what man doesn't have a fly in the ointment, once you get to know him? Teddy has swarms of them. Teddy is typhoid, when it comes to flies in his ointment.

I've been to Milton's house twice before to meet with his pretty mother, whose worry lines show up more in her home than at my meetings. Linda Beyer's a powerhouse professionally, rumored to have found Billy Joel an estate or two on the far, exclusive end of the Island. But at home, she's just another anxious parent. I've sat in her living room, the decor thoughtful and perfect, the touches personal and telling—a bronzed baby shoe on a table, a robin's nest on a windowsill. Milton is her only child. I've seen his bedroom, which has a teddy bear on the bed and a poster of Britney Spears on the wall. We've spoken in Linda Beyer's elegant rooms about the "success in the workplace" Milton might aspire to. Her expression is pained when I define success as donning a bright green smock with the word SAVEWAY emblazoned across the chest.

"Milton," I call softly into the backseat, "we called your mother, but she isn't home. We're just going to stop by now, and see if someone's there."

Milton doesn't answer me. I check my rearview mirror and discover he's asleep. I know that driving him home is a wild goose chase, but what else am I supposed to do with him?

"Wait here," I tell Milton, even though he's still sleeping, and then I get out of the car, walk up the beautifully landscaped front path, and try his front door. No answer. I leave a note for Mrs. Beyer with my phone number, tucking it halfway through the handsome brass mail slot. Then we back out of the long brick driveway and head for the Ronkonkoma Arms.

On the way home I'm thinking of Teddy, of the first time we ever made love, after a Christmas party at Inga's apartment. How Inga introduced Teddy, an old friend from her Stony

Brook days, that very night at her party. How Teddy looked so sweet, so big and clunky and muscular, in the way that all the best breeds of sports dogs do, and how I fell instantly in love with his square, manly chin, and that vulnerability he wore between the open top buttons of his red flannel L.L.Bean shirt. How trembly I was later, unbuttoning that shirt, as he sat me on his lap in his tiny Northport basement apartment. And then, I'd slept with him. Just like that. I was no party girl, but I knew it was all right, that he was the one I was born to marry. At least, that's what I'd thought back then. Now here I am driving around husbandless, a retarded man in a pink blanket sleeping on my backseat. What has happened?

Milton is difficult to rouse, once we're parked at the Ronkonkoma Arms. I try shaking his shoulder, but he doesn't stir. I bend over the top of him, wrap my arms around, and pull. Milton exhales suddenly, spewing flu germs at my nose and mouth. His glassy eyes open and grow wide.

"Miss Plow!" he whispers. "Oh! Miss Plow!" His arms rise and encircle me, before I can react.

"Oh, Miss Plow!" Milton says again, and then my face is crushed into his hot body, somewhere between his neck and armpit.

"Milton!" I cry, but my voice is muffled against his chest. My feet are still on the ground outside, but they are in danger of rising. Milton guides my face to his with his hand beneath my chin. I'm pinned to his body by his other arm when he presses his lips to mine and kisses me.

It is a warm, feverish kiss. I hear him breathing hard as his mouth moves against mine. I smell his sickness, but also his

baby shampoo. I can't think, and then I can. I think about the
flu I'll be getting next week. I think about how Milton is my
client. I think about how nicely this developmentally challenged man kisses. I wonder if this is sexual harassment, then
realize that I'm the one trapped, and then wonder who is ha-
rassing whom. I manage to brace my hands against his chest
and push free.

"Milton!" I say. "I was not trying to kiss you. I was trying to
wake you up!"

Milton smiles a flushed jubilant smile and sits up in the car.
"Oh, Miss Plow," he says, pulling the pink blanket around him,
"I was trying to kiss *you.*"

He beams at me with pure love for every hair on my head,
every blemish on my body, every last pound of me. It warms me
in an odd way. He is my Mr. Right with the wrong brain.

"Come on, Milton," I say. "Let's go inside and wait for your
mother."

He climbs out of the backseat, blanket trailing, and slowly
we make our way through the rows of parked cars toward my
apartment. He's hunched forward a bit, shuffling toward the
elevator like he might topple over any minute.

"We're almost there," I tell him, as we enter the elevator. He
bundles himself against the mirrored wall.

"Where?"

"My apartment."

The elevator whines as it climbs.

"Your apartment?"

"Yes."

"Your *home*?"

"Yes."

"Oh, Miss Plow! I've never been to your home before!"

"Well, Milton, your mother isn't home right now . . ."

"She makes me toast. Will you make me toast?"

He rubs his arms briskly beneath the blanket, either cold or excitement, or both.

"I'll make you toast," I promise him, "and then you can rest."

The elevator door opens on my floor. Before we can step out, a man's voice travels toward us from somewhere down the corridor. "Hold that for a moment, will you?" Milton's finger jabs the DOOR HOLD button, but I freeze.

I know this voice.

I peek out the elevator door and there he is, bounding toward us, rolling his brown leather desk chair along ahead of him.

Surprised does not describe Teddy's face when he catches sight of Milton and me. The overstuffed chair is rushing toward us inside the elevator.

"Don't hit us!" Milton yells when he sees it. Milton raises his hands to his face and the pink blanket drops to his feet.

I pick up the blanket. "What are you doing here?" I ask Teddy. But it's obvious what he's doing here. He's taking things out of our apartment, emptying out our home of everything he considers his. He's doing it the sneaky way: no call first, no prior arrangements made with his spouse. He's wrestled his surprised expression into submission and now his cool lawyer look overtakes his face. He's wearing a flannel shirt, not unlike the one I met him in at Inga's Christmas party. The shirt is tucked into too-tight Levi's, as if he were a teenager, as if he were on his way to the local high school to show off his butt to the girls. This is what extramarital love has done to him. He's put on a little weight in the face, maybe too many Almost Cookies, but his butt still looks good in the jeans. He's got it facing us now, as he attempts to maneuver the desk chair into the elevator. He hasn't even waited for Milton and me to get out. As if we're his elevator operators, a woman in a pleated skirt and a man in a pink blanket. I am upset by how good his butt looks. If there were a God, his behind would be ruined for Inga. *Something* would be ruined, something besides me.

I wave an open hand at the chair, slapping the air the way I'd like to slap him. "Are you going to finish paying for that, now that you're taking it away?"

Milton has moved behind me now, breathing virus cells on the top of my head that gently tickle the part in my hair.

"Who's he?" Teddy asks, and I sense Milton's weight shifting the tiniest bit.

"This is Milton Beyer, and he is sick with the flu."

Teddy makes a face.

"So you're bringing sick men up to your apartment now?"

He's smirking behind the chair that smells like him. He thinks he's made a funny joke. This is what makes my hand fly out and push him, palm against flannel, but it is his own weakness that makes him stumble then bounce against the closed door, until suddenly he is sitting on the elevator floor with the giant upturned seat wedged into his crotch.

"Jesus Christ!" Teddy cries.

"Miss Plow!" Milton moans. "Oh, Miss Plow, I don't like this."

Teddy's gaze moves from me to Milton. "Oh, he's *retarded*," he says, almost apologetically. "You didn't tell me he was *retarded*."

"I never told you you were a jerk, either," I say, and then the stupid faucet starts up again, flooding my eyes, automatic as rain. I'm sniffling like a baby when I feel the weight of Milton's heavy arm circling my shoulders and neck like a noose.

"Don't you be mean to Miss Plow," I hear Milton tell my husband. It's a whole new voice coming out of him. Growling, deep, formidable. Teddy rises quickly, brushing himself off and then the chair. "Look now, pal," he says, in a horrible patronizing voice, "everything's fine here. You don't need to worry about Miss Plow . . ."

"Jerk!" Milton hollers. "Jerk! Gay jerk! Retarded jerk!"

I whirl around in our tiny crowded space and look at Milton's beet red face. He stands with his fists curled, a big man, bigger than Teddy, the fine hairs on the sides of his neck standing straight out. Teddy's smiling sheepishly behind his brown leather chair. Cover your balls, I think. You really should.

My finger finds the DOOR OPEN button. "Let's go, Milton," I say.

"Okay, Miss Plow. We'll make toast." I feel his heavy arm go around my shoulders again. He drags me down the hall in his protective custody.

"Milton," I tell him, when we've gotten to my open door. "It's time to remember your work manners again."

"Okay," Milton says, letting go.

"Milton."

"Yes, Miss Plow."

"Good work."

"Thank you."

I lock the door behind us when we're in the living room. I put on the dead bolt. Teddy's junk mail is sprawled across the pink couch cushions. He's forgotten his leather bomber jacket, too, the one I bought him for his birthday at the Sharper Image. The TV's still there, but there's a gap along the kitchen wall where the butcher-block microwave cart used to be. The oven rests on the floor now, a bunch of my cookbooks stacked on top. I settle Milton with a clean blanket on the couch, make him tea and cinnamon toast. He sighs contentedly as he eats his toast, his plate resting on his belly. The crumbs fall on his blanket and outline his mouth in a fine curry-colored mist.

"This makes me so happy," he says.

There's a timid knock at the door, but we don't answer it.

the lunch special

aren't you curious about what's on today's menu?"
Marcie asks as she whisks me away from the EPT parking lot in
her ancient Isuzu Rodeo. Big Red, she calls it, and yes, it is big,
and it's red, but it's also the most uncomfortable vehicle I have
ever ridden in. Marcie takes a speed bump at forty miles an
hour, pretty much assuring that we'll both never have children
or at least never have full range of motion in our necks again.
She cuts off a Hummer exiting the lot, and the driver blares his
giant-sized horn at us.

"Ass monkey," Marcie says.

It's Wednesday afternoon, and our mystery lunch date is in
high gear.

"Doesn't this thing have shocks?" I ask Marcie, then add:
"How can I guess what's on the menu if I don't know where
you're taking me?"

Marcie reaches across me to the glove compartment and
pulls the lever. It springs open unnervingly and a brown bag

falls onto my lap. "There's another one in there, too," she says. "Our lunches. We'll be eating them on the way."

"On the way to where?"

"On the way to Teddy and Inga's new house."

My head springs forward a little, either a pothole or Marcie's announcement.

"*Are you crazy?*" I ask her. "Pull this truck over!"

"We're just about there," Marcie says calmly.

"Pull it over! Pull Big Red over! Now!"

I am almost sorry that she obeys me. Marcie jerks the wheel hard to the right and lands us in someone's driveway. It occurs to me, for the first time, that we have been driving through a residential neighborhood—a *nearby* residential neighborhood—not two miles from the EPT office building.

"We're only three blocks away," Marcie says.

I gaze at the spaces between her bristles of hair. She's letting the blond grow in by ruthlessly chopping off the black. Now each individual spike looks like a candy corn in black and white.

"Don't you want to see?" Marcie asks, her voice gentle and cajoling. "Don't you want to know?"

"How do *you* know?" I ask her.

"It's easy to find out who's bought a house if you work in the county office building."

"You went to the Registry of Deeds?"

"No, but I could have. I just went online and searched grantees in Nassau and Suffolk County. Two seconds later, up popped Inga's name!"

She tells me this in the cheerful tones of a children's librarian. Meanwhile, my stomach feels like it's in a meat grinder.

"It's not possible," I manage to utter. "Teddy only told me they were looking for a house a few weeks ago . . ."

Marcie doesn't seem to be listening. "Bitch-Inga, I call her," she says. "*Bitchinga.* Don't you think that has a nice ring to it? *Hola, Bitchinga!* It has a Latin flair, I think. Something the Buena Vista Social Club might sing . . ."

"Marcie! Stop!" I put my hands over my ears, but it's really my eyes I want to cover. I don't want this house to exist. It *can't* exist. Not yet.

"They must have been planning this for months, while he was still at home," I say, suddenly aware of the ugly truth. "While he was still in my bed, hogging the comforter. While he was still eating the dinners I cooked him, while I was still washing and folding his underwear, sorting out his socks . . ."

"Yup." Marcie nods. "He was probably getting laid over there, too. By Bitchinga. The guy needs a twelve-step program. A ONE LAY AT A TIME bumper sticker, a . . ."

"Marcie, stop!" Now my hands have moved to my eyes, and my palms are wet with tears.

"Hey, hey, little sister," Marcie coos, rubbing my back in big swirly strokes. "He was no good to begin with. You know that."

Of course I know it, but what does it have to do with this terrible moment in the front seat of Big Red? My sobs are coming out in big gulps now. I wipe my eyes and see that I have elbowed my brown bag lunch into a squashed pancake. Not that I could ever eat it. Not that I could ever eat again. Well, maybe at least not for a couple of hours.

Teddy. His name tastes like poison on my tongue. Stracuzza. A loser. A total loser.

Marcie waits a minute until I have somewhat regained my composure. Then she pats my hand and shifts into Reverse. "Ready?" she asks.

"Why do we have to do this?"

"Because I am your friend, and I can see that you have been making an ass out of yourself over this dude, Rosie. You've got to look the truth in the eye, girlfriend! And I'm going to help you do it."

I think Marcie has the Japanese symbol for truth tattooed somewhere on her torso. It's big with her. I should get it tattooed on my ass, so I can continue to sit on the truth, the way I have been doing for months now. I turn to Marcie with new resolve.

"I'm ready," I tell her.

"Good. We're almost there."

We back out onto the residential street and drive three blocks, past hideous garrison ranches with pillars that look like two-by-fours, even though the houses probably go for half a million. We make a right onto a street call Bluebell Lane, and Marcie tells me this is the street.

I rename it Dumbbell Lane, because Teddy will live on it. Bitchinga Court is nice, too. I'm culling my brain for other lame witticisms when Big Red abruptly stops, in front of a pink monstrosity with the two-by-four-type columns gracing the front. It's a garrison, its heavy overlay of a second floor hanging over the top like a pregnant belly. The skinny faux-Georgian columns look like they might buckle beneath the weight. It's a Pepto-Bismol nightmare, a house that only Long Island could spawn.

"This is it?" I ask needlessly.

"Yup, twenty-one Bluebell Lane."

"Looks like anyone over twenty-one would know better than to go near it."

"That's the spirit," Marcie says, rewarding me with one of her beautiful smiles.

She does have a beautiful smile. So why, I wonder for the zillionth time, is she sleeping with Sean Zambuto? My reverie is halted when a sleek BMW pulls up behind Big Red. I am shocked to see Linda Beyer stepping out of the car.

"What is Milton's mother doing here?" I ask.

Marcie smiles mischievously. "Don't worry. She didn't sell the house to Teddy, but she used to work at the realtor's. She knows everyone there. I just called her up and asked her if she'd do you a favor."

"Do *me* a favor?"

"Yes. She loves you. You're so good with Milton, and you did take him home with you last week, when he was sick."

"What? Do *me* a favor?"

"Want to go in?" Marcie asks. She's opening her door to step out and greet Linda Beyer. I pull up my jacket collar as high as it will go, but there's no hiding my flushed, stunned face. Linda Beyer is waving at me through the window. What can I do but step out of the vehicle?

"Hello, Miss Plow," she says, looking perfect in Burberry. Her gorgeous legs shoot from the bottom like picturesque flower stems. She strides smartly in her Marc Jacobs, shoes with tips sharper than steak knives, shoes that would cripple me, should I ever try to cram my size nine-wides into them.

"This wasn't my idea," I quickly tell Linda, casting swords with my eyes at Marcie.

Milton's mother squeezes my hand. "I kind of figured it wasn't. But isn't it nice to know that Mr. Stracuzza and Ms. Stockholm bought such a dog?" She glances over at the pink monstrosity. "Not only that, but the basement leaks. This house'll be smelling like the bottom of a clothes hamper in no time."

Marcie snorts with laughter. "That is so great," she says.

I am not laughing along. I'm frozen to the curb, trying to make sense of this field trip Marcie and Linda Beyer have arranged for me. How much does Linda Beyer know? And why the hell is Marcie telling her my business? Does her sphere of influence include not only the office, but everything that touches it?

Linda Beyer seems to read my thoughts. She pats my shoulder and looks at me. "Roseanna," she says, with a new frankness in her voice, "I can only imagine how hard this must be for you. And it's not fair. You're a good person." She smiles before concluding her comments. "The least we can do is have a look at this place. I think, after you do, you'll feel better."

"So we're going in now?" Marcie asks.

Linda Beyer nods.

"Oh, goodie!" Marcie claps her hands together like a child at Disneyland. She skips up the front path ahead of us. Linda guides me up the flagstone, like the scarecrow leading Dorothy. It figures my own personal Oz is a hot pink garrison ranch. I stare down at the patchy lawn, wishing my husband and best friend crab grass, ants, rot. Linda turns a key in the front door lock and then we walk through rooms of low ceilings and bad wallpaper. Aluminum casement windows. Stained wall-to-wall carpeting in bad colors like avocado and gold. I think of my mother, and how she resisted all these color trends of the sixties, seventies, and eighties, sticking instead to her beige for all things. My mother seems like a genius now, as I poke my head into a chartreuse bathroom.

They would paint it, of course. I can imagine Inga in her little short shorts and halter, stretching adorably with a paint roller in her hand. "I've had enough," I announce to Marcie and Linda. Marcie looks disappointed but Linda nods gravely, and we make our way back to the front door.

"Isn't it gross?" Marcie asks gleefully as we walk to the cars. "I could smell mildew already."

"What are they going to do with all that room?" I absently ask no one, but then I am sorry I've said it. It's obvious to all of us what they'll do with that room. They'll fill it with little blond children. Tears spring to my eyes. Marcie grabs my hand.

"He's a schmuck," she says.

"He is," Linda Beyer agrees.

I place myself wordlessly back on the car seat. Linda Beyer says something else, maybe something about Milton, but my hearing seems not to work. I nod idiotically and wave, and then she vanishes.

We sit, staring at spindly town trees planted along the curb. "Why did she go along with this?" I ask Marcie, looking straight ahead through the windshield.

"Have you ever met Milton's father?" Marcie says in response. "Do you even know if he *has* one?"

Come to think of it, I never have met Milton's father. It is always his mother, the glamorous Linda Beyer, who shows up at our monthly parent meetings, wowing the other parents with her killer body and expensive Caribbean-hued suits.

"You know what *he* did when he discovered his son was retarded? He walked. Now he's married to some bimbo Manhattan socialite, and they send their perfect daughters to the Dalton School."

It is almost impossible to imagine a man leaving Linda Beyer, incomprehensible to imagine *anyone* leaving Milton. Milton, who was placed on this earth to spread the love, to remind you that you are beautiful, to smile at you with chocolate brown eyes.

"How do you know all this?" I ask Marcie.

Marcie fires up Big Red. "I know everything," she says.

We're suddenly moving again, driving off Bluebell Lane onto some other identical street, then onto the Vet's Highway and back to the office. My heart is aching like a bruise. We're driving back from Teddy and Inga's house. Marcie parks in the lot and cuts the engine. We sit in the car a while. Finally, she turns to me and says, "You didn't eat your lunch."

"Neither did you."

"I have Snickers bars in my desk."

We sit quietly a moment.

"So you're actually sleeping with the boss," I say.

"What?"

"You're sleeping with Sean Zambuto?"

Marcie looks down at her lap. I seem to want to pry into her life, as deep as I can go, in return for her having done the same to mine. But I'm also curious. I *want* to know why Marcie is sleeping with Sean. He's no prince, and he's forty-one. On an island that spawned Seinfeld and the Baldwin boys, Sean is merely the usual Long Island recipe of Irish and Italian, like lasagna boiled in a corned beef pot. No glamour there. His hands are little. His olive skin clashes with his Irish pug nose. And yet, here he is, a middle-aged social worker, sleeping with the most beautiful young woman I know. If a man like Sean Zambuto can get a woman like Marcie, what hope is there for me to attract anyone other than, say, a butcher?

"I have never heard him crack a joke," I tell Marcie. "He's never even laughed at the *right* part of your jokes."

She's twisting the hem of her brown paper bag. "It's possible I'm bored at times, for a teeny tiny second maybe," she says. "But when he looks at me with those little darty eyes, I know he loves me."

"*Any* man would love you," I remind her, "even with your stupid hairdos."

"Not *love* me," she says. "Just lust me."

"What's so bad about that?"

Marcie exhales thoughtfully, then turns and pats my hand.

"You want to know why I love Seanie?" she asks. "I'll tell you. He lets me tell him what to do."

"That's it?" I ask. I'm stunned, watching Marcie's eyes grow moist with appreciation.

"With Seanie, I always know how it's going to be," she says.

"Ah," I say. "Not like with Teddy."

She shakes her head resolutely. "Seanie would never do anything like that."

We both seem to know it's time to get out of the car. We slam
Big Red's doors shut and slowly traipse back to the building.
Marcie swings open the heavy glass door and holds it for me.
Sean is waiting at her desk, his thick black hair sitting on his
long head like a feather duster. He's as patient and smiling as
an Irish setter, and Marcie looks grateful for the sight of him.
I'm happy for her though I, of course, wouldn't want an Irish
setter waiting for me at my door. Not that I have this option.

lunch redux

So how's your love life?" my mother inquires on the phone.

"Why don't you ever ask me about my *work* life?"

"It's your love life that's going to hell in a handbasket. Why should I be interested in your work life?"

I'm lying in my half-empty king-sized bed on Saturday morning, not feeling so hot. I suspect I might be coming down with Milton's bug. The sun shines cheerfully through my bedroom window.

"I've been wanting to talk to you about your father," my mother says.

I sit up, suddenly interested. "I've tried to call him a gazillion times."

"And?"

"And then *you* get on, and start grilling me about my love life."

"Hmm," my mother says. Then: "Look, if you want to know

what's going on with Dad, why don't you pick me up for lunch? We can go to that Acropolis Diner on the Veteran's Highway. They have a nice Greek salad over there."

The last thing I want is another lunch date. Not after my last lunch date with Marcie.

"I might be sick," I tell my mother.

"I might be old," she says. "So what? You gotta eat."

She seems awfully keen on this lunch idea. Perhaps she needs my moral support, someone special to talk with about my father.

"I do want to know about Dad," I concede.

"Then get dressed and come pick me up. And wear something nice. And wash your hair and blow dry it."

She hangs up, leaving me with an uneasy feeling. Either she thinks I ordinarily go out filthy or she has something up her sleeve. Chump that I am, I haul myself from my nice safe bed. I head for the shower and then for the car.

I pick my mother up by honking the horn in front of the house, maybe payback for her telling me to wash. She stomps out of the house in a dotted yellow shirtwaist dress, looking like *I Love Lucy*, only half a century too late.

"You can't come in and say hello to your father?" she asks, when she's settled in the front seat.

"I'll see him Sunday," I say. "I want to talk to you first. How is he?"

"You've had a whole lifetime to research that question. You want the Cliff's Notes, now that we're in the car?"

"I mean his illness."

"What illness?"

"He is being checked for prostate cancer . . ."

"That's right, Missy. He's being *checked.*"

"You mean he's not ill?"

"No, I mean he's being checked? Okay? *Checked.*"

My mother's back is so straight, she looks like a large sitting Barbie doll on the car seat. Her breasts jut out like two missiles. She turns her mouth to me, painted lips pursed in a frown, and I see that I'm treading on her one soft spot, my father. But isn't that why we're having lunch today, to talk about my father? Now I'm not sure. My mother extracts a Salem Light from her purse and lights it. I roll down a window and we drive the rest of the way without talking.

When we get to the Acropolis, my mother starts giving me grooming tips again. "Your blouse is all bunched up in back," she says. "Pull it down."

I yank at the back of my pink tank top until it brushes the waist of my jeans. Next her fingers come soaring toward my head. "Here," she says, stabbing them through the front of my hair. "That's better."

"Ma! What are you *doing*?" I walk away from her, stomp up the diner steps ahead of her. She scoots in front of me through the glass door as I swing it open.

And then I see him. And then I know what she is doing.

Mickey Hamilton waves from a booth along the row of front windows, just where my mother likes to sit. She does the fakest-looking double take I have ever seen in my life, throwing her hand over her heart and breathlessly exclaiming, "Oh! Isn't that the fella you work with? At the SaveWay? Well! Will you look at that!"

I stand like a statue in the diner's foyer. My mother has done some manipulative things in the past, like wearing a navy blue pants suit to my wedding, for instance, but this is the lowest of low. This is mortifying, insulting—perhaps even on Mickey Hamilton's part, for going along with it. And yet, I am surprised once more to notice that Mickey Hamilton isn't as boring-looking as I'd once suspected.

My mother is flouncing over to Ham's booth, flushed with excitement, the polka dots on her full skirt bouncing up and down. Ham is rising in faux surprise and delight. I can hear him mouthing his faux spontaneous invitation for us to join him for lunch. When did she orchestrate this? I suddenly re-member her telling me—repeatedly—how it's worth it to drive the extra few miles to the SaveWay to get her meat and produce. And to get her Rosie a new boyfriend, too.

I could wrap my hands around her little polka-dotted collar and throttle her.

Just the same, we all have to eat.

You'd almost have to say Mickey looks *hot* in his black V-necked T-shirt, which stretches nicely over his biceps and brings out glints of gold in his hair. Nothing beige about him to-day. I pull down the front of my tank top, this time possibly on purpose. A nice line of cleavage smiles up at me. *Hello!* Some-times I like being full-figured. Sometimes I hate my mother.

I make my way, as dignified as possible, to the booth of the co-conspirators. Mickey rises a second time. His Polo tee is tucked into linen chinos and the flatness of his stomach is something to see. His seventies sideburns still look awful. His father must have had the same ones when Ham was born. I imagine Ham Senior coming home from his job at the slaughterhouse, telling little Mickey, *Son, someday this will all be yours.*

"Ms. Plow," Mickey says, shaking my hand and smiling. "I'm glad I ran into you"—he turns to acknowledge my beaming seated mother—"and my favorite customer here, of course. Because I was going to call you about Milton anyway."

Bullshit, I think, smiling my biggest smile, the charming one with lots of teeth. "Milton's doing fine," I assure him. "His mother thinks he'll be back at work in a week."

"Great," Mickey says. "I can't tell you how much I miss him. Three customers have had accidents in the parking lot with the empty carts, and two of them have been stolen."

"Customers were stolen?"

"No. Carts." He smiles.

"You two have so much in common," my mother trills.

My eyes shoot darts at her. Bullets. Land missiles.

"Sit down," Mickey says, gesturing graciously at the seat across from him. My mother's already tucked in by the window, hands demurely crossed on her skirted lap. When we leave this place, I will kill her.

A waitress shows up amid my homicidal thoughts and Mickey orders us three beers. Presumptuous, if you ask me, but my mother is charmed.

"Isn't that thoughtful of you," she says. When the Millers arrive, she thanks him again, lifting her bottle and holding it beside her face. She's Miss Rheingold of the new millennium. She smiles her nineteen-fifties smile: gay, cool.

Mickey hands us each a hundred-pound menu and my mother dives right into conversation.

"So, Mr. Hamilton," she says, opening her menu and pretending to study it. "I run into you all the time at the SaveWay, but I'm not really sure what you do."

This is such a lie. I kick her beneath the table but she keeps smiling.

"Well, I *was* a butcher," Mickey says. He winks at me, our little joke. "And now I'm the store manager."

"I *thought* you might have been a butcher," my mother observes.

Mickey grins.

"You know, Roseanna's uncle was a butcher."

"Who?" I ask.

"Well, he wasn't really her uncle," she says, not looking at me, "but a close friend of the family. Barney Kroener. He was *like* an uncle."

"Mom," I say. "He was a *neighbor.*"

She ignores me. "He's dead now, poor man," she tells Mickey Hamilton. "Had the high blood pressure. Was on the medication for years. His wife used to tell me how the medicine affected his, ahem"—she sips delicately from the mouth of her beer bottle—"his performance, so to speak."

"Ah," says Mickey.

"This was long before Viagra," she adds.

"Ma," I plead.

"Not that they didn't try to rectify the situation, mind you. In those days, it was a bit more challenging. Marge Kroener would send him off to the veterans hospital for his shot . . . you know, one that would give a man his . . . ahem." She sips her beer again.

"*Ma!*" I cry again.

"But *you* know where that hospital is, Mickey. It's all the way down the Seaway, halfway to Montauk! All those traffic lights, that big intersection by the North Shore Mall. By the time he got home, the shot would be worn off and they'd be right back in the same boat where they started!"

My mother laughs merrily, mixing her metaphors and helping herself to another swallow of her beer. Mickey laughs along with her. He catches my eye and winks again. I don't know what this wink means. Maybe he thinks my mother is demented.

"Oh, Mrs. Plow," he says, "you are quite the cut-up."

"Thank you, dear," she effuses. "But it's Pulkowski, not Plow." She casts me an evil sideways look. "That's this one's real name, in case you'd like to know."

"I *do* like to know."

"But you can call me Helen."

He pats her hand twice. "And you can call me Ham."

Later, when Helen leaves to powder her nose, I put my fork down and glare at him. "This is the lowest trick my mother has ever pulled on me."

"What trick?"

"The surprise blind date trick."

Mickey is fiddling around with his French fries, but I know he's listening. "Is it that bad, having lunch with me?" he asks the potatoes.

"That's not the point!" I bang my fist down on the table, a little too emphatically. A jelly-covered toddler in the booth behind us stares at me with an open mouth full of toast. "Mama!" he says, loud enough for the entire diner to hear. Then he just stares, a child of the damned.

"I think your mother's hysterical," Mickey says. "I thought you'd think her blind date idea was funny. I really thought I knew your sense of humor."

"Why would you think you know *anything* about me?" I snap.

"Well, I know your mother's a piece of work."

Now I feel bad. I haven't enjoyed my lunch with Ham, but it hasn't been his fault. He's been really sweet. This might have been nice, without my mother. And we could have lived without the story of Barney Kroener's sex life.

"High maintenance, huh?" Mickey adds, almost as if reading my mind.

I still don't answer him. I'm too confused to answer questions. Do other people's mothers set up blind dates for them, and then attend?

"I'm sorry this has been so unpleasant for you," he finally says. Then he rises, removing two twenties from his wallet and throwing them down on the table. "Look," he tells me, "we just tried to have some fun. *I* enjoyed lunch, anyway."

I grab the twenties to return them to him. "Please, no," I tell him. "Wait! You don't have to leave. I'm just—"

He holds his hand up like a crossing guard, halting my explanation and refusing the money. "I'll see you at work when Milton comes back."

"But . . ."

"Later, Ms. Pulkowski."

The toddler and I stare after him as he makes his way past diners and waitresses and rotating trays of pie. "Bye bye!" the little boy shouts, waving his sticky hand. Then Mickey Hamilton is swallowed into the lunch crowd, like Barney Kroener in traffic.

who's your daddy?

Where's ham?" my mother asks when she emerges from the ladies' room, her bright red lipstick replenished.

To avoid strangling her, I rise and head for the diner door, bringing the check along with me. I hear the *click! click! click!* of her high heels behind, but I don't turn and I don't wait up. I thrust my credit card at the cashier, then stuff Ham's two twenties into my purse. Now I'll have to give them back to him when I see him at the SaveWay.

"Well?" my mother persists. "What happened? Did you two have a disagreement?"

The woman at the cash register withholds my receipt until I answer. I snatch it from her fingers, and her lips purse into a small suck hole of disapproval. "Thank you," I seethe, then stomp out the door. My mother follows me as I head to the parking lot. I have possibly never been angrier with her. The thought of her sitting in the car beside me for another fifteen minutes is intolerable. Before I unlock the doors, I whirl around to face her.

"I don't want you smoking in the car," I snap.

"*You're* the one smoking," she says. She crosses her arms defiantly in front of her polka dot bodice. "I had no idea you were so fervently against male company."

"What were you thinking, inviting him here? And what were you *smoking* when you decided to tell your little cute-ass Barney Kroener story?"

My mother cringes a little. "You're the one who hid a marijuana cigarette in your underwear drawer."

"Ma, I told you! That was *not* my joint! It was Cousin Arthur's. And he was smoking in my bedroom because he couldn't stand *listening* to you anymore at the dinner table!"

"Humph," my mother says, unconvinced.

"And what were you doing in my underwear drawer anyway? I was sixteen! Even then, you couldn't stay out of my business! You *can't* stay out of my business, Ma! Why is that?"

In response, my mother unsnaps her purse daintily and extracts a Salem Light.

"I don't want you *smoking*. Period," I tell her. "What's a seventy-four-year-old woman doing smoking? Can you answer me that? Don't you read the news? It's bad for you, Ma. It can kill you."

My mother makes me wait while she lights up and takes a few puffs. She shoots her exhaled smoke in a smooth jet pointed toward the sky. She's not wasting any words on me. I rave on, unstoppable. "Dad has cancer, doesn't he? He's got cancer, and here you are, standing in the parking lot, smoking."

My mother says nothing, but the faintest glimmer of defiance flutters across her face. She's not talking. Which, to me, means something bad. We pull out of the lot when she is finally done with her cigarette. Then she says, in a tone she tries to make friendly, "The problem with you, Rosie, is you don't want anyone helping you."

I gun the car into the flow of traffic. There's really no room to enter, but I cut off a darting little sports car, and he merely horns me.

"Up yours," I mumble.

"Very nice," my mother says.

"You are impossible," I tell her. "You're pathological! Helping and interfering in one's personal life are two very different things, you know. But, no, I don't expect you to comprehend that."

"Oh, here she goes, Miss Social Worker with all the big words." My mother shifts in her seat, readjusting her wide skirt. "What is more personal than a mother and a daughter? It isn't *interfering* when *one* shows a concern for *one's* daughter."

"Is that why you call Marcie at EPT each week?"

"She's my friend, Missy. All right? Do I not get to call friends up in your screwy version of the way the universe should work?"

I jerk the wheel, almost giving us both whiplash, pulling the car roughly off the road into a parking lot. My mother lets out a little gasp and her hand flies to her throat. I shift into Park, pull on the emergency brake, and we sit there. "I don't want your interference," I finally say, when my hands stop shaking. "I don't want your help. I don't need your maternal wisdom any more."

"Children always need their parents' help."

"I'm an adult!" I scream. "Would you please *get* that? I'm thirty-two years old and I know how to find my own men!"

"You don't know anything," my mother murmurs, in a voice that makes me turn and look at her.

"You don't know the first thing about your own life." She looks me full in the face. "You don't even know who the hell you are." There are tears in her eyes, and one runs down a line in her cheek that I'd never noticed was there.

"Ma, why do you say things like that?"

"Because I am not your mother," she says.

"Oh, now you're disowning me? I don't deserve to be your daughter because what? I want to know about my own father? I want you to stay out of my personal business?"

"I'm your grandmother," she says simply. "Your own mother is God knows where, and has been since you were an infant."

I study her face, looking for that twinkle she sometimes gets when she's teasing me. It's not there.

I feel my hand fly from my side, whether to hit her or to gather her in my arms, I don't know. I don't know a lot of things, like what that noise is, suddenly coming out of my mouth. Or why little pinpricks of light are circling my head.

"Ma," I croak, grabbing her hand, which suddenly feels frail as a bag of twigs between my fingers. "What are you saying?"

She wipes her eyes with her free hand before she looks up at me. Her mascara is a mess. Her eyes look ancient, tired, deeply recessed. She looks as though she has lived a million years.

Who is this woman? I stare at a face that has been imprinted in my mind from birth, but whose face is it?

It is the face of my mother's mother. That is what she's telling me.

There is a knock on my car window that startles us both, and I turn to see a grinning man pressed close. I lower my window reluctantly, and the man says, "You ladies interested in buying a car?" I look behind him and see the giant BUICK sign then, suspended from a pole, surrounded by gleaming cars.

My father is my grandfather, I think.

The man in the window is smiling patiently in his wrinkled white shirt. His red tie is flapping in the outside breeze and a stain at its center hypnotically sways back and forth, back and forth, before my glazed eyes. I try to make the moment real. I am finding out who my mother is and my father isn't, in a Buick car lot.

"We're all set, dear," I hear my mother tell the man. "You can run along now, sir," she adds.

Her voice has regained the strength and authority we are all used to, but when I look at her face, I see that her eyes are still pink. The muscles around her jaw seem slack, as if collapsed in defeat. She looks like a grandmother. *My* grandmother. But who is my mother?

My grandmother turns to me, when the salesman has left, and the next thing she says gives me my first real hint at the answer. "I've spent the last three decades of my life trying to make sure you don't turn out like your mother," she tells me coolly. She runs a hand through her pin curls. "Wherever the hell *she* is."

• • •

Hours later, the sun mercifully set, I am back in bed idly flipping through magazines. Women's magazines, news magazines, book reviews, gossip rags—these are my Prozac, my Valium, my lithium and Ritalin. My skin feels clammy. I wipe my eyes with Kleenex with aloe while rhythmically turning page after page after page as though I might find, if I search hard enough, the article entitled ROSIE'S PARENTS REVEALED.

Lord knows Helen hasn't told me who they are. Or were. She seemed to go into a fugue state in the Buick lot, once she'd made her last pronouncement about my mother. It was useless to attempt to find out more, not that I didn't ask.

I try to focus, try to breathe normally. I reach for the little book I keep on my bed stand, *The Slow Person's Guide to Buddha*, and read:

> It is better to spend one day contemplating the birth
> and death of all things than a hundred years never con-
> templating the beginnings and endings.
>
> —BUDDHA

I squeeze my eyes shut and think about this. I close the Buddha book. I pick up the first *Cosmo* from the pile. Advice abounds from the glossy pages.

BE A FLIRTY FUN FEMALE! the opening article encourages. Further browsing discloses that this apparently means I should flaunt my big breasts. I could possibly do this, but . . .

I don't know who my parents are.

The phone rings. It rings again and I still don't answer it, even though it could possibly be Ham. I am sure it's not my mother, as she didn't seem to be speaking at all when I dropped her off some hours ago. It doesn't matter. She isn't my mother anyway.

Must. Read. Magazines. I flip some more pages. GUY WITHOUT SHIRT features this month's "half-naked hunk." I stare at his buttered bare chest, his six-pack gleaming like organ pipes, his teeth blindingly white. His smile seems incredibly insincere. I turn to an advice column for *Cosmo* Guys, things your man should never say to you, all right there in black and white. The list seems basic, the obvious gaffes men shouldn't make when they're out with their *Cosmo* Girls. *Have you gained weight? Our waitress is cute! You want to split this dinner bill?*

Your mom is a bitch.

I close the magazine. How many times did Teddy remind me of this, in the four years of our marriage? But what was it Ham had said about Helen, today at the diner? *Your mother is a piece of work. High maintenance, huh?* That's the nicest way a man has ever called my mother a bitch. Even though she's not my mother.

I push aside my cold cup of tea and pull the comforter higher to my chin. Lights out, but sleep won't come. How can I sleep when I don't know who my parents are? When I don't know why my own mother took off or why Helen is glad I'm not like her? *She came down the canal sideways,* my mother has always told the mailman, my teachers, the neighbors, anyone who would listen. But whose canal? Not Helen's. And who is my father? Is he some kind of loser, too? I flinch, remembering against my will the gaps in the kitchen that Teddy has created: the missing microwave cart. The stack of cookbooks on the floor. The butcher-block table yanked away from the wall like a bad boy yanked from the school line. I certainly *married* a loser. It stands to reason that I would be spawned by one.

Eyes squeezed shut again, my gentle giant of a father-slash-grandfather wafts into my mind. I suddenly see how lucky I was to have had him for all those growing up years. The giant hand that used to hold mine as I crossed streets. So warm! It was like putting my hand in a fur muff, the kind Jo wore on her bracing winter coach rides in *Little Women*. My Daddy Pulkowski. And me, his little Winona Ryder. And Helen, who won't talk about what's wrong with him now. It makes sense that she planned today's ridiculous outing at the Acropolis Diner. She always gets busy when she's upset.

"Oh, shit," I moan to nobody. Then I sit up in bed and find the phone. It is Helen who picks up, of course.

"Ma," I say, unsure if I should still use this title. "I want to talk to Dad."

"I was just watching *The Swan*. They took a woman who looked like the north end of a southbound horse and gave her a new caboose."

"Put Dad on, please. I want to speak with him."

"She had buck teeth just *like* a horse's. I felt like giving her an apple."

"Mom, put Dad on."

"I don't understand it. If we decide to make the whole world beautiful, who will the homely people be? Where is the sense in all of this?"

"Are you going to put him on the line?"

"For your information, Miss Plow, Pulkowski is sleeping."

I take a deep breath, then exhale. "Then I'm coming over to get him up."

The clunk of the phone is deafening. I imagine it landing on her Formica counter, holes up, gaping at the ceiling like a small injured animal. I hear my father's breathing before I hear his voice.

"Rosie," he says.

"Dad. How are you?"

"Fine. Is everything all right?"

"That's why I'm calling you. Is everything all right with you?"

His breath again, thick as radio static. Slowly drawn in, steadily wheezed out.

"I have a bit of the cancer, honey."

The hair on my neck tickles as it rises.

"You what?"

"The prostate. They found something. Just a bit."

"Does Mom know?"

"Don't go upsetting your mother, honey."

"Does she know?"

"She knows."

"Ah. Daddy."

"Honey."

He exhales like a train whistle, lonely and far away.

life in the express lane

Once, when I was sick—it must have been the first year we were married—Teddy went out to a place called the Kosher Carry-Out and brought me back a quart of matzoh ball soup. It was the sweetest thing a man could have done for a woman with a red nose, pink eyes, and seriously un-shampooed hair. He had so much fun playing doctor that day! It was like a role he'd been given in a play, and he went after it in a big way. "Open up, babe," he'd said, cupping his hand beneath my chin and spoon-feeding me the steaming Jewish penicillin, as though I were an infant. He smiled at me with such a blend of love and pity. I couldn't tell if the dizziness I felt was him or the fever. Teddy *was* my fever, that perfect sniffly day. If ever I knew anything in life, I knew for certain he loved me in that moment, in that room, on that germ-infested bed.

He hasn't called since the furniture heist. He doesn't even know that his mother-in-law is really his grandmother-in-law.

I sigh aloud, then pick up the phone and dial the SaveWay, determined to handle the things that I can.

"How's Milton doing?"

"Is that why you're calling?"

It's raining like a son of a bitch this awful Monday morning, and Mickey Hamilton is going to make it hard for me to apologize. I haven't left my house in two days, since our little lunch outing. I haven't even had my little protein milkshake. I'm trying to make one thing right before I go to the office, and Mickey Hamilton seemed the easiest.

"Is that a nice way to say hello?"

"How may I help you, Ms. Plow?" he says.

Ham is in a mood. I slip a shoe on. "I wanted to give you your forty dollars back."

"I don't want my forty dollars back. I told you."

I sit down on the side of my unmade bed. "I also want to apologize," I say. There's a hit of silence on the other end.

"That I'll accept, Ms. Plow."

"Good. It really wasn't about you. It's . . . just a tough time for me and my mother right now."

"You're having a tough time with everyone these days, it seems."

I stare down at my lap. My knees poke hopefully from the hem of my skirt. "Look, my life's a mess right now. Why can't you just accept my apology, and let's go on."

"Let's go on with what?"

I pause, sliding my second foot into an Amanda Smith pump. "With our usual cordial, professional friendship."

"We can't do that, Ms. Plow."

I rise, sighing, my brain pounding with a headache. "And why is that?"

"Because we don't have a cordial, professional friendship. You have feelings for me, Ms. Plow. I saw it at the diner, over your plate of chicken fajitas."

"Christ, Ham," I start, but then I stop. I stop because I'm afraid he might be right. Or because he might be wrong. I'm so confused that I sit back down again.

"See? You're calling me Ham now."

When I don't respond to this, he continues. "Why don't you come by this morning? I've begun Milton on bagging, since it's pouring out. Your lessons with him have been excellent. He re-members to put the heavy stuff in the bottom of the bags. But still, it's his first day. Don't you want to come over and see how he's doing?"

This sounds infinitely better than walking into the offices of EPT, my newest trauma written all over my face, Marcie ready to pounce, Sean giving me that placid look that may be even worse.

"I'm leaving right now."

"Great. Oh, and Ms. Plow. I had a very nice time with your mother Saturday."

"No, you didn't."

"Yes, I did," he insists.

No, he didn't, I think, hanging up. He hasn't even met my mother. Any more than I have. I skip my protein milkshake and slide into my raincoat.

•   •   •

I can see Milton through the rainy plate glass at the end of the express counter. He is shaking his hands in front of him, as though jangling invisible bangle bracelets before the customer at the end of the line. The woman has her purse clutched to her chest like a shield. A half-filled grocery bag stands between them. A young cashier has her arms crossed in front of her register. I hurry inside.

"Are you the one that works with him?" the cashier asks when I reach them.

"Yes," I say. I plunk down my briefcase on her conveyer belt to look more official.

"Well, he's starting it again. Counting the items?"

Inches above her cropped yellow hair is the sign. PLEASE!! 8 ITEMS ONLY! Milton is panting lightly, eyes darting from the sign to the customer and back again. "Eleven!" he's wheezing. "It's not eight!"

The offending shopper lowers her purse when she sees me. She looks partly relieved, but mostly angry. "I was trying to explain to him that the cat food is *four* for a dollar ninety-nine." She is speaking too loudly, enunciating her words slowly and correctly, the way some people talk on their telephone answering machines, the way most people talk to the developmentally challenged. This makes me dislike her, and her cat.

"I stacked them that way, *four* in one pile, making them obviously *one* item. The eighth item."

"Yes, I see." I hate her blue sparkly reading glasses, perched on the edge of her nose like a roller coaster car, ready to take the dive. "I see how you slid in the last three items."

The woman's penciled eyebrows rise. "Well, you *could* put it that way. Are you the manager?"

I'm tempted to lie, but shake my head no. I turn my back to her instead and address the cashier. "Go ahead and bag the rest of this," I say, then I take Milton by the arm and begin moving him toward the office.

"Miss Plow," he says. "Miss Plow, she was breaking the rules!"

"I know, Milton." I try to sound firm but understanding at the same time. "It must be hard for you to follow so many rules and then watch other people break them."

"She should be fired. She's gonna get *fired*!"

"She's the customer, Milton. She can't get fired."

Milton socks his fist into the palm of his other hand. "The rules! She can't buy eleven!"

"Strawberry Fields" is playing, and bland violin chords are flittering down into the meat section where we're walking. Women's backs are bent over displays of steak and lamb. Above the women's heads are rows of teriyaki sauce and sales posters, and one additional poster that announces the week as National Depression Week. GET A FREE SCREENING, the poster advises in pink letters. We open the door to Mickey Hamilton's office and Milton precedes me in.

Ham turns his head from where he sits at his desk. He rises and limps across the small room to the table in the center.

"Milton. Ms. Plow. Sit, please."

I sit, but Milton stands.

"What's wrong with your leg?" Milton asks.

"Nothing. A dog bit it, but now it's fine."

"A *dog* bit it?" He rubs his arms nervously in the front of his green smock.

"But it's okay now. Let's talk about your work."

I watch him study Milton with steady gray eyes.

"A dog *bit* it?"

"Milton. What happened?"

"A lady wants to cheat. On the express line."

"Ah. You were counting, huh?"

"Eleven!"

"Well, you know what, Milton? That's okay when they do that. You don't have to tell them they have too much."

"They can break the rules?"

"It's not really a rule. It's more like a suggestion."

Milton looks shocked. "It's a rule! Miss Plow says there are rules!"

"Yes, but customers' rules are a little different from workers' rules."

"They can break them?"

"Some of them. That one."

Milton's angry eyes find me. "They can have eleven when it says eight?" He turns to Ham again. "I don't like you."

"Oh, you probably do," Ham, tells him gently. "You just don't like me saying that customers can cheat on the express line. I don't blame you, buddy. But you know something? If the customers have *too* many items on that line, the cashier will tell them to move."

"*I'll* tell them to move."

"No."

"Why not?"

Ham takes in a breath, thinks carefully as he exhales. "Because we need you to think about the bagging. We need you to think about that."

"That's a rule?"

"You do it the best."

"I do it the best," Milton says.

Ham smiles at him, the sweetest smile I've seen in months. "Right. Now let's get going back to work. You're on the clock."

"I'm on the clock," Milton says. "No kissing." He pushes a chair out of his way and leaves.

In the silence that follows, I walk around the table to where Ham is sitting. I take his face in my hands so the sideburns are covered. And then I kiss him. I kiss him long enough for two kisses, hard enough to say thank you. And then, when I pull away from his warm surprised lips, that is just what I tell him.

"Thank you," I say.

He lets out the breath he's been holding. "No problem."

"You were wonderful with Milton and you were wonderful with my mother."

"I could be wonderful with you, too," he says.

"I'm sure you could. My husband just bought a new house so he can live in it with my best friend."

"Ouch."

"Why am I telling you this?"

"Beats me," Mickey Hamilton says, rising and wrapping his arms around me.

"My father has cancer."

"I'm so sorry, Rosie."

"And we've just broken the no kissing rule."

I smell his aftershave as he moves in close to kiss me again. His arms are strong and he is warm. He doesn't seem to mind an ounce of me in my supersized raincoat.

"I'm not sorry about that," he whispers into my hair.

"When did you get bitten by a dog?"

"That's another story," he says. "I like this story better."

meet the family

"**the first horror movie** I ever saw was *The Ten Commandments*," Mickey Hamilton tells me, lying on his side on the vast expanse of mattress I once shared with Teddy. We're talking about our childhood traumas. Mine was being bitten by a dog. A boxer, to be exact, when I was seven.

Ham had a boxer named Duke when he was a boy. He was a sweet boxer, he tells me. They called him Dukey, back before this was another word for dog doo. Dukey had teeth like the wax mouths we used to wear at Halloween, and the taut coiled body of a discus thrower. But he never bit anyone. Not like the dog at the SaveWay that bit Mickey's leg. Dukey just guarded the house, like a teddy bear in a scary mask.

"I wouldn't exactly call *The Ten Commandments* a horror movie," I tell my new lover, rolling on my side to face him. "Moses isn't exactly Chucky."

He kisses me, the way he has these last two weeks: hard and

long, yet soft and dreamy at the same time. Adultery agrees with me.

"My mother loved that movie," Mickey sighs. His face is nice, close up. In these past days of dating and bedding him, I have resisted a constant urge to attack his sideburns with an electric razor while he sleeps.

"She found it in a video store owned by some rabid born-again. She ruined my childhood with it."

"You got something against religion?" I run a hand down his chest. "What if Helen invites you to Mass with her?"

Mickey smiles and strokes my face. "I hardly ever see your mother at the store these days. Seems like you don't see her, either."

"I see her," I say. "We just took my father to his first radiation treatment."

"Yes, but you don't pick the phone up when she's chatting with your answering machine."

I move away slightly. "It's more complicated than you think."

Mickey lets this go. I am glad. "It's not the religious aspects of the movie that bother me," he says, getting back to *The Ten Commandments*. "It's this scene where they tie a guy's arms and legs to four horses pointed in opposite directions. Then someone cracks a whip and, even though you don't see the guy being drawn and quartered, you hear this ear-piercing scream. *Aaaaaagh!*" Mickey's arms are flailing outside the blankets as he illustrates this for me.

I am surprised he was so sensitive to this scene. When I think of those sealed packs of quartered chickens I pass every day at the SaveWay, I wonder how he could have been a butcher.

I haven't told him yet about Helen being my grandmother. I have this feeling that it's a bad way to start a relationship. There's a lot I don't know about Mickey Hamilton yet, but there's even more he doesn't know about me. Still, he's nice and he's patient, and he doesn't seem to mind my sharing little with him but sex. Sometimes when I'm in his arms, I imagine I am Inga, enjoying a thrilling extramarital fling with someone like . . . Teddy.

Mickey wraps a strong arm around me, pulling me in, fixing me with those gray eyes I once found boring. Nice eyebrows, thick as forefingers, furrow in concentration, or maybe in lust, on my face. I don't feel the slightest bit fat. I move in and kiss him hard on the lips. His hand slips under the comforter and finds something nice.

Then we hear knocking at the door.

I glance at the clock, which says 8:59 A.M.

She couldn't even wait until nine o'clock.

"Who is it?" Mickey asks, hands withdrawn, eyes on the bedroom door.

"I don't know," I lie.

He sits up, his smooth muscled shoulders looming above the comforter. The sight of him, so big and tall in the morning sunlight, still slightly alarms me. I am used to being a physical match for the man who sits beside me in bed.

The knocking continues. I hate the corny rhythm she pounds out on my door. *Shave and a haircut! Two bits!* It's a grandma rhythm, not a mother rhythm. I should have known, just by the way she's knocked on doors all these years, that she could not have been my mother. Mickey leaps from the bed and heads for the bathroom.

"Aren't you going to answer that?" he asks.

It is too early in our relationship to tell him how I would like to answer the door. I would like to swing it open, naked as a pin-up, and order the person on the other side gone. Out of the Ronkonkoma Arms! Off the property! I'd like to tell this person who has shamelessly called herself my mother, and now balks at telling me the full story of my real parents, to go find another project. Leave me alone. Find your own boyfriend.

Instead, I wrap myself in a robe and go to the door. I glare at her through the peephole, where her head looks large and her body tiny. Her eyes bulge distortedly, like an insect's under a microscope.

"What do you want?" I scream through the door. Maybe it's not a scream. Maybe the scream is internal. But the question is hostile enough, and I watch her move back a bit and shift something that is tucked beneath her arm—the one that doesn't have a large purse in it. It looks like a photo album.

I'm just glad it's not a book of poetry. Never again will I admit into my home a woman with a book of poetry. The large insect face looks up at me, sad and a little desperate. Before thinking, I unlatch the lock and swing open the door.

"Come on in, Ma . . . I mean, *Helen*," I say.

Helen steps inside in her beige car coat. In perfect symmetry, Mickey steps into the living room wearing a mauve towel around his waist. He smiles at Helen calmly, as though she is an irate shopper demanding a refund on her dented can of tomato paste.

Helen's glance moves from Mickey's towel to me, then back to Mickey.

"Hi, Ham," she says. "It's about time you got here."

"Hello, Mrs. Pulkowski," Mickey says. "I was just leaving, but it's very nice to see you."

"I'll bet it is," Helen muses, staring brazenly at Mickey's caboose. He pats me on my behind as he exits the room, then laughs a little, a small hoot, a sound so relaxed and unfrazzled that I believe for a second I am in a *Twilight Zone* episode.

"My timing is great, then," Helen says after him. "Rosie and I have some things to talk about."

"No time like the present," Mickey tells her, then pauses at the bedroom door, turning around. He seems to be enjoying modeling his mauve towel. "Rosie thinks the biggest trauma in her life was being bitten by a dog." He fixes me with a penetrating look straight out of a daytime soap opera. "But I think there might be something else."

"Right," my quasi-mother says. "There's always something else with Rosie."

I plop down on the couch, which coincidentally matches Mickey's towel. "Maybe you should go home and watch *The Ten Commandments*," I snap at Mickey. "Then you'll have some idea of what I'd like to do to you later."

"Rosie!" Helen says.

"Don't worry," I tell her. "It's PG."

"Make me some tea, Rosie, and then get dressed," Helen says. "I've got something to show you."

Back in the bedroom, Mickey is sitting on the bed, innocently putting on a sock. He gives me a hug as I'm en route to the shower, then calmly finishes dressing.

"Save me the best pork roast!" I hear Helen call to him, as he's leaving. "I'll be in later to pick it up."

"You want the bone in it, Mrs. P.?"

I don't hear her answer.

I dress and find Helen at my dining room table. She has made the tea for us herself, using a bone china tea service that was a wedding gift. Teddy always hated it. He loathed the delicate pastoral pattern, the glinting gold around its edges. On our honeymoon, he'd bought himself a masculine-looking Italian espresso set, all straight lines and bright red.

"I saw your wayward husband at the post office this week," Helen says, pouring the tea and reading my mind. "It's right next to Dad's radiation center, you know. On Jericho Turnpike."

"How's Dad?"

"He's fine."

"Was Teddy with Inga?" I can't help myself from asking.

"No." She pats my cheek gently. "What do you care? You have a nice fellow now. Drink your tea."

"Ma, I don't think you should be asking Mickey to save roasts for you. He isn't a butcher anymore. He's a store manager."

"Oh, Ham doesn't mind."

She slides a cup and saucer toward me, then opens the black album sitting on the table beside her own cup. Pinpricks of excitement travel up my arms. So this is it.

"I don't blame you for taking a little break from me," she says, gazing down at the collage of black-and-white snapshots affixed at their corners with little black triangles. It's a photo album I've never seen before. Helen sighs and flips a page, then flips back again to the first one. "I have come to see this is no small piece of news I have given you," she says. "About your mother. And me. And your father."

Something, a little furry animal, scuttles between my ribs. "You haven't told me anything about my father."

"I meant Pulkowski. Your grandfather, technically. Well, *actually*, I suppose."

She wrings her hands together, flashes of red nail polish appearing and disappearing. I have a sudden moment of empathy for the small woman sitting across from me.

"He looked like hell," Helen says.

"Who?"

"Teddy."

Of course. She would never say Pulkowski looked like hell.

"His hair was sticking up all over the place and his shirt tail was hanging out of his Farmer Brown jeans . . ."

"So, Ma," I try again, for the hundredth time in two weeks. "Who is my father?"

"My Pulkowski was a lot like your Ham when he was young," she says, ignoring my question.

"He's not my Ham."

"Whose Ham is he, then?"

"We're just dating."

"In bed."

I can't believe I'm having this conversation with my grand-mother.

"Who is my father?" I ask again, and again she doesn't re-spond.

She turns a few pages of the album instead, until she has found the snapshot she is looking for, then passes the book to me. "There," she says, pointing to a photo of a young Pulkowski in his Air Force uniform, tall and broad shouldered and strap-pingly handsome. "Can you see the similarities with Ham?"

It bothers me that I can.

"They say most women marry their fathers," Helen contin-ues. "And I'm afraid you did, too. Now, though, you're dating your grandfather."

"Ma!" I say, closing the book, afraid of the book. "I liked it better when you talked to me about my weight."

"Your weight is fine," she says, reopening the album to the first page again. A faint odor of mildew rises from the ancient binding. "There," she says, and a half-smile plays across her lips. She pushes the album toward me.

I see a photo of a young Helen on the beach, the kind of movie star legs they don't make anymore. The skirt of her dark one-piece bathing suit is frozen in a flutter against slim hips. The surf is behind her. I see a pretty brunette, a definite Miss Rheingold, squinting in the sun with a bundle in her arms. I see the half-moon curve of a baby's cheek peeking from the bunting in the crook of her arm. I see the great happiness on Helen's hopeful face.

"God, you were beautiful," I say.

"You should have seen your mother."

Now my small grandmother, this powerhouse of my childhood, is rocking ever so slightly, as though the rigid Scandinavian chair she sits on is really a rocker, and the baby in the photograph is once more in her arms. She stares at the photo with glazed eyes, gently rubbing an index finger over the snapshot's ragged edges.

"Ma," I say. "Who was she?"

"This was at Montauk," she tells me. "Pulkowski and I used to rent one of those little dollhouse cabins they had along the old Route 27."

I don't know the old Route 27. I have never been with Helen and Pulkowski to Montauk. I was always shipped off to Sag Harbor during my childhood summers, to a sleep-away camp where Disney movies were shown on a stretched white bed sheet and there was always sand in the sandwiches.

"That's my mother in your arms?"

"It was her first time at the shore," Helen says. "She was only six weeks old. I was afraid a wave would take her away."

A moment of jealousy registers somewhere in my stomach. "What's her name?" I study the snapshot again, see my grandmother's perfectly flat stomach, six weeks after giving birth to the watermelon baby in her arms. Whose child am I anyway?

Helen keeps rocking. "She got such a diaper rash from all that sun and sand! Pulkowski had to drive the Studebaker all the way to Hauppauge to find her some ointment." *Rock, rock, rock.* She has fallen into a hole a half-century deep.

"Ma," I say. "What's her name? Where is she? What happened?"

Helen looks up as if surprised to still find me sitting beside her at the table. "Oh, my darling Miss Muffet," she sighs, and then tears fill her bottom lids. She pats my palm with her small cold hand. "Sitting on your tuffet, eating your curds and whey."

"Ma. Her name."

I am gentle with her, but now I feel tears in my own bottom lids. I turn from Helen's sad face and back to the snapshot, studying the tiny arc of infant face, looking for something there, anything familiar, or comforting, or more revealing than my grandmother. But what can a fifty-year-old thumbnail of face disclose? Nothing. A tear runs down my cheek. I wipe it away before it hits the album.

"Alexa," Helen suddenly says. "It was an old family name on the Pulkowski side."

I look up at her. "Alexa? This is my mother's name?"

Helen pats my palm again.

"Where is she? What happened? Is she alive?"

"Along came a spider who sat down beside her."

Now Helen is gone. She is too deep down the hole. "You drive to Hauppauge and get the ointment," she tells someone. "You take the tangles out of her hair with the Toni cream rinse so you won't hurt her. You fight with her teachers . . . pack her lunch box, hem her party dresses . . . you defend her, protect her, educate her, worry like *hell,* and for what?"

She looks at me. "For what?" she asks again, her eyes burning with bewilderment. "You spend all those years raising and loving your girl only so you can hand her off to some . . . *boy*? Some rough, undeserving boy?"

That would be my father, then.

"Who was he?" I ask.

"A bum," she says.

"A bum? My mother slept with a bum?"

Helen waves her hand dismissively. "He was some boy in her high school. That's all."

"And that makes him a bum?"

"She met him on a *school* bus! He wasn't even going to college."

"And that makes him a bum?" I repeat. I feel something stir in my gut, and realize that, for the first time in my whole life, I am defending my father.

"He wanted to be a *carpenter*!" Helen shrieks.

"Jesus was a carpenter!" I shriek back, pulling the Catholic card to shame her, this woman who goes to Mass every Sunday without her husband.

"Jesus didn't knock up my daughter!"

I feel the two of us spiraling, higher and higher, into our long overdue mother-daughter knockdown fight. "And what's wrong with a carpenter, anyway?" I seethe. "I married a *lawyer* and you called him a putz. Now I sleep with a *butcher* and you call him a prince. What did this daughter have to do? Bring home a president who knew how to carve a roast?"

"She was a child! She wanted to *marry* him!" Helen yells, standing now, and gesticulating as though she wants to hurt something. "Sixteen-year-old girls in the National Honor Society don't marry carpenters and settle down with babies!"

"Ma!" I shout, standing myself. "Maybe she loved him! Maybe she *wanted* to marry him!"

Helen's hand swings way back this time, then cracks me

hard across my cheek. "I didn't want my baby marrying Johnny Bellusa!" she yells, tears spilling down her face. "Is that okay with you? Is it?"

I hardly feel the sting where she has hit me.

Johnny Bellusa.

This is my father's name. Here is my life, then: I have gone from a Stracuzza to a Bellusa.

I feel Helen's arms go around me as I stand beside the dining room table, staring at a gold-rimmed teacup, a white paper napkin, a spoon, my shoulders suddenly shaking.

"She had the baby at the Little Flower Home for Unwed Mothers," she tells me, stroking my back, crying into my neck. "Breech birth. Almost killed her."

"Down the canal sideways," I sob.

"She wouldn't let us put it up for adoption. She brought it home and then she left."

I lean into her small bones, suddenly wanting my grandmother to call me by my real name. I want to be Roseanna Plow to her, not the *it* that was left behind by Alexa Pulkowski. A giant sob escapes me and Helen Pulkowski, the only mother I have ever known, pats my back gently, the way you might pat a baby's. That is, if you didn't leave the baby to go away forever.

Then we hear keys in the door and Ham walks in. "I forgot my wallet," he tells us, and I know, until the day I die, that I will never be sure if he is making this up or not. He walks over to Helen's and my little huddle and gently extracts me from her arms and into his.

"Hello, Rosie," he whispers into my hair.

I hang on to him like a lifeboat.

that's what friends are for

rosie? it's about time you picked up. I was beginning to think you broke your hip in the shower and were lying there in the soap scum."

I glance at the clock, try to remember what day it is. Why is Marcie waking me on a weekend morning? Okay, a weekend afternoon. I sit up, begrudgingly. The sun pouring through the slats of my shades is blinding. "Marcie, what's up?"

"Don't give me 'what's up.' You know I talked to your mother. You looked like shit when you left the office yesterday. As a matter of fact, you looked like shit when you *arrived*. Your shoes didn't match your purse! I was afraid you were going to go home and stick your head in the oven. I would have called you last night, but Seanie took me out to dinner for our anniversary."

"What anniversary?"

"The six-month anniversary of our first doing it."

"You're kidding me, right?"

"No I am not. Some people celebrate the day they met. We celebrated the day we first slept together. It's more romantic, let's face it. But that's not the point. The point is, you look like a psycho these days, and we haven't had a chance to talk."

I get out of bed and wrap a robe around myself, still holding the phone to my ear. I'm tempted to tell Marcie I'm all right. But I'm not all right. I'm exhausted from *acting* all right. Maybe that makes me a psycho.

"So anyway," she tells me, as I wander from bedroom to dining room, aimlessly looking for some purpose for being awake, "I am coming by to pick you up in twenty minutes. We're going back to my place, and we're going to eat lots of pasta and ice cream and drink lots of wine, and talk and laugh and eventually gossip about our coworkers."

"I can't—"

"You can and you will. Even Ham thinks it's a great idea."

"You spoke to Mickey?"

"I ran into him at the SaveWay. Where do you think I got the pasta?"

Instead of staring at a dining room chair, I sit on it. It's the same one Helen sat on a week ago, when she told me my father was a bum and my mother abandoned me without a second thought. I tilt back on the grandma chair, realizing I don't have the energy to argue. A part of me feels touched that Marcie cares enough about me to set up a Girl's Day on her six-month sex anniversary with our boss.

"Get dressed!" she says. "I'm on the way."

But it isn't just she who comes. It's Sean, too. Sean, whom I have never seen outside the confines of his office. The surprise I feel, swinging open my door and finding him standing there in baggy jeans and a Yankees cap! Sean Zambuto's head was not made for a Yankees cap. It is shaped like a kidney bean. It is the head of the Head of the Department of Social Work.

He smiles kindly at me, hands stuffed into pockets, head slightly bowed. "Roseanna," he says, in the same courtly voice he uses in our staff meetings. He removes one hand from a pocket and extends it. I have never shaken hands with him while wearing plaid pajama pants before. I feel foolish in my knockoff Uggs from Payless.

"Seanie," Marcie orders, "grab her purse and bag." She envelops me in a hug, my coat already over her arm. "Let's go," she says, and I obey mutely, allowing her to deliver me from my empty apartment to the backseat of the warmed-up Big Red.

"Take us straight home, Seanie," Marcie orders, once we're buckled up. Seanie pulls out of the Ronkonkoma Arms parking lot. Marcie dives straight into treatment.

"Roseanna," she says, using the inflections of a therapist, the deep breathing techniques, the good eye contact, "our mission is to normalize things for you today, so you can see how really *minor* this news flash of your mother's is."

"She's not my mother."

Marcie waves a dismissive hand. "Big fucking deal. Get out the Zoloft." Sean's eyebrows rise a little in the rearview mirror, reminding me of Pulkowski.

"She's told you everything, hasn't she?" I ask.

"I called her. Friday. When you came in looking like shit again. We had coffee at her house. Well, *your* house, I guess. Or your grandparents' house, anyway."

I rub my temples. I am not ready for other people to know my story. Mickey is enough. He's been kind and has asked no questions. He's cooked a lot of meat for us, as though this would help. But I am lost in my own reverie anyway, whether something is broiling in the oven or not. After work each night, I lie in bed ignoring him, trying to imagine whose womb I traveled in when my bones were fully formed, my fingers separated from their webbing, my legs strong enough to kick at the stomach of a woman I've never known. I have turned my back on Mickey and his roasts, but my obsession of these past weeks has been my own private hell, and I have held it close to me and cherished it with a masochist's bittersweet delight.

Marcie's mouth has stopped moving and we are all mercifully silent for a moment. The *ping ping ping* of Big Red's turning signal is the only sound in the car. Helen must wonder the things I wonder. Like: what has become of Alexa Pulkowski? What did she do with her honor society mind?

"You were raised by a wonderful mother," Marcie says after a moment. "She's really suffering, Rosie."

Good, I think, but I say nothing.

"Your clothes were always clean and so were you. No one ever hit you. You were sent to college."

Did my real mother ever go to college? Where was she living

now? *Was* she living now? How had Helen lost track of a sixteen-year-old girl?

"You were raised in a two-parent home at a time when close to half of all American families were raised by a single parent."

I move slightly toward the window in the backseat, as though I believe this will stop Marcie from talking. But it doesn't.

"Now," she sighs, "moving on to your marriage." She glimpses up at our driver. "Seanie! Hold your ears." I see Sean's bashful smile in the rearview mirror.

"Okay. Your husband was an ass clown."

"I thought you said he was an ass *monkey*," I object.

She waves away the distinction. "So. One out of two marriages in this country ends in divorce in the first four years. *The first four years!*" Her eyes narrow behind her thick black glasses. "You are right on target with yours."

Her ridiculous comment stirs me momentarily from a numbness as thick as cotton batting. "So you're saying my marriage is screwed in a statistically appropriate way?"

"Don't be a smart ass," she says. "What I'm saying is the demise of your marriage is unremarkable. You are no more or less remarkable than Helen, for keeping her marriage to a sphinx together for half a century."

"That's very comforting," I assure her.

"I hope so." Marcie sighs contentedly.

We pull up the driveway of her rented Cape house, which looks a lot like Inga's rented Cape house, which makes me sad.

"Now that we've talked about all the hard stuff," Marcie announces, "we're going to go inside and pig out."

"I'd rather just go home and get some rest."

"Bullshit. You'd rather curl up under a quilt and die. And that is absolutely impermissible."

"Well, I may fall asleep here, then."

"Fine," Marcie says. "But I doubt it. I've got Ben and Jerry's in there."

Sean opens the door for us, as a good chauffeur should, then carries my stuff inside. He walks ahead of us, my leopard-skin plush slippers bobbing up and down at the top of the bag.

"Isn't he great?" Marcie swoons, and I am once again amazed at the appeal these silent men types have for certain women. Here she has just called Pulkowski a sphinx, and in the next second she's decreeing Sean Zambuto great.

"He lives here now," Marcie confides as I shuffle along beside her in my Payless Uggs. "My little Zambie, sharing my mailbox." She sighs and turns to me, her expression changing. "Where does Ham live?" she asks.

"In Manhattan somewhere."

"You've never been there?"

I shake my head, noticing for the first time that I've never asked Mickey to bring me there.

"He drives back and forth to the Island every day?"

"He used to, I guess. Now he mostly stays in Ronkonkoma."

"So your boyfriend sort of lives with you, too."

I shrug. "Basically, I guess."

• • •

We've drunk a bottle and a half of wine by three o'clock, snuggled into opposite ends of the living room couch, Sean nowhere to be found. We've watched *SpongeBob SquarePants* and a DVD of *Family Guy*. We've eaten a box of Cap'n Crunch, a bowl of green grapes, and some buffalo wings that magically appeared on the coffee table sometime during the afternoon, delivered by Sean.

"Seanie!" Marcie calls now, over the din of a Lucky Charms commercial, "Go out and get us some more wine, hon!"

Seanie emerges from his new home office with his coat on, detours to the couch to receive a kiss from Marcie, then swings open the front door and leaves.

"He's such a doll," Marcie burbles, and I can't help myself from commenting.

"He's certainly a nice person," the three-quarters bottle of wine begins saying, "but he's a forty-one-year-old guy who's never been married and takes orders like a waiter."

"And your point is?" Marcie asks, smiling brilliantly.

"Marcie, you could have anyone . . ."

"And I have. I assure you."

I let this sit a minute, chewing on a cold buffalo wing. "My actual mother was in the National Honor Society," I say, apropos nothing.

"Oh, I know the type," Marcie comments, twisting a clump of two-tone hair. I don't know if she's complimenting my mother or dissing her.

"And how about you? What type were you?"

"What do you think?" Marcie asks. "A cheerleader, of

course. Don't tell me you don't see it. I have cheerleader genes, just like you have honor society genes."

Maybe it's the wine, but this makes sense to me.

"I used to jump around, cartwheeling and leaping from pyramids of other cheerleaders, and they loved me, they *adored* me."

I don't even have to ask her who. *Everyone* loved her and adored her. It's the cheerleader's destiny. Marcie is twisting the hem of her Scooby Doo pajama pants. "I went out with any boy I wanted," she says. "The captain of the football team. A state champion wrestler. A student teacher named Edward X. Wilson. We had to keep that one quiet. His middle name was Xavier and he was uncircumcised. He was no different than the others. They looked in my eyes and saw my crotch. I was the girl who did the splits in the little pleated skirt. That's all I was to them—blond hair and a crotch." Marcie absentmindedly takes a swig from the empty wine bottle. "You get tired of that after a while, Rosie."

My mind flashes back to my own tormented high school days of sitting on the bleachers in my big-boned body, watching girls like Marcie leap and clap and twirl, feeling so lonely, so wrong, so undesirable that, later in my life, I would accept the imperfect affections of a man like Teddy. There was once a popular boy who really liked me, but he couldn't admit it. He sat beside me in the study hall held in our poorly lit school auditorium, the overflow of students from the over-filled classrooms. He was the type of boy Marcie went through like Kleenex, but for me, he was the *only* boy whose destiny had touched upon football playing and popularity and yet still took an interest in me. Each day he'd flop into the fold-down seat beside mine, smiling in a way that didn't disguise his delight in seeing me. In the safety of dim lighting and high seatbacks, he told me of his mother's unhappiness and his father's philandering, his fear of flunking chemistry and his waning interest in his girlfriend, a girl named Marissa Olsen who was, of course, a cheerleader and a nominee for Homecoming Queen. One afternoon, right before school ended, he grabbed my hand impulsively. "Oh, I wish you were prettier so I could go out with you," he exclaimed. Then he became shy again and pretended to do geometry homework on his lap. I carried his outburst in my heart for the rest of my high school days. It was a warm and glowing nugget of gold that no one could take away from me. If only I'd been prettier he would have loved me!

The door swings open, letting in a burst of cold and Sean Zambuto. He squeezes Marcie's shoulder on the way to the kitchen. She turns to me and says, "See? That man truly loves me." Sean returns with an uncorked bottle of Shiraz, then disappears. We start drinking again.

Hours go by, a blur of television noise and ice cream and dozing off and Marcie lecturing me about seeing Helen outside of radiation appointment hours. Mickey shows up just as Seanie is carrying a platter of pasta, smothered with sauce, to the coffee table. I look up from my haze and there he is, my sideburned savior, standing above me with a SaveWay bag in one arm, smiling down at my plush leopard-skin slippers, each one half the size of his dead dog, Dukey.

"Well?" he says. "How was your day of love and healing?"

I leap to my feet, almost knocking over the coffee table and the spaghetti on it, and throw my arms around his neck. He grips me with his one free arm, the other still holding the gro-

cery sack. I cling to him like a baby baboon. He somehow puts
the bag down. I don't even try to speak; that would only be an
embarrassment. I'm sure he smells my Napa Valley breath,
and I'm sure he's taken in the wonder of my outfit: the pink
plaid pajama pants, the gray T-shirt with the little holes in the
hem. He smells so nice, like crisp autumn air and an old
man's aftershave and Bounce dryer sheets. He is mine for the
taking. He doesn't try to escape, like the rest of them, or tell
me lies, like some of them, or bemoan the fact that I am not
pretty enough. Life has thrown me some curve balls but it also
has tossed me an ex-butcher with buns of steel and a heart of
gold.

"And a heart of gold!" someone is blubbering. Apparently it
is me. Apparently, I am telling him this, rather than just thinking it. Apparently I am very, very drunk.

"You're a sweet drunk," Mickey breathes into my ear, and
this is how I know that I'm telling him about his buns of steel,
instead of just thinking about them.

"If I tell you I'm healed will you take me home?" I ask him, a
little too loudly and a little too urgently.

"Sure," Mickey says, "but first you have to eat some of this
nice dinner."

"Who the hell are you, my father or something?" I ask,
segueing from sweet drunk to ugly drunk, but Mickey just
laughs, and Marcie pipes in, from somewhere behind us, "She
probably suspects *everyone* of being her father this week."

This, for some reason, unleashes a bubbling fountain of
laughter from some perverse hidden chamber inside me. I am
shaking with laughter, rolling with it, convulsed by it to the

point where Mickey must gently set me down on Marcie's couch until it has passed. The wide alarmed eyes of Seanie pass above me, but he no longer worries me, he is such a total and complete lapdog of this friend of mine, Marcie. This friend of mine, Marcie! Now *there* is a girlfriend with a real and true concern for Roseanna Plow. Not like Inga, that turncoat, that bitch, that emaciated wannabe poet who sleeps with my husband while noshing on seaweed Fritos in an ugly pink house in Hauppauge.

When my hysteria has subsided, I feel Mickey guiding my arms through the sleeves of my coat, apparently willing to forgo the pasta and just get me home. He is thanking Sean and Marcie profusely for the day, offering them the contents of his SaveWay bag in exchange for their services, then hefting me to my feet with one strong arm and moving me toward the door.

"Don't forget to call your mother!" Marcie hollers merrily from somewhere behind me before the door closes. "She loves you, you know."

the tree of abandonment

So i'll see you at the store later?" Ham asks, hugging my sluggish body where it lies on my couch, fully dressed. "Rosie, are you listening to me?"

"Of course I am." I try to sit up, but something like a pot lid bangs my forehead. "I was just thinking about my training session with Milton today," I lie.

Mickey frowns as if he doesn't believe me.

"Okay, and I'm a bad drinker. Marcie gave me really bad wine."

"Rosie," he says. "Let me just say something without your getting mad."

Bang goes the pot lid. I rub my head and look at him. "It's about Helen," I say.

"Just listen," he repeats. "As you go through life, people you care about deeply are going to piss you off. And then, eventually, you forgive them." He reaches out his hand to touch me, then seems to think better of it. "You forgive your boss, you forgive your friends. Why not forgive your family?"

"You mean I should forgive Teddy?"

Mickey laughs. "Rosie, you know I'm not talking about Teddy."

Of course I do. I sink in the couch cushions again. This is more *call your mother* stuff. Mickey has been dishing it out since he dragged my sorry carcass home Saturday night. *Call your mother. Call your mother. Call your mother.* The fact that she's *not* my mother skims past him like a mosquito over the surface of a pond. Mickey looks great in his tweed sports jacket this morning, but he can't seem to turn off his Dr. Phil. I guess the good news is I've finally acquired a problem that is worthy of Oprah: not knowing who my parents are.

I tug on Mickey's tie and pull his face down to me. "You have a scrumptious ass," I say. I end the therapy session by kissing his nice mouth.

"Yes, and if I were to piss you off, you'd probably forgive me, if even for my ass alone. So why not Helen?"

"First of all, her ass doesn't impress me," I say, but Ham doesn't laugh. I sit up again with a lot of effort. A gaunt ray of sun streaked across the carpet is killing me, causing something behind my eyes to throb. "And secondly, I don't even know what to forgive her for! I don't know if she's kept me from the best parents in the world, or if she's saved me from being beaten with wooden hangers."

"Maybe you've already had the best parents in the world."

A loud sigh escapes me. "I thought you were one of those guys who didn't talk."

"What?" Ham looks puzzled.

I tug on his tie again and kiss him, this time longer. "You're a saint," I tell him.

He smiles, but looks a little disappointed. I don't think he's bucking for sainthood. I think he wants to hear something else, some proclamation of love, but he's barking up the wrong tree. The broken tree. The messed-up tree. The tree of abandonment. It'll be months before anything blooms on this tree. Besides, if he wants me to fall in love with him, he shouldn't act like he's my therapist. And he should invite me to his apartment in the city sometime. It's not that I want to go there so badly; it's just that Marcie got me thinking: he's never asked.

"There's fresh coffee," Mickey says before he leaves.

After he's gone, I get up and pour myself a travel cup of coffee, suddenly glad to be heading to the SaveWay instead of the office. I can't bear the thought of another lecture from Marcie. Then there's Sean, or "Zambie," whom I would have a hard time thinking of as an authority figure today. Lord knows what he thinks of me. How are we supposed to work together, now that he's seen me being dragged out of his house in pink pajamas? Better just to see Mickey again, and perhaps steal another kiss in his office.

In the SaveWay lot, the autumn sun is casting halfhearted light on the chrome of parked cars, bright enough to tweak my headache. I tug my coat closer around me, and clip-clop toward the store in my sensible high heels. Sturdy Zones they're called, built like "career shoes" on the outside and old lady shoes on the inside. It used to be I wouldn't be caught dead in these shoes, a gift from Helen, of course. But today they feel just right, the perfect blend of shame and comfort.

Once inside, I search for Milton in the food aisles, where he should be working today. He has asked me to get him off shelf work several times. He's not even that crazy about cart collection these days. What he wants is his bagging job back, and I fully expect him to ask me again today. He is happiest interacting with the customers. He has learned to let the express counter customers cheat on their number of items without saying a word. He has learned to make eye contact while asking customers, "Paper or plastic?" He doesn't ask children in the carts for a bite of their candy anymore, but bagging still requires a lot of supervision, so mostly he's assigned to other duties.

I find him dusting a shelf of dog biscuits with a yellow feather duster in aisle six. "Yummy yummy yummy in my poochie's tummy!" he sings, a little dog food jingle he's heard on TV. His hair has fallen across his forehead in the casual way of young male leads. He's incongruously beautiful. He could be cast as James Bond, if 007 liked babies as much as babes.

"Hello, Milton," I say, and he turns and rewards me with a nice warm smile.

"Miss Plow!" he says. "Happy Thanksgiving!"

"Soon," I tell him. "In another few weeks."

"No, *now*." He lowers his feather duster, spins around and points to a mountainous stack of canned squash at the end of the aisle, a paper Pilgrim smiling from the summit. "See?"

"I guess you're right," I tell him, too zonked to explain how these holiday specials come out weeks before the event. His eyes devour me like a lover's.

"No snow yet," he says.

He's right again. I parked the car in a swirl of dead leaves in the SaveWay lot. Long Island will probably be gray and dusty on

Thanksgiving, instead of white and glittery. Teddy and Inga's first holiday together will probably be crummy. They'll have brown lawns, bare trees, and dirty cars to remember, none of the world's imperfections covered up in sparkly whiteness. There's that, at least, I think, cheering myself a bit. Milton is tickling himself beneath his chin with the yellow feather duster, but he's staring at me intently.

"Are you sad?" he asks.

"No. Just tired."

"Sad because there's no snow?" His brown eyes are gravely studying me.

"How do you like dusting the shelves?" I ask.

"I want to bag the groceries."

"Well," I say. "Why don't you continue your excellent work here for a few more minutes, while I speak to Mr. Hamilton?"

"How many minutes?"

"Five."

"Five?"

"Right."

He looks mournfully down at his wristwatch. "Okay."

I leave him there and head for the dairy aisle toward the manager's office. I'll ask Mickey if I can supervise Milton as a bagger for a little while and maybe even get my extra kiss. Then I'll go home again and sleep until they find me. Long tubes of fluorescent light glow down on the bricks of cheese, causing the headache behind my eyes to return. I knock once on the office door before walking in.

"Come in," Mickey says. It's his friendly voice, but I hear that little edge of business in it. I adjust my eyes to the room's dim light and then I smell the perfume. It's a light flirty scent I'm familiar with from the free samples inside my *Cosmo*s. I look in the gloaming to see who is wearing it and find Mickey standing across the table from a woman with blond hair. She's a definite *Cosmo* Girl. Her eyes seem to be lilac but it could just be contact lenses. She's very pretty, though it could just be her expertly applied makeup. She's wearing a burgundy wool coat, very handsome. No outline of her body is visible, but it's pin thin under there.

"Rosie," Mickey says. "This is Jane."

Jane smiles, like a nice person. "Hi," she says.

I extend my hand for a Ms. Plow handshake, wondering how my hungover pallor compares to her rosy smooth skin beneath the artificial lighting.

"Well," Jane says, patting Mickey's hand. "Be good, Michael." Before she leaves, she turns to me once more. "Nice meeting you," she says. "I've heard all about you." Her smile is quick but approving. "All good stuff!" she says, and then, in a flash she's gone, leaving a burgundy aura in the space where she'd stood beneath the light.

"Michael?" I say.

"Sit down," Mickey says, waving a hand toward a chair.

"I can come back later." I slap Milton's manila folder down on the table.

"No need for that. Jane just dropped in to say hello. It's not the first time."

"Jane?"

"She's my ex-wife. We're friends. I know that sounds like an oxymoron to you."

I glance at his face. Calm as a pond in August. "Jane comes by often? I'm surprised you've never mentioned it, Michael."

"You've never been here when she's come. And it's no big deal if she does. What's to mention?"

"Nothing. Nothing at all."

"Maybe I have mentioned it and you just haven't heard me. Lately you don't listen to me anyway. You just walk around with your little cloud of self-pity over your head."

I'm caught off guard by the sharpness of his voice. I've never heard Mickey sound annoyed with me.

"Maybe you see her more often at your apartment in the city," I hear myself say.

"What?" Mickey looks sucker punched.

"Is that why you never invite me to stay there?"

"Roseanna, you don't know what you're talking about."

"Whatever," I say. "Here's Milton's file."

"I don't *want* Milton's file—"

The door groans and opens and Milton stomps in.

"Mr. Hamilton!" he calls. "Mr. Hamilton, it's been seven minutes! Is Miss Plow in here?" He's panting and looking around.

"Milton," Mickey says sharply. "How many times have I asked you to knock?"

Mickey's tone turns Milton to stone. He is frozen in his green apron. His eyes turn left and right, first at Mickey and then at me.

"Miss Plow! Are you all right?" His cheeks grow pink with concern.

"Miss Plow! You said five minutes!" Milton is scrutinizing

me with alarm now. "What's the matter? Did that bad man with the chair come back?" He clasps his hands together anxiously. "That man in the elevator?"

Mickey looks at me. "What man in the elevator?"

"Not your elevator," says Milton. "Miss Plow's elevator."

"What elevator?" Mickey asks again.

"He means Teddy!" I snap. "He saw my husband in my elevator, okay?"

"Miss Plow!" Milton gasps.

Now it's Mickey's turn to pout. He's got his arms crossed and is staring at the floor.

"It was a long time ago," I tell him, disgusted at his denseness.

Milton cautiously walks over to me. "Oh, Miss Plow. You are very, very sad. Maybe I could make you some toast."

"So you didn't think it was worth telling me about?" Mickey fumes.

"He was stealing a chair!"

Milton is beside himself now. He rubs his hands together and cries out in an anguished voice, "If you two can't learn to get along, you can both just take a time-out!"

"Fine," I say, picking up Milton's folder again. "I'm taking my time-out."

"Take all the time you need," Mickey calls after me as I leave. I storm out of his office like I have somewhere to go. But where, I wonder, once I hit the parking lot. And then I see that there is only one place I can go.

tiny moments of brilliance

i find helen in her kitchen, already preparing dinner. The lunch dishes are drying on the dish rack and the sun is pouring through the windows. Pulkowski, she tells me, is out running errands.

"Does he feel well enough to run errands?" I ask her.

"He feels fine," she tells me, not looking up from her counter. I watch her roll raw rice into the center of raw meatballs. "Porcupines" she calls this meal. Pulkowski loves it. She will brown the meatballs before simmering them in tomato sauce. The rice will swell and soften like a hidden treasure inside the meat. Later, my mother will scoop them onto Pulkowski's dinner plate, infusing the color back into his cheeks. Then his prostate cancer won't be so bad, because of the porcupines. This is the way their love works. I rub my arms, thinking about it.

Helen says nothing about my showing up in the middle of the day. She doesn't comment on the fact that I've been boy-

cotting her for weeks. In exchange, I don't say a word to her
about her daughter or Johnny Bellusa. She scans my face and
sees everything, possibly even my hangover. But she is silent.
We've got the small TV going that sits on the counter of her
kitchen. An old *I Love Lucy* is on. Ricky is trying to wake up
Lucy to go fishing. "Come on!" he says. "You'll miss the sunrise!"

"Sunrise, sunset, it's all the same thing," says Lucy. "One
goes up, the other goes down." Lucy makes a face. "Tra la la! The
dance continues." The studio audience swells in laughter.

"Brilliant," my mother says. "That thought is brilliant."

I look at her as she works. Her shoulders are hunched,
stretching the dotted print of her cotton blouse tight across her
small back. "Women have these tiny moments of brilliance that
go unnoticed," she says, "even sometimes to themselves." She
is rolling the meat as she speaks to me. She talks in a soft cooing
voice, as though she is telling me a story. "Oh, it's true, Missy,"
she says. "Who's there to listen to a woman's life?"

I'm stirring the sauce the porcupines will go into, register-
ing Helen's point. So much of women's work turns out to be
lonely work.

"I used to have them, little perfect moments of insight,
when you kids were young. Right in the middle of making your
sandwiches or vacuuming a rug or something."

When we kids were young. That would be Alexa and me, I suppose. My mother's two girls.

"Like once," she continues, half talking to herself now,
"when I was listening to one of you sneeze with a cold, I realized

that most humans sneezed in sets of two. Did you know that? It's not just *a-choo*. It's *a-choo! A-choo!*"

She drops the first six meatballs into her frying pan, standing beside me at her stove. "If some putz at Stony Brook University came up with that discovery, everyone would hail him as a genius. I told your father about it when he came home from work that night and I remember he was very unimpressed."

The smell of the hot olive oil fills the air around us.

"Probably thought I was daft. Easy for him to think I was daft. He was at work all day in his nice busy office."

She jabs at a porcupine with her spatula and I see that she is angry with him. What the hell was Pulkowski doing, sitting there with his legs shooting over the end of the examination table, getting radiated week after week? Who did he think he was, getting cancer? I realize something else, too, that Alexa Pulkowski and I could have been raised as sisters in Helen Pulkowski's house. We could have been *us kids*, for a few years, anyway, until my mother ran off into the twilight. But it didn't happen that way, and I don't even know if Helen or Alexa had wanted it to happen or not.

"He just wanted his dinner, not some little moment of brilliance from me," Helen mutters, and I look down at her scalp and see how the hair is thinning at the back.

"Well, men, you know," I say. This is my way of consoling her, without actually laying my spoon down and putting my arms around her. She looks up at me with wet eyes, and we are back.

•   •   •

Mickey is waiting for me in the living room when I arrive home. His hulking frame rises awkwardly from the mauve couch cushions, like a huge G.I. Joe doll bent all wrong at the joints. He grimaces at the sight of me, as though my presence gives him gas. He's still feeling bad about this afternoon. I toss my briefcase onto a chair, unsure as to whether we're about to launch into tearful apologies or round two.

"Hey," he says, squeezing his hands together like he's wringing out a washcloth.

"Hello," I reply carefully. "I went to see Helen."

"Excellent," he says. Then he sighs. "Rosie. You knew I was divorced."

I say nothing, just remove my coat.

"Do you really think I still see her?"

"That's your business," I lie.

Mickey reaches for me, pulling me onto his lap. It feels warm and safe in the little cave he makes for me there. "And we have no business together?"

I disengage myself and stand. "Why don't you ever invite me to your place?" I check his face for changes, some sign of discomfort, but Mickey's sideburns don't rise an inch.

"Do you think it's because I've created a love nest there with my ex-wife?" He puffs air out of his mouth, a derisive sound I've never heard come from him before. "That's your ex-husband's style, not mine."

This stings. Since when has Mickey begun saying things that sting? "So now we're going to start dissing my husband?"

There's a long beat of silence in my Ronkonkoma living room. We can hear trucks going by on the Long Island Expressway. Neither of us can believe I am defending Teddy.

"It's not as if your fabulous ex isn't a constant third party in our lives," Mickey says rising from the couch.

"He's not my ex. He's still my husband."

"And that means . . . what?"

I cross my arms and begin pacing, "It means that he's not completely *gone* yet! He hasn't asked for a divorce. Who knows what he might decide to do?"

Even to my own ears I sound crazy. Perhaps I *am* crazy. Or maybe I'm just cycling through the stages of grief with my gears stuck in pissed.

"Rosie, hey." Mickey takes me into his arms and presses me against him. He waits until I am still before he speaks. "Listen. I think you should acknowledge that it's over with Teddy, whatever you think of me. Your husband lives in a pink shoebox with your best friend."

"Okay!" I shout, and tears start running down my face, wetting his nice white shirt. "But he's still my husband. We share the same tax forms. He is *associated* with me in a legitimate way. He's a real, if shitty, husband, unlike Helen, who's a fake, if wacko mother . . ."

Sob, sob, sobbing like a baby. Hangovers are a terrible thing. I know it's not just the after-effects of Marcie's bad wine that jumps around in my gut, but also some point I'm trying to make, and then Mickey makes the point for me.

"A lot of people in your show have left the stage," he says, and I think, *damn* him for getting it so right. He strokes my hair and waits for me to compose myself. I smell the SaveWay on him, a subtle combination of cheese and refrigeration. I cannot stand his kindness. I pull away from him, cross my arms again, and give him my fiercest look. It is the look I reserve for Milton when I find him kissing the babies in the shopping carts.

"What are you hiding in the city, then?"

"I'm hiding nothing, Rosie. I don't *want* to hide anything from you."

I shake my head and begin pacing again.

"I told you," he says. "It's over with Jane and me."

"Do all men prefer blondes in the end?" I ask.

"Look," he says. "I have to see her again. She's selling the house we lived in. There are papers to be signed. It'll be quick and formal. That's why she was at the office."

"Fine," I tell him, noticing this is not fine. "I may have to see Teddy again soon, too."

"Fine," he says, crossing his own arms. He studies me a moment and says, "Except nothing's fine, is it?"

The way he says this, I know we have crossed a line, some arduous, tired line that will takes miles of travel to cross back over again. I see this as clearly as I see the plump mauve couch cushions behind him, and suddenly I'm sorry that I've used my sweet Mickey as a punching bag. "I'm just a little confused now," I tell him, by way of an apology, but I know it's too late.

I watch Mickey grow quiet, scratching his chin with his big mitt. "You know what, Rosie?" he says after a moment. "Maybe we're moving too fast. Yes, I think we're moving too fast. So here's what I'm going to do. I'm going to go home now. I have a lot of work to do. I'll just go to my place and stay there tonight."

I sit on the couch, a little stunned. "You'll just stay at your place tonight?"

"I think it's best."

"We can't have a fight without your leaving?"

"It's not because we're having a fight."

"What if I want to come with you? To see your place."

"You can come another time."

"Fine," I say.

"Fine," he agrees, getting his coat.

"When are you meeting your ex-wife again?"

"Tomorrow. At the Pasta Café."

"Doesn't she work?"

"We're meeting on her lunch break."

"Fine," I say. "You'd better get along then."

"Fine," he says, and he doesn't try to kiss me.

"Good night," I tell his back, but he just closes the door behind him. I sit on the couch, in the indentation he has left. The apartment is so still, I can hear the heat rising from the heating ducts. If Inga were here, we'd eat a quart of Häagen-Dazs now. But strangely enough, I find I'm not hungry.

• • •

"Why are we eating lunch at Starbucks?" Helen asks, at 11:59 the next day. We are seated at our table, a little round disc, surrounded by well-dressed people sipping lattes and double lattes and cappuccinos. The whole world smells like coffee beans and the plate glass windows are seriously steamed. This does not block the view of the Pasta Café, though. You can see its glass doors and the people coming and going.

"Why are we eating lunch at Starbucks?" Helen repeats.

"Ma, they have plenty of food here."

"You're still calling me Ma?"

I shrug my shoulders. "It's who you've always been."

"Good." She pats my hand. "Now let me explain something to you. I can get a can of Chock Full o' Nuts for a dollar ninety-nine." She places her huge winter purse on the tabletop, obliterating its little disc surface. "So explain to me, please, why would I pay three dollars here for a cup of tar?"

She's talking too loudly, of course. "Ma," I say, trying to model for her our indoor voices (I'm beginning to see why I went into the field that I did, training challenged people to have normal social skills), "there are other things you might like to try besides the coffee."

"Like what?" She crosses her legs in pleated wool slacks and fur-lined ankle boots.

"Well," I begin, scanning the menu on the wall. "Have you ever tried the chai tea?"

"The *what* tea?"

"Chai."

"Chai?" Helen's eyes squeeze shut in mirth. "Sure. I'll have that and the lemon toffee delight bar." She begins snickering. "That ought to handle the four food groups for my lunch."

Now she's laughing out loud. People are baldly staring, peering over the rims of their laptops. I see how this was a mistake, bringing Helen along on a surveillance mission. I'd imagined us healing our rift as we sipped Costa Rican, rebuilding our relationship as we inadvertently, but sort of on purpose, "spotted" Mickey and Jane. Of course, I haven't told Helen why we're sitting here today. It's really not her fault that she doesn't know we're supposed to be having fun.

Although, she does seem to be having fun. At my expense.

"Ma," I whisper hoarsely, trying to quell her hysterics. "There's a reason we're here at Starbucks."

"Is it the Heath Bar mango-crunch muffins?" she asks, collapsing back into laughter.

"Ma, please. I'm trying to tell you about the little spying mission we're on."

Helen falls silent. She turns to me with sharp eyes. "What spying mission?"

"It's Ham and his ex-wife. They're going to meet across the street any second."

Helen stops smiling. Her eyes move to the unsteamed part of the window.

"They sold their house and Mickey has to sign some papers."

Helen's mouth sets in a firm straight line.

"You'll get to see her, the ex-wife! Isn't that fun?"

"And why are we here?" Helen asks. "Just to invade their privacy?"

"Well . . . yes."

Now she is frowning hard. "And do you think he still loves his wife?"

"No . . ."

"Can't you see that he loves *you*, you little moron?"

I sit back hard in my chair. "Ma, you of all people shouldn't be judgmental about today's outing. Are you forgetting how you dragged me to the Acropolis to meet Ham?"

"That was for your own *good*, Missy! Nobody got hurt. You

think no one's going to get hurt today if they see us looking out this window?" She stands abruptly and grabs her purse from the table. "What's your purpose here, Rosie?" she asks. "Are you trying to screw things up with Ham, just because *I* introduced you? Or because the man actually loves you . . . unlike that dimwit Teddy you married?"

Now I have bolted to my feet as well. "You're a fine one to lecture me on deceitful behavior! Don't you think so, *Grandma*?"

Helen doesn't turn to respond. She's already clip-clopping toward the door on her high-heeled boots, her coat flowing like a cape off one shoulder. I am left alone to make my mortifying exit. I creep past the stunned faces of our peanut gallery.

Now I'm running down the sidewalk, trying to catch up to Helen. I try to calm myself by thinking of how my clients cause scenes like this all the time, and how I just sit them down afterward and ask: *what have we learned today?* I zip my coat against the frigid air and think about this. But Helen is steaming down the sidewalk, making headway, and no tiny moment of brilliance illuminates me.

gobble, gobble, happy turkey day!

mickey has boycotted me, true to his word. He has not stayed over once since our little blowup, nor have I asked him to. It has been almost three weeks. I cannot believe I am again counting the days since a man has left me. I have no idea how the paper-signing with Mickey's wife went. I've begun to grow used to my huge empty king-sized bed. There is plenty of room to move around. Maybe this is just what I need—room to move around, without a man to bump into.

Helen doesn't think so. She is outraged to hear that Mickey is no longer modeling my mauve towels in the morning. Marcie has told her this, of course. Marcie of the big heart and the big mouth. Helen's taken the bull by the horns and invited Mickey to Thanksgiving dinner.

Now this great family holiday has arrived, filling my bedroom window with gray skies and morning drizzle. I lie beneath my comforter, counting the many ways that today will be awkward for Mickey and me. His navy bathrobe still hangs from a hook on my open bathroom door. *How are we supposed to act?* I ask it, lying in bed, staring at it. The slumped shoulders remain droopy and still.

Mickey and I are technically not together anymore—something even Milton has sensed, and responded to by sitting among the potted ferns and rose bouquets in the floral department again. Yet I wouldn't really say that we're broken up, either. We're just taking a hiatus, Mickey says. I sigh and pull the comforter higher. Milton and I remain depressed.

The phone rings incessantly. I nestle deeper into my Martha Stewart linen, envying her her time in prison. At least they left her alone in there. The phone rings and rings. With great reluctance, I drag myself from my designer swaddling and pick it up.

"Should I bring your mother a pie or something?"

It's Mickey, wondering about a hostess gift. I feel the little hairs on my arms standing. It is so easy to say the wrong thing, strike the wrong tone, give the wrong impression when you don't really know if your boyfriend still loves you.

"I don't think so," I tell him carefully. "She bakes her own pies."

"Ah. Maybe some flowers then."

"Let's see . . ." I say, trying for humor. "How long have you and Helen been dating now? Three months? Yes, flowers would be perfect."

"Ha ha," he says. "Then what should I bring?"

His voice sounds wonderful. I remind myself that he hasn't really dumped me. We're just taking a break.

"Some candy, maybe? A plant?" he asks.

"Pulkowski gives her all that kind of stuff."

"Yes, but maybe this year, he won't be feeling up to it."

"He's *fine*."

I have snapped at him. Now I sound bitchy. "The treatments are really working," I assure him. I'm making this up, of course. It could be that Pulkowski is getting worse. "A bottle of Scotch," I advise. "Buy her some Chivas. She loves it."

"Chivas?" he says. "As in Regal?"

"She's too cheap to buy her own. She buys the off-brands, like Old Smuggler, and pours it into her empty Chivas bottle."

"That Helen . . ." Mickey says.

There is a beat of uncomfortable silence.

"Are you glad you're going to see me today?" Mickey asks.

"Helen certainly is."

A second beat of silence. My joke has not gone over. But what if I *am* glad to be seeing him today and he's not glad to be seeing *me*?

"I'll see you later," Mickey says.

I hang up, exhausted. I still have to shower, put on fancy clothes, figure out how to look happy.

In the bathroom a tired-looking face stares back from the mirror. I look pasty, and slightly lumpy. Teddy has done this, or maybe Mickey. Or maybe Helen. Holiday stress has taken its toll on my skin. A nice long bath will steam the pores.

I lie in the bubbles, trying to think of ways I can change everything about my whole life. I remember a nun I had in third grade who taught us we could do this, could change the whole world with small actions. She did it one day as we sat at our desks, practicing our cursive. With my pencil squeezed between my fingers, I watched her take down the Stations of the Cross that were hanging on our classroom walls. Then she pulled a small hammer from the folds of her habit and began pounding new nails, mounting the little plaques in the reverse order. "I'm a lefty," she explained to us, when she was finished. "By hanging these backwards, I have slightly changed the world." I remain in the tub long after the last bubbles are gone, thinking about this.

Eventually I begin the ritual of holiday dressing up. First I apply face cream. Then I fiddle with a contact lens the thinness of cellophane, almost not there in the palm of my hand. All this effort because I am a woman, susceptible, as most females are, to the belief that I am a slovenly loser who deserves what I get if I don't make the mighty effort to *improve* myself. I once had a client whose husband took her head in his hands and slammed it against their white enamel kitchen sink. When I visited her the next day in the hospital, she was applying lipstick to her smashed lips. "I'm a vain woman," she'd said, smiling sheep-ishly beneath her black eyes and mummy bandages. So much, we want to be loved.

Mickey rings the buzzer, just as I'm done drying my hair. He comes in carrying a SaveWay pie in a box.

"I thought I told you my mother bakes her own," I greet him—the wrong greeting, of course. I smooth down my rust-colored silk skirt, try to regroup.

"May I say you look beautiful?" he asks.

I glance up at him. I like the way his eyes settle on my hips and not my contact lenses. He is a man who appreciates the things I've come equipped with. What a shame if I have lost this man.

"I got her the Chivas, but I thought maybe I should give her something Thanksgiving-y with it," he says.

"It's a nice gesture. But she'll throw that pie out the minute you leave."

"Well."

I glance at the box. "Hold on."

I pull my phone directory out of my work purse and dial up Eleanor's group home.

"Gobble, gobble! Happy Turkey Day!" someone answers. It's one of the residents. She puts me on with the day counselor, and when I identify myself, her voice grows cold.

"Please hold," she says, and then the phone is roughly dropped. No matter. Eleanor loves pumpkin pie, and when I tell her I'm coming over with one, she whoops loudly into the phone.

"It's right on the way to Helen's," I tell Mickey.

"I don't mind," he says. "I like getting an inside look at what you do."

"Same here," I tell him. "Maybe one day you could bring me into a meat locker."

Mickey laughs, and I almost relax. He holds my coat out and I lace my arms through the sleeves. "Ready?" he asks.

I smile at him nicely, like a normal person.

There are construction paper pumpkins on the doors and windows of the Cooperative Living group home, a large Colonial house that sits on a block of residential homes, all of which could use a good painting. Eleanor's face is pressed against the largest window, flattening her nose and cheeks and making her eyes look even more startling. She lets out a yell when she sees us and then disappears toward the door.

"You have the pie?" she asks, flinging open the storm door. She is dressed in a yellow cotton dress, way too light for almost winter. She rubs her hands together as her eyes dart from the pie to Mickey to the pie again.

"Who's he?" she asks. "Is he your boyfriend?" She rubs her hands together more briskly.

"Eleanor," I say. "Aren't you going to ask us in?"

"Come in!" she shouts.

We enter a foyer lined with rows of sneakers. It smells like turkey and Lysol.

"Where's your counselor?" I ask Eleanor.

"Watching TV," Eleanor says.

She squeezes the hand of a woman standing beside her, a small fiftyish woman with gray hair and pink fuzzy slippers. "That's her boyfriend," Eleanor tells her, pointing at Mickey with her free hand.

"Mmm. Nice," the woman says. I don't dare look at Mickey.

Eleanor throws her arms around my waist, almost crushing the pie box between us. "She's mine," she says, hugging me tight, and I am thankful this Thanksgiving Day that I have Eleanor's affections back.

I introduce Mickey to Eleanor and her friend. Eleanor kisses Mickey on the cheek and leads him toward the dining room. "Come on!" she commands, and our small troop follows.

The table there is set with an orange paper tablecloth and a paper turkey centerpiece with a fold-out fanned tail. The ancient yellowed wallpaper warms the room like cupped hands. I place the pie in the center of the table, wishing I could stay. Perhaps one Thanksgiving at the Cooperative Living group home could slightly change my world for the better.

"Eleanor baked a super cool cake," the woman in the fuzzy slippers says. "But we'll eat your pie, too."

"I decorated it special!" Eleanor says, hanging a one-eighty and rushing toward the old house's pantry. She reemerges carrying a lopsided layer cake, iced in chocolate, with a plastic green Shrek figurine stuck on top, slightly off center. A swirl of icing crusts Shrek's noggin like a bad toupee. "I love his smile," Eleanor confides. "He's better than a turkey."

After mucho hugs and pats and kisses, we're finally back in the truck, heading toward Helen's in silence. I stare out my drizzly window at a dull gray sky, watching brown lawns and naked trees fly by. I find I'm teary all of a sudden. I keep my face glued to the window but Mickey, damn his touchy-feely soul, senses I'm sad anyway.

"Are you all right?" he asks, squeezing my hand.

"Yeah," I tell him, my voice coming out in a whisper. "I think I just wanted to stay there, is all."

"Why's that?" Mickey asks, but I have the feeling he knows why and just wants me to say it out loud.

"Because I'm feeling crummy these days. About . . . everything."

There. I've accommodated him with the truth. When Mickey doesn't say anything for another minute, I turn the tables on him.

"How did your little business meeting go with Jane?"

"Didn't you see us when we came out?" he asks. "Oh, that's right. You and Helen left early."

My stomach flip-flops a little with guilt, or maybe it's

shame, I've never understood the difference. Growing up with Helen, I never had enough time to examine the difference. "That was a mistake," I confess, wanting to come clean. "I was still mad at you. That's why we did it."

"You mean Helen went along with it?"

"Nah." I rub my arms, suddenly chilled. "I didn't tell her why we were going to Starbucks. When she found out, she stormed off."

"Hah!" Mickey's laughter surprises me. "Well, Jane never knew you were there, so it doesn't matter."

We listen to the tires hum and bump for a while. Then I say, "So you're really all finished with your divorce now?"

"I already was finished. We just hadn't decided what to do with the house."

"So what did you?"

"I gave it to her."

"You gave her the house?"

"Yes."

Why do I feel as though Mickey has just thrown a bucket of water at me? I know why. It's because some husbands, even if they are lowly store managers, give their wives houses. While my husband simply walked out of his. No, it's worse than that. He bought another house with Inga.

"I don't know how the hell we're going to get through this Thanksgiving dinner," I find myself blubbering, my eyes stinging and my hands balled in fists.

"Is it that bad to spend a whole afternoon with me?" Mickey asks. I sense he knows my emotional outburst is not about him, but more about the fact that I was married to a putz—a putz I happened to eat turkey with, every fourth Thursday in November.

I look at Mickey through carefully applied eyeliner that now must be smudged. "How many Thanksgivings has it been since your divorce?"

"Enough," he says. "I'm used to it. But for you, this is the first one, of course . . ." His voice trails off. He pats my hand. "You'll get used to it."

"Goddamn it," I say, punching the plush seat of his truck. "Why can't people learn to live with each other in a married state?"

"Most people can . . ." Mickey offers.

"Then what the hell happened to yours?"

Mickey frowns into the windshield and says nothing. I can't blame him for this. He is my dinner guest and I am, in essence, complaining that each of us isn't having dinner with our estranged spouses. I know I am being unreasonable, but something about seeing that turkey with construction paper feathers tugs at my heart like a toddler yanking his mother's skirt, making me obstinately believe that some things in life shouldn't *change*. They just shouldn't.

Mickey's slowing his truck down, pulling into the parking lot of a 7-Eleven. He averts his face from me, but I can see his pain anyway, almost as if it is radiating from his sideburns.

"Do you really want to know?" he asks.

"Yes, I do," I say.

Mickey cuts the engine and stares straight ahead. We watch three teenagers out front sipping from their soda bottles.

"It's not a horror story," Mickey begins. "No one did anything awful."

"I understand," I say, though I really don't. Of course some-one did something awful. That's why they're divorced.

"I met her when I was fourteen," he says, rubbing his hands together. "By the time we were thirty, we'd been together more than half our lives. We were like kids who grew up together, and now we wanted to get out of the house."

"So what happened?"

"One of us did."

"Which one?"

Mickey looks down at his lap.

"Me. Not that it matters."

"Sure it doesn't," I tell him.

"She was actually relieved that one of us finally did some-thing. She's seeing someone now. I'm happy for her."

I narrow my eyes at him. "Did you leave her for someone else?"

"No."

"I'm supposed to believe this?"

Mickey takes my hand in his, where I allow it to reside, inanimate as a lump of coal. "You can believe what you want." he says. "There wasn't anyone else because I hadn't met you."

I pull my hand free. "What's that supposed to mean? That we're sort of *not* broken up?"

Mickey starts the engine again. "Rosie," he sighs, "let's just get through this dinner today."

"That'll be fun," I snap. "The two of us from our broken marriages being served by a woman who's lied to me my whole life."

Now Mickey turns and looks me full in the face. "Rosie," he says. "It's not always about fault."

"I know," I tell him, smiling my holiday smile. But my heart hardens a little, for I am unwilling to agree with him on this point.

all aboard the chili choo choo

his ass looked cute in his new slacks. He bought your mother good Scotch and he loves you. What's your problem, Roseanna?"

Marcie's sitting on the edge of my desk on Monday morning, dissecting my Thanksgiving with a stack of folders on her lap.

"How do you know his ass looked cute?" I ask.

"I know everything," she says, pushing her black horn rims up her nose. "I talked to your mother."

"My mother told you his ass looked cute?"

"Well, not in those exact words. She said he had a nice tush."

"I guess once she's told you she's not my mother, the rest is easy."

Marcie swipes the air between us dismissively. "Poor Rosie. Bitch-slapped by life! So she's your grandmother. It's no reason to sit around looking like a Prozac commercial."

I rise from my chair, almost hitting the back wall of my

claustrophobic office. "It means that I have a mother and a father I don't even know!"

Marcie runs a hand through her spiky black-and-blond hair. "So you have an interesting life story. Call the National Guard."

"Your head looks like a cabbage," I lash out, flopping down in my desk chair again. "Are you ever going to *style* that pathetic crew cut?"

"I'm just going to let it grow out," Marcie answers, unfazed. "Sometimes you just have to give things *time*, Rosie." She looks at me significantly, then rises to leave.

"Wait," I say. "Answer me this. Are you saying that if you found out you didn't know who your mother or father was, you would just wait for your hair to grow out and forget about it?"

Marcie snaps a suspender thoughtfully with her free hand. She appears to be wearing Sean's suit trousers today, topped with a stretchy pink number that ends above her navel. I glimpse a single ray of the Aztec sun tattooed over her behind as she stands with her back to me, mulling. She turns around and faces me, then comes back in and reclaims her seat on my desktop.

"Look," she sighs, "if you want to find out who your parents are, then go ahead and find them. It isn't that hard to do. Go online. Google them! Try SuperPages! Think how easy it was for me to find Teddy and Inga's house."

I wince at the reminder of Teddy and Inga's house. Especially in light of the phone call this morning from Teddy himself, asking me to meet him for lunch. It bewilders me as to why I've agreed to join him at our old haunt, the Chili Choo Choo, where we often met for lunch in better days. I don't even like chili, something I never told Teddy, in the course of our four-year marriage. Now I don't like Teddy, either. And yet I've told him yes, I'll walk the eight blocks to the restaurant, maybe because I need just one last shred of evidence that it's over, that his absence at Helen's Thanksgiving table wasn't a mistake.

"I can help you find them," Marcie says, interrupting my thoughts.

"Huh?"

"Your parents. I can find them. Helen loves me. I can ask her things you can't possibly even broach."

"I don't want to do this through Helen. And I don't need a translator."

"I see myself more as an ambassador." She frowns thoughtfully. "Ambassador to the Republic of Pulkowski. I could get the whole outfit. The epaulets, the gold buttons . . . and, *oh yes*, . . . one of those cute little hats with the brim . . ."

"Marcie, this is serious!" I screech.

Marcie rises from the desk a second time. "Everything is serious, Rosie. You have Gil Fortinier coming in at two, and he's just been fired from his plumber's job. That's serious, don't you think? Let me know if you want me to help you."

She pats my arm affectionately. I follow her retreating Aztec sun to the door. "Thanks," I call after her.

She turns and frowns. "And why isn't Ham staying over at your house again?"

"He says we're not ready yet."

"What is he? A nun?"

"What are you?" I retort. "A cross-dresser? Do you really think Sean's suit pants are becoming?"

Marcy smoothes a hand over the behind of the trousers. "You sound like Sean now. My answer to both of you is yes." She sashays out doing the one-two step.

I pull Gil's file and try to concentrate. Gil is one of my "special needs" clients who doesn't fall into the category of developmentally challenged. In other words, he's not retarded. But Gil's got this major auditory processing problem. He simply cannot hear two things at the same time. If the television is on while the faucet is dripping, the plunk of the water might as well be a road worker outside Gil's open window, running a jackhammer full throttle. I am fascinated by learning disabilities like his. My problem has always been the opposite. I've always been able to hear two things distinctly at the same time. My problem is sorting out the truth.

I browse through Gil's file and others, wasting away my morning. I think about Marcie's offer to find the elusive birth parents, and about my awful behavior in the parking lot of the 7-Eleven. I think about how Helen gazed at Mickey with such ardor across the turkey platter, at Thanksgiving dinner. I think about Pulkowski, and how his color looked a little better. Sometimes I even think about my clients.

At some point my wall clock says it's time to head for the Chili Choo Choo, where Teddy will be waiting with God knows what kind of new bomb to hurl my way. Maybe Inga is pregnant. Maybe they want me to be the godmother. I pull on my coat and head for the elevator. Marcie is on the phone, but waves and mouths a "good luck!" as I pass. I have no doubt she knows where I'm going. Marcie knows everything.

• • •

I see Teddy waiting at a round table in the back of the Chili Choo Choo, sipping a cup of coffee. I see him before he sees me, and there are all the things I've always loved: the liquidy hazel eyes, the creamy olive skin, the errant snippets of brown hair above his ears. He spots me and flashes his insincere smile, and there are all the things I've always hated: the weakness of his chin, the promises of the moon that have passed through those thin lips, the tiny row of white teeth, as though his teeth refused to grow after the age of seven.

Bowls of chili circle the room, resting in their freight cars. They travel behind his head, then disappear into a wooden bridge. It's a "theme" restaurant, like so many others now on Long Island. Teddy loves "theme" restaurants. He loves themes in general, like the lawyer theme of his supposed career, and now, this schmaltzy *The Way We Were* theme I imagine him hoping our luncheon will have. He rises as I approach and hugs me with lots of squeezing and back patting. All I can think is that he wants the microwave oven, to go with the stolen cart.

"Roseanna," he sighs, like this is his big scene in the movie, and I know with certainty that this lunch isn't about kissing and making up.

"How have you been?" he asks, inside of his insincere hug.

"I've been better," I say, breaking free of him.

He pulls out my chair, though he has seldom done this in the four years of our marriage.

"You look wonderful," he says.

"Teddy, please. Just cut the crap."

He does. His whole face changes. His eyes grow dark and downcast, and he seems to travel far from me, right there in his chair.

"I hear you're dating some store guy," he says.

"I'm not *dating* anyone," I tell him. "And people who sleep with their wife's best friend don't really get to say things like that."

Teddy and I are silent for a moment. He looks a little steamed. *Some store guy.* He should know all the things Ham is that he is not.

"Well, since you're not into small talk, let me get to the point here. I, uh, actually, would like a divorce."

I open my mouth to say something, but nothing comes out. The train of chili bowls rattles by above us. Into the small cacophony I try to absorb what Teddy has told me. Then I grow quiet, waiting for my reaction.

"I'm sure this comes as no surprise to you," he continues. "Considering. I thought we might be able to talk a little today about getting our affairs in order."

"Excellent idea," I say calmly.

"What?" I glance at Teddy and he looks confused.

"Let's get our affairs in order," I hear myself repeat.

Teddy eyes me sharply. "Are you going to make some off-color joke about *affairs*, Roseanna, because if that's where you're going here . . ."

Poor Teddy. The guilt. I let him stew in it a minute. "No," I finally say.

This baffles him further. "You mean you're . . . not going to contest this?"

I shake my head. Tears sting my eyes.

Teddy seems momentarily bewildered. Then he looks up at me and says, "I wanted to speak to you today about, you know, the arrangements."

I wipe my eyes with the back of a hand.

"I suppose this doesn't come as a shock to you, then."

"It doesn't," I tell him, and realize it's true.

"Inga and I have this house now, you see . . ." Apparently he feels he must explain further. He looks at me guiltily, but then corrects his expression. "I guess I'm wondering what you'll be wanting to do now, with the apartment and all."

"What I'll be wanting to do?" I twist a cloth napkin while I rack my mind for an answer to Teddy's question. What will I be wanting to do, now that Teddy and I will be divorced? Will I want to continue living around the corner from my ex-husband and ex-best friend, working only minutes away from their new house? Will I want to resume a relationship with *some store guy*—that is, if he'll have me? It occurs to me that I don't really know what I'll be wanting to do with the rest of my life. The only thing I know for sure, sitting across from my husband now at the Chili Choo Choo, is that our marriage is over.

I seem to be glued to the restaurant chair, gulping like a guppy out of water. Now I hear myself crying. Is this what it means to really say good-bye to a part of your life? Teddy is staring at me, horrified. He digs into the deep pocket of his DKNY shirt and comes up with a handkerchief, which he hands me, and which I accept.

"May I ask you something?" I simper.

Teddy nods, looking a little frightened.

"With what money have you bought this house?"

The color drains from his lips. "Inga's money," he says, " if you must know. For now, anyway."

All those little bags of chips, I think. Almost this and Almost that. I smile to myself, and then I'm breathing better. Teddy looks down at his menu, frowning as though he is studying a legal brief. "Just as soon as you and I get our affairs in order in a civilized way," he says defensively, "I fully intend to get my name on the deed and pay my fair share."

I smile again. This is the second time Teddy has asked me to behave in a civilized way. Although he's the one who has moved into a house with my best friend, I entertain the possibility that it is I who might be uncivilized. I, who teach the developmentally challenged to fold their napkins on their laps and hang up their coats on hangers and shake hands politely at interviews. I roll a saltshaker between my hands. The chili bowls continue to thrash around on their tidal wave and Teddy stares solemnly at his menu, his toughest lunch task over. It won't be so hard to not be his wife.

A waitress comes over with a pad. She is young and pretty, in a Long Island kind of way. A train engineer's hat sits on top of her big hair like a stranded fishing boat on a sand dune. Teddy shows her some teeth and my memory flashes back to the Christmas party at Inga's house. How he'd smiled at me that night, just like this. Teddy tears his eyes from our waitress and looks back at me.

"May I get you something?" the waitress asks.

"Nothing at all," I reply. I rise, pat Teddy on the arm, and leave. "We'll have to get our affairs together in a civilized way some other time," I tell him.

I squint against a stinging wind as I walk the eight blocks to my office. I pass a woman pushing a stroller with dirt bike wheels. I pass a black man with a yellow Lab talking to a white woman with a black Lab. I pass SUVs, lots of SUVs: Cherokees, Navigators, Range Rovers, Hummers. Almost always women are behind the wheels, as though these trucks are substitutes for the men they wish they'd gotten—powerful, protective, big men, willing to kick some ass for the woman who loves them. It all makes me wonder why I'd never gone out and bought one myself, while married to Teddy Stracuzza.

Back at EPT, I walk past Marcie's desk, which is empty, then spy the choppy back of her head in the window of Sean's office. When I open my office door, there is my two o'clock, Gil, slumped like a sack in the orange plastic chair. He's early this time. He nods, my last client of the day, a depressed plumber with a learning disability.

"Yo," he greets me. The blue tendrils of an escaped tattoo shoot from the collar of his shirt. "I pulled the plug on your clock," he says, gesturing toward the Baby Ben that sits on my desk. "I hope you don't mind, but the noise of it was truly ball-busting."

"How are you?" I ask, modeling good eye contact.

Gil picks at a hangnail, looking unhappy. "This lady puts on a Tony Bennett album and then she starts telling me what's wrong with her sink. I'm on my knees in her kitchen and the guy's nonstop singing." Gil sighs. "Best I can understand, her sink is lost in San Francisco. 'You need a fucking washer!' I tell her, 'cause I'm yelling over the damn music. The lady starts yappin' and yappin'.'" He waves his tattooed arms around—skulls, swords, hearts—it's amazing. "So," he says, "I'm fired."

"You're fired?"

"She tells me to leave. She says I look demented." He raises his chin a little.

"People in the suburbs think everyone is demented," I tell him kindly. "Don't take it personally."

We talk for fifteen more minutes. I remind Gil about swearing in front of the customer, but when he winces at my mild admonition, I stop. So much hurt in the world. Do any of us escape it? I tell him to come back in a week, and we'll watch *Job Skills for Success*. He leaves in a blur of blue ink and leather. I lock the door after him and go looking for Marcie.

"Yes?" she says, looking up from her computer.

"I want you to do it," I tell her. "Find them."

Marcie snaps a suspender and smiles. "Done," she says. "Just promise me you won't let this little adventure fuck up anything with the butcher."

"I promise," I tell her. "And he's a store manager."

"Good," she says, turning back to her computer. "Now give the dentists a call in Mineola. Things are escalating in the lingerie department. Eleanor's nightwear is apparently moving toward Frederick's."

do i look like anyone you know?

"**Zambie! get the door!**" Marcie bellows. She's riveted to her computer screen where it sits on the sleek, long oak desk in her home office. We've been in the chat room for the Little Flower Home for Unwed Mothers all Saturday morning, reading heartbreaking stories of the motherless, the abandoned, the still-searching.

"Look at this one," Marcie says, pointing to the computer screen.

HI IM LOOKIN FOR MY SIS TYESHIA JONES IM HOPIN U R IN GOOD SPIRITS AND HEALTH. The post is by someone named Shondel P. An even more pathetic one follows, from a woman named theresa617. *Do I look like anyone you know?* Posted is a photo of the pale-faced Theresa, holding up a toy poodle in a red devil's suit.

"This is depressing," I say, rising from my chair beside Marcie's. "Why are we looking at this stuff? I *know* who my birth parents are. I just don't know *where* they are."

Marcie is wearing baggy gangsta pants today, which hang a full inch below the lacy elastic of her thong. "This was your port of entry," she explains. She is speaking to me as though I am developmentally challenged. "Don't you want to know who your homies were?"

"These people aren't my homies!" I tell her for the hundredth time. "Being born at a home for unwed mothers isn't about the bonding."

Marcie doesn't buy it. For Marcie, being an abandoned baby is exotic. A home for unwed mothers is retro—something that should give you fashion ideas. She can't tear her eyes from her computer. "I'm trying to give you some perspective here," she tells the screen. "You were taken home. By your real mother! What if you were poor Theresa with the poodle in the devil's suit?"

Sean walks into the office holding a pizza box. Marcie turns and grins at him. "Seanie, does Rosie look like anyone you know?"

"I'm sorry. No," Sean replies nervously. Marcie instructs him to put down the pizza on the other end of the desk. He leans his kidney bean head over the box, and I imagine it clad in one of those plaid wool hats with the furry flaps and bill, the ones the wimpy boys' mothers used to make them wear to school. He always seems to show up at the most intimate moments of disclosure in my life.

"Get us some napkins, Zambie," Marcie orders, and my boss just nods and shuffles toward the kitchen.

"What I want to know," I tell Marcie once Sean is gone, "is how to find my parents without asking Helen or Pulkowski."

"That's simple," says Marcie. "*I* ask them."

"No," I tell Marcie again. "They have enough on their plates. And I don't even know if Helen and I have made up or not."

"That's because you brought her along on your stupid field trip to Starbucks. Good one, Ace."

"Do you know *all* my personal business?" I ask.

"Look," says Marcie, pulling a slice of pizza from the box and handing it to me. "We're gonna find these dudes one way or the other. I've already started a national search online. You just go state by state, and I'm already up to Illinois."

I put the pizza slice back in the box. "The problem with your search is that she may not be Alexa Pulkowski anymore. She could have any last name by now."

"That's why I'm starting with Johnny Bellusa," Marcie says. I feel her eyeing me as I stand beside the pizza box. "Hey, girl-friend, you're gettin' skinny. Do people stop eating when they discover they're illegitimate?"

Sean walks in on cue, of course, plopping down a stack of napkins and acting like he hasn't heard Marcie.

"I'm not illegitimate," I declare loudly. But is it true?

"Seanie," Marcie says, "will you give Roseanna a slice of pizza, hon? She's getting too thin, don't you think?"

Sean steals a glimpse at my physique but doesn't respond. Am I losing weight? I pull at the waist of my jeans and find an inch of spare room there that I don't remember before. Am I actually thinner? My whole life I've believed that thinness equaled happiness. Could this miserable time in my life be, in fact, happiness? I put the slice Sean has handed me back in the box for the second time.

"I gotta go," I tell Marcie. "I'm training Eleanor at the Seacrest Diner."

"On a *Sunday*?"

Sean's eyes rotate like fruit in a one-armed bandit, from lovesick boyfriend to boss. "It's the only way they'll try her out," he says. "They don't want her if she can't handle a weekend crowd."

Marcie turns from the computer. "So it didn't work at Dr. Sharpe's?"

"The jury's out," I tell her. "The dentists are sort of amused and sort of not with the nightgown thing."

"I think she's on to something," Marcie says, swiveling her desk chair to Sean and wrapping her arms around his undefined waist. "Baby, don't you think we should wear our jammies to work?"

"Absolutely not," Sean says.

I'm happy to leave for the Seacrest Diner, where I can do something simple and successful, like teaching Eleanor to wipe down the booths after the diners have left. Marcie's orphan patrol was becoming too intense. Watching her and Seanie together is never easy. Being home is no better, with Mickey calling each night, wanting to talk about Teddy and the divorce and how I'm feeling. I can't tell if he means how I'm feeling about him or about the divorce or about my being a motherless child. Nor can I tell if he wants me to ask him to stay over, or if he is happy that I don't protest when he puts his coat on after a visit and leaves my apartment. It's an unsettled time in life. Watching Eleanor swab tabletops with long sudsy streaks is soothing.

At the Seacrest, I follow the path of a waitress strong-arming her way through the usual weekend crowd, searching for Eleanor among the tables. I spy my client's broad back bent over a window booth. The table she's scrubbing looks clean enough to perform an appendectomy on. She looks up, pretty in a pink blouse and white apron, and flashes me her famous half-moon smile.

"A fine job you're doing here," I tell her, admiring her work.

"I'm the bomb," she replies, cheeks flushed by her efforts. "That's what Mrs. Bingle tells me."

"Who's Mrs. Bingle?"

Eleanor brushes stray bangs back with a rubber-gloved hand. "My director."

"Director for what?" I ask, a little alarmed. Are there other social agencies working with Eleanor that I'm not aware of?

"The Special Theatre Group!" Eleanor exclaims, as though I'm some kind of idiot. An elderly woman in the booth behind us turns her snowy head.

"That's great, Eleanor. I didn't know you were in a theater group."

"I am." Eleanor claps her rubber hands. "The Special Theatre Group!" The old woman gives us a curious look. Her hair is sprayed into a little lacquered nest, stiff as an Easter basket.

"I sing! I'm in the show! All of us at Cooperative Living who *want to* are in the show." Eleanor's cheeks flush an even brighter pink as she drops her sponge and throws her shoulders back and takes a deep breath. Then she bellows, loud enough to bring the house down:

Give my regards to Broadway!
Remember me to Herald Square!

Tell all the gang at Forty-second Street
That I will soon be there!

She really knows how to hold her endnotes. Heads are turning and now even the cooks are coming out of the kitchen to
hear what's going on.

Whisper of how I'm yearning!
To mingle with the old time throng!
Give my regards to old Broadway
And say that I'll be there e'er long!

"That's lovely, dear," the old woman says, clasping her
hands over her empty plate.

"There's more," Eleanor informs her. She turns back to me
and asks, "You want more?"

"Hell, yes!" yells one of the cooks, a big-bellied man with a
stain on his apron that looks like a target.

"We're trying to eat here," grumbles a man at a table of six,
but someone at the counter hollers, "Beautiful!" and the cook is
waving his spatula and Eleanor's moment goes into two. She
takes her praise with her head held high, a lesson to us all.

While Eleanor's minivan is on its way back to Cooperative
Living, I call over there to find out more about the Special Theatre Group. Turns out Mrs. Bonnie Bingle is a volunteer who
used to perform in the supper theater circuit. They'll be putting
on a show in a month called *Don't Count Me Out*. I jot down the
date in my agenda and head back home, trying hard to generate
excitement for my sexless evening ahead with Mickey. Like

usual, he's coming over to cook. He'll prepare some meat he brings from work, as if he believes that roasting a hunk of flesh will heal everything. When dinner's ended, he'll put on his coat, hug me really nicely, and leave. He apparently feels I still need the time-out, or perhaps he's not anxious to witness another one of my tantrums, after the 7-Eleven.

I call him on my drive home to see if he's at the apartment yet. He is. I tell him I've been at the Seacrest Diner, but I don't tell him about Marcie's and my afternoon.

"I wish I could have heard your client singing," he says.

"Want to stay over tonight?" I ask.

"Maybe."

He won't. I'm sure of it.

Back at the Ronkonkoma Arms, I find him in the kitchen, cooking our dinner with the radio going on the counter. He's still in his work clothes, and his tie dangles dangerously close to the roast beef he is basting in the oven. "I forgot to ask on the phone. Did you go to Marcie's this morning?" he says, closing the oven and smiling at me. His cheeks are flushed with the heat and the radio is blasting some hopeful love song. He is a perfectly good man, preparing me a delicious dinner for no reason other than the fact that he might love me. Why shouldn't he stay over tonight?

"She was researching the Little Flower Home for Unwed Mothers," I answer, putting down my briefcase. I wish he would come over and hug me, but he doesn't. And then I think of something to ask him.

"Do you think I look thinner?"

"You always looked great to me," he says, closing the oven door.

It's at times like this that I sort of miss Teddy. He would tell me if I really looked thinner, just as he never hesitated to say when I looked fatter. And then I have this idea. "Wait right here a minute," I tell Mickey.

I race into the bedroom and close the door and lock it. I pull at the waist of my jeans before unsnapping them. That extra inch of denim is still there. Encouraged, I pull open the top bureau drawer and begin searching for the red underwear. I strip quickly, leaving my clothes in a pile on the floor, then scramble into the thong. This time, the thin strip of lace glides more easily over my hips. Undeniably more easily. I hook up the bra and notice less lava spilling from the volcanoes. There's an overflow, just not so much of it. I can tell. I can really, really tell.

"Oh my God!" I shout to no one. I run to the closet, open the door, and examine the image in the full-length mirror.

I hear myself gasp. The woman in the mirror looks good. Really, really good. Good means not too fat. Good means the thong's elastic is no longer recessed in soft pockets of flesh, but resting against the nearly unearthed bones of my hips.

I press my hands to my breasts and feel their fullness over the top of the bra. My belly doesn't jiggle at all! If I were a lesbian I would love me. I look sexy, I'm a hottie, I look great! Joy like a rapid transfusion flushes through me. I am not what *Cosmo* would call "pin thin," but I am not fat, either. Not at all.

I decide in an instant to show Mickey my new body. I am tired of sleeping alone and I miss the solidness of his body beside me. I even miss his sideburns. He may love me just the way I am, but just the way I am is getting *better*! I fling open the bedroom door, stand at the threshold and throw back my shoulders, like Eleanor before belting out a song. Then I run back to the closet and find my sluttiest shoes. They're open-toed stilettos, and I quickly step into them, glancing again in the mirror. I look even hotter! I throw my shoulders back a second time and stride proudly into the kitchen. The music is really blaring now. Someone is singing, along with the radio. "Shake it like a Polaroid picture!" the voice sings. But wait, that can't be Mickey singing. That's a woman's voice singing. And I am walking right toward her in my bra and thong and slutty shoes.

"Rosie!" Marcie cries, slamming down a wine glass a little too hard.

"Aaagh!" I yell, covering myself like Eve in the garden.

"Yikes," I hear Mickey say.

Sean, sitting at the kitchen table in his Yankees cap, says nothing.

"See, Seanie?" Marcie says. "I told you she looked thinner."

"When the hell did you two show up?" I scream, futilely wrapping a dishtowel over my shoulders.

"Just a minute ago," Marcie says. "I thought you'd want to hear in person that I've found your father."

old cape cod

he does stay over, but I'm not interested in sex, not anymore. I am obsessed. I toss and turn. I click the lamp on and off. I hog the blankets.

"I'm going to find him," I finally tell Mickey, sitting up in bed. "I'll use my sick days. That will give me plenty of time to look for him and to, well, whatever."

Mickey lies on his side, chin propped in one hand, frowning."Rosie, are you sure you want to do this? I mean, you just found out where he is."

"Don't you think I've waited long enough to meet him?"

Mickey rests a hand over mine. "Yes, but we don't know, Rosie, if he's ready to meet *you*."

"You think I should write him first? Send him a party invitation? *'You're invited to a reunion with your bastard daughter! Time: Three o'clock! Date: As soon as possible! Bring a gift! Bring thirty-two of them!'* "

Mickey sighs. "Do you think you might be a little angry with him?"

I sit up taller, the covers fall from my naked body. "I'm not angry at him! I'm just a tad disappointed. He has a daughter he's never met! He has a *kid,* for God's sake! Don't you think he'd have wanted to find his kid?"

A wan strip of moonlight falls across Mickey's forehead. It makes him look worried.

"Do you even know where Cape Cod is? Wouldn't it be better to drive up there with someone?"

"There are maps," I say. "And MapQuest."

"Rosie," he sighs. "Come here." I allow him to hold me in his arms, settling into the smell of sheets and warm skin. "Why don't you let me go with you?"

"No."

I've responded too quickly; I've probably hurt his feelings. I try to change the subject. "That was humiliating tonight," I say, "when Marcie and Sean showed up while I was in my underwear."

Mickey breathes into my scalp, says nothing.

"Wasn't that bad?" I ask.

He lets out a long breath before he speaks. "You know what's bad, Rosie? What's bad is that you won't let me into your life."

"That's ridiculous," I say, even though I know it isn't. "You're here in my bed. I invite you to stay over. We're snuggling close."

"Fine, if we don't get too close." His voice is low and sad. I hate that he's right. I feel I owe him an explanation, no matter how lame.

"It's not that I don't want you too close. It's just that it's so soon after my marriage has crashed and burned. You said it yourself. I *do* need time to straighten out and think right."

"Fair enough," Mickey says. "But we've been together for months, Rosie. And we've had our time-out. Now important things are happening in your life. And you don't want me to be part of them."

"You won't show me your apartment," I shoot back. Cheap shot.

I sit up again and look at him. The sliver of light has risen, like a halo, to the crown of his head. "Is this about me wanting to find my father by myself? Because if it is, Mickey, frankly, I don't see how you can't understand."

Mickey shakes his head slowly. "It's not about that. Not just about that." I watch him leave my bed, his moonlit back rising like a cresting whale. He slides a strong arm into the robe he's left at my house. "I don't want to be your rebound boyfriend, Rosie," he says. "I care too much about you."

"What are you talking about?" I ask, but I know what he's talking about. He's talking about not feeling loved by Rosie Plow. Am I doing to him what Teddy has done to me?

I hold out my arms and he sits on the side of the bed and allows me to embrace him.

He breathes into my neck, then slowly pulls away.

"Are you leaving?"

Mickey nods. "Call me when you get there."

. . .

Five hours and twelve minutes, MapQuest assures me. Two-hundred seventy-nine miles between Ronkonkoma and my father. It's 9:45 in the morning and Cape Cod in early winter looks like the set of an apocalypse movie, everything wind-torn and deserted, as though awaiting the arrival of a flood or perhaps Godzilla. Mini-golf windmills turn their flimsy blades along a cluttered tourist strip in Buzzards Bay. I pass Quik Marts, go-cart tracks, lobster stands, used auto lots, finding little of the romance I was expecting in this vacationland of the Kennedys. It could be the day, which is wintry and overcast and snowless. It could be the fact that I've been on the road since 5:00 A.M., when I hastily threw clothes into a gym bag (much as Teddy did when he left. How much easier it is to recall this now without pain!) and drove away from the Ronkonkoma Arms in the blackness.

Once Mickey left, there was no hope of sleep. *You've sent home the only man who's ever loved you!* my mind screamed, louder than Helen, louder than a Pentecostal minister. I'm not sure that my urgency to leave at five was only about finding Johnny Bellusa. I was desperate to exit that empty bedroom.

Whatever. If I find my father right away, it gives me five days to spend with him. I can return to Long Island in time to accompany my other father to his oncologist's appointment. I can be there for Pulkowski, the way he has always been there for me. And maybe I can even make things better with Mickey.

I glance down at the crinkled paper on the passenger seat, on which Marcie has scribbled her online notes. John Leonard

Bellusa was born in 1954 at Holy Innocents Hospital in Kings Park, New York. Mother: Rose Annunziata. Father: Anthony Bellusa. My paternal grandparents. Had I been named for my paternal grandmother? Would the Bellusas and Teddy's parents have been *paesanos*? Too late to know now. Too late for so many things.

I pull into a Dunkin' Donuts for a third cup of coffee, knowing I'm stalling. Truth is, I'm a little scared. As the miles between my car and Woods Hole shrink to double digits, I wonder how this reunion will actually go. Am I prepared to meet this father I've never known? Isn't this what Mickey was trying to ask? I settle into a window booth, sipping my coffee and watching cars go by.

Whisper of how I'm yearning!
To mingle with the old time throng!

Eleanor sang those words with such conviction. I shuffle to my feet and head for the door. A sleepy waitress smiles at me.

"See ya," she says.

According to the map spit out by my computer at 4:30 this morning, it's a straight shot now to Woods Hole. Then, it's just a question of finding an address. The search engine Marcie used was able to locate a town and state, but no street address for John Bellusa. I suppose I'll just ask around when I get there. How did he end up in Woods Hole in the first place? All questions I should have written down. I'm plowing toward this reunion the way I've plowed through everything my whole life.

Charming shuttered Capes and white clapboard churches whiz by left and right. FALMOUTH, the green sign says. Picturesque gift shops crop up in clusters, some of them closed for winter, others selling taffy and thimbles and those flags people hang from their front porches, announcing the next holiday with bunnies or snowflakes or Labrador retrievers. Woods Hole is next, according to the sign. I pass by an oceanography institute that bears its name.

Soon the road bends left and the wooded residential areas give way to the sea. I look across a bay and see a giant ferry docked in the distance, a huge parking lot with glinting cars on the shore. The road curves right, taking me past a few restaurants, a red brick post office, a village bookstore. Woods Hole residents with turned-up collars hurry from one door to another, their faces chapped by the wind or, who knows, maybe by the sea. Will my father's face be chapped by the sea? How long has he lived here? Doesn't a boy with a name like Johnny Bellusa really belong on Long Island?

A left turn just before a small bridge brings me to the parking lot by the Martha's Vineyard ferry. I find a spot, turn off the engine, and sit. Maybe never have I been this physically close to my real father. Would I recognize him if he got out of the car next to me, if he walked past me in the village?

When the car gets too cold, I lock it and head for the Sea Shanty, a breakfast and lunch nook I spot across the street. A cowbell rings above the flimsy storm door and three diners arched over coffee turn from the counter to look at me. Exposed wooden walls and rough-hewn ceiling beams make the place feel claustrophobic. There are a few small tables wedged by the door up front and I grab one and sit. A tired-looking woman in anklets and sneakers drags herself over and hands me a menu.

"Thanks," I tell her, smiling nervously, as though I am guilty already of some subterfuge in her town. She says nothing in response. I stare blankly at the breakfast selections, the Ahoy Matey, with three eggs, the Anchors Away, with two and the corned beef hash, and the Bow and Stern Reducer, with only cottage cheese and fruit. I order the Anchors Away, though I have possibly never eaten corned beef in my life. I watch the washed-out waitress retreat again, her dyed hair the color of her faded orange capris. I've asked her nothing about Johnny Bellusa. It doesn't seem likely I will. I suddenly wish Mickey were here with me, or maybe, better yet, Helen. Helen would get the job done. And Mickey, I might allow him to bring me home again.

I chew mouthfuls of toast, tasting nothing. I swirl around the hash and break the egg yolks with my fork, so it looks as though I've eaten something. I don't deserve to have Mickey bring me home again. And I've accomplished nothing, hurrying this far away from him. I hand the waitress a ten-dollar bill without saying a word to her, without the name of Johnny Bellusa ever passing my lips. She waves limply as I leave. I have no idea where I'm going next.

I turn my collar up as I hit the street and wander through the village. A hot surge of anger, and then impatience, pulses through me, the only thing warming me this bitter cold noon. Wind pierces the seams of my coat, assaulting my face like any other resident of this seaside town. What is Johnny Bellusa *doing* here? What am *I* doing here? And why haven't I asked anyone for help?

A teenaged boy approaches on the near-deserted sidewalk,

head shaved and chains dangling from his baggy pants. On impulse, I block his path and finally get my mouth to open. "Excuse me," I say. "Do you know anyone named John Bellusa?"

The boy's soft face looks incredibly young, even though he is dressed to be dangerous. He shrugs his shoulders, surprised, and asks, "Wow, is this like a reality show thing?"

"I'm just looking for someone who lives in town named John Bellusa."

The boy looks disappointed. Nothing ever happens to him in Woods Hole. He shrugs and says, "I think my old man used Bellusa to build his porch."

He might as well have said I've won the state lottery.

"Used Bellusa? As in a construction company?"

"Something like that," the boy says, then wafts away, pant legs billowing like sails.

Heart hammering, I duck into the post office ahead and look for a phone book. I find a tattered one chained to a pay phone in the back. I leaf through the white pages first, and then the yellow. I try Remodeling, then Carpentry, and finally, under Construction, my finger hits pay dirt: TIP TOP CONSTRUCTION, CARPENTRY, AND REMODELING: NO JOB TOO BIG. NO JOB TOO SMALL. JOHN BELLUSA, MASTER CARPENTER. My hands shake as I write down the number and address. I let out the breath I've been holding before I put the coins in and dial, exhaling so loudly that a woman at the counter turns to look at me. I smile at her pleasantly.

I'm not surprised when I get voice mail. It's twelve noon on a Monday, a time when all good carpenters are at their work sites. I *am* surprised when the voice begins to speak, a warm, deep male voice, a voice with a trace of Long Island in it, the voice of my father.

You have reached the offices of Tip Top Construction Company, where your next construction, remodeling, or carpentry project is never too big or too small.

The vowels are hard in the man's pronunciation. It's *oaw-fi-sus* and *caw-pun-try*, just like a New Yorker would pronounce the words. The message winds down in the usual way:

Please leave your name and number and we'll call you back shortly.

My hand squeezes the receiver. Should I leave a message? How would I begin? I clunk the phone down hard. The woman at the counter stares again. I race out of the post office with my precious scrap of paper.

I'm shivering now, standing on the street. I should have left a message, but what would I have said? *Hi, this is Roseanna Plow. Remember Alexa Pulkowski? Remember that baby she had? Well guess who's in town?* I can't do it. So what's left? I'm not the type who circles a house, waiting for someone to come out. Perhaps if Marcie were here I'd do it, but what if he has a wife? What if little half-brothers and half-sisters are playing on a swing set in the front yard? Do I really want to show up with my New York license plates, rubbernecking out a rolled-down window? Do I have any other choices? I begin walking toward the car again.

ALL SHELL'S BREAKING LOOSE CRAB HOUSE, a bright red sign

above my head reads. I open the door and walk in. I don't want to go to my car. I need to think. I need to actually *eat* this time. It's after twelve and I've had nothing but coffee and a piece of toast since leaving Long Island. My hands are freezing and I'm still shaking.

"Lunch?" a kind-looking woman says, and when I nod, she leads me to a small booth overlooking the street. "Some coffee to warm up?" she asks, and I nod again, even though this will be my eightieth cup.

The woman studies me, looking concerned. "I'll go 'head and get that, hon," she says, patting my hand like she knows something. I gaze out the window, my clenched fists resting on the red and white tablecloth.

The waitress returns with coffee and a menu, and this time I don't even open it before I ask her my question. "Do you happen to know someone in town named John Bellusa?"

The woman's blue eyes seem to follow the flight of a hummingbird. They wander that quickly, and I know that she has heard of my father. She frowns a second in thought, creating crinkly lines in the happy places of her face. She's at least fifty, but her eyes are lovely and her soft blond hair is pretty as a twenty-year-old's. "Do you mean the carpenter?" she asks.

Yes! Yes, I mean the carpenter! I silently scream. "I believe so," is what I tell her, hoping to sound calm, rational, not too eager. The waitress smiles knowingly.

"You're looking for Johnny, hon?"

Johnny. The hostess calls my father Johnny.

"Well, not exactly."

Yes! Exactly! the internal voice screams.

"Uhh, yes, in a way, I suppose I am." I gulp the hot coffee without adding milk. It burns my lip and tumbles to the sour place in my stomach. The woman is still studying me, almost as if contemplating what she'll tell me next.

"They're building a house over on Albatross," she says. "But you wouldn't know where that is, would you? Being from out of town and all."

I just about jump out of my seat. "Do you know where it is?" I ask. "Could you direct me?"

She pats my hand again, her palm warm against my icy knuckles. "Why don't you eat something first?" she says. "And then we'll get you there."

I force down the lobster roll she has suggested. When my plate is empty, she rewards me with a folded-up placemat, directions to Albatross Lane on the back.

"Thank you," I sniffle, and the stupid automatic tears start producing in my eyes. I almost hug her.

She pats my arm as I'm standing by the door in my coat. "Take care of yourself, hon," she says. In a sweep of blond hair, she turns away and is gone.

The penciled directions on the placemat lead me down rutted roads bordering the sea, beaches on my right, huge houses sitting in sand dunes on my left. When I look across the water, I can almost make out small islands on the horizon. Martha's Vineyard? Nantucket? Maybe nothing? I have no idea. I come to the next turn, onto a road called Heron, which will lead me to the house being built on Albatross. Which will lead me to my father. Who will look at the woman behind the wheel of the car with New York plates and see . . . what?

I pull over a little too roughly, swerving onto a stretch of sandy shoulder. Fatigue flushes through every muscle in my body. I rest my forehead on the steering wheel. Only adrenalin keeps me awake, urges me to lift my head again, to pull down the visor and check my makeup in the mirror. The face looking back seems as unsettled as the winter sea. The auburn hair is windblown and lopsided. The skin is deadly pale. There I am, a thirty-two-year-old woman stopped at the side of a pitted beach road, applying blush for a daddy I've never known.

hey! where ya headin'?

there is a white pickup truck glinting in the winter sun. It's parked beside the skeleton of a house, fully framed on a small knoll beside the sea. The house is a huge lumbering thing, all bones and bay windows. When the dots are connected, it will have dormers and skylights and even a widow's walk. I imagine the wealthy doctor, the affluent lawyer, who will plant his family here, among the townies, for their long sunny weekends.

I sit and wait. My car doors are locked, as though I'm protecting myself from whatever happens next. The wind delivers the scents of wood shavings and the sea through my cracked windows. I hear someone moving around in there. A hammer creates a staccato rhythm. *Bang! Bang! Bang!* I take a deep breath, peer through the two-by-fours, search for the person who is hammering. Nothing. I flip down the visor for one more glance in the mirror. My cheeks glow with artificial pinkness. I've applied blush as though it were a balm, a disguise, a product to transform me, but to transform me into what?

What does a man want to see when a woman walks up to him and says she is his daughter? Does he want to see someone who looks like him? Or would he rather see the curve of the chin, the startling eye color of his forgotten love? I rub my cheekbones with spittled fingers, trying to remove the blush. Would he want his daughter to be beautiful? Or sexy? Something seems wrong with that. Women are sexy for their lovers, not for their fathers. But still, pressing fingers into raw flesh, I admit the truth: I yearn to look beautiful to him. I yearn to look worthy.

I have no control over any of it. A man may walk out of that house, take one look at me, and feel only a sense of disappointment, see only unwelcome evidence of an early mistake in his turned-around life. A cold tickle runs up my arms, just thinking about it. What if I am only a mistake?

The banging suddenly stops. A seagull's single caw is the only sound in the universe. There are a few seconds of silence, then a radio booms to life. A jingle plays loudly.

Hey! Where ya headin'?
We're off to Frankie's Fish Bar!
Where the tastiest fish and clams are . . .

A figure walks toward the space that will one day be the house's front door. It moves closer, until I make out a red shirt, blue jeans, giant dusty work boots. I grip the steering wheel as my mouth goes suddenly dry. *Hey! Where ya headin'?* The man braces his arms in the door frame and glances out toward the sea. Then his eyes move toward me. I look down into my lap. I feel him advancing.

I press down the lock button, but my car's already locked. This seems silly, since I've come all this way in hopes of having this figure approach. I press the button again and the doors unlock. The man moves closer. I lock the doors again but roll my window down. Cold winter air seeps in. I stare straight ahead, sensing, more than seeing, the man draw nearer. After seconds that feel like hours, a plaid flannel arm comes to rest on my window ledge. I hear myself gasp.

"Are you all right, Miss?"

My head snaps forward. What is this? There is a boyish quality to the voice, not the honeyed bass I heard on Johnny Bellusa's answering machine. I force myself to turn toward the window and find a young man staring at me, his brown eyes crinkling with curiosity. He can't be more than twenty-two. He's a very handsome boy. His chin is impossibly cleft, like a movie star's. I sit up very straight. The young man has a day-old beard, mussed-up brown hair, shoulders as broad as Mickey Hamilton's. I can't get my mouth to work.

"Are you lost or something?" The young man scratches an unshaven cheek. I can't believe I let Mickey leave like that—just get up from my bed in the middle of the night and go.

"Is there anything I can help you with?"

Focus, I think. *Speak*. "My name's Roseanna Plow," I announce, as though this is an explanation for everything. But apparently, it is not. The handsome boy waits patiently for more. I am tempted to tell him that I came down the birth canal sideways, something Helen would do at a moment like this.

"I'm Peter DaSilva," the man says helpfully. He extends his hand through my open car window and I shake it. I can't get over the sight of him. He is *Cosmo* Hunk of the Month material. I imagine turning the page on a glossy shot of his bare six-pack.

"I'm looking for Johnny Bellusa," I tell him.

"I work with Johnny. Well, *for* Johnny, actually."

"Is he here?"

"Sorry," he says, "but it's only me today. Johnny's on the Vineyard, lining up electricians for a project over there."

"The Vineyard?" Visions of Johnny Bellusa, squashing grapes, flitter through my addled mind.

"Martha's Vineyard," Peter says. He points his perfectly cleft chin toward the ocean. "You can see it out there on a clearer day than this."

Of course. Martha's Vineyard. Why shouldn't my birth father be on Martha's Vineyard? "It's where all the really big jobs are," Peter explains.

"When will he be back?"

"Not today. But he should be here tomorrow morning."

There is a brick on my chest that I decide is disappointment. But what's another day to wait, after thirty-two years? I take a deep breath. "At what time?" I ask, but Peter DaSilva is smiling at me.

"Soon as it's light out, I imagine. Is there some message I can give him?"

I shake my head no.

"Okay," he says. "I'll just tell him a pretty lady from New York was looking for him."

"Thanks." I reach for my emergency brake so he won't see me blush.

"You're welcome, Roseanna Plow," he says.

• • •

My name is Roseanna Plow, and I'm driving over the Cape Cod Canal better than I came down the birth canal. I'm driving straight and carefully, staying in my lane on the Bourne Bridge, not even looking at the choppy winter waters beneath me. I am driving the afternoon away, in hopes that I can burn up my jitters the way I'm burning up gas. Over the bridge and back again. Heading toward home, then heading toward Woods Hole again. Am I coming or going? Have I ever known?

Back in Woods Hole, the Sand 'n Surf Motel has so many vacancies that the desk clerk offers me a selection of rooms. "One-thirteen has better cable reception, but no water view," the old man in the angora sweater confides, pushing glasses up his nose.

"Whatever you think," I say, tapping my fingers on his desktop.

The rumpled clerk gives me a bemused look, then turns and takes a key from the pegs on the wall, his baldpate glowing in the fluorescent lighting. "Most folks like the water view, but I guess it *is* winter," he muses.

Five minutes later I am sinking into a fatally soft mattress in a room without a view. The sun is dipping low in my window. The day is escaping, the world turning gray. I lie on a gold plaid bedspread, still buttoned into my coat, eyes squeezed shut. Weariness floods me. I breathe in and out the smell of Pine-Sol and the sea, wondering why I didn't leave Peter DaSilva a phone number to give to Johnny Bellusa. It would have been better to speak to my father on my cell first, safely locked in this room with the seashell wallpaper, before deciding what to do next.

Instead I've set up a situation where I face the same unnerving scenario twice: the long-lost daughter arriving at a half-built house, gaping from a car with New York plates.

I'm suddenly missing Mickey. Wouldn't it be nice to drive down Albatross in the morning with him in the passenger seat?

Too late now. I will myself to sleep. With any luck, I won't face life again until morning.

Unless, of course, the phone rings.

The "Roll Out the Barrel" polka is suddenly blaring in my ears. A silly phone ring, selected to tease Helen, then never replaced. I wake up in total darkness, flailing around, finally finding my cell phone on the nightstand.

"Hello?" I manage, sitting up groggily in my buttoned coat.

"Roseanna?"

Happiness floods my sluggish veins. I knew he'd call! I knew he wasn't leaving me for good!

"It's Mickey," he says.

"Ham!" I cry.

He doesn't respond.

"Mickey, I'm so sorry about last night."

He doesn't respond this time, either. I rub my eyes, try to clear my head. "What time is it?"

"It's eight o'clock. Where are you?"

"I'm in my motel room. I was sleeping."

"You were asleep at eight o'clock?"

Something's wrong. I sit up taller, at attention. "I had a rough day," I begin.

"That's why you went to bed without even letting me know you got there?"

"I didn't exactly go to bed," I explain. "I was just resting . . ."

"Well, I only called to tell you about Milton. He was in an accident today."

"What?" I spring from the too-soft bed, landing on wobbly feet.

"He's okay. And it was minor. A shopper backed her Volvo into him and his shopping carts. But he was asking for you, so I thought I should call you."

"He's really all right?"

"Yes."

"Did he see a doctor?"

"Yes."

"And his mother was called?"

"Yes. Some of us make the expected calls."

Oh, the coldness in his voice.

"Mickey. I miss you, I really do. I hope you understand that this is just something I needed to do alone."

"Then go do it," he says. "And we'll talk about us when you're through." The line goes dead. Something inside of me goes dead. I run my fingers through a tangled clump of hair.

Nobody picks up when I call Milton's house. My stomach begins growling. It's impossible to stay in room 113 any longer. I splash some water on my face at the sink in the tiny pink bathroom. With my coat already on, I leave to find some dinner.

The old man behind the desk is gone. When I ask the new clerk for a dinner recommendation, she directs me back to All Shell's Breaking Loose. "It's the only thing open off-season," she tells me. I thank her and head for my car.

The restaurant's blinking sign is visible a block away. I

hurry down the sidewalk through a bitter winter wind. The place is really hopping, almost unrecognizable in the evening. Lights are dimmed and tables are packed. There's a band in the back, playing ZZ Top tunes and other songs I imagine the Hells Angels might enjoy. Semi-drunk people are laughing and shouting over the music. Through a cloud of steamy air, I spot my blond hostess from lunch, cozied up on a barstool with some guy who looks like he should have FISHERMAN stamped on his forehead. His sinewy arms are covered in tattoos, almost as if he's the Popeye of the new millennium. Somehow, in all the noise and activity, a scrappy-looking brunette with a body like a fireplug spots me at the door. She ushers me to a table not far from the bar crowd, mercifully removed from the dance floor. Just as I'm seated, just as the band inexplicably segues into a Tim McGraw country ballad, I catch sight of a red plaid shirt at the bar, three stools down from my lunch waitress. I recognize the shirt immediately. It's not the kind a girl from Long Island sees every day.

I order a cosmopolitan and the brunette waitress has it back for me in a jiffy. I'm sucking down the last of it, waiting for my fish burger, when Peter DaSilva turns from his barstool and flashes me an adorable smile. Then, for the second time in one day, he begins advancing. I take a minute to savor the situation. An absolute stud, ten years younger than Roseanna Plow, is bearing down on her, and his eyes don't say "big-boned" or "old" or "full-figured," either. I want to slap myself for not being more excited.

"Good evening, Roseanna Plow," my new friend says, hovering above me, shouting over guitar chords. When I look up into the smoke and lights and those luscious brown eyes, I notice for the first time that the room is spinning.

"Hello, Mr. DaSilva," I say, and my voice sounds goofy to my own ears.

"Can I buy you a drink?" Peter asks, grinning lasciviously.

The goofy voice says yes, and Peter raises a hand to get the waitress's attention before plopping himself down in the seat beside me. The brunette returns, and her eyes gleam at the sight of us. "Kimberly, honey," Peter says. "A Bud for me and"— he turns his big wet eyes on mine—"what's your pleasure, Roseanna?"

"She's drinking cosmopolitans," Kimberly informs him.

"Then make it another," Peter says.

Kimberly leaves us and I am not so drunk as to misunderstand where my evening is heading. I mentally resolve to take charge of the situation, but am unclear as to where I want to take it. I yearn for my second drink to arrive quickly.

"How ya doing tonight?" Peter asks.

"I've been better," I tell him honestly. "Way, way better."

"Is it Johnny Bellusa?"

I don't answer, the only wise thing to do under the circumstances.

"Are you in love with him?"

"What?"

"Are you in *love* with him? 'Cause it would break my heart if you were in love with him." He winks, then gives me a country western kind of look—half yearning, half lust.

"I don't even know him," I confess. "I came here to meet him."

Peter waits to speak again until after Kimberly has delivered our drinks. His rapt expression makes me feel as though I am that *other* kind of woman, that Inga or Marcie kind.

"Why do you want to meet Johnny?" he finally asks, after taking a long pull off his beer.

I take a healthy slug of my second cosmopolitan. "Do you know him well? Is he nice?"

"He's a nice guy. But . . . isn't Johnny a little too old for you?"

"Too old for what?"

Peter laughs. "Now, now," he says, patting my back. "Whatever's going on, it can't be all that bad."

He's already touching me and for some reason I find it comical. *Pat, pat, pat,* like a papa bear. I sip my drink to stem off a wave of the giggles. I yearn for Helen at my table, to glare at me critically and tell me to *snap out of it!*

"Someone I care about very much was hit by a Volvo today," I say.

"That's too bad," Peter says, looking a little confused.

"Plus," I add, "Johnny Bellusa's my father."

"He's your *what?*" Peter says, pushing his chair back and staring at me.

"He's my father," I repeat. I finish off my drink. "Only I've never met him."

Peter's mouth falls open. "Holy crap," he says. "Does Johnny know you're in town?"

"No."

"Where are you staying?"

"At the Sand 'n Surf."

Peter whistles softly. "What a day Johnny's in for tomorrow."
I look at him. "I almost drove out of town today. After we met."
Peter crosses his arms and considers this.

"Do you think I should go back there in the morning to meet
him?"

His forehead creases in thought. "I guess so," he says. "I
mean, I imagine so." He scratches his chin again. "I don't really
think I know."

"Me neither," I concede. "Is Johnny Bellusa married? Does
he have kids?"

"Not that I know of," Peter says. Something in his expression changes, but then he corrects it quickly.

"What?" I ask.

"Johnny's more the ladies' man type," he says.

My eyes instinctively move to the bar, where my blond waitress from lunch sits with her Popeye. Peter's gaze follows. "Is
that one of his ladies?"

"How'd you guess?" Peter says, laughing a little.

It's not funny! I want to scream, but Kimberly plants a plate
in front of me and the smell of the fried fish turns my stomach.
I stare at it a minute, trying to absorb this new bit of news. My
father is a barfly. My father is a mover.

"Can I get you anything else?" Kimberly asks, looking at me,
and then at Peter, and then at me again.

"Nothing," I say, and she reluctantly walks away.

"Could he possibly walk in here tonight?" I ask Peter, pushing my plate away. "My father, that is?"

Peter shrugs. "Anything's possible. But would that be so
bad?"

Something stiffens in my tired, slack spine. The thought of meeting Johnny Bellusa in this loud, smoky crab house is intolerable. "*Very* bad," I say, rising so quickly, I almost tip the table. "I'm not meeting my father in some bar."

"I understand," Peter says, guiding me gently back to the chair. He waves again at our waitress, pointing at my plate. "Kim?" he says. "Could you wrap this up, honey? I think we're gonna take it out."

Five minutes later, I am driving to the Sand 'n Surf Motel with a carpenter following in a white pickup truck. I am fleeing the possibility of meeting my father in an oyster house, but also leading a man back to my room, a man I hardly know, a pinup boy who knows my father better than I do. Why shouldn't I bring Peter DaSilva back to my room, the drunken part of me asks. How wise is this, the sober part responds. A friend of your father, whom you haven't even met yet. I brush away the sober input like flies from a salad. Why shouldn't I, a healthy unattached thirty-two-year-old woman, bring a *Cosmo* Hunk back to the Sand 'n Surf? Mickey is possibly through with me anyway. Teddy wants a divorce. I'm finally, finally thin. I'm finally, truly . . . alone.

The brightness of approaching headlights brings a surprise round of tears to my tired eyes. I squeeze the steering wheel, suddenly wanting Mickey, just five minutes of him in the seat beside me, so I can think clearly again. The motel lights gleam ahead, and I pull into the lot and cut the engine.

Peter DaSilva pulls his truck into the space beside mine. I hear him slamming his door, as my own heart slams against my rib cage. I feel him walking toward my side of the car while I remain frozen to my seat, hands gripping the wheel like I am saving my own life. In a second more it will be rude to remain in the car, but I can't seem to open my door. I roll down my window instead and gaze up at the most handsome face that has ever looked at me with this kind of lust. Backlit by the Sand 'n Surf's red VACANCY sign, his hair glows pink in the soft light.

"Peter," I say, hearing a new solidness, but also a sadness, in my voice. "All my life I have dreamed of a man like you following me home. And now, do you believe it? I just can't invite you in."

i'd know you anywhere

roll out the barrel" awakens me at 7:30 A.M. It's the first time I've used the alarm feature on my cell phone, and I'm glad it's worked. I stretch in my soft saggy bed, feeling rested, reviewing in my mind the previous day's events: the house on Albatross, Mickey's call, Peter following me home. Something else, too.

Milton.

I punch his number into the cell phone. Milton picks up on the first ring.

"I can't believe the lady didn't see me!" he exclaims, speaking so loud I must hold the phone away from my ear. His child's disbelief, coupled with his deep male voice, fill my motel room with a whiff of wonder. "Oh, Miss Plow, it was bad. It was *bad!* Despicable driving. Despicable driving."

He's repeating himself the way he used to, when I first met him, when he was most anxious about holding a job and suspicious of my motives in getting him one. "I'm glad you weren't hurt."

"Where *are* you?" he demands. "Why weren't you at the SaveWay?"

"I'm on vacation," I tell him gently, feeling I've failed him. "Just like you were last summer, when you took a week off from the SaveWay and went to the beach with your mother."

"Sunken Meadow," he says. "Sunken Meadow Beach. You *can't* take a vacation when there are despicable drivers!"

"I'll see you very soon," I promise him. "Now could you put your mother on?"

"Okay, hon," he says inexplicably, as though I have suddenly been promoted from his vocational counselor to his sweetheart.

"Linda, I'm so sorry," I say, lost for what else I could possibly tell her.

"I don't want him on carts anymore," she says. "I want him bagging."

"You got it," I promise. But I wonder, after we hang up, how much clout I really have with Mickey anymore.

He doesn't answer the phone, the four times I call him. The morning is escaping and I've yet to accomplish my mission on Albatross Lane. There is nothing to do but to get into the shower and go. I let the hot water pour on my hungover body for a long time. Then I blow my hair into long, glossy, shampoo-commercial curtains of auburn. I put on makeup for Daddy, then pull up my jeans. They're still amazingly loose. I turn from the mirror, satisfied. It's showtime.

The sun is high and the morning air crisp as I drive once

more down seaside roads that already feel familiar. Today, when I turn onto Albatross, I see two trucks glinting in the sun—Peter's white pickup and a long red Chevy Suburban with gold lettering on its panel. My father's truck. It has to be. I pull up behind it.

No waiting this time. I slam the car door a bit too loudly and stand, fully exposed, in front of the skeleton house. Then I throw back my shoulders and start walking. I keep my eyes on my shoes as I navigate upturned earth and empty soda cans and bits of wood on the path. I can feel blood pulsing in my forehead and my vision seems to be gone at the sides of my head. I hear my breath going in and out, labored sounding, almost panting. I practice in my mind: *My name is Roseanna Plow and I am your daughter. My name is Roseanna Plow and . . .*

"Can I help you?" a voice asks.

I know this voice, not only from the answering machine, but from somewhere deep inside my glued-together molecules. I raise my eyes and there he is, looming. Is he tall, or is it the height of the stairless foyer that makes him appear to take up so much space, to take up so much sky, to take my breath away? How could someone absent so long occupy so much space?

I try to see his face through a mist of tears freshly risen in my eyes. It is a kind face with regular features, a strong even jaw line and expressive lips. It is my face. No one could miss it. The resemblance leaves me speechless.

I take a step back. He reaches out and I accept his proffered hand and allow him to pull me up, over the door's high threshold, into the house with no walls. "I'm John Bellusa," he says, studying me with my own eyes. "You must be Roseanna."

His face crinkles into a handsome weathered smile. He is truly tall, the founder of my big bones, even when we stand at the same level. He is big-boned, but also the slightest bit bent. There is a small stoop at the back of his neck, as though he has carried too many two-by-fours for too many years. As though he has carried too much.

"So Peter told you I'd be coming," I say. I take his hand in mine and squeeze it. Now there are tears in Johnny Bellusa's eyes, too. He pulls me toward him and hugs me.

I have a thousand questions for this man who smells like sawdust and Dial soap, but in his embrace, I find answers as well. I feel I'm in the arms of a kind man, an imperfect but good man, a man who recognizes his own young. My tears wet his corduroy shirt and I see how my carefully applied makeup is all for nothing. When we finally pull apart—Johnny looking a bit sheepish, his shirt stained with mascara—I ask him the question that has been on my mind since the day Helen told me she'd had a daughter name Alexa.

"Where is she?"

"I don't know," he says.

I lean against the spine of a wall, gasping a little.

"When did you see her last?"

"The day before she ran away."

I look up at him. "So you knew me? When I was a baby?"

Johnny Bellusa's face crinkles into a smile again, this one sadder. "I saw you once. When Alexa brought you home."

My back slides down the two-by-four that supports me, until I am sitting in sawdust on an unfinished floor. *Alexa.* He uses the name so naturally. He makes her more than a story—a person who truly exists. A sea wind whistles around us but I can't feel any cold.

"I still do know you," he says. "I'd know you anywhere."

"How?"

He shrugs. "You're my daughter."

We both feel awkward, once his words hit the air. Then I feel something harden in my heart, something stubborn and hurt. Does a man get to call you his daughter if he was never there? He is a sperm donor. He's my biological father. But that doesn't make me his daughter.

"Where were you when the training wheels came off my bike?" I ask him.

He looks down at his steel-toed boots, but the pain in his face can't be hidden.

"Why weren't you at my graduation?"

"I thought about your graduation," he says quietly.

"Why didn't you ever call, or write? Why weren't you ever there?"

Johnny Bellusa bows his slightly stooped head in quiet grief. "Your grandmother didn't want me there," he says in a sad voice. "I wasn't calling the shots. I was a kid who had done a terrible thing. I had gotten the girl I loved pregnant. And then she ran away."

"Did she love you?"

He runs a rough hand over his eyes, leaving it there a second. "She did."

"Then why didn't she ever find you again?"

Johnny Bellusa turns his pained face away. "I was hoping maybe you could answer that."

We're quiet a moment. Then Johnny says, "Did you know your grandparents moved after she left? All the neighbors knew there was a baby in the house that wasn't Mrs. Pulkowski's. So they left Islip and moved somewhere."

To Commack, I think. To the house with the beige walls, my childhood home. They did it for me, so Helen could go on suspending fruit in Jell-O molds without the whiff of scandal tainting our food. I'm deciding whether to tell Johnny Bellusa this (Does he deserve to know it? Couldn't he have found out for himself?) when the staccato rhythm of a hammer begins, and I remember we're not alone.

"Where is Peter?" I ask him.

"He's sheet-rocking the basement."

"A funny place to put up walls first."

"He wanted to give us some privacy."

The handsome face of my father looks pale. I study the even features, the chapped neck, the slight stoop. "Peter told me you were a ladies' man."

"Hah!" my father laughs. "I've just never married is all. It's lonely sometimes, so I take women out." He casts me a quick anxious look. "That's all right, isn't it?"

"I'm not your mother," I tell him curtly. "You can do what you like."

"You're mad at me," he says. "I don't blame you. Allie and I made an awful mess of things."

Now he looks truly miserable. It's not right that such a big man should look so vulnerable. I find myself feeling bad for him, and I think, perhaps, we're all victims when it comes to love. We're all perpetrators, too. Throw in a little sex, and marriages crash and burn, over too much, or too little of it. People hurt each other, use each other, infect and inseminate each other because of it. Lovers suffer. Babies are born by mistake. Cribs fill up at places like the Little Flower Home for Unwed Mothers.

"Who doesn't make a mess of their lives?" I ask him. "You should only know the half of mine."

Johnny Bellusa seems unhappy to hear me say this. He scrutinizes my crumpled form where I sit on the floor. "I'll bet you have a fine life," he says. "I know your mother would be proud of you if she met you today."

"You don't know anything," I tell him, wiping my eyes with the back of my hand.

"I know what I see," he says.

I realize his words are meant to comfort me, but you don't get to disappear from a child's life for three decades, then sweet-talk your way back in. It doesn't seem right, even if the words are sincere. I pull myself to my feet and brush off the seat of my jeans. Maybe we've had enough for one visit.

"How are Mr. and Mrs. Pulkowski?" he asks.

"Oh, tired," I respond. "I don't think they figured on raising another kid after your girlfriend."

"I bet they didn't. But they probably did a good job. Better than I would have done."

"You could have married my mother," I tell him, with all the tenderness of an executioner.

"Yes, I suppose that's true." His voice sounds no louder than a sigh now. "But that didn't happen, did it?" He rubs his eyes again. "I guess we're not having a very good reunion, are we?"

"As good as can be expected," I say, stepping down from the threshold and out of the house. "Maybe we should stop the visit now, and just sit a while with our thoughts."

"We could have dinner tonight," Johnny Bellusa suggests. "I'd like to take my girl to dinner."

"You like to take all the girls to dinner, according to Peter."

He scratches his cheek and smiles. "You've got a lot of your mother's spirit, Roseanna. By the way, what's with the *Plow*? Are you married?"

"No. Yes. Sort of. But Plow's not my married name."

Johnny looks puzzled. "You go back now and decide about dinner. You can let me know and either way, I won't be offended." I watch him bend to pick up a hammer. "But there's one thing I want you to know," he says, "in case you decide not to see me tonight." The hammer hangs limply in his left hand as all of Johnny Bellusa's attention focuses on me. "I was really happy your mother didn't let them take you away. She looked her parents and a fleet of nuns in the eye and said, 'No, you can't put my baby up for adoption.' Do you know what kind of guts that took, in 1975, in a Polish Catholic household?"

I nod. I know exactly what kind of guts it took. His girlfriend wasn't the only person raised by Helen Pulkowski.

gone

Sleep happens on Cape Cod, a lot more than *shit* does, despite the claims of innumerable T-shirts displayed in the gift shop windows. When Mickey still does not pick up his phone after what is possibly my thousandth try, sleep beckons me. Lie down, it says. The sun may be bright, you might need lunch, but you're tired. So sleep. Sleep away fathers and boyfriends. Sleep away the sound of Mickey's phone ringing, unanswered. Sleep away your grandparents packing their possessions in boxes and whisking you away from Islip to another town where no one knows you. Okay, I say. All right, I will. I close my eyes and the world inside my eyelids turns burnt orange, but this does not deter me from falling off, floating away, leaving my life and sinking into a too-soft bed in room 113 at the Sand 'n Surf.

My cell phone awakens me to early winter darkness. It can't be more than five o'clock, but the sun has long ago tidied up its desk and exited. There is a chill in the air that sends bumps up my arm as I scramble for the screeching little phone. Then I think it might be Mickey. Hope sits me upright on the soft bed.

"Hello?"

"Rosie?"

"Mickey!" I cry, trying to pack everything—love, remorse, the happiness I'm feeling—into the one word.

"Rosie?" he says again.

He's called me Rosie! Twice!

"I'm so glad it's you! I've been trying to call you all day!" *Breathe, Rosie, breathe.* "I wanted to say how sorry I am for not bringing you on this trip. And I want to tell you about meeting my father. But most of all, I want to tell you how much I miss you, and how much you mean to me, and that I . . ."

". . . Rosie."

". . . love you. What? Something's wrong."

"Rosie, it's bad."

"What's bad?" Even as I ask, I know the next thing Mickey says will be hard.

"Sit down," he says.

"Mickey, what?"

"I'm sorry, Rosie. Your mother."

"What about my mother?"

There is a red line woven through the plaid on the bed-spread. I follow it with my eyes, knowing that this will be the last thing I see in my life as I now know it.

"Helen . . . she . . . died this morning."

Very calmly, I click on the bed stand light. The red in the bedspread is even brighter than I'd imagined. "She what?"

"She had a heart attack this morning. Rosie, I am so sorry."

I listen as he exhales into the phone. Then I rise from the bed with the phone beneath my chin and begin smoothing wrinkles from the spread. I tuck the top edge carefully over the pillows, patting, smoothing, everything very smooth, very careful.

"Rosie? Are you still there?"

The trick is to get a nice sharp crease beneath the pillows. Helen has always said this. I jab my hand in there, then jab it again, then again, harder.

"Rosie? Rosie?"

Jab. Jab. Jab. "I'm making the bed," I tell him. My voice sounds small and strangled.

"Why don't you sit down, sweetheart. Why don't you let me come and get you?"

Helen would love this bedspread. The nice gold earthy tones would go perfect with beige. "Perfect," I say out loud. "Perfect," I hear myself say again. I pull out a hard desk chair and lower myself into it.

"Do you want me to tell you what happened?" Mickey asks gently.

I take a deep breath. "I met Johnny Bellusa today," I say.

"Do you want me to tell you?"

"Yes."

"Are you sitting?"

"Yes."

"Good." Another breath. "Pulkowski called around seven this morning. He asked me to come over to the house. He said that Helen had gone to the kitchen. She was making coffee and she . . . fell. I asked him if he'd dialed 911, but he said he knew. He said he knew from the war when someone was gone."

"She was gone?"

"Yes."

"Gone." The strangled voice again. I stand and smooth the spread over the pillows again. Impossible, I think. She cannot be gone. Helen is everywhere—in my thoughts, in my business, in the closets and drawers of my apartment, in the house on Albatross with no walls. She could never be gone, anymore than air or grass or cars could be gone. She was just making coffee! She was getting ready to pour a cup and bring it out to her TV tray in front of her television, where she would watch her morning shows in her beige living room. *Gone* isn't a word that could ever describe Helen. Gone is where I am, in this Cape Cod motel room, sitting on a hard chair.

I call Johnny Bellusa and leave a message that I can't make dinner. I find myself telling him why, almost as if I want him to suffer. I throw my things into my bag and leave the Sand 'n Surf Motel. Scrubby pines rush by on Route 28, their droopy branches waving as I pass. *Get out of town!* they moan, shaking their piney fists. *She's dead!* they wail, though I don't believe them. What do scrub pines know? Who knows Helen better than I do?

No one knows her better than I. Not even Alexa. Does it matter whose birth canal I really came down? I stayed. I endured. I loved when it was hard. I am Helen's daughter, more so than my mother was. *I* get to say who's gone and who's not. She can't be gone when I didn't get to say good-bye to her. When Pulkowski still needs her. When the last time I saw her, she was wrapping Saran Wrap around the leftover Thanksgiving turkey and putting it away.

On the phone Mickey had stuck to his story, no matter what I said to dissuade him. She was in the kitchen. On the floor. Pulkowski knew. McClain's Funeral Home. Come. Come. Do you want me to get you?

Of course not, I told him. I have a car. I can drive. Now I am racing back to my childhood home, reversing my MapQuest directions, so I can be with Pulkowski, sit with him, make our plans to bury Helen. Mickey says he'll be there when I arrive, and the thought of being in his arms tonight fills me with a guilty pleasure that slices through my pain.

Johnny Bellusa will have to wait. As for Alexa, his runaway girlfriend, she doesn't even know our mother is dead.

so long, miss rheingold

around midnight i turn the key in Helen's front door and tiptoe into the living room. There is Pulkowski in his La-Z-Boy, gently staring into space. I sit quietly across from him on the nubby old couch that Helen never saw fit to replace.

"Daddy?" I whisper. He stirs, as if awakened from a trance.

"Oh, honey," he says, then leans forward and hugs me hard.

"I'm home," I whisper.

"It's so late," he says. "Your mother would have been worried."

Mickey walks in bearing a cup of tea while I'm weeping into the scent of Tide on my daddy's shirt. He sets it down on Helen's TV tray, next to Pulkowski. His hair is mussed and his eyes look tired but his face is the most wonderful sight I have seen for days. He pulls me in his arms and holds me close.

"Rosie," he breathes into my scalp. "You're here." He holds me like a man who might love me, but who knows? He is a kind man. This could only be Helen's death.

We all sleep poorly on pieces of living room furniture. Pulkowski stays in his La-Z-Boy, tilting it back like a dentist chair. He dozes open-mouthed, as if awaiting the dentist himself, or perhaps a last kiss from Helen. When his breathing steadies, I curl up into Mickey's chest on the scratchy sofa and sleep there.

We eat breakfast in a state of numbness the next morning. Mickey flips French toast as Pulkowski and I sit holding hands at the table. Helen seems to be among us, wafting in the steam of our coffee, fiddling with the television's volume. We feel her, but we can't see her. It silences all of us.

After breakfast, Mickey and I set out for McClain's Funeral Home with the bag of clothes we've helped Pulkowski put together. We sit in a small office papered in burgundy flock, separated from the funeral director by a heavy dark wooden desk. The dress Pulkowski has chosen to bury Helen in raises an eyebrow of even old Frank McClain. He probably hasn't seen a beaded white shirtdress with a full skirt since 1959. But Helen loved her bowling league formal dance dress and so does Pulkowski. I hand it to the funeral director along with Helen's single strand of pearls. In the paper bag on my lap are her Robin Red lipstick and nail polish and her Evening in Paris eau de parfum.

"You want us to prepare Mrs. Pulkowski using these items?" he asks tactfully. *Damn straight*, I'm thinking. *You're laying out a woman who could have been Miss Rheingold.*

"Yes, please," Mickey replies, then he takes my elbow and escorts me out of the funeral home.

I am weeping soundlessly as we drive home. Mickey pats my

hand, but this only causes my crying to become louder and sloppier. I pound the dashboard of his truck with my fist, and all the anger and sadness held in for the sake of Pulkowski comes pouring out in buckets. "Damn it to hell!" I cry. "This is *so* Helen. Did she do this because I went to find Johnny Bellusa?"

"Don't be silly," Mickey says, then he pulls into the parking lot of SaveWay's competition, the King Kullen. He glides so smoothly off the road that it almost seems he was expecting my breakdown. We pull into a space at the end of a row and Mickey hands me a white handkerchief, something even a man twice his age wouldn't ordinarily carry anymore. I blow my nose, but can't stop crying.

"Did I hurt her feelings?" I ask, blowing my nose a second time. "Did she think I didn't need her anymore, just because I went looking for my parents?"

Mickey takes my chin in his hand and turns my face to look at him. "Rosie," he says. "You didn't *kill* her. She just died."

"You don't know anything!" I cry, pulling away from him. "You didn't know Helen the way I did! She would do *anything* to get your attention . . ."

". . . like drive twenty miles out of her way to buy a pork roast, just so she could get her Rosie a boyfriend? I think I knew Helen."

"She didn't *torment* you the way she tormented me."

"She loved you, Rosie."

It's the way he says this that makes me stop. There is an assuredness in his voice, the kind that comes from actually knowing something.

"And you loved her," he concludes.

I am left speechless. Could this be the simple truth of all of it? Can two people fight, sulk, try to please each other, withhold important information, hurt each other, run away, overeat, undereat, and still, at the bottom of it, do it all because they love one another?

It appears so.

How stupid, how pointless, the dance suddenly seems.

"She died of a heart attack. Her smoking probably caused it. Not you."

My breath comes more slowly now. I can feel how swollen my eyes have become. "Did she know I went to find my father?"

He looks down at his lap before he answers. "I told her. She called the store looking for you while you were gone. So I told her the truth."

"You don't really *get* my family, do you?" I say. "Nobody tells anyone the truth."

"She kept the truth from you because she loved you. It may have been a mistake, but her intentions were good."

"We can put that on her tombstone," I tell him. "SHE LIED TO EVERYONE BUT HER INTENTIONS WERE GOOD."

I find I am crying again. This time it feels like a great release after what is perhaps a practical joke. Life *is* perhaps a practical joke. My sobbing comes louder.

"Rosie, come here," Mickey says. He takes me in his arms and I breathe in deep the smell of his skin, the warmth of his chest. We stay like this for a long time, or maybe it just seems long. He just holds me and rocks. Holds me and rocks.

It must be that I fall asleep this way. We're still sitting in his

truck in the King Kullen parking lot when I awaken. But somehow, my eyes open to what feels like a freshly made world. It's a
world that no longer holds Helen, no longer requires that Ham
hold the best pork roast with the bone in it. Mickey and I are
sitting in a truck, but a few miles down the road an undertaker
is dressing Helen in her bowling dress. A town away, Pulkowski
is weeping in his easy chair. Two states away, a man named
Johnny Bellusa is pounding nails, thinking about the daughter
he's just met.

And I am sitting beside a man named Ham. I notice this,
too, and how I feel safe in the cab of his truck, glancing at his
stupid sideburns. Bright sun shines on chrome shopping carts
and a brilliant blue sky spreads like an umbrella above us. I
turn and look at Mickey, and even though the time is wrong and
Mr. McClain may be applying lipstick to my grandmother's
dead lips, I have to tell him what I have discovered.

"Mickey," I say, "I figured out something major while I was
on my little road trip."

Mickey looks tired. His day-old beard glints like gold around
his jaw. "What's that, Rosie?" he asks, sounding like Mr. Rogers,
sounding like he is handling the overtired, upset child sitting
beside him in his truck.

"Mickey." I sit up straight and look at him. "It turns out
we're not dating."

A look of alarm crosses his features.

"No, wait. I've said this wrong." I rub my eyes with my fists
and my hands return covered in mascara. "I mean," I explain,
"that I'm not sleeping with you just because it feels good to
sleep with a nice guy after your husband turns out to be a putz."

"A putz?"

"Helen's term. But this isn't about Teddy. It's about you. And us." I squeeze his hand. Mickey looks confused. He studies me, no doubt seeing a demented raccoon, with all that mascara smudged around my eyes. But it doesn't matter. I'm his raccoon, if he'll have me. Nothing deters me now from telling him what I know.

"When I was driving up to see Johnny Bellusa, I missed you so much my stomach ached. I drove away from ten Dunkin' Donuts without purchasing a single doughnut. Not a Munchkin! That's when I discovered I wasn't just seeing someone. You could get down a cruller if you were just sleeping with some guy and he didn't matter to you. But you matter to me." I stare straight at him. "You rendered me doughnut-less." I squeeze his hand again. "That's what you've done to me, Mickey Hamilton. It turns out, somewhere between the Bourne Bridge and Falmouth, I discovered I was in love with a butcher."

I kiss his mouth hard. "We're in a relationship, Mickey!" I say, coming up for air. "Isn't that great?"

Mickey doesn't respond. He certainly doesn't look smitten. He looks more like a guy flummoxed with his tax forms.

"We're in a relationship, Mickey!" I repeat again.

Again I wait for him to react, pray that he'll pull me into his arms and shout *Eureka!* or *Hot damn!* or *It's about time, you crazy bitch!* But no, none of this happens. He seems to be thinking about something, hashing something over in his mind.

"Rosie," he finally says, exhaling his decision through his mouth and nose, "I was going to wait to tell you something, but I want you to know right now."

I grip the dashboard, suddenly light-headed. *I was going to wait to tell you something?* When has a man ever said these words without breaking your heart in the next sentence?

"Please," I beg him, my fingernails pinching deep dimples into the padded dash. "Don't tell me. Tell me another day. I've had enough for one day, going to the funeral home and all."

Mickey appears not to be listening. He's pulling out of our spot at the King Kullen. "Put your seat belt back on," he says. "I'm taking you somewhere."

save me

I'm shocked when Mickey flicks his blinker and swings the truck onto the expressway ramp. "What are you doing?" I ask. "Don't we have to get back to Pulkowski?"

Mickey reaches across me and pops open his glove compartment, retrieving a cell phone I have never seen before. It's tiny, not much bigger than a box of Tic Tacs. I watch him speed dial while expertly merging into the westbound lane. He holds the phone against his strong jaw, nestling it into a sideburn. "Are you in today?" he asks someone. "Good. Stay there for another hour, will you?"

Are you in today? Who is in? Mickey's doing seventy-five. I run a hand through my tangled hair, daring not to ask, but trying to think.

The doctor is in.

The ex-wife is in.

The chairman is in.

"Who is in?" I blurt out, but Mickey only shakes his head.

"Just be patient," he tells me. "And give me Marcie's number."

I do. He calls her cell and asks if she would mind going over to Pulkowski's. Then a smile like a sunrise breaks across his face. "She's already over there," he says to me. "Thanks," he tells Marcie, "we'll be home in a couple of hours."

Home. Does Mickey now consider Pulkowski's house his home? Did Helen adopt him while I was out of town? It doesn't matter. A warm feeling flushes up my neck at the sound of his words.

"Are you finally taking me to your apartment?" I ask.

"No."

I rub my eyes, fighting back confusion and fatigue. "Are you going to tell me where we're going?"

"Did you know I have an autistic cousin?" Mickey asks, ignoring my question. Outside the window, mileposts and exit ramps whiz by us. "My family has this summer house in Connecticut, not far from Stockbridge, in Massachusetts. It's on a lake in the Berkshires. We kids used to play there in the summer while the grown-ups drank martinis on the porch."

Mickey whips his truck onto the exit for the Clearview, and now we're heading for a bridge while he's heading down Memory Lane.

"Was Dukey the dog at the house?" I ask.

He smiles. "His real name was Duke of Edinburgh the Third and he was the son of two AKC champions."

"You named your boxer after Prince Charles?"

"Prince Charles is a *prince*, and the Duke of Edinburgh is a *duke*," he explains. "Anyway," he continues, pulling his truck

into the E-ZPass lane of the Throgs Neck Bridge. "My cousin
Amelia would come each summer. She was a beautiful little
redhead, younger than your butcher friend here."

The Long Island Sound is glistening beneath us as we cross
the bridge. The crisp winter sun gives everything a sharpness
that hurts my eyes. I try to keep my mind on Mickey's story, but
suddenly I realize I'm on the same bridge I crossed last night,
in my hasty exodus from Cape Cod to be with Pulkowski.

"Mickey," I say again, "Where are we going?"

"Patience, babe," he says, patting my knee.

Babe? Does this mean he's accepted my professions of love
in the King Kullen parking lot? Does it mean our time-out is
over? Or are we merely surpassing the speed of time on 95
North?

"You probably know all about these *rituals* autistic kids
have," Mickey says, going on with his totally-unrelated-to-
anything story from his childhood. "The patting and the repeating and stuff. Sometimes I see it with Milton. Have you ever
watched him straighten up the Laughing Cow cheese in the
dairy case? He fiddles with it each time he passes."

"How's Milton doing?" I ask, remembering his accident
and his agitated conversation on the phone. Was that only two
days ago?

"He's fine," Mickey says. "He wanted to come back to work
today, but I told him to take a few more days off."

This is just like Mickey. So thoughtful. So caring.

"So anyway," Mickey says, "I just loved this little cousin of
mine. She was beautiful, and she had these little dimples when

she smiled." Mickey frowns into the windshield. "It wasn't a touchy-feely time for autistic kids, though. Her family was down with this 'tough love' treatment plan, always slapping Amelia's hands and grabbing her face to get her attention."

Mickey's own face seems to harden a bit at the memory. "I used to try and sneak her out of the house, and onto the porch, or the lawn, where I could protect her a little and, you know, just *watch* her." He exhales sharply as we switch lanes. "If you just sat with her awhile in her little world, she would pat you on your head and smile, sort of even *at* you."

The tires hum and the car is silent and I'm amazed to see tears in Mickey's eyes. How could a guy who would grow up to cleave carcasses in two have been so upset by a slap on the wrist? Mickey leans toward me now and kisses my cheek, almost careening the truck into a small blue Mini Cooper. "Careful!" I cry. He straightens the wheel but kisses me again.

"I've always loved the way you work with Milton and your other clients," he says. "I've always loved that about you."

I am quiet for a moment. Then I say, "Well, how come you didn't go into special education or social work then? Instead of, um, butchery."

Mickey laughs. "Hang on," he says. "You'll understand everything."

We take an exit off the Merritt Parkway. I cannot believe he has driven me all the way to Danbury, Connecticut, ninety miles away, to bring me to a SaveWay supermarket. It's not even as nice as the one on Long Island. It's an older store, about half the size of the one Ham works in. The fancy neon sign glitters like too-large jewelry on an ancient dowager. The whole facade looks as though it has had a facelift that didn't quite work. "This is the original store," Mickey comments, shifting the truck into Park in a front row spot in the lot. "Come on. Let's go."

There comes a time in even the most patient person's life when she runs out of patience, when enough's enough. Gazing at the original SaveWay, I realize this time has come. I am glad that Mickey thinks I am nice with my clients, but I'm suddenly flushed with a wave of fatigue. Riding in its wake is the guilt I'm feeling for being so far away from Pulkowski. My butt remains firmly ensconced in the passenger seat of Ham's truck. I'm not going anywhere.

My grandmother died yesterday. I turn to Mickey, who has already got the car door open for me, and remind him of this fact. "Please," I say, hearing the weariness in my own voice. "Take me home now." I touch a sideburn gently. "We can work our stuff out later. After we bury Helen."

Mickey's eyes are sparkling with something I don't understand and my words don't seem to affect the glitter level at all. "Trust me, Rosie," he says. "Helen would *love* this. She would *want* you to be just where you are at right this minute."

I let out a long breath. "I don't think so."

"Rosie, please. Just give me ten minutes, no more, and I promise I'll bring you right home." He hugs me quickly, then releases me. "Please?"

"All right."

He rubs his thumb beneath my eyes and smiles. "You're so beautiful," he says. "Let's go."

I trundle behind him through the parking lot, hugging myself to stay warm. As we approach the front doors, Mickey takes my hand and pulls me toward the back of the building.

"Aren't we going in?" I ask.

"Not the store," he says, tugging on my hand like a child. He leads me around the side of the supermarket. And then I see it.

Behind the store a three-story office building with mirrored windows rises like a mirage at the far end of the parking lot. "There," Mickey says, and I follow him like Dorothy through the poppy fields. Mickey opens the glass doors and leads me inside. From the pocket of his jacket he extracts a card and swipes it like a Visa at another door. This one is polished wood and chrome. A woman Helen's age sits at a desk beside it, smiling at us. "How are you, Michael?" she asks.

"Fine, Jean," he says, and then he puts a hand on my back and guides me through the door. He leads me down a short carpeted corridor, past a potted plant, and knocks on a door with a brass plaque. He swings it open, then grabs my hand to follow him. "Are you there?" he calls. "Pop?"

At the far end of a large office I glimpse the back of a man's head. A thick head of white hair turns, revealing the handsome face of . . .

Ham.

The face is older and the crinkly lines around the mouth deeper when the man smiles, but there is no mistaking that this is Mickey Hamilton's father.

"Michael," the man says, rising from his chair. At six-foot-something, he gives "big-boned" a whole new meaning. There is something aristocratic in the man's bearing, the way his shoulders are thrown back the slightest bit as he walks toward us, the way his cuff links wink on the cuffs of his starched white shirt. But his hands are rough, like Mickey's, hands that weren't born to the cuff links. Butcher's hands.

"So this is the famous Rosie Plow," he says, his voice sonorous and warm. And then I am in his embrace, which is a lot like Mickey's embrace. I relax into it, perhaps because I'm exhausted, or perhaps because this moment is no stranger than any others in this strange day.

"I am so sorry about your grandmother," he breathes into my ear, and I believe him. "Michael told me how much you loved her."

Tears soak the front of his nice clean shirt. I know I should say something, but my bewilderment has rendered me speechless. It's liberating, in a way, to be speechless. All you have to do is stare at the two men who are now smiling at you.

"Sit down, please," Mickey's father says, and a chair appears behind me, and Mickey is lowering me into it. "I know you can't stay long," Ham Senior says, sitting across from me on his side of a long mahogany desk. "But I am so pleased to meet the woman who has captured Michael's heart."

"Michael?" I manage to mutter, but the man in the white shirt is studying me, appraising me with sharp, if kind, eyes. His desk is beautiful. Heavy carved wood, beautiful grain, buffed to a high shine. There are plaques and portraits all along the cream colored walls, and it doesn't take me long to find the portrait of Mickey in a serious dark suit, right beside the one of his father.

My eyes must grow wide. "Are you all right?" Mickey asks, squeezing my shoulder. I stare again at the desk. There's a Waterford crystal paperweight resting on top, centered between two pen sets. A gold embedded coin stamped with the SaveWay logo floats in the glass. I squint at the etching: 75 YEARS. I look up at Mickey.

"Yup," he says, resting his hands on my shoulders. And then I see how my butcher friend is really Mr. SaveWay Junior.

"Rosie," he says, "I didn't bring you here to tell you about the stores. I just *had* to bring you after, well, our little conference at the King Kullen . . ."

"The King Kullen?" Ham Senior sounds alarmed.

"Don't worry, Pops. It's not treason." His eyes, his beautiful eyes, go back to me. "I've been wanting to bring you here for months, Rosie, to meet my father. Every week we're in our meetings and all I can talk about is you."

"It's true," Ham Senior confirms. "He's been useless as a business partner. But his accounts are straight about *you*. I ask him for figures and he tells me you're beautiful. I ask him for a report and he tells me you're funny."

"But . . . ," I try.

"And now I see he's right, of course." Mickey father rises from his chair. "But you two have to go now." He clasps my hand in his big mitt. "Go. Take this Ham with you. I am truly sorry about your grandmother."

·   ·   ·

"Want to see my place in the city?" Mickey asks, as we approach signs for the Throgs Neck Bridge. "I could take the tunnel and show you real quick. It's in the Village, and there's actually street parking in my neighborhood now and then."

The heat is blasting in the truck, but I'm still shivering. Apparently I am in shock. Mickey has wrapped his ski jacket around my shoulders, over my own coat. It's the first time I've noticed the lift tickets dangling from the zipper. Mount Snow. Bretton Woods. All of them from last year. Who is this guy?

"Rosie?" he says. "I know the timing was bad on this, but still, it felt right."

I say nothing. My gloved hand is wrapped around the smooth glass of the SaveWay paperweight. Mickey's father insisted I take it, almost as if it were Mickey's dowry. *Keep it,* he'd said, handing it to me. *I know it'll be in good hands.*

"Think of how Helen would have loved this," Mickey says.

"Did she know you were the SaveWay Boy?"

Mickey laughs, swinging into the lane for the bridge. "I'll take you to my apartment some other time," he says. "Let's get you home to Pulkowski. And no, Mrs. P. didn't know. Although, you've got to admire her instincts. She always told you I was a prince."

"She told me you were a butcher, like Barney Kroener."

"Barney Kroener?'

"The neighbor who couldn't get a hard-on."

Mickey hoots in laughter, making his sideburns rise. "No, that was your uncle."

"He was *like* an uncle."

Now we're both laughing. I slip the ski jacket from my shoulders. I'm beginning to warm up. "So why didn't you ever tell me about any of this?"

Mickey's face changes. He stares straight ahead, squeezing the steering wheel. "Well," he begins, a little warily. "Remember that day in my office when we discussed Hams and Fishers and Plows?"

I stare down at my lap, at my newly streamlined knees. That was not my proudest moment, that afternoon in Ham's office. I was mourning the loss of a man with a law degree while disparaging a very nice guy's profession—or, at least, what I *thought* was his profession. It's painful to think about how I must have sounded. For a counselor working with the developmentally challenged, Roseanna Plow showed no evidence of "understanding diversity" that day. "You thought I was a snob," I tell Mickey, stroking his father's paperweight miserably.

"Well," Mickey says. "I *thought* I knew you better than that, but just in case I was wrong . . . you know, blinded by your beauty or something, I figured I'd hold my cards close to my sleeve."

"Fair enough," I concede. "But is that an insult, that 'blinded by your beauty' line?"

Mickey turns his face to me, eyes wet and full of love. No, it was not an insult. I take his free hand in mine and press it to my cheek. This is my way of telling him I love him. "I'm sorry," I say, "that I was an ass."

"You're *my* ass," he replies, which, of course, makes us both laugh.

"So why are you managing a SaveWay in Ronkonkoma," I ask, "instead of living in a villa in Venice?"

"Is that what you think we SaveWay Boys do?"

"Well . . ."

"I have worked in every store my family owns. Three states. Seventeen stores. Every department." The truck slows as we creep through the tollgate for the bridge. It creates a temporary stillness between us. "I've done every job Milton has," Mickey says. "Every one of them. And I've ordered produce and manned the courtesy desk and swabbed out the refrigeration units, when necessary. I've done every job my grandfather did, when he ran his little grocery store on a street corner in Newark, seventy-five years ago."

"The birth of the SaveWay," I say.

"Yup," Mickey concurs.

I lean my head against his shoulder. "Save me," I say.

"I'd be delighted to, Ms. Plow."

• • •

The two of us look like hell when we arrive home. We drag our wrung-out selves into the house, where Marcie's voice can be heard, chiming loudly from the kitchen. We find her standing at the stove in a ripped VH-1 T-shirt, her horn-rimmed glasses tucked into the neckline. Her face is wet and her eyes are as pink as a rabbit's. She waves hello with her free hand while flipping a grilled cheese sandwich with the other.

"Mr. P. and I were just talking about that time Mrs. P. dragged you to the Acropolis to meet Ham."

Pulkowski is bent over in his kitchen chair, shaking with laughter.

"Did you know she was going to do that?" I ask Marcie.

"I knew everything," Marcie says, sliding the sandwich on a plate and placing it in front of Pulkowski. "Helen and I had our talks. I remember this one conversation where she told me she thought you should dump your husband because he was a putz . . ."

Now Marcie is shaking with laughter, too. She stands over Pulkowski, slapping his back, the two of them convulsed in hysterics. "A putz, she called him! A little Yiddish weenie!"

I'm almost jealous of her, the way she gets Pulkowski to laugh. When she finally stops, straightening up beside his chair, she scrutinizes Mickey and me with her discerning eye.

"What's with the paperweight?" she asks, as I put it down on the counter. I don't answer her. It feels good to have a secret that Marcie doesn't know.

"More food is on the way," she says. "Seanie's out getting us chop suey."

"Thanks," I manage, but Marcie's still scrutinizing.

"Look at you," she says. "Helen wouldn't believe how *skinny* you are."

"Too skinny," says Mickey, grabbing my waist and smiling.

"Helen," Pulkowski says, with an ocean of feeling. "Helen."

Such love. I have never seen the equal of it in my life.

what separates us

Pulkowski and i sit side by side in the front row, staring at Helen's open casket, thanking friends and relatives as they arrive. I keep my arm looped through his, as if to anchor him to this earth. Mickey and Marcie play host and hostess, greeting people at the door, bringing them over to us, relieving us of their presence when we've had enough. Helen smiles serenely from her nest of velvet pillowing, as though she knows about my trip to Connecticut, and she knows she looks good in her bowling dance dress, and she knows that all the flowers are for her. I can feel her still hovering, supervising the day's events. My heart drips like a soggy sponge with how much I miss her. I am immersed in these feelings when I hear the hesitant footsteps of Mickey behind me, and someone else, too, and turn to find Teddy frowning down at us. Mickey flanks his side like a security guard, studying my face for clues for what to do. Teddy smiles weakly but adorably, his tiny bottom teeth flashing. He is wearing one of his shiny suits, the suits that were supposed to bring him great success in the law, but brought us monthly bills from Barneys instead. He looks ruffled and nervous, but also sincere and sad. He's come to the wake of a woman who has never said a kind word about him. It was decent of him.

I smile at Mickey and squeeze his hand. Only then does my butcher leave us. He walks to the side of the casket where he stations himself, watching over Helen like a Beefeater at Buckingham Palace. Teddy takes my grandfather's hand in his. "I'm so sorry, Mr. P.," he says. Pulkowski nods his thanks.

"Rosie," Teddy says.

"Thank you for coming," I say. Then I rise to my feet and hug him. I smell his aftershave, his skin, the starch of his white shirt, all scents that used to be a part of my life, my thoughts, my bed, my future. They strike a sweet note of nostalgia, as if I am glimpsing a movie I once was fond of watching, but they do not make me want to go home with him again.

Putz! Helen silently seethes from her cushiony casket, the pillows beige, the lining beige, everything beige and more expensive than the white but, what else were we going to get for Helen? *Putz!* she says again, but no, Ma, I tell her, *I* get to decide who the putzes are. *I* do.

Teddy's all right, I tell her. He came today to pay his respects. And if he wants to spend the rest of his life with Inga, the Almost girl, that's all right, too. Really.

Mickey is still standing guard at Helen's side in his own expensive suit, looking far more comfortable wearing it than I ever would have imagined. It feels so wrong that I never got to tell Helen how much I love him. But, as *Cosmopolitan* once advised, it's the curve balls that drive us home.

A little laugh escapes my lips and Teddy looks worried. His brow furrows in that five-year-old way of his. He'll never be a killer lawyer. He's got vulnerable written all over him. Still, he used to be my Teddy. In many ways, we grew up together. And then one of us left the house, just the same as in Mickey's marriage. Maybe Mickey is right after all. Maybe it isn't always about fault. Although, a husband could leave the house in a lot nicer way than Teddy left.

"Thanks for coming," I tell him again, walking him down the aisle toward the door.

"Well," he says, "she was a part of my life."

"She certainly was," I agree, though I'm sure we're imagining different parts. When we've reached the door, I say, "You're very sweet to pay your respects." I lean forward and kiss him on the cheek. "My best to you and Inga."

Teddy's mouth falls open.

"Are you planning to have children?" I ask.

"What?" Now his expression is one of naked shock.

"You and Inga. Will you have children? That pink house is pretty big."

Now he looks frightened. Perhaps his ex-wife is going crazy at his mother-in-law's wake. Not that Helen is his mother-in-law, really. But this is none of his business.

I enjoy the tiniest bit watching Teddy struggle. "Rosie," he finally says. "I know it's not the time for this discussion, but I want to say that I'm sorry about the way this whole thing played out."

"This whole *marriage* thing, you mean?" I can't resist tormenting him a teeny bit more.

"I don't know what to say," he says, his face coloring in the setting sun. "I just hope you know that I once loved you . . ."

Can a face burn any redder?

". . . I mean I'll *always* love you, but . . ."

Even I can't watch him struggle further. I open the heavy oak door and a rush of cold air comes in. "I wish you well," I tell him. "We had a good ride there for a while. Send me the papers whenever you're ready."

Another guy might have hugged me back, or said thank you, but Teddy's just not that smart.

"You all right?" Mickey asks when I return to the room. I run my fingers down one sideburn, tug at his tie, pat his chest.

"I'm fine, my big handsome SaveWay Boy," I say.

●　　●　　●

"Daddy, would you like to go for a little walk?" I ask Pulkowski, now that Teddy is gone. The old man nods and slowly rises. We shuffle past neighbors and mourners and through the dark corridor that leads to McClain's front entrance. We stand beneath the black awning, allowing the winter air to revive us. The sun dips low in the afternoon sky and a few passing cars already have their lights on. It has been a long day—exhausting hours of hello, hello, hello while simultaneously saying good-bye, good-bye, good-bye to Helen. People I'd never met from the neighborhood where Alexa lived have peppered the afternoon. They've gazed at me with wonder and open curiosity. *Yes*, I've wanted to say, *that's Johnny Bellusa's face you're looking at.* I've almost felt like apologizing to them for causing Helen to leave their neighborhood. But isn't that really Alexa's fault? I turn and look at Pulkowski, who appears lost in his own thoughts, hands dug deep into the pockets of his suit jacket. He looks strong and solid, but he's an eighty-year-old man with prostate cancer. How much longer will I have him?

"Daddy?" I ask. "Do you miss Alexa?"

It is a stupid question, but something in me wants to hear it asked out loud. It is also a stupid time to ask, with Pulkowski carrying so much fresh loss on his shoulders. But his face lights up when he hears his daughter's name. He turns his tired eyes on me, then folds me into a bear hug.

"Of course I miss my other little girl," he says.

"Would you like me to try and find her?"

He exhales warm air into my scalp. "What if I told you I know where she is?"

I pull away from him, feeling the blood pulsing through my own veins. "What?"

"Your mother and I know where she is. But she won't see us. She's afraid we might . . . well, try and do something."

My heart feels punched. A wind lifts the corner of my jacket but I don't feel it. "Try and do what?" I ask.

"She lives on some sort of commune in Washington State."

"A commune?"

He smiles. "Yeah. And she only eats vegetables." Pulkowski's grin crinkles wider. "That bothered your mother no end."

A car swishes by with its lights on. I blink, looking down.

"They grow broccoli," he says. "On the commune."

"She's never come back?"

"Nope."

"She never wanted to see me?"

Pulkowski is silent for almost a full minute. The wind picks up as the sky grows a deeper shade of navy blue, but neither of us makes a move to go inside. "That's the kind of question there's no good answer to," he finally says. He takes my chin into his big hand, as if I were a child again, and rubs away tears with his thumb. "But it's not about you."

"What else could it be about?" I weep, not sure if I'm crying for myself or for Helen or for the mother I've never known.

"If I told you about it, would it help?" my grandfather asks.

His arms are around me again. I wrestle with my anger, but maybe it's not toward him. "She was my little sweetheart," he says, "but she was a strange girl." I hear him breathing slowly, as though he is collecting his thoughts, arranging his words, trying his best to find a way to explain things. "She was sharp as all get-out, Allie was, but she was troubled, too. Nowadays they'd have some fancy label for it. You might even know what it was."

I pull back and look at him. "You mean some psychiatric label?"

My grandfather nods, sadness creasing his eyes. "As a little girl she was sweet as sugar. But as Allie got older, she would go into this sort of state, where she didn't talk and she looked sad and no one could reach her, not even Helen."

The thought of Helen unable to reach anyone saddens us both. We're quiet a minute.

"She took a bottle of pills once," he says softly. "Your mother found her in her bedroom. She was real smart, though. All A's in high school, all the hardest courses." A wisp of a smile

crosses his face. "I don't know where she got the brains from."
He laughs his Pulkowski laugh, but it's short. "She started getting involved with this group of kids who were—what would you
call them?" Pulkowski's brow creases. "Hippies, I suppose. She
didn't really seem to like them, though. The only friend she
ever truly liked was the boy on the school bus."

"Johnny Bellusa?"

A grave nod confirms that yes, my father was the boy on the
school bus.

"She talked to him all the time. Every night. On the phone.
In his car, in front of the house."

"Did you like him?" I ask, knowing I sound pathetic, like
some little kid who wants you to like her new bike. My grandfather doesn't answer me.

"Your mother tried to get Allie some help when she came
back home with you. She wanted her to go into this program at a
hospital for adolescents with . . ."

"Psychiatric problems," I finish for him.

Pulkowski nods. "She left." He crosses his arms, like he's
trying to keep pieces of something together. "She did okay for
herself, got some kind of midwife training in Oregon . . ."

A car with a bad muffler passes on the street, but it's not its
noise that sends ice water through my veins. It's my mother. A
midwife. My birth mother delivers other mothers' babies while
placing a whole continent between herself and me.

"She paid off her own loans, even contacted us when she was
all done and working," Pulkowski says, oblivious to the fact that
my insides are frozen, my muscles contracted, my joints locked
with rust and grief.

"But she never had what you'd call a normal life. Well, not by Helen's or my standards anyway. And she never"—he pauses and takes my hands in his—"well, she never wanted to come home again."

Big tears are rolling down my cheeks. Purple shadows collect in the pain on Pulkowski's face.

"Oh, honey," he breathes. "Far as we know, she never got any help for her problems so, you see, it really isn't Alexa who doesn't want to see her little girl. It's her sickness that keeps her from wanting it."

"So she'll never want to see us?" I sob into his sports jacket, not sure if I'm crying for myself or for Helen or for the mother I've never known. But Pulkowski can't answer my question. I know this. He can pat my back, as he does now, gently swirling his big hand in circles. He can wipe my tears with his thumb. But these are the most words that have passed between us in our whole lives together. He has said all he can to comfort me. And a person doesn't have to talk all the time to tell you he loves you.

•   •   •

The next morning we stand at a gravesite at Calverton Military Cemetery, where Helen will wait for her World War II sweetheart to join her one day. It's a cold, crisp winter's day and snow clouds hang in wait above us. Mickey has his arm around my shoulder. We've all just laid a single red rose on Helen's casket. *Good-bye, Ma!* When a young soldier begins playing taps, Pulkowski's knees seem to buckle a little. *Good-bye, Miss Muffet!* He clasps his hands together like a man who has nothing to hold. I stand beside him with my arm around him. A light snow falls on the shoulders of our winter coats, dusting the flowers atop the gleaming wood of the closed casket. A priest, shoulders hunched with cold, raises his hand over Helen in a final blessing. I feel a smile playing on my lips. He's probably some spoiled Jesuit, I think. Someone's probably bringing him his tea and his brandy and wiping his behind for him.

don't count me out

the morning of Eleanor's performance with the Special Theatre Group, I pick up the phone and dial Johnny Bellusa.

"Roseanna?" he says, when he hears my voice. "Is that you?"

I smile from beneath my pile of comforters. "Did you think it was one of your girlfriends?"

"There you go," he laughs. "Talking just like your mother."

"I'm sorry I couldn't have dinner with you," I tell him.

"I'm sorry about your grandmother. How's Mr. Pulkowski doing?"

"He's in the next room, if you'd like to speak to him. He's been staying with us since she died. Should I put him on?"

There's a beat of silence on the other end. "Oh, no," Johnny says. "I wouldn't know what to say to him after all these years."

"He knows where Alexa is. He's seen her from time to time."

"Is that so?"

I tell him it's so. I repeat everything regarding Alexa's

whereabouts that Pulkowski has told me, even as I wonder why I am doing it. Naturally, I hope for a fairy tale resolution to my parents' ill-fated romance—the carpenter and the midwife rushing from their respective coasts to finally come together. What child doesn't wish for this?

"You want to hear something funny?" I ask Johnny Bellusa. "My mother is a vegetarian and I'm in love with a butcher."

Johnny laughs, and I can almost see his slightly stooped shoulders moving up and down. Mickey rolls over in his sleep, throwing a wild arm across my waist.

"I've got to go," I tell Johnny. "But I wanted to ask you something first." I take a breath and then say it. "Did you know my mother was a little . . . well, emotionally unstable, back when you knew her?"

I can hear my newfound father sighing into the phone. "Your mother was like a princess to me," he finally says. "Like Princess Diana, let's say, walking into a voc-tech high school boy's life." He pauses. "I always thought she was perfect." His voice cracks a little on the word *perfect*.

I pull Mickey's arm tighter around my waist. "I'd like a rain check on that dinner," I tell Johnny after a moment.

"Anytime, sweetheart," he says. "Anytime you're ready."

I pass Pulkowski on the pullout couch in my living room, on my way to the kitchen to make coffee. A mauve pillow half ob-scures his sleeping face. I gaze at him a while, realizing I don't need more than him, not for now. One day I might be tempted to board a red-eye in search of my mother in a Washington State broccoli patch. But for today, I am happy knowing I have these two sleeping men in my life. And I had Helen, too, a blessing that perhaps a child can only really appreciate in retrospect.

I bend down and kiss Pulkowski's forehead. It's been a big week for him, medically speaking. The report came back; he is cancer-free. The irony is he's not sure what he's staying alive for anymore. Talk about your curve ball: the woman he adored took tender loving care of him, but she also smoked a pack of cigarettes a day. Now she's gone and he's just got me.

He's also got Mickey, of course. And Marcie. Even Sean makes it over here some Sunday afternoons to play some cards with him. We're getting by. The apartment is crowded but he hadn't wanted to be alone right away. Now he says he's ready to go home.

Today, after the show, Marcie and I are going to bring him over, fill his cupboard with groceries, buy him a new *TV Guide* and empty out some more of Helen's closets and drawers. We'll leave him a list of telephone and cell phone numbers and make sure his car has gas in it. It's his idea. Well, his and Marcie's. She's been filling his freezer with Stouffer's frozen dinner entrees for weeks. She's already begun on Helen's closet.

Today's a big day in Eleanor's life, too. Mrs. Bingle, director of the Special Theatre Group, has given her a starring role in *Don't Count Me Out*, no doubt because of her booming singing voice. All of us are going to see her in her show. Mickey's coming from the SaveWay and bringing Milton with him. Even Marcie and Sean will be in attendance, since they're both off on weekends, and since Eleanor is an EPT client.

Pulkowski seems a little confused about what a "Special Theatre Group" is. It's at times like this I miss Helen most. She would just tell Pulkowski we were going to hear some retards singing today, and not feel the slightest bit bad about saying it.

I start the coffee brewing and set out three cups. Mickey's bought me a new microwave cart (butcher block of course) and the kitchen looks much more put-together again. We're turning Teddy's study into a guest room so Pulkowski can come back as much as he likes. It's not as though he's any trouble. He hardly talks, after all.

Since I'm the first one up, I jump into the shower, and while the warm water's running over my nice slim body, I hear the glass door open, and Mickey gets in. "Hey," he says, and he wraps his arms around me. He is wet and warm and furry in all the right ways. "Hey," I tell him back, kissing his lips and tasting soap. He runs a hand over my almost flat stomach. "We could make that guest room a nursery, you know," he says. I've never told him that this is what I'd always hoped Teddy would say. I kiss him again, and this time taste shampoo. "I just got thin," I tell him.

"You were always beautiful," he says. "I like a big-boned girl."

Butcher pillow talk. It's all about the bones and the cuts of meat.

At ten o'clock Mickey is already gone and Pulkowski and I are driving over to the Cooperative Living group home. The sky is a great gray batting of clouds, and you can almost smell the snow that will soon fall. Pulkowski looks sharp in the nice Arrow dress shirt I have ironed for him, starching the collar and cuffs just as Helen would, starching also the front panel where the buttons are. We pull into the already crowded dirt parking lot behind Eleanor's house and watch as residents' parents and families slam car doors and hurry in, some of them carrying flowers, one of them carrying a bottle of sparkling grape juice packaged to look like champagne.

"Mr. P.!" we hear someone shout, and we turn and find Marcie running toward us, covered from head to toe in a man's brown overcoat, big as a tent and billowing in the winter breeze. Sean walks briskly a few paces behind, wearing a winter cap that makes his head look like an egg. The four of us step into a foyer crowded with boots and jackets, a huge papier-mâché star suspended from the ceiling and countless other paper stars taped to walls and windows. DON'T COUNT ME OUT! a large poster reads in crayoned bubble letters. Eleanor comes running over with a smile on her lips and a face full of stage makeup. She's wearing what would have to be described as a prom gown. It is peach colored, with more tiers than a wedding cake. She looks like a princess. "Get over here!" she yells, then throws her arms around me and hugs me.

"Eleanor," I say. "I think you meant to say hello."

"I'm the bomb!" she says, releasing me. "Hello."

"You certainly *are* the bomb," I tell her, puffing up one of her leg-o-mutton sleeves. "And a beautiful bomb at that."

I introduce her to Pulkowski, who stands in the midst of developmentally challenged madness and pre-show jitters, a swirl of shouting, exclaiming special needs actors and their families, smiling serenely at Marcie. When I look at Marcie's outfit, I see why he is so transfixed.

She looks perfect in Helen's Swiss-dotted shirtwaist dress. The patent leather belt at her waist is buckled in just the same hole. The skirt falls from her slim hips in a pleasing swell of yellow dots and pleats. The little white half-jacket hangs crisply from her shoulders, its three-quarter length sleeves pressed with sharp lines.

"Is this the hottest outfit you've ever seen in your life?" she says.

I don't know whether to throttle this crazy best friend of mine, or to collapse in hysterics at the sight of her. I take the middle road and stand in the foyer with my mouth open.

"You look lovely," Pulkowski breathes.

"Check out the shoes," Marcie says. She clicks together a pair of vintage open-toed high heels, probably the ones that Helen wore to my christening. Her toenails are painted red. "Your mother has some awesome hats," she says, "but they all seemed too summery for today."

"Yes, it *is* February," I manage.

"I hope you took them," Pulkowski says. "The hats. She'd want you to have them."

"What hats!" Eleanor yells, then she takes me by the hand and drags me into the dining room.

What a sight that is.

The walls are covered with old movie posters of Rita Hayworth and Joan Crawford and Clark Gable. The largest poster shows Fred Astaire and Ginger Rogers, mid-dip in their dance. HOORAY FOR HOLLYWOOD! the crayoned banner in this room reads. On the table, beside a vase of yellow roses, are markers and name tags to be filled out by guests, and at the table's center is a giant sheet cake, made, no doubt, by Eleanor.

Absolutely no doubt it is made by Eleanor. Only Eleanor

would decorate a sheet cake with footwear. I move a step closer to make sure I am seeing right. There is a silver character shoe pressed into the hot pink icing. The shoe doesn't look new, either. Its frayed ankle strap drags in the icing. Nobody seems disturbed by this, or maybe today's guests are too polite to say anything.

"Look," says Eleanor, lifting a few layers of her dress to expose her own silver character shoes. "Same shoes as mine. They're only for dancers. *Only* for dancers." She wags an index finger back and forth.

"They're lovely," I say. Then, pointing at the cake, "Whose shoe is that?"

"I don't know!" Eleanor exclaims, as though I am an idiot for asking.

I feel hands on my shoulders and turn around to find Mickey standing behind me. "Don't ask me to train this one at the SaveWay," he whispers in my ear, staring at the hot pink cake.

"Pipe down," I tell him, kissing his cheek. Milton looks crestfallen standing beside him. He's rubbing his hands together as though he has just witnessed a murder. It has been hard for him to understand that Miss Plow will soon be Mrs. Hamilton.

"Hello, Milton," I say, shaking his hand very formally.

"You can't put a shoe in a cake," he says, rather loudly, really.

"Yes you can, if you're an actor," Eleanor corrects him. "Who are you?"

"This is Milton," I say. "Milton, this is Eleanor."

"I'm the star of the show," Eleanor tells Milton. "Don't count me out."

"Well, a Volvo hit me once," Milton says.

This seems to intrigue Eleanor.

A trim woman in a black dress whom I take to be Mrs. Bingle calls for all the actors to join her immediately in the parlor. The dining room empties out in seconds, leaving only bewildered parents and guests behind.

"Who *was* that girl?" Milton asks, following the cloud of peach crepe in Eleanor's wake. Mrs. Bingle reappears and urges us to take our seats in the parlor at once.

Mickey nudges me with his elbow as we file in. "Is this the start of a beautiful thing for Milton and the baker?"

"I don't know," I tell him. "I got the butcher."

"I love your flank steaks," he says, patting my newly svelte behind.

"Hush," I tell him, settling into a folding chair between him and Pulkowski.

"Can I sit next to Miss Plow?" Milton asks, leaning over Mickey in the next seat.

"No," Mickey says.

"Would you like to sit with me?" Seanie asks, surprising us all.

"No," Milton says, and Marcie bursts out laughing.

An elderly woman in a turquoise jumper settles herself behind a beat-up piano at the front of the room. In a burst of chords, the Special Theatre Group comes dancing in, singing their hearts out.

Give my regards to Broadway!
Remember me to Herald Square!

Tell all the gang at Forty-Second Street
That I will soon be there!

Eleanor stands in front of the others, belting out her song. The others sing and dance behind her, executing some fairly difficult choreography better than I ever could, hoofing it like there's no tomorrow in their shiny tap shoes and glittering character shoes.

Give my regards to old Broadway
And say that I'll be there e'er long!

Eleanor spreads her arms out like Al Jolson, skirt bobbing, eyes glowing, her cheeks pinker than the icing on her cake. Pulkowski takes my hand in his and we sit and watch it all.

After the show, we all eat the cake, removing the silver pump before cutting into the icing. Milton gazes mournfully as Mickey hands me a cup of fruit punch.

"Miss Plow?" he asks. "Will I ever have a girlfriend like you?"

"Well," I tell him in a low voice, "you know you're a stud. *Someone* ought to snatch you up."

"I know I'm a stud," he shouts, as I glance around the room, looking for any house staff who might be listening, "but I have *challenges*."

"We all have challenges," I remind him, but this doesn't seem to comfort Milton. I pat his arm and look straight into his chocolate eyes. "I wish I could see into the future," I tell him. "I'm only your counselor."

"Oh no," he says, "You're not just my counselor. You're the lady with the beautiful face."

• • •

Mickey and Milton must get back to the SaveWay. I walk them out to Mickey's truck, the lady with the beautiful face. Milton strides at a brisk robotic pace ahead of us. Ham has given him the keys to unlock the doors, and he is taking this responsibility seriously. Mickey and I stroll behind at a slower pace, enjoying our snippet of time alone together.

"I can make us dinner tonight," I suggest. "I'll be home from my father's early enough." The snow hasn't begun to fall yet, but the storm feels so close a shiver of anticipation runs up my arms. We walk hand in ungloved hand through the parking lot, both of us imagining our first night in weeks alone at the apartment.

"Feel like anything special for dinner?" I ask.

"You," Mickey says, squeezing my hand.

Well, we know he is a carnivore.

"Remember that little red get-up you once modeled for Marcie and Seanie?"

I nod. My cheeks grow hot enough to melt snow.

"Why don't you put that on when I get home?"

I squeeze his hand back. "Why don't I, Mr. Ham?" I say. "Why don't I do that?"

When we reach the truck, Milton already is buckled in. His beautiful anxious face peers out the window at us. I give Ham's hand one last squeeze and let him go. They'll drive back to the SaveWay and he'll get Milton resettled at his bagging station.

I'll drive Pulkowski back to my childhood home and, with Marcie's help, we'll begin making it a place where he can live again. Then, this evening, as my grandfather experiments with his first full night alone, I'll slip into fire-engine-red lingerie, skimpy as rubber bands, a gift from my ex-husband, and make love to a man with funny sideburns, the man whom perhaps I was born to love.

Back in the Cooperative Living dining room, I find Pulkowski pleasantly ensconced in a ladder-back chair, surrounded by Eleanor and her homies, some of them still wearing their stage makeup. The little white-haired resident I'd first met on Thanksgiving is patting Pulkowski on the head, beaming at him with pleasure. "You're so cute!" she keeps saying, again and again. Pulkowski doesn't seem to mind. It's the first time I've seen him smile in weeks.

"Take home this cake!" Eleanor shouts at me, rushing over with a Saran-Wrapped wedge on a paper plate. There is a square dent in the icing, where the heel of the shoe once rested. I thank Eleanor and take the cake, tell her again how wonderful she was in the show. She gives me a hug that would injure a smaller person. But I am big-boned and my heart is full, and even if Eleanor wears pajamas to work for the rest of her days, even if they fire her, I can't help but notice the excellent growth in this client of mine.

I settle Pulkowski in the car with the cake on his lap. "Ready?" I ask, turning over the engine. He nods, flashing me his famous Daddy smile.

"Marcie will be there to help us," I remind him. He nods again.

Eleanor is waving from the big picture window as we pull out of the lot of the Cooperative Living group home. We're off to re-open Helen's house. The snow has finally begun in earnest. Brown lawns are covered with a thin layer of white, delicate as lace. I tune the car radio to Pulkowski's favorite station and we listen to Peggy Lee sing "Fever," her voice sexy and strong, her phrasing seductive. My grandfather taps his knee in time with the music. I can almost hear Helen calling him, louder than Peggy Lee, far more suggestively. *Get over here, Pulkowski, and help me with this goddamn zipper!* The snow falls. The windshield wipers swish. Pulkowski's hand goes *pat, pat, pat.* As Helen once told me, on a day less happy than this one, life can't be all veal Parmesan and violin music. But as lives go, in this very or-dinary moment, I find mine to be delicious.

2.5

ERNST KÄSEMANN

THE TESTAMENT
OF JESUS

A Study of the Gospel of John
in the Light of Chapter 17

D1174897

FORTRESS PRESS

PHILADELPHIA

In Memory of Muriel S. Curtis

Translated by Gerhard Krodel from the German *Jesu letzter Wille nach Johannes 17,* published 1966 by J. C. B. Mohr (Paul Siebeck) Tübingen.

First American edition by Fortress Press 1968
Second printing 1969
First paperback edition 1978

ISBN 0-8006-1399-6

7049A78   Printed in the United States of America   1-1399

CONTENTS

ABBREVIATIONS

BZ	*Biblische Zeitschrift* (Paderborn)
ET	English translation
FRLANT	Forschungen zur Religion und Literatur des Alten und Neuen Testaments (Göttingen)
HzNT	Handbuch zum Neuen Testament, ed. H. Lietzmann (Tübingen)
JThC	*Journal for Theology and the Church* (New York)
KeK	Kritisch-exegetischer Kommentar über das Neue Testament (Göttingen)
NF	Neue Folge (=New Series)
NTD	Das Neue Testament Deutsch (Göttingen)
NTS	*New Testament Studies* (Cambridge)
SBT	Studies in Biblical Theology (London and Naperville)
ThLZ	*Theologische Literaturzeitung* (Leipzig)
ThR	*Theologische Rundschau* (Tübingen)
TU	Texte und Untersuchungen zur Geschichte der altchristlichen Literatur (Berlin)
ZNW	*Zeitschrift für die neutestamentliche Wissenschaft und die Kunde der älteren Kirche* (Berlin)
ZsystTh	*Zeitschrift für systematische Theologie* (Gütersloh)
ZThK	*Zeitschrift für Theologie und Kirche* (Tübingen)

PREFACE

THE LECTURES PUBLISHED here were given as the Shaffer Lectures at the Yale Divinity School on April 26–28, 1966. They endeavour to give an answer to the question which has interested me for almost forty years, namely, into which historical situation should the Gospel of John be placed? As early as my inaugural lecture at the University of Göttingen entitled 'Ketzer und Zeuger', I tried to find an answer. Since my solution proposed there was generally rejected, even by my friend Ernst Haenchen who repudiated it as a 'stroke of genius',[1] this made me hesitate for a long time and forced me to engage in self-criticism which resulted in relinquishing several too daringly constructed hypotheses. However, the intensive study of different Johannine interpretations as well as my own exegesis compelled me in the end to take up my former approach with modifications, limiting myself to the Gospel and pursuing my goal more thoroughly. One need not be a frog to jump twice into the same pond. Furthermore, my arguments are to a large extent not new, but only dug up again and properly aligned. Naturally, it is not my intention to discuss, much less to solve *all* the problems of the Fourth Gospel. While the question which I raise must keep the whole Johannine problem in mind, not every detail needs to be discussed. I am satisfied with probing into the centre of the complex of historical problems, either by taking the much-travelled route or by climbing along undiscovered paths. The wide landscape on both sides of the road can afterwards be surveyed anew.

My study is dedicated to the memory of a woman who, during the years 1947–8, preserved people totally unknown to her from hunger and collapse and who also made my theological work possible. Mrs Muriel S. Curtis represents that overwhelming hospitality which I experienced during more than eight months in my travels in the United States in 1965–6. To some of my new friends in the New World, these lectures may perhaps appear offensive and unsuitable as an expression of thanks. Anglo-Saxons are especially fond of the Gospel of John and radical criticism at this point may offend. But

[1] *ThR*, NF 26 (1960), pp. 281ff.

true dialogue depends on meeting, irritating, and stimulating each other precisely where the stakes are the highest. A mere stroll over uncontroversial fields would seem to me inappropriate both to the riches of the impressions which I received in America and to my expectations from the impetuous new generation of young theologians.

I would like to thank my friend Professor Gerhard Krodel, of the Lutheran Theological Seminary in Philadelphia, for his well-considered translation.

Tübingen   ERNST KÄSEMANN
Pentecost 1966

I

THE PROBLEM

I WOULD LIKE TO begin this study with the unusual confession that I shall be discussing a subject which, in the last analysis, I do not understand. Not without irony, one could point to the history of exegesis as offering the proof that only occasionally has exegesis achieved lasting results. If true understanding had actually been realized, then the great problems of New Testament interpretation would not need to become the object of diligent research in each new generation. But the enormous quantity of books and articles which are continuously appearing indicates that our interpretations only occasionally reach the desired goal. One could add the portentous generalization that everywhere in life true understanding is rather difficult and rare, while reciprocal misunderstanding usually characterizes the human situation.

The historian, however, should limit his horizons lest he substitute the general structures of life for concrete historical objects. I can therefore formulate my problem more precisely: Historical criticism has demolished the traditional opinion that the Fourth Gospel was written by John, the son of Zebedee. However, historical criticism has not offered us an acceptable substitute for that outdated view. All of us are more or less groping in darkness when we are asked to give information about the historical background of this Gospel, information which would determine our understanding of the whole book and not merely of individual details. Nowhere else in the New Testament do we find ourselves in a greater dilemma than in John, even though everywhere in the New Testament we encounter such riddles that introductions to the New Testament could, to a great extent, be placed into the literary genre of fairy tales, their dry tone or their pretence of factual reporting notwithstanding. The Evangelist whom we call John appears to be a man without definite contours.

We can hear his voice, a voice distinct from the rest of primitive Christianity, and yet we are unable to locate exactly his historical place. Much of what he says is quite understandable and frequently we are deeply moved by it. But his voice retains a strange other-worldly quality. Every age in the Church's history has felt that other-worldliness and for this reason has esteemed his Gospel especially. The historian, however, cannot be content with that. His work pre-supposes the categories of time and space. A world without shadows and historical contours cannot be investigated. He must be able to localize an historical object in order to recognize it. Men can stand only when they have ground under their feet and this ground is also the presupposition of understanding. But here lies our problem: In a way, since the second century, the interpreters of the Fourth Gospel have been endeavouring to discover the forgotten historical situation in which this Gospel arose. The numerous conflicting and, to a sur-prising extent, diametrically opposed interpretations prove better than anything else that the quest for the historical situation of the Fourth Gospel has so far been unsuccessful. This is not to deny that new possibilities of understanding are continually opened up, possibilities which in part raise real issues and in part mark new progress which cannot be surrendered. But, on the other hand, im-partial analysis will also establish that sheer fantasy and ignorance are just as busily and continuously reburying what others have dug up. The purpose and the chaos of scholarship are here reflected equally[1] and only a few participants show serious concern because of it. Historically, the Gospel as a whole remains an enigma, in spite of the elucidation of individual details.[2]

It is the intention of my lectures at least to contribute to the recognition of this fact as a challenge addressed to us. To be sure, experience might teach us that there is little hope of mastering at long

[1] In this connection we should not forget the work of F. Overbeck, *Das Johannes-evangelium* (1911). He comments sarcastically on p. 79, 'Modern scholarship in the case of the Gospel of John is like a bear dependent on licking its own paws to get something.' Similarly J. Wellhausen, *Das Evangelium Johannis* (1908), p. 3, 'We strain at the gnat and swallow the camel.'

[2] R. E. Brown, *The Gospel according to John*, Vol. I (1966), pp. cxxviff., would find little support for his affirmation that in view of the New Testament's diversity, it is not difficult to locate John within the mainstream of Christian thought. C. H. Dodd is more correct when he says in *The Interpretation of the Fourth Gospel* (1953), p. 6, 'There is no book, either in the New Testament or outside it, which is really like the Fourth Gospel', or E. Hirsch, *Das vierte Evangelium* (1936), p. 145, 'It is really that book of the New Testament which has sealed itself most tightly against superficiality.'

last that which lies unconquered before us.[3] But the historian can as little resist the fascination of tackling unsolved problems as a mountain-climber can resist the challenge of the peak rising before him. Experience will teach him that he will have to seek more audacious paths, if those that were followed in the past did not lead to the goal. Yet it is also true that the bolder the paths, the deeper could be the fall. But new endeavours could also open up new vistas. At least they can enable us to recognize the magnitude of the problem more clearly. Even if nothing else were gained, such an endeavour would not be in vain. For the raising of the right questions (because the difficulties are recognized more clearly) is the necessary beginning of scholarship and frequently its most important result.

John 17 serves as the basis and guidepost of my lectures. Regardless of how the question of the original position of this chapter is answered, it is unmistakable that this chapter is a summary of the Johannine discourses and in this respect is a counterpart to the prologue. It should be rewarding to unroll the problem of our Gospel almost, as it were, from the end, beginning with chapter 17. Of course, this cannot be done now in a detailed exegesis. I shall rather select certain key words from the context in which the distinctive Johannine themes are focussed and I shall analyse these themes; namely, the glory of Christ, the community under the Word, and Christian unity. They are treated successively, even though they are so closely interwoven in chapter 17, as well as in the whole Gospel, that they cannot be isolated from each other. Repetitions as well as omissions therefore cannot be avoided in this type of argumentation. The Johannine eschatology will be treated under the aspects of christology, ecclesiology and soteriology. However, a theological interpretation of the Fourth Gospel is not our ultimate aim. Rather, I shall unfold the complex of theological problems only so far as it can serve as a key for the historical question of the historical situation out of which this Gospel grew. The theological problems must, after all, point to a specific sector of primitive Christian history and, conversely, we must be able to deduce it from them.[4]

---

[3] E. C. Hoskyns, *The Fourth Gospel* (1947), pp. 20, 49f., endeavours to show that, on principle, the encounter with eternity conceals the historical situation and he accuses historical criticism of a lack of understanding in this matter. However, each encounter with eternity is bound up with a specific situation.

[4] So also R. Schnackenburg, *Das Johannesevangelium* I (1965), pp. 101, 134f.

II

THE GLORY OF CHRIST

IN THE COMPOSITION of chapter 17, the Evangelist undoubtedly used a literary device which is common in world literature and employed by Judaism as well as by New Testament writers. It is the device of the farewell speech of a dying man.[1] Its Jewish antecedents are represented by the Testaments of the Twelve Patriarchs. Within the New Testament this device is found in the farewell speech of Paul to the elders of Ephesus in Miletus (Acts 20), in the pseudonymous tract known as II Timothy describing the ideal bishop, and in the eschatological tract known as II Peter. It was also introduced into the story of Jesus' passion, where, in Mark 13, it served to provide a place for apocalyptic material. In Mark 13, Jesus, as he went to his death, anticipated his disciples' future in prophecy, warning and reassurance. If the Fourth Gospel took up this Synoptic tradition, then John transformed it to an unusual extent. For apocalyptic instruction, which dominates the testament of Jesus in Mark 13, has disappeared from John. In its place we find four long chapters, roughly one-fifth of the whole Gospel, which are connected by the motif of the farewell discourse and which thus received an importance unsurpassed even by John's passion and resurrection narratives.

What prompted John to emphasize this form of presentation? It is not sufficient to answer that the farewell discourses were composed as a clever transition to the concluding section of his work. For this form of presentation is essentially paradoxical. The whole Gospel pictures Jesus not merely as a miracle-worker who heals the sick, raises the dead and remains unassailable by his enemies, but also as the one in whom eternal Life and Resurrection appear personified. A

[1] Compare E. Stauffer, *Die Theologie des Neuen Testaments* (1948), pp. 327ff, (ET *New Testament Theology* [1955], pp. 344ff.); W. Bauer, *Das Johannesevangelium* (1933), pp. 207f.; O. Michel, 'Das Gebet des scheidenden Erlösers', *ZsystTh* 18 (1941), pp. 521–34.

testament in the mouth of the Prince of Life is, however, most unusual and we can hardly suppose that the Evangelist failed to reflect
on this paradox. Therefore we must investigate the basis and the
purpose of his manner of presentation. Why did he choose to clothe
his thoughts in the form of a testament? The first thing we recognize is
that here the Evangelist was marking an epoch not merely in the life
of Jesus, but also in the history of the community. This can be seen
in the fact that John 17, in distinction to the previous chapters, was
composed in the form of a prayer. Again, this is not merely the
clever use of a literary device. For the prayer of Jesus does not play
the same important role in John as in the Synoptics, and John 11.41f.
gives us the reason for it. Jesus has no need to ask the Father because
his request is always heeded at once. Thus actually he can only give
thanks. His prayer, therefore, differs from ours in that, like his discourses, it, too, witnesses to his unity with the Father. He lives in
royal freedom and in the certainty of his immediacy to the Father
and therefore he has no more care. To be sure, John 17 contains
individual petitions, but it does not become a prayer of supplication.
Rather, his majestic 'I desire' dominates the whole chapter. This is
not a supplication, but a proclamation directed to the Father in such
manner that his disciples can hear it also. The speaker is not a needy
petitioner but the divine revealer and therefore the prayer moves
over into being an address, admonition, consolation and prophecy.
Its content shows that this chapter, just like the rest of the farewell
discourse, is part of the instruction of the disciples. The presentation
of the instruction in the form of the prayer, however, indicates that
the disciples' fate does not rest in their own hands. The decision
about them has been made in heaven, and the Johannine Christ
appeals to the throne of God on their behalf that this decision may
remain in force. In this respect, he exercises that intercession which
in Rom. 8.34 and in the Letter to the Hebrews belongs to the
heavenly High Priest who has been exalted to the right hand of the
Father. In John, the disciples become witnesses to the dialogue
between the Son and the Father, in which their future course is
being determined, and thus they themselves are drawn into a fundamentally heavenly activity. The one who speaks here is, in the last
analysis, not the one who is about to die. The dying of Jesus comes
into view only as the presupposition of the farewell situation, of his
departure from the earth. Therefore this chapter is not a testament
in the sense of a last will and bequest, but rather in the sense of a

final declaration of the will of the one whose proper place is with the Father in heaven and whose word is meant to be heard on earth. In a certain sense, the proclamation of the eternal gospel, spoken of in Rev. 14.6, is also taking place here. To be sure, in John 17 and Rev. 14, the situation, the content and the recipients differ from each other, but in both instances we encounter the motif of a heavenly proclamation, concise in form and ultimate in significance.[2]

Here a new problem arises. John 17, like the farewell discourses in general and in contrast, for instance, to the Sermon on the Mount, is a secret instruction to the disciples. Its scope encompasses the total earthly history. But only the disciples can hear it and understand it. Insight which the world cannot and may not have is granted to them, even though the message as such is not enigmatic. It is no accident that in v. 3 the key word 'gnosis' already appears. Apparently this 'gnosis' does not refer to the anthropological and cosmological mysteries as they are communicated through apocalyptic proclamation. Nevertheless, the truth with which we deal here, the knowledge and acceptance of which places man under obligation, is revealed only to the enlightened and the elect and is therefore communicated in the form of a secret discourse. The community addressed is actually joined more closely to heaven than to earth. Even though it still exists in earthly form, it belongs in its very essence to the realm of the Father and the Son.

These introductory remarks will have to suffice to indicate the peculiar atmosphere in which the problems of the Fourth Gospel arise. We shall now focus our attention on the text itself. The beginning of John 17 is dominated by the key word 'glorification' of Jesus. With this key word, the message of the whole Gospel is taken up once more in our chapter. The prologue in 1.14 has already summarized the content of the Gospel with 'We beheld his glory'.[3] Consistently with this, the book closes with the confession of Thomas (20.28), 'My Lord and my God', and with a reference to the many other signs and miracles of Jesus which could be reported. It has always been recognized that no other Gospel narrates as impressively as John the confrontation of the world and of the believers with the glory of Jesus,

[2] The prayer is therefore neither an integral part of Christ's enthronement, as stated by T. Arvedson, *Das Mysterium Christi* (1937), pp. 132f. and C. H. Dodd, *op. cit.*, pp. 419ff., nor should it be limited (see Hoskyns, *op. cit.*, pp. 494ff.) to a prayer of consecration.

[3] See my article, 'Aufbau und Anliegen des johanneischen Prologs', in *Exegetische Versuche und Besinnungen* II (1964), pp. 155–80.

even in the passion story. In view of this it is astonishing that even though Jesus' glory is recognized as being already manifest, nevertheless at the same time, in a certain respect, it is also regarded as still being in the future, for his glory will be perfected only with his death.[4] What is astonishing is not so much the tension between both affirmations as such. We find this in many other parts of the New Testament, inasmuch as we meet there the phenomenon of a twofold eschatology, of realized and futuristic eschatology. Its intention is to proclaim the end of the world as already breaking into the earthly present reality now with Christ. The twofold eschatology is connected with christology elsewhere in the New Testament in that the earthly Jesus is distinguished from the returning Judge of the world, or the crucified one is distinguished from the resurrected and exalted Lord. In short, John stands here within a firm tradition, but, as is his custom otherwise, he develops this tradition further in an astonishing and even paradoxical manner. While Paul and the Synoptics also know the majesty of the earthly Jesus, in John the glory of Jesus determines his whole presentation so thoroughly from the very outset that the incorporation and position of the passion narrative of necessity becomes problematical. Apart from a few remarks that point ahead to it, the passion comes into view in John only at the very end. One is tempted to regard it as being a mere postscript which had to be included because John could not ignore this tradition nor yet could he fit it organically into his work. His solution was to press the features of Christ's victory upon the passion story. At any rate he does not describe the journey of Jesus as a process which leads from lowliness to glory. Despite the stress on the agreement in structure between John and the Synoptics, especially in Anglo-Saxon scholarship, John is hardly based on a pattern according to which the Galilean teacher enters Jerusalem with Messianic honours before he is shown hanging shamefully on the cross, then, in an abrupt change of fortune, to appear in the glory of the resurrection. Of course, John knew of this tradition and did not despise its pattern when it appeared useful or necessary to him. But he employs it with the greatest freedom and ruthlessly breaks it up when his viewpoint demands it. Therefore the cleansing of the temple is found at the beginning of Jesus' activity and many journeys to Jerusalem take place for various feasts. The miracle of the raising

---

[4] This problem dominates the investigation of W. Thüsing, *Die Erhöhung und Verherrlichung Jesu im Johannesevangelium* (1960).

of Lazarus opens and is the cause of the passion. Theological themes dominate the structure of this Gospel. It is obvious that the category of the Galilean teacher does not apply to the one who, like a mystagogue, with long-drawn-out monologues, symbolic speeches and cryptic intimations confronts the world, provokes its misunderstandings and precipitates its judgment. Neither historical reminiscences nor a concentration on Jesus' own development dominate the writing of the Fourth Gospel. Certainly one can and must raise the question how far this Gospel is parallel to the Synoptics and how much it reflects their emphasis in its details.[5] But if this is done in the interest of showing the closest possible approximation between John and the Synoptics, rather than of drawing the contrast between them, then the peculiar Johannine accents and stresses are shifted and the interpretation falls under the domination of apologetics. Here, as in other places, one can see that the victory march of historical criticism became possible within the field of New Testament scholarship only because fundamental questions had not been thoroughly discussed. The method was confined to tackling surface problems with an attempt at harmonization, rather than a quest for different nuances and divergent viewpoints. Historical criticism has won a total victory today because it turned out that it could successfully be domesticated *ad usum Delphini*. Its task is then no longer to lay bare offences and trouble-spots, to indicate the problems involved in traditional viewpoints, but rather to undergird the conservative approach, bringing it into an advantageous position at a stage prior to actual theological investigation and thus drawing the teeth of radical higher criticism at the earliest moment. Nowadays, the battles are often fought in the theatre, using blank cartridges. The 'happy ending' is not merely wishful thinking, but the condition tacitly agreed upon for the historical-critical enterprise, and even satires of this technique of transformation would offend against good manners. The Gospel of John is the favourite playground for such practice.

What customary scholarship endeavours methodologically, namely to show that John approximates to or complements the Synoptic tradition, is then expressed in practice, quite remarkably, through the almost universal attempt to find a christology of humiliation even in the Fourth Gospel. It is typical that a discussion based on the kind of liberal interpretation which characterizes the Johannine Christ as

[5] Cf. C. H. Dodd, *Historical Tradition in the Fourth Gospel* (1963), as representative of this.

God going about on the earth[6] is generally omitted, or confined to comments on exegetical details. Yet here we meet one of the most important issues, if not the decisive problem of Johannine interpretation. Unless this problem is dealt with thematically, the suspicion arises that one has not even recognized it. Problems cannot be replaced, like clothing, simply by creating a new fashion. The problem of the divine glory of the Johannine Christ going about on earth is not yet solved, but rather most strikingly posed when we hear the declaration of the prologue: 'The Word became flesh.' For what reasons is this statement almost always made the centre, the proper theme of the Gospel? Of course, it introduces and establishes the possibility of writing the earthly story of Jesus. However, we must also ask: In what sense is he flesh, who walks on the water and through closed doors, who cannot be captured by his enemies, who at the well of Samaria is tired and desires a drink, yet has no need of drink and has food different from that which his disciples seek? He cannot be deceived by men, because he knows their innermost thoughts even before they speak. He debates with them from the vantage point of the infinite difference between heaven and earth. He has need neither of the witness of Moses nor of the Baptist. He dissociates himself from the Jews, as if they were not his own people, and he meets his mother as the one who is her Lord. He permits Lazarus to lie in the grave for four days in order that the miracle of his resurrection may be more impressive. And in the end the Johannine Christ goes victoriously to his death of his own accord. Almost superfluously the Evangelist notes that this Jesus at all times lies on the bosom of the Father and that to him who is one with the Father the angels descend and from him they again ascend. He who has eyes to see and ears to hear can see and hear his glory. Not merely from the prologue and from the mouth of Thomas, but from the whole Gospel he perceives the confession, 'My Lord and my God'. How does all this agree with the understanding of a realistic incarnation? Does the statement 'The Word became flesh' really mean more than that he descended into the world of man and there came into contact with earthly existence, so that an encounter with him became possible?[7] Is not this statement totally overshadowed by the confession 'We beheld his glory',[8]

[6] F. C. Baur, *Kritische Untersuchungen über die kanonischen Evangelien* (1847), pp. 87, 313; G. P. Wetter, *Der Sohn Gottes* (1916), p. 149; E. Hirsch, *op. cit.*, p. 138, represent this view.

[7] So F. C. Baur, p. 97.

[8] So again F. C. Baur, pp. 94ff.

so that it receives its meaning from it? I am not interested in completely denying features of the lowliness of the earthly Jesus in the Fourth Gospel. But do they characterize John's christology in such a manner that through them the 'true man' of later incarnational theology becomes believable?[9] Or do not those features of his lowliness rather represent the absolute minimum of the costume designed for the one who dwelt for a little while among men,[10] appearing to be one of them,[11] yet without himself being subjected to earthly conditions? His death, to be sure, takes place on the cross, as tradition demands. But this cross is no longer the pillory, the tree of shame, on which hangs the one who had become the companion of thieves. His death is rather the manifestation of divine self-giving love and his victorious return from the alien realm below to the Father who had sent him.

This line of argumentation is not contradicted by pointing out that the Fourth Gospel clearly speaks of the obedience of the one whom the Father has sent.[12] It cannot be denied that we meet here the tradition of a christology of humiliation as known to us through Phil. 2.7f. It is, however, questionable whether John would permit us to base on that tradition an interpretation of the whole Gospel in terms of a christology of humiliation. Not even Paul should be understood in this way, as if Christ's obedience were, for Paul, merely the sign of his lowliness. For according to Rom. 5.12ff., Christ as the obedient one is at the same time the new Adam and the heavenly *anthropos*. Correspondingly, for John obedience is the mark of the Son of Man who not only participates in the mission of God, but also fulfils it. He finds his food in the fulfilment of the divine will, a food which exempts him from earthly food, and unites him with the Father. Therefore in John, the obedience of the earthly Jesus is not, as in Phil. 2.9, rewarded with his exaltation,[13] but rather is finished and brought to a close by his return to the Father. Obedience is the form

[9] As examples of this view see E. C. Hoskyns, *op. cit.*, pp. 17f., and C. H. Dodd, *Interpretation*, p. 249. But more or less all modern interpretations of John follow this line, dominated by the idea of the incarnation.

[10] Cf. 'He tabernacled among us' (1.14), which is taken up by the paradoxical 'a little while' of the farewell discourses in 14.19; 16.16ff.; as already in 7.33; 12.35; 13.33.

[11] The misunderstandings in 6.42; 7.27; 7.35f.; 8.48, 53; 9.29; arise from the problem of the humanity of Jesus.

[12] As is done by E. Haenchen, 'Der Vater, der mich gesandt hat', *NTS* 9 (1962/3) pp. 208–16, and earlier by Dodd, *Interpretation*, p. 254.

[13] Thüsing's interpretation is completely oriented on the pattern of Phil. 2.6ff. In this orientation may lie the decisive error of his investigation (see Thüsing, *op. cit.*, p. 223).

and concretion of Jesus' glory during the period of his incarnation. During this time the divinity he claims is misunderstood, provokes objection and requires a final revelation. The formula 'the Father who sent me' is, lastly, neither the only nor the most typical christological formula in the Gospel. The Baptist, too, according to 1.6, is 'sent by God'. To be sent by God means, to begin with, nothing else than 'to be authorized'. Yet, according to the rabbinic maxim, the delegate is the representative of the sender and as such the recipient must accept him as equal to the sender. In the Gospel, the formula 'the Father who sent me' therefore alternates continuously with the concept of the oneness with the Father, and the former receives its peculiar christological meaning through the latter. Jesus is the heavenly messenger who acts out of his oneness with the Father. In unique dignity as the Father's 'exegete' (1.18), he surpasses everyone else who may otherwise have been sent. A truly subordinationist christology can by no means be deduced from this, regardless of how relevant the distinction between the Father and the Son might be for John. This distinction is, however, important for his concept of revelation, which holds that there is no access to the Father except through Jesus and, correspondingly, that Jesus has no other function and authority apart from being the revealer of God. If the formulae of his commission through the Father and his unity with the Father are isolated from each other, the result will be subordinationism or ditheism. Both formulae are correlative and complementary, because only together do they describe the truth that Jesus is nothing but the revealer and, on the other hand, that Jesus is the only revealer of God and therefore belongs totally on the side of God even while he is on earth.

The road travelled by the Johannine Christ should consequently not be presented as a development from lowliness to glory. But may we then speak instead of the paradox of a glory hidden in lowliness? Such an interpretation is commonplace today.[14] It is again surprising how rarely the basic problems of the interpretation of the Fourth Gospel are carefully thought through. In general, the interpretation is so greatly interested in balancing the extremes of possible explanations that it eagerly grasps for formulae which permit the establishment of a dialectical balance.[15] It is precisely through this

[14] Typical representatives are Hoskyns, *op. cit.*, pp. 81f.; C. K. Barrett, *The Gospel according to St John* (1955), p. 77.

[15] This approach is reflected in T. W. Manson, *On Paul and John* (1963), pp. 131ff., 152ff., where history and dogmatics, experience of love and metaphysics, divinity and humanity subjected to it are brought into balance.

method that the greatest danger arises. One-sided interpretations usually dig their own graves, or else they start a discussion leading to their correction. But dialectical formulae, such as the paradox of lowliness and majesty, are so vague and grant so much leeway to our understanding, that all sorts of different divergent notions can be attached to them. Clarity of thought is then replaced by the fascination exercised by the slogans. It is obvious that a real paradox between the lowliness and the glory of the earthly Jesus can only be affirmed if we seriously speak about Jesus' afflicted humanity exposed to the world, to suffering and to death.[16] The disguise, the hiding, of a divine being in lowliness may appear paradoxical, but it is not really paradoxical at all. Such concealment, in the last analysis, is to make communication possible between what is unequal and therefore separate, between heaven and earth, God and man. As the possibility of communication such hiding is something very proper and very purposeful and quite rationally understandable. It indicates condescension, but not antinomy. It is, of course, right to argue that the notion of Jesus' humiliation is found also in the Fourth Gospel, because his mission necessitated his descent from heaven to earth and this descent, his humiliation, is brought to an end through his return. But lowliness and glory, humiliation and exaltation, do not remain separated like two stages on a journey, so that when one is here one cannot be there. They are rather united with each other in that the earthly Christ who enters the world of suffering and death does not lose his unity with the Father. He does not really change himself, but only his place. Human fate is thrust upon him so that in a divine manner he may endure it and overcome it. Individual development cannot take place for the one who is himself the way, that is to say who is both the beginning and the goal for his followers, the resting place for those whose hearts are troubled without him. Because he himself is the Life and the Resurrection, the world of suffering and death has no power over him even in his dying. To him the Father has given power over all things. The world is for him only a point of transit and humiliation simply means being in exile. His humanity may time and again arouse misunderstanding and offence. However, it is not his humanity as such which does so, but rather his humanity as the medium of the call to acknowledge the Creator by believing

[16] The notion of the paradox is thought through in this sense only by R. Bultmann; cf. *Die Theologie des Neuen Testaments* (5th ed., 1965), pp. 399f. (ET *Theology of the New Testament* II [1955], pp. 47f.).

in the Son. The combination of humiliation and glory is not paradoxical as such, because the humiliation makes the epiphany and presence of glory possible and represents its concretion. Only the exclusive, absolute claim through which Jesus binds salvation to his message and person is offensive and paradoxical.

The Synoptic writers, Paul and even Hebrews endeavoured to find a balance between the cross and the exaltation, and they have done so in various ways. John is, to our knowledge, the first Christian to use the earthly life of Jesus merely as a backdrop for the Son of God proceeding through the world of man and as the scene of the inbreaking of the heavenly glory.[17] Jesus is the Son of Man because in him the Son of God comes to man.[18] It is characteristic of John's radical reinterpretation that he uses this title which designated the apocalyptic World Judge to refer to the earthly existence of Jesus. The Son of Man is neither a man among others, nor the representation of the people of God or of the ideal humanity,[19] but God, descending into the human realm and there manifesting his glory. Eighteen centuries have been fascinated by this picture of the Johannine Christ, and in their faith have concurred with the prologue and the confession of Thomas. The Church of all ages acknowledges the statement 'We beheld his glory', and consequently accepts the Gospel which illustrates this sentence.

We have taken a long detour in order to grasp adequately the problem of John's characteristic of a twofold eschatology and the christology resulting from it. The usual beginning is to point out the preponderance of the so-called present or realized eschatology which is a special characteristic of the Gospel. In this connection, the question of the frequency and importance of the remnants of a futurist eschatology remains controversial. It is acknowledged that John knows no imminent expectation nor a cosmic drama of the end in the sense of apocalypticism. His place in the third Christian generation shows itself in the reduction of futurist eschatology to the realm of anthropology. This holds true, even if the present form of the Johannine text is regarded as original, that is, if those texts dealing with the future resurrection are not excluded as later interpolations.

[17] We must therefore (contrary to Barrett, *op. cit.*, p. 58) speak of a 'higher' christology, if we cannot follow Barrett, p. 77, in emphasizing the humanity and the subjection of Jesus to the Father.

[18] Cf. R. Schnackenburg, 'Der Menschensohn im Johannesevangelium', *NTS* 11 (1964–1965), pp. 123–37.

[19] Contrary to Dodd, *Interpretation*, p. 248.

Since ch. 21 does testify to a redactional revision of this Gospel, the possible presence of interpolations within the rest of John cannot simply be excluded. A point in favour of regarding the futurist texts as interpolations is the fact that these are only a few verses which are cast into stereotyped form and are detached from the theological complex as well as from the context. But even if the text is accepted in its traditional form, we still have no more than a few meagre relics of pre-Johannine beliefs which do not constitute a real counter-balance to specifically Johannine ideas but merely restrain their extreme development. In that case, the Evangelist would have failed to outgrow completely the relics of the past and would have retained the individual hope of a future resurrection when he forsook the apocalyptic expectation of the imminent end and of the arrival of the new world.[20] We shall see later that such an interpretation is not totally impossible.

The problems touched on here force us to reflect more thoroughly upon the specifically Johannine proclamation at this point. We see its peculiarity in 5.24, which states most emphatically that the believer 'has already passed from death to life'. The following verse underlines this: 'The hour is already here when the dead shall hear the voice of the Son of God and those who hear it will live.' John 3.36; 6.47; 8.51; 11.25f. state with the same certainty that eternal life is now already present in the believer. This eternal life cannot even be touched by earthly death. John 3.18ff. draws a line from here to the extremely radical statement that the final judgment, which had traditionally been expected to happen on the last day, has happened already with the coming of Jesus who, in John 11.25, personifies the Resurrection and the Life. We have been accustomed to understanding sentences such as these in an edifying, more or less 'spiritual' manner,[21] and to tone down their cutting edge by harmonizing and balancing them with the Church's futurist eschatology. In doing this, however, we fail to recognize the apparently polemical character of the Johannine proclamation and its eschatology as it is expressed, for instance, in ch. 11. Above all, we also generally fail to see or at least to express the fact that statements like this grow out of a firm tradi-

[20] H. Strathmann, *Das Evangelium nach Johannes* (1954), p. 18: 'Eschatological thinking has achieved a permanent footing in the Church's thought.'
[21] E. Gaugler, 'Die Bedeutung der Kirche in den johanneischen Schriften', *Internationale kirchliche Zeitschrift* 14 (1924), pp. 97–117; 181–219; 15 (1925), pp. 27–42, interprets this in a liberal vein (p. 112): 'For the loving community the concept of a final judgment has disappeared.' But in that case, what about the concept of the final resurrection of the dead?

tion which the New Testament frequently preserved. We meet this tradition in the baptismal proclamation of Col. 2.12f. and Eph. 2.5f., where it is even connected with a statement about the heavenly enthronement. The pre-Pauline existence of such traditions in Hellenistic enthusiasm is also confirmed by Rom. 6.4ff., where Paul takes up that tradition and modifies it by changing our resurrection and life with Christ from the perfect tense into the future tense. With respect to the present, our resurrection with Christ has, for Paul, only a metaphorical meaning and validity, namely as a figurative expression of the new obedience of the Christian. The *Sitz im Leben* of this view becomes quite clear when enthusiastic members of the Corinthian congregation reject, not Christ's resurrection, but the believer's future resurrection. Undoubtedly they held this view because they thought that through baptism they already participated in the resurrection world and eternal life, and therefore could contemptuously encounter earthly death. Our chain of historical evidence is complete when II Tim. 2.18 counters this heretical proclamation that the resurrection of the dead has already taken place. It is quite disturbing that the Evangelist, at the very centre of his proclamation, is dominated by a heritage of enthusiasm against which Paul had already struggled violently in his day and which in the post-apostolic age was branded as heretical. John, however, was too independent and too critical to accept without modifications a heritage which in the deutero-Pauline writings had already been adjusted to the Church's eschatology. John detached it from the context of the understanding of baptism as an initiation into mysteries and placed it in the service of his christology. The *praesentia Christi* is the centre of his proclamation. After Easter this means the presence of the Risen One. All the Gospels presuppose Easter, and therefore they develop a post-Easter christology of Jesus as the Son of God. It may also be right to say that all the Gospels understand Jesus' miracles in the light of Easter, whether in the sense that bodily healing sets men on the horizon of the dawning new world, or else in the sense that the power of the miracle-worker is interpreted as the energy of the divine spirit and the power of the resurrection. John's account is not totally new, but it does have radical consequences. Not only is it presented from the perspective of the resurrection of the dead which had been anticipated in Jesus' resurrection, but it also affirms what the enthusiasts of Corinth and the heretics of II Tim. 2.18 had proclaimed, namely that the reality of the general resurrection of the dead is already present now. The reason for this affirmation lies in the fact that Jesus is known only in his resurrection existence. Unlike Luke, John has not yet learned to understand Jesus' resurrection as an individual event limited to Jesus only. At this point he remains faithful to the apocalyptic view which he otherwise left behind and holds that Jesus' resurrection is the beginning of the general resurrection of the dead. But he forsakes the apocalyptic view in that he no longer separates the beginning from the end, but rather, like the Corinthian enthusiasts, has the beginning and end focussed in, and coinciding with, the today of the presence of Christ. The world of the resurrection has broken into this earth with Christ and is present only within the realm of Christ's influence. There, however, the resurrection is present in such manner that the believers, too, are grasped by it and reborn. Earthly death is insignificant wherever Christ appears. The man who belongs to Christ still has this death before him and around him, just as he still must sleep. Yet this is only the appearance and the shadow of the power of death which has already been overcome. The reality of death lies behind the believer, even if, like Lazarus, he should still die. In the presence of Christ, the reality and the threat of death no longer exist. We must continually keep in mind that John does not understand this metaphorically, spiritually or as edifying oratory. John's point of departure here is not his anthropology, so that one could argue that in this case the believer's hope is proleptically anticipated. Rather, his point of departure is his christology. Its reality is seen in Christ's world-wide victory over all his enemies, as expressed in various christological hymns of the New Testament. Wherever Christ is encountered, man has come into the realm of his victory and participates in it so long as he remains in this realm as a believer. The shift in eschatology becomes apparent. Primitive Christian eschatology was prepared through the message and activity of Jesus and constituted through Easter, and in this sense the primitive eschatology was always christologically oriented. For John, however, eschatology is no longer the force that determines christology; the opposite is the case. Christology determines eschatology and eschatology becomes an aspect of christology. In Christ, the end of the world has not merely come near, but is present and remains present continually.

If this is so, then the distinction, gained from cosmology and anthropology, between realized and futurist eschatology in the Gospel of John can be maintained only with difficulty, and, in the last analysis, is no longer appropriate. This distinction no longer characterizes the centre of Johannine theology but, at most, its periphery. Therefore, time and again John's interpreters have had to note the pre-eminence of so-called realized eschatology and regard the futurist statements as last testimonies, or as relics of an older tradition which are trailing along, but are no longer an organic part of John's theology, or even to delete them as glosses. Bultmann's famous formulation[22] that Easter, Pentecost and the Parousia coincide in John is absolutely correct from the perspective of John's christology. At most, one could find fault with Bultmann's formulation because it does not recognize the complexity of the situation. His remark does not indicate that in John the earthly life of Jesus also belongs to this category. But Bultmann could never include Jesus' earthly life in it, because he interpreted the Johannine incarnation radically as an entry into a totally human life. His interpretation is oriented on the pattern of humiliation-exaltation and he sees both concepts paradoxically related to each other. But can one really avoid that pattern? Even if the career of Jesus may not be understood as a process of development and growth and even if the use of the catchword 'paradox' becomes questionable in view of the emphasis on the divinity of Jesus, one must still agree that John speaks of Jesus' glory both as present reality and future reality. Furthermore, in John the passion appears as the peculiar and proper hour of his glorification. The interpretation which dwells on the lowliness and humility of the earthly Jesus refers to this fact as its strongest support.[23] There is no real clarification of the eschatology and the christology of the Fourth Gospel so long as no precise understanding has been attained at this particular point. Consequently we return once more to our initial question and formulate the problem anew: In what relationship does Jesus' earthly life stand to his passion, and, furthermore, what is the nature and character of his passion if the resurrection and the life already appear in the earthly Jesus?

The second question receives its answer in that the comprehensive and, for John, characteristic description of Jesus' death is given with

---

[22] Bultmann, *Theologie*, p. 410 (ET II, p. 58).
[23] So especially in Thüsing, *op. cit.*, pp. 46, 48ff., 201ff., who consequently postulates two 'time-spans' of Jesus' glory. He sees the first under the sign of his death, pp. 100, 192, and the second under the sign of his 'new status', p. 207. Of necessity he thus regards the glory of the pre-existent one as problematical. Similarly Dodd, *Interpretation*, p. 208, who interprets the earthly glory under the aspect of love. Similarly W. Bauer, *Johannesevangelium*, p. 203, and Barrett, *op. cit.*, p. 418.

the verb *hypagein*, to go away. This verb includes exaltation and glorification in so far as it refers to the separation from the world and the return to the Father, which is at the same time the return to the glory of the pre-existent Logos. The aspect of his obedience is not eliminated here. On the contrary, obedience is and must be constitutive because through it his passion is connected with his earthly life. From this perspective, Jesus' death, in the Fourth Gospel as in Phil. 2.6ff., is the completion of his incarnation. But in distinction from Phil. 2.9, the exaltation in John does not appear as a divine reward for the earthly obedience rendered, and one should avoid contrasting earthly obedience with exaltation.[24] John himself uses neither the noun 'obedience' nor the verb 'to obey'. Instead he has the formula 'to do the will', which corresponds to the other formula, 'to hear the word'. We may paraphrase both with 'obedience', but it should then be clear to us that this may not be understood moralistically,[25] and above all that it has nothing to do with what we usually mean by humility.[26] Instead, both formulae express a commitment to the heavenly realm, to remaining in that truth which opposes subjection to the power and deceit of the earthly realm. If we want to call this obedience, then lowliness is expressed through it only in so far as this commitment to the heavenly realm and to the divine truth must exist on earth, seeking life with God in conflict with the earthly rebellion against God. Obedience is then the manifestation of the divine Lordship, of the divine glory, in the realm below which is alienated from God. For Christ, obedience is the attestation of his unity with the Father during his sojourn on earth. For this reason Jesus' passion must be described as a triumphal procession in John instead of a *via dolorosa*. Lowliness in John is the nature of the situation, of the earthly realm which Jesus entered. In entering it, he himself is not being humbled. He retains the glory and majesty of the Son until the cross. There once more he judges his judges as he has always done before. When he is given up by the Father, he demonstrates more clearly than ever that the earth has no power over him.[27] In summary: The glory of Jesus is not the result

---

[24] Contrary to Hoskyns, *op. cit.*, pp. 449f., 464. According to him the earthly life of Jesus is separation from the Father.

[25] Contrary to Barrett, *op. cit.*, pp. 60, 72; Thüsing, *op. cit.*, p. 239.

[26] Contrary to Barrett, *op. cit.*, p. 262.

[27] Therefore I find it impossible to agree with R. Bultmann, *Das Evangelium des Johannes* (1941), p. 377, that the glorified one is always the incarnate one, if this statement is interpreted to mean: 'The Exalted One is the lowly one and the humiliation and lowliness is not extinguished with the return to the heavenly *doxa*.'

of his obedience, so that, as in other New Testament writings, his glory could be defined from the perspective of his obedience. On the contrary, obedience is the result of Jesus' glory and the attestation of his glory in the situation of the earthly conflict.

If this is so, then the Johannine phrase 'the hour of Jesus' may not be interpreted as being nothing but a reference to his passion.[28] John 2.4; 4.21, 23; 5.25, 28 refer beyond doubt primarily to his hour of glorification, while 7.30; 8.20; 12.23, 27; 13.1; 17.1 refer primarily to his passion. But these two sets of references are not unconnected. In John 12.23; 13.1; 17.1 the hour of his passion is in a unique way the hour of the glorification of Jesus and from this viewpoint we can include all references to the hour of his passion as being allusions also to the hour of his glorification. But again this use of 'the hour' in John does not indicate that in the passion the humility of Jesus or his communion of love with the Father are most thoroughly realized,[29] nor does it indicate that, paradoxically, the exaltation begins in the deepest humiliation. John 13.1 clearly interprets the meaning of the passion. The hour of the passion and death is in a unique sense the hour of his glorification because in it Jesus leaves the world and returns to the Father.[30] Here we can see the result of our investigation thus far. John distinguishes the earthly glory of Jesus from that glorification which takes place in the passion. But this distinction is not a contrast and could not be one, because for John the earthly Jesus already personified the Resurrection and the Life. But neither is the earthly glory an anticipation of the glory bestowed on him in the exaltation;[31] at any rate, the catchword 'anticipation' does not express what is decisive in John at this point. The misunderstandings of the interpreters have their origin in an uncritical transfer of the pattern of a 'now already—not yet' eschatology to Johannine christology. One cannot, of course, object to this transfer as a working hypothesis, and historically it may even indicate the origins of John's christology, but everything depends on a correct insight into the modifications made by the Evangelist. The pattern of the 'now already—not yet' eschatology is christologically shattered by placing the glory of his pre-existence beside the glory of his earthly life and of

---

[28] Thüsing, *op. cit.*, pp. 76ff.; O. Cullmann, *Urchristentum und Gottesdienst* (1950)' p. 67 (ET *Early Christian Worship*, SBT 10 [1953], p. 66).

[29] Contrary to Dodd, *Interpretation*, pp. 208, 262; Thüsing, *op. cit.*, p. 182.

[30] In this respect, the death of Jesus does have the character of a centre of gravity, contrary to Bultmann, *Theologie*, p. 405 (ET II, p. 52).

[31] Contrary to J. Dupont, *Essais sur la Christologie de St Jean* (1951), p. 273.

his passion. More precisely, John understands the incarnation as a projection[32] of the glory of Jesus' pre-existence and the passion as a return to that glory 'which was his before the world began'. The glory of the earthly Jesus manifests itself in time and space and in a world of rebellion against God. In this respect, features of lowliness are connected with his glory. His glory is perfected through his death, since limitations cease and the realm of lowliness is left behind. This Johannine view really has nothing in common with the old futurist eschatology. The one who walks on earth as a stranger, as the messenger sent by the Father, the one who passes through death without turmoil and with jubilation, because he has been called back to the realm of freedom, has fulfilled his mission, as his last word from the cross indicates. Neither the incarnation nor the passion in John have those emphases and contents which were taken from ecclesiastical tradition. They do not mark a change in Christ according to his nature, but only a change in terms of 'coming' and 'going', of descending and ascending. Incarnation and passion indicate the change of space and thus of the scope of the manifestation of Christ. Since all his words and deeds manifest his being, always and everywhere, the one who reveals himself in them is the one who is always and everywhere one with the Father, the pre-existent Logos in his heavenly glory. If we wish to characterize this truth on the basis of the pattern of a twofold eschatology, then we may no longer regard the tension of the suffering and of the exalted Jesus as constituting the centre of that eschatology. In that case, the centre must rather be sought in the relationship of the eternal Logos to the revelation in the earthly Jesus. In John's eschatology, in so far as it is christology, the direction has been reversed, so that his eschatology no longer emphasizes the end and the future, but the beginning and the abiding. Because it is measured by the eternal, the temporal therefore has the character of the transitory. The basic problem is no longer the sense in which the crucified one is the Son of God, but rather the reason why God came into the flesh and gave himself to death. The answer to this question is given with the two words, mission and return.

We cannot register this change in perspective without raising the historical question as to the factors which made the change possible. We have already stated that John was dependent on an enthusiastic piety which affirmed a sacramentally realized resurrection of the dead in the present. To be sure, John unfolded his own proclamation

[32] I am using an expression of Dodd, *Interpretation*, p. 262.

of the resurrection not from the sacrament but from his christology. Beginnings for this perspective can be found in the primitive Christian tradition. Already prior to John, hymns that had developed within the same enthusiastic piety described Jesus as a pre-existent heavenly being whose earthly existence was but a stage of a journey to take him back to heaven. Some of these hymns supplemented the mythological picture by transferring to Jesus the attribute of the mediator of creation as found in the Jewish Sophia myth. In so doing, they gave content and weight to his pre-existence. In this way a protology, a doctrine of the first things, was placed beside the eschatology,[33] and the latter was reflected in the former. Now the presupposition had been created for the centre of gravity to shift. When the place of the apocalyptic eschatology was taken by some sort of balance between protology and eschatology, then eventually the protology could move into the centre of the Christian message. Jesus then had to become the divine mediator of creation who came near to man in the incarnation and withdrew again from him in his passion. It is exactly this view which is consistently developed in our Gospel and which is made into the dominant motif.

From this point of view, the tradition of the miracle stories is transformed. For John, too, miracles are indispensable. They are not merely concessions to human weakness.[34] If that were the case, it would have been unnecessary to heighten them to the very extreme. Nor would Jesus' passion, with deliberate intention and contrary to all traditions, have been triggered off by the miracle of the raising of Lazarus. It would also ignore the fact that the Johannine miracles in general are clearly and emphatically described in terms of demonstrations of the glory of Jesus. Human need is, to be sure, the occasion for the miracle, but the meeting of human needs is at most a subsidiary aim. God does not manifest himself on earth without the splendour of the miracles which characterize him as the Creator. It is indeed correct to point out that John attacks a craving for miracles. This is not done, however, on the basis of a criticism of miracles in general, but in the interest of his one and only theme, namely, his christology. His dominant interest which is everywhere apparent is that Christ himself may not be overshadowed by anything, not even by his gifts, miracles and works. Jesus alone is the true divine gift to

[33] Cf. H. Hegermann, *Die Vorstellung vom Schöpferungsmittler im hellenistischen Judentum und Urchristentum* (1961).
[34] Contrary to Bultmann, *Theologie*, p. 409 (ET II, p. 56).

which all other gifts can and should only point. The isolated miracle is, from this perspective, just as illegitimate as the isolated sacrament, the Old Testament absolutized over against Christ, or the fathers and the witnesses in so far as an independent significance is ascribed to them. The presence of the miracles narrated by John cannot be explained by John's faithfulness toward the tradition. John took up that tradition freely. It was not accidental that he omitted demon exorcisms as not being illustrative enough of Jesus' glory and that he selected the most miraculous stories of the New Testament. He would hardly have done so had he wanted to use them as mere illustrations to the speeches of Jesus and thus been disinterested in the miracle itself. We must not forget that Thomas is referred to the faith which does not see, only after he has seen and touched. The intention here is to bind his faith to the word which conveys Jesus as the personified Resurrection, and not to isolated facts of salvation. At this point, interpreters generally modernize more than is permissible for the historian. No Christian at the end of the first century could have come to the idea that God could enter the human scene without miracles, or that the rebirth should be the sole miracle which is appropriate to him. The Johannine criticism of miracles begins and ends where Jesus himself is sought or forgotten for the sake of his gifts. On the other hand his glory cannot be without miracles and the greater and the more impressive they are the better. For his community confesses: 'From his fulness have all received grace upon grace.' There is no reductionism about the miracles in the Fourth Gospel!

Like the miracles, John's discourses are composed on his christological theme, which is also their centre and to a large extent their only content. Certainly the Evangelist collected the christological titles in order to present through them the different aspects of the universal significance of Jesus. But just as certainly they are all brought in line with the Johannine declaration of the unity of the Son with the Father. The possibility of misunderstanding this declaration is clearly brought out when the Jews regard it as blasphemy and when even the disciples are unable truly to understand, right up to the end. But the misunderstanding does not only cling to the declaration as such. It is misunderstood and ambiguous, like the miracles, because here, as in the miracles, the stranger from the world above reveals himself, while the world below continuously seeks to capture him in the net of its own categories and experiences. Regardless of how many features of the Hellenistic miracle-worker were transferred to the

Johannine Christ, he is still not a Son of God as that age understood it. For in that case he would have sought his own glory, and his unity with the Father would then have dissolved. Consequently, it is not his intention as a heavenly being to gain acceptance into the company of the great founders of religions who have come in their own name. For only as God's revealer does he remain one with the Father. Through him God is glorified, because only through him does it become clear who God is, namely, our Creator. His unity with the Father has a soteriological function. Only the one who is sent can reveal the one who has sent him. Only in the Son does the Father show himself as acting and speaking. Christ is the only 'exegete' of him whom no one else has ever seen. We shall have to ask later what that means concretely. Now we must recognize not only the exclusiveness of these declarations but also John's willingness to employ mythological language to express that exclusiveness. Once again, all attempts at modernization at this point grasp John's message only inadequately.[35] While the insight that the unity with the Father has soteriological functions is correct, it is insufficient to state merely that. The soteriological function remains the spearhead of the kerygma, but it now receives a tremendous new depth. With the christological mystery is connected what later times called the mystery within the Trinity. If this is true, however, then the mythology used in the Fourth Gospel, in distinction from the other New Testament writings, no longer merely has the purpose of proclaiming the world-wide and saving-historical dimension of the christological event. The Johannine mythology is at the same time an expression of the beginning of dogmatic reflection in the strictest possible sense and thus opens the door for patristic christology.[36] The problem of the nature of Christ is discussed thematically in John, to be sure still within the frame of his soteriology, but now with an emphasis and a force which can no longer be explained on the basis of a purely soteriological interest. The internal divine relationship of the revealer as the Son is just as strongly emphasized as his relation to the world.[37]

[35] This even includes Dupont, *Essais*, pp. 231, 267ff., 287f., who plays off mission against nature; Bultmann, *Theologie*, p. 414 (ET II, p. 62), who takes offence at the mythological notion of pre-existence; also all interpretations of the unity between Father and Son in terms of love.

[36] The embarrassment of the modern exegete is illustrated in T. W. Manson, *op. cit.*, who on p. 131 speaks of 'a dogmatic reconstruction cast into the form of history', whereas on p. 134 he states that, nevertheless, John stands closer to Paul than to Nicaea. Such triviality means nothing, even if Nicaea is relevant at all.

[37] Contrary to T. W. Manson, *op. cit.*, p. 135; Dupont, *op. cit.*, pp. 287f.

In this way, the exclusiveness of Jesus as the revealer receives its foundation and its safeguard.

The dogmatic emphasis of John is reflected even in the style of his discourses. In distinction from the Synoptics, the Johannine discourses are not collections of originally separate sayings, but rather lengthy monologues, which, under various aspects, revolve time and again around the same centre of the divine mission and nature of Jesus. Dogmatic reflection is their cause, meditation their form, definition their peculiar and outstanding feature. Movement enters into them almost exclusively through polemic, and the polemic is expressed through the literary device of absurd misunderstandings. Only in Paul do we find the same passionate theological discussion. But while the actual life of the Pauline communities evoked the problems with which Paul dealt, the discourses of John show the reverse. In John, a theological complex of dogma is forced upon the everyday life of the community with unmistakable harshness. A dogmatic controversy is taking place.[38] This controversy is directed against Judaism, as one would expect if the controversy is to be carried on by the earthly Jesus. At the end of the first century, there was ample reason for it, not only in Syria. On the other hand, we may not forget that in the Fourth Gospel the Jews are the representatives of the world as it is comprised by its religious traditions. The controversy with the Jews as the representatives of the world, therefore, has an exemplary significance for a larger, more extensive religious realm. At least we shall have to be more careful than in the past in evaluating the possibility that a struggle within the Church is reflected and hidden in these debates with the Jews. Such evaluation is all the more meaningful and mandatory if the origin of the Fourth Gospel in such circles of Hellenistic enthusiasm as are opposed both by I Cor. 15 and II Tim. 2.18 should prove to be correct. This does not mean that our Gospel had to be written against representatives of a different christology. It could well be that John was endeavouring to combat a development in the Church which in his opinion did not take christology sufficiently into account. If so, the controversy dealt with the slogan *solus Christus*, Christ alone. We cannot yet answer that question, but we shall take it up later in a different context.

If the unity of the Son with the Father is the central theme of the Johannine proclamation, then that unity is of necessity also the proper

---

[38] Wellhausen, *op. cit.*, p. 53, and Wetter, *op. cit.*, pp. 96, 169f., were already correct here.

object of faith. Nowhere else in the New Testament is faith described with such force, repetition, and dogmatic rigidity. Faith means one thing only; to know who Jesus is.[39] This knowing is not merely theoretical, for it verifies itself only in remaining with Jesus. Nor does it take place in one single act of perception from which everything else would automatically follow. It means discipleship, following on that way which is Jesus himself, following through a hostile world. In this pilgrimage it is necessary time and again for Jesus to come to us, promising, calling to remembrance, teaching, warning and comforting, and it is necessary for us time and again to recognize and acknowledge him anew. Such a description of the *fides qua creditur* should not, however, prompt us to try to define the confession of faith exclusively on the basis of the situation of decision. Neither our experience nor our decision determine who Jesus is. This is always established already for us as the *fides quae creditur*, as dogma, and therefore it can be formulated in a manner which transcends the situation of personal decision. John does not present us with a model of a Christianity without dogma. John's peculiarity is that he knows only one single dogma, the christological dogma of the unity of Jesus with the Father. Therefore one should not play off the kerygma against the dogma.[40] John neither proclaims the veneration of a new god, nor does he demand mere assent to the Church's dogma, even though God's revelation may have hitherto been hidden and Christian faith may be formulated in doctrinal statements. The reason why the individual believer is not in danger of losing himself to a philosophical world-view or a religious tradition or a Church dogmatics lies in the fact that his salvation is based on Jesus alone. Precisely for this reason, it may not be left to the individual to determine who Jesus is, otherwise world-views, religious traditions, and the ever-changing Church dogmatics would be at their most dangerous. Faith does not limit itself to theology and theology cannot guarantee faith, much less be a substitute for it. Without theology, however, faith cannot be kept alive and proclamation cannot rightly be made. All theology, even if it does not want to admit it, deals with dogma, because theology must remain related to the Jesus who was prior to our faith, and theology has to formulate who this Jesus was and is.

John did that in his own manner. In so doing he exposed himself

[39] Barrett, *op. cit.*, p. 58; Brown, *op. cit.*, p. LXXVIII; and earlier F. C. Baur, *op. cit.*, p. 183.
[40] Contrary to Bultmann, *Evangelium*, pp. 213, 298, 412.

to dangers which are an element of life and also of theology. One can hardly fail to recognize the danger of his christology of glory, namely, the danger of docetism.[41] It is present in a still naïve, unreflected form and it has not yet been recognized by the Evangelist or his community. The following Christian generations were thoroughly enchanted with John's christology of glory. Consequently the question 'Who is Jesus?' remained alive among them. But those generations also experienced the difficulties of this christology of glory and had to unfold and deepen its problems and, in so doing, had to decide for or against docetism. We, too, have to give an answer to the question of the centre of the Christian message. From John we must leran that this is the question of the right christology, and we have to recognize that he was able to give an answer only in the form of a naïve docetism. Thus we ourselves are forced to engage in dogmatics. An undogmatic faith is, at the very least, a decision against the Fourth Gospel.

[41] F. C. Baur, *op. cit.*, pp. 233, 286, 291, 373; Wellhausen, *op. cit.*, p. 113; Overbeck, *op. cit.*, pp. 30, 344, 364f.; Hirsch, *op. cit.*, pp. 8of. The assertion, quite generally accepted today, that the Fourth Gospel is anti-docetic is completely unproven.

IIII

THE COMMUNITY UNDER THE WORD

O NE OF THE many surprising features of the Fourth Gospel
and perhaps the most surprising of all is that it does not seem
to develop an explicit ecclesiology. By formulating the problem in this way, I am already indicating that I cannot conceive
that Christian proclamation, including proclamation in the form of
a Gospel in which christology is central, could be without ecclesiology. However, John does not unfold the kind of ecclesiology which
the historian would expect to find in a representative of the Christian
Church at the end of the first century. We cannot fail to see that even
Luke made the epoch of the Church the centre of history and that
Ephesians gave an impressive theological basis to this concept. Can
John's proclamation neglect a theology of the Church when it so
strongly emphasizes the glory of Jesus as a result of its orientation on
the exalted Lord? Can it neglect a theology of the Church when it
represses the apocalyptic hope as a result of being part of the trend
towards early catholicism? It would be wrong to object that we
should not expect a doctrine of the Church in a narrative of the
earthly history of Jesus, since such a doctrine could only be introduced with difficulty. For after all, John changes the Galilean
teacher into the God who goes about on earth;[1] would he not also
be capable of picturing the circle of disciples from the perspective
of the later church organization, as was done in part even by the
Synoptic writers? Apparently the Fourth Gospel does not share in
this development. Even the basic elements of congregational life,
worship, the sacraments and ministry, play such insignificant roles
that time and again John's interest in them has been doubted. Just

[1] Thus J. Grill, *Untersuchungen über die Entstehung des vierten Evangeliums* I (1902),
p. 36; W. Heitmüller, *Das Johannesevangelium* (Die Schriften des Neuen Testaments
IV, ³1918), pp. 11, 27.

as the concept 'Church' is absent, so are the titles of honour such as
the 'family' or the 'people of God', the 'heavenly building' or the
'Body of Christ'. Correspondingly, the disciples seem to come into
focus only as individuals,[2] and all the titles of honour which we miss
with reference to the church organization are applied to them as
individuals. They are the friends of Jesus, the beloved of God, the elect,
those who are sanctified through the Word. They belong to the
realm of truth, of light and life, in short, they belong to heaven. The
same idea is present in Ephesians, which also set the Christian community in the heavenly sphere. All these observations have often
been made already. Therefore it is all the more surprising that here,
too, interpreters of the Gospel are usually satisfied to make the
observations without dealing with the historical and theological
problems inherent in them. Alternatively, they are more interested
in harmonizing and striking a balance with the customary primitive
Christian views than in analysing the 'concrete, the individual, the
peculiar' features as F. C. Baur[3] so urgently demanded. Historical
criticism has become a gadget for anyone to use. It no longer testifies
to the passion and the intellectual horizon of the historian for whom
tradition as such has become questionable, but now shows that texts
can be manipulated by the specialists. Therefore, before dealing with
our theme, we must be aware of and resist efforts of apologetics which
endeavour to level off and gloss over the peculiar and the unique.

In the Fourth Gospel, too, Peter is regarded as the representative
of the historical circle of disciples. John 20.6ff. still contains a slight
indication that Peter's position is connected with the tradition that he
was the first witness of the resurrection. Odd as it may seem, this
connection is not brought out in a manner corresponding to the importance of the tradition. On the contrary, the resurrection stories in
John tell of Mary Magdalene, of all the disciples and of Thomas, but
are silent about Peter. Can this really be unintentional, especially
when we remember the events of 20.4ff.? It is not Peter, but the
other disciple (who is probably meant to be the Beloved Disciple),
who reached the tomb first, and yet it is Peter who first enters it. Is
the purpose of this last comment to strike a balance with the historical

[2] D. Faulhaber, *Das Johannesevangelium und die Kirche* (1935), pp. 51, 58f., 65;
E. Schweizer, 'Der Kirchenbegriff im Evangelium und den Briefen des Johannes',
Studia Evangelica (1959), p. 371 [also in *Neotestamentica* (1963), p. 254] (ET in *New
Testament Essays: Studies in Memory of T. W. Manson*, ed. A. J. B. Higgins [1959],
pp. 230ff.); Bultmann, *Theologie*, p. 444 (ET II, pp. 91f.).
[3] Baur, *op. cit.*, p. 75.

tradition? If so, the introduction of the Beloved Disciple means that here, too, the Petrine tradition is placed in the shadow of the Beloved Disciple. Whatever may be the significance of the Beloved Disciple elsewhere, it is obvious that he obscures the significance for the Church of the Prince of the Apostles.[4] Peter no longer towers above the other disciples, as is shown in exemplary fashion in 20.21. There all disciples receive in like manner the commission, the Holy Spirit and the authority to forgive or retain sins. The Johannine community has and acknowledges an office effected by the Spirit and endowed with specific authority. The commission given by Jesus leads not only into the world but also into the community, to its service, and even to its discipline. Our Gospel presupposes an organized communal life, and with the absolution it also takes for granted the institution of an office through the risen Lord. However, this office is not reserved for Peter, nor for the circle of apostles—the word apostle in its technical sense does not even occur in John—and therefore does not have to be transmitted through delegation by the apostles, as in the Pastorals. Interpretations of John 20.21 have often read the closed circle of 'the twelve' into the text.[5] John, however, speaks of the disciples. It is typical of his Gospel that it introduces new figures like Philip, Nathaniel, Nicodemus, Lazarus, Thomas, and—what is especially significant—women, like the Samaritan woman, Mary and Martha, and Mary Magdalene. These new figures press into the foreground and enlarge the circle of apostles. That is to say, they eliminate the theological significance of the apostles as a unique group. The memory of the historical past is not eradicated, but it is weakened into a typical pattern. The disciples who receive commission, Spirit and authority from the risen Christ are simply the representatives of the Christian community. In this community, each one is commissioned by being called to discipleship as narrated in John 1.41ff. and confirmed in 17.18ff. Unmistakably, John represents a Christianity in which ministerial functions are not yet connected with privileges. As in Paul, so here, the priesthood of all believers[6] is maintained, which is rather surprising at the end of

---

[4] Cf. A. Kragerud, *Der Lieblingsjünger im Johannesevangelium* (1959), pp. 53ff., 68ff.

[5] Barrett, *op. cit.*, pp. 79ff.; F. Mussner, 'Die johanneischen Parakletsprüche und die apostolische Tradition', *Biblische Zeitschrift*, 5 (1961), pp. 76f.; R. Schnackenburg, *Die Kirche im Neuen Testament* (1961), p. 30 (ET *The Church in the New Testament* [1965], p. 31).

[6] E. Hirsch, *op. cit.*, pp. 114, 346, 451; E. Schweizer, *op. cit.*, p. 373 (ET, pp. 237ff.).

the first century.[7] For John this doctrine is even more self-evident than for Paul, whose doctrine of differentiated charismata clearly indicates that the apostle was quite familiar with the problems contained in such a view. When John 3.34 engages in polemics against the Jewish arguments that the Spirit is always received only 'by measure', we have a clear indication that he is not at all interested in a differentiation of the gifts of the Spirit as the basis of a church order. There is no other writing in the whole New Testament of which this can be said. Was there ever a time when the Church was not troubled by questions of its order? In post-apostolic times, the problem of the Church's order moves into the foreground everywhere. Where is the situation, the locale, in which, at the end of the first century, one can be untouched by a problem like that? In view of this difficulty, it is understandable that the authority of the apostles is read into this Gospel, too. At any rate, this is more comprehensible than ignoring the difficulty altogether and locating the Johannine community, like a phantom, between heaven and earth. No church can be that invisible, not even the one from which the theological notion of the invisible Church may be deduced. If the apostles are honoured only as the first disciples retained in the memory of the historical past, then it must be possible to find a different kind of community structure which would agree with that outlook, a structure which would explain the seemingly anachronistic disinterest in forms of ecclesiastical organization. And indeed John does give us an indication, when again in an astonishing and to some degree anachronistic fashion he persistently calls the Christians 'disciples' and in so doing takes up the earliest Christian self-designation and employs it as a substitute for all ecclesiological titles. The expression 'the disciples' is, to be sure, part of the tradition. Its stereotyped use, however, makes it clear that the expression is taken up thoughtfully and deliberately and that it is meant to characterize the nature of the Johannine community at its very core. The verbs connected with this expression demonstrate that the aspects of hearing, learning, serving and following after are contained in it. In short, it really refers to 'the pupil'. Therefore, Jesus himself can be designated teacher, even though this designation falls short of the ideas contained in the title 'Son of God' in the Gospel. The self-understanding of the Johannine community inevitably produces far-reaching consequences. On the basis of this self-understanding in terms of 'the disciples', it becomes

[7] Kragerud, *op. cit.*, p. 64.

evident that the community is viewed primarily not from the aspect of its corporateness, but rather from the aspect of its individual members, while the general trend of later times is to incorporate the individual into the realm of the Church by organizational, sacramental and cultic means. The disciples are addressed from a peculiar esoteric aspect as 'friends'[8] in John 15.14f., and III John 15 shows that this address is used as the most intimate self-designation of the 'brethren' among themselves. If all are disciples, brothers, and friends of Jesus, then differentiations among them can no longer be decisive. The relationship to the Lord determines the whole picture of the Johannine Church to such an extent that the differences between individuals recede, and even the apostles represent only the historical beginnings of the community. Perhaps the most interesting feature in this connection is the role in the Gospel of John of women who are presented quite emphatically, like Mary Magdalene, as witnesses of the Easter event, or, like the Samaritan woman, as servants in the ministry of the proclamation of the Word. Paul had already expressed his veto against active participation of women in the worship of the community in I Cor. 14.34ff., even though women were used by him and in the succeeding periods for ministering to various needs and probably also for mission work within the women's quarter. But only heretical circles in the later strata of the New Testament entrusted the public proclamation or even the leadership within the community to women. The candour and frankness with which John in this instance swims against the stream characterizes his historical position.[9] Again we recognize him standing in the enthusiastic tradition, whose slogan and battle-cry is: 'There is neither male nor female.' In Corinth the most daring consequences had already been drawn from this slogan and as a result the later Church, which claimed the apostles as its foundation, retreated from any notion of Spirit-effected emancipation of women while, on the other hand, the heretics continued the older tradition.

If we review our investigation thus far from this aspect, our individual observations can be assembled into a picture. The community which knows itself to be governed by the Spirit can let the apostolate, the ministry and its organization melt into the background and

[8] Gaugler, *op. cit.*, p. 29, correctly called attention to the fact that in later times only mystical circles used this predication to indicate that personal fellowship with Christ determines them. It is no less significant that the 'friends' understand themselves as free men. Cf. Bultmann, *Evangelium*, p. 418.

[9] Hirsch, *op. cit.*, p. 305.

understand itself in the manner of a conventicle which is constituted through its individual members and which designates itself as the circle of friends and brothers. This community may take up and use the oldest self-designations and traditions of primitive Christianity, traditions which at the end of the first century appear outdated and obsolete, and thus come into conflict with developing early Catholicism. In short, John stands within an area of tensions in the Church.

His situation is also expressed in his understanding of cultic matters, especially the sacraments. The spirited controversy about John's relationship to the sacraments may perhaps at this moment have exhausted the argumentation on the basis of detailed exegetical analysis. It appears highly unlikely that the most extreme positions will permanently prevail.[10] Worship and sacraments do not play a dominant role in our Gospel.[11] On the other hand, however, there is no reason to assign all references to the sacraments to a redactor.[12] To be sure, the presence of redactional work in John may be demonstrated from chapter 21 and can hardly be denied for texts such as 6.51b–58. Yet undoubtedly the Evangelist not only knew of Jesus' baptism, but also presupposed the practice of Christian baptism and of the Lord's Supper in his community. If there are allusions to the sacraments in John 3.3ff.; 6.32ff. and in other texts, they are hardly surprising at the end of the first century. On the contrary, one would expect to find a multitude of sacramental allusions in a Christian document of that time. But it is not proper to read our expectations into the text of John, so long as a non-sacramental interpretation is possible. We gain nothing if we indulge in eisegesis, but only magnify the Johannine enigma at this very point. We must ask: Why does the same John who, as we are told, continuously indulges in sacramental allusions, and who, as we are ready to admit, did indeed presuppose the practice of the sacraments in the Christian community, nevertheless not narrate the institution of the sacraments? Why does he substitute the narrative of the foot-washing for the words of institution

---

[10] Compare H. Köster, 'Geschichte und Kultus im Johannesevangelium und bei Ignatius von Antiochien', *ZThK* 54 (1957), pp. 56–69 (ET 'History and Cult in the Gospel of John and in Ignatius of Antioch', *JThC* [1965], pp. 111–23); E. Lohse, 'Wort und Sakrament im Johannesevangelium', *NTS* 7 (1960), pp. 110–25.

[11] Contrary to Cullmann, *op. cit.*, p. 38 (ET, p. 37); W. Wilckens, *Die Entstehungsgeschichte des vierten Evangeliums* (1958); also Barrett, *op. cit.*, p. 69.

[12] Contrary to Bultmann.

of the Lord's Supper? Apparently this did not happen by accident, but rather by design. The *disciplina arcani*,[13] the endeavour to protect the sacredness of the Eucharist and eucharistic words from profanation would indeed explain the absence of the words of institution in John. However, it cannot be proven that this discipline already existed at that time.[14] Above all, those secrets in which John himself is truly interested are unfolded in wide-ranging monologues in the form of the secret discourse. Apart from 6.51b–58, there are no such monologues about baptism and the Lord's Supper. The theme of 3.3ff.; 6.32ff.; 15.1ff. is not the sacrament as such. On the other hand, we find in John many rather primitively constructed narratives which serve the Evangelist as points of departure for his own thoughts. Important features of primitive Christian faith and life and central contents of the primitive Christian proclamation are silently passed by in John, as a comparison with the Synoptic Gospels and with Paul reveals. This implies that the peculiar relationship of our Gospel to the sacraments and the cult may not be investigated and determined in isolation. It is rather a characteristic aspect within the total context of John's relationship to the earlier tradition. Simple and extreme solutions do not do justice to the problem of the use of tradition in John, which is quite complicated and should be approached dialectically. The exegetical controversy about the meaning of particular details, verses and sections cannot come to an end so long as the exegete endeavours to overcome the dialectics inherent in John by emphasizing either one or the other side of this Gospel.

The debate really centres upon John's conception of history, within the context of his doctrine of the incarnation. This is recognized by almost everyone, since everyone brings the problems of the Church, the ministry, the sacraments and tradition in John more or less clearly into relation with his doctrine of the incarnation, so that these problems are answered on this basis. Unfortunately most interpreters usually do not sufficiently consider the consequences of this kind of approach. For if the incarnation is really the pivotal point of all the problems under consideration here, then at this point, too, the primacy of christology has come to the fore, that christology which is the unmistakable feature of John's theology. Christology and history cannot simply be co-ordinated in this Gospel as though they were

[13] So J. Jeremias, *Die Abendmahlsworte Jesu*, 3rd ed. (1960), pp. 119ff. (ET *The Eucharistic Words of Jesus* [1966], pp. 125ff.).

[14] Lohse, *op. cit.*, p. 122.

more or less independent entities which can be brought together, placed side by side or separated. Still more important, christology may not be injected into history as though it were an eschatological novelty and history could be known without it. Incarnation is not merely a miraculous event within history. Incarnation rather means, as the prologue unmistakably indicates, the encounter of the Creator with his creature. This, however, implies that history and the world must be understood in this light and from this perspective. Without it, they cannot be understood at all. It is exactly this idea that is demonstrated by John on every single page of his Gospel. However, if this is so, then we pose the wrong questions when we investigate the significance of history in John without taking this aspect into consideration, or when we carry our historicist, existentialist or 'saving-historical' notions and conceptions into the Gospel. Of course, we cannot stop others from doing that, and, as a point of departure, even the raising of false questions may be fruitful. It should, however, be recognized that the premises in this case contain the problem and that the results at best reveal only part of the dialectical truth, and cannot do justice to all the Evangelist's intention. In the confrontation with the Creator, history ceases to be what we imagined it to be. John placed this idea at the very centre of his presentation and developed it with many variations. This idea is the perspective from which he composed his Gospel and therefore it is the hermeneutical key to its interpretation. This idea produced the dialectic which we must now develop in detail.

The statement 'The light shines in the darkness' does not differ basically from the statement 'The Word became flesh.'[15] The first sentence declares what becomes of the world as it encounters its Creator. This encounter reveals the world's whole past, present and future as darkness, in so far as it does not enter into and remain in the brilliant stream of light. The Gospel, therefore, describes the world as the realm of deficiencies and defects, of sickness and death, of lies, unbelief and misunderstanding, of doubts and sheer malice. This it is, perhaps more distinctly than anywhere else in its religious sphere, which in John is represented through Judaism. Because of this situation, the characteristic feature of this world cannot be a history which arranges the world's epochs and signifies its immanent path. The world has 'fathers' to which it appeals. Yet for the world, its fathers are only the projections of its own attitude into the past, just

[15] Compare Käsemann, *op. cit.*, pp. 161f.

as Christ projects this attitude metaphysically into the work and sphere of the devil. The end of the world is, therefore, always present in death, appearing in many different forms and faces. Historicity is not really an attribute of the world as such. Historicity is present where the Creator acts in and on the world. Only God, in manifesting himself, truly brings about history, just as he alone can give life.

This statement that only revelation produces history must be put more precisely. It is characteristic of John that he refers to the creation of the world only in traditional formulae, except in the prologue. He does not mention Adam's fall at all and when he deals with Old Testament figures, which happens rather seldom, he does so in a manner which leaves them without clear historical features. Like John the Baptist, they are mentioned only in their function as witnesses of Jesus. We also occasionally find traditional formulae which speak of the general resurrection of the dead as the goal of history. Yet in these instances we may be dealing with later interpolations. Finally, only the traditional miracle stories which John took up depict individual persons in vivid colours. All other figures lack individuality and distinct features, because they characterize, from a functional viewpoint, the attitude and response of the world or of the Christian community to the encountered revelation.[16] In view of these facts, to interpret John in terms of salvation history is indeed more than risky, and permissible only if this kind of salvation history is clearly distinguished from other types such as the Pauline or the Lucan salvation history.[17] Of course, one can reduce the most diverse things to their lowest common denominator, provided one harmonizes, formalizes and ignores the differences. The task of exegesis, however, demands the bringing out of different emphases and distinct profiles. The Johannine salvation history is, to be precise, in its very essence the history of the Logos who overcomes or increases the world's resistance to its Creator. The fact that this resistance and its conquest are always depicted in typical scenes is further evidence that John's whole emphasis falls upon the revelation as such. The history narrated in his Gospel happens, to be sure, on earth, that is to say within time and space, and the Logos therefore requires human opponents and human partners. Apart from the traditional material, the reality of the Logos' opponents and partners is limited to the

[16] This is shown in principle, if somewhat exaggeratedly, by A. Loisy, *Le quatrième Évangile* (1921).
[17] Cf. Cullmann's interpretation.

function of reacting. Thus they can disappear as suddenly and abruptly as they appeared. They are 'drawn' either from below or from above and they act almost like puppets in the blindness of their foolishness. The light from above, falling upon them, puts them in motion, and only in the circle of this light do they have life. Thus, the history represented here can be regarded as a process only in the most external and superficial sense. Jesus is pictured as the one who is on the way and this picture is repeated on a higher level, since his way on earth is simultaneously his way back from the earth *via* the cross to heaven. The dimension of the past is retained only in so far as it points forward to his presence; all of the future is nothing but the glorified extension and repetition of this presence. History remains the history of the Logos, since it is the sphere of his past, present and future epiphany. The sole theme of history is the *praesentia Christi*. What else may happen on earth is only scenery and props for this theme. These earthly events are in part only intimated or roughly sketched, so that some narratives recede into twilight. Dogmatic reflection determines the structure and the subdivisions within this Gospel. Consequently the place of events can time and again be Jerusalem. Many of the traditions important to the Synoptics are uninteresting to John. The cleansing of the temple can be moved to the beginning, and the miracle of Lazarus' resurrection opens the passion story. The narrative material is used to illustrate Jesus' words and to introduce the long monologues of his discourses. Compared with the reality of everyday life, all of this is quite artificial.

If we keep this in mind, then John's relationship to the tradition as a whole also becomes intelligible. An evangelist who desires to narrate Jesus' earthly history cannot, as a matter of course, dispense with traditions. More astonishing is the fact that John, living at the end of the first century and situated, it would seem, not too far from Palestine, possibly in Syria, in all probability does not know the Synoptics themselves, but rather a tradition whose purer and more original form is preserved in the Synoptics, and which is known to him in a version which has to some extent run wild. Again, this would point to a time and place in the history of primitive Christianity where the currents of the emerging early Catholic Church are not very strong. The peculiar feature of the Johannine use of tradition, however, is that he deals with what he has received more freely and more vigorously than anyone else in the New Testament. It would be false to argue that John is contemptuous of tradition, or that he engages in a basic criticism of tradition by contrasting the Spirit with tradition. If such a contrast was to have been drawn at any time in the history of primitive Christianity, then it would have had to be relatively soon after Easter, when, for instance, the circle around Stephen transgressed the Jewish cultic law for the sake of missionary work among the Gentiles, or when the Corinthian enthusiasts with their realized eschatology, based on the efficacy of the sacraments, broke up the traditional Jewish-Christian apocalyptic frame. John no longer belongs to this stage, even if certain roots of his do reach into the past. The alternative 'tradition or Spirit' is quite alien to his thought. For him, the Spirit calls the words of Jesus to mind and he himself actualizes that by writing a Gospel which in form and content has many parallels with the Synoptics. He did not despise the use of the Old Testament[18] even though he can get along without it in large sections and he always puts it into the shadow of his traditions about Jesus. He probably took over at least in part and without great modifications narratives from a source containing miracle stories, and the same is true with regard to the core of his passion and Easter accounts. With all of this, John discloses that tradition is absolutely necessary and that without tradition the Spirit becomes spiritual falsehood. Here again we recognize that it is not a matter of alternatives, but rather of shifts in emphases and perspectives. Such shifts can be seen in the fact that the voice of the Spirit is not limited to tradition and that the tradition is not, as stated in II Peter 1.12; 3.2; Jude 3, once and for all time fixed in the apostolic tradition. Jesus who comes again in the Spirit is identified through the tradition, but Jesus is more than tradition. His guidance into all truth cannot be separated from the tradition which witnesses to his work with his first disciples, but it is not exhausted by this tradition. For his work grows, and the glory of succeeding times is greater than that of the beginnings. Finally, we must take note that the tradition of the apostles is nowhere directly and unmistakably encountered as such. Wherever exegesis affirms the contrary,[19] it operates within the categories of fantasy. Just as the eleven represent the Christian community and beyond that have only historical significance, so their work and heritage is not basically differentiated from the work

---

[18] Compare N. A. Dahl, 'The Johannine Church and History', in: *Current Issues in New Testament Interpretation. Essays in Honor of O. A. Piper* (1962), pp. 124–42.

[19] A representative of this view is Mussner, *op. cit.*, pp. 66ff.

of the Samaritan woman or the work of later times, for instance in the case of the Hellenists in 12.20ff. The sole qualification of genuine tradition is that the voice of Jesus is contained in it. Tradition is not an end in itself, but the means of the witness which is legitimated neither through the name and rank of the witness-bearers, but through its content and object. If tradition has but this sole function —namely, to retain Jesus' voice, then it is at the same time limited and relativized by this function. The voice of Jesus, which is to lead the community ever anew into all truth, can never have tradition as its substitute. On the contrary, the primitive Christian tradition stands under the same motto as everything that is earthly: 'It is the Spirit which makes alive, the flesh is of no avail.' Whatever does not serve as a witness for Christ is cast away, regardless of how important it may have been historically. Even the tradition which is acknowledged is ruthlessly moved into new contexts, as the whole Gospel proves, because it is not the past which sanctions and legitimates a tradition, but rather its possible usage in the present. It is not at all sufficiently emphasized that John must be seen in the historical and theological context of a Christian prophecy whose characteristic feature, according to I Cor. 14, is the actualization of the Christian proclamation.[20] Just as this prophecy is determined by the particular situation as it teaches, admonishes, rebukes, comforts and interprets anew the tradition to its own time, so likewise John carried the Gospel with prophetic ruthlessness and one-sidedness into his present situation, using as much or as little of the tradition as suited his purpose. In John, polemic is more than merely a literary device for his speeches.[21] The prophet must discern the spirits. This also includes the repudiation of what is antiquated in order to remain faithful to the one who abides. Zinzendorf's confession also holds true for John: 'I have but one passion. That is He, and only He.' Obvious as it may appear to us, such a confession was precisely what was not self-evident in the history of Christianity. It rather marks the important exceptions, and quite frequently it points to a sectarian type of piety. While such a confession does not necessarily imply a criticism of the received tradition, it can easily lead to that. Above all, it preserves the Lord's freedom over against the ecclesiastical tradition.

We have to pause here for a moment and voice our opinion that

[20] Kragerud, op. cit., p. 114, has seen that, even though I cannot otherwise agree with his analysis.

[21] Barrett, op. cit., pp. 11f.; Mussner, op. cit., p. 64; Brown, op. cit., p. LXXVIII.

these observations indicate the historical situation in which this Gospel arose. If it more or less clearly presupposes the conditions and trends at the end of the first century, even if its own concerns and purposes do not easily accord with those conditions and trends, then the Gospel would fit best into a side tributary apart from the general stream yet connected with it. The fact that only occasional glances are cast in the direction of the Church's situation and that many points at issue run counter to it should be interpreted as polemic on the part of John. Does the key to the problem of the seeming lack of a historical context and of the other-worldly quality of this Gospel, which has puzzled all church history, actually lie in the explanation that the Fourth Gospel did not grow up within the realm of the Church known to us through the New Testament, the Church on which all John's interpreters focus their attention? Of course, no universal church organization existed at the end of the first century. The independence of the communities and the differences of their conditions and expressions can hardly be exaggerated. Yet in spite of all the differences, the independent and divergent communities were pressing toward unity and did so in various ways, with varying clarity of purpose and varying degrees of speed. Paul had already endeavoured to manifest unity. The Book of Acts and the Letter to the Ephesians draw up a theological programme for it. The formation of the New Testament canon was possible only because the Christian past was seen naïvely and perhaps even ideologically in the light of this trend toward unity. Finally, the progress in the formation of the Catholic Church is clear up to the middle of the second century. If the Fourth Gospel fits least well into this development and is first discovered by the gnostics, then the reason for this may be that John is the relic of a Christian conventicle existing on, or being pushed to, the Church's periphery. The historian at least may not discard this possibility, even though it contradicts the high esteem in which our Gospel has always been held in the history of the Church, and may cause difficulty for the theologian. Historical scholarship always has disillusioning and demythologizing results. We have seen how our assumption of John's historical position throws light upon his christology. The difficulties of his ecclesiology and the peculiar dialectical relation to tradition can also be more thoroughly understood on the basis of our assumption. The man who lives on the fringe of the prevailing development of the Church can oppose its trends and simultaneously be subjected to them, as his very reaction shows. Turning to the past, he can take up old traditions and at the same time prepare the way for new developments, provided his reaction is not sterile, but fruitful. By contradicting the present in his faithfulness toward the past, he is already contributing to the scaffolding of the future. Sectarians also participated in the formation of the early Catholic Church and they were more influential than orthodoxy was at any time willing to admit. Admission to the canon means the acknowledgment of a writing, not of the atmosphere and environment in which it grew up. The productive and the unproductive errors are likewise part of a realistically understood history of salvation under God's providence.

It would be foolish to deny that obviously John also sets out an ecclesiology. But his ecclesiology is not designed on the basis of the forms of church organizations. As a result, the institution as such is not glorified by means of that mythology which is abundantly present in John's christological thought. For John, the Church is basically and exclusively the fellowship of people who hear Jesus' word and believe in him; in short, it is the community under the Word.[22] All other ecclesiological definitions are oriented on this one and significant only in so far as they give expression to it. But this also means that the Church is viewed here with strange emphasis from the perspective of its individual members. To hear, to believe and to follow is something that only the individual himself and not his representative can and must do, even if he does it within the Christian brotherhood. Pointedly, but not exaggeratedly, we take note that John, as the first theologian, passionately rejects the principle that it is sufficient to believe with the Church and to be supported by the Church as the mother of the individual. John, therefore, could not base salvation upon the tradition as such. Tradition calls attention to Jesus, and in this respect it is indispensable. But tradition remains fundamentally misunderstood when it does not instruct one's own faith. Tradition always remains dangerous because of its tendency to pass itself off as the voice of the Good Shepherd and to drown his voice. Our relationship to Jesus cannot be moved into the historical dimension and be made dependent on our relation to the Church, even though the voice of the Good Shepherd is heard in the Church and transmitted by it. The voice of the Good Shepherd is not qualified or limited by the Church's transmission, nor does his voice receive its authority from tradition. It is his voice which qualifies, limits and empowers the

[22] Most strongly emphasized by A. Schlatter, *Der Evangelist Johannes* (1948), and R. Bultmann.

Church as the community under the Word. Thus John 4.39, certainly not without polemical intentions, denies the idea that the mere witness of faith transmitted only by men creates a sufficient relationship to Jesus.[23] The mark of true faith, according to John, is that a man has himself seen and heard Jesus and is following him. Otherwise one would still be in the situation of the Jews who hold on to the faith and the traditions of their fathers and in this very way close their hearts against Christ.

Of course, the question now arises how, after Jesus' death, it is still possible to see and hear for oneself and in this sense to be the Church. The answer is given pointedly, in that Thomas is challenged to a faith which has not seen. The answer is not really paradoxical, because Thomas had indeed seen before and the farewell discourses in 14.7ff.; 16.16ff.; and 17.24 promise the disciples that they shall also see in the future. It is therefore not the case that two stages are contrasted, the first determined by seeing, the second by not seeing. Rather, John's call to believe without having seen clearly indicates that for John the object of seeing is not the historical Jesus as we call him.[24] The promise of seeing Jesus even after his exaltation establishes that the faith of later generations is not dependent to such a degree on the Church's proclamation as assent to dogmatic propositions would have to be. True faith goes beyond the mere word of men, even though it be the word of Spirit-filled men and of the Church. Even if after Easter faith can arise only on the basis of the Church's proclamation, faith must still come to Jesus himself, just as the Samaritans had to meet him directly after the woman's proclamation. Faith is thus guarded against misunderstanding on two sides. For John, faith is neither *fides historica* nor *fides dogmatica*. But how can this be maintained, when on one hand faith has already been evoked by the historical Jesus, having him as its object and content, and when, on the other, as shown earlier, it is none other than John who determines the nature of faith dogmatically, that is, as faith in Jesus' divine Sonship, and when all post-Easter faith arises only on the basis of such dogmatically oriented proclamation? It is one of the most important tasks of Johannine interpretation to raise this problem and to answer it exactly. One can hardly affirm that recent

[23] Compare Bultmann, *Evangelium*, pp. 148f.; Hirsch, *op. cit.*, p. 153; R. Walker, 'Jüngerwort und Herrenwort', *ZNW* 57 (1966), pp. 49–54, is not convincing.

[24] Contrary to Cullmann, *op. cit.*, p. 112 (ET, p. 115); Barrett, *op. cit.*, p. 72.

interpretation has advanced very far at this point. In general, it has suppressed either the one side or the other, and thus missed the dilemma which confronts us here. Modern Johannine scholarship had to argue in one-sided fashion because it was fascinated either by the notion of the incarnation or by John's supposed spirituality and as a result interpreted the christology accordingly. Here it becomes evident that John's christology may not be interpreted on the basis of our ideas about the nature of incarnation or about his supposed spirituality, but on the contrary, incarnation and what is commonly called spirituality or mysticism must be understood in the light of his christology. His christology alone finally determines whether the problems of our Gospel have really been recognized and properly solved. Neither is the case when, as is customary, the alternative of humiliation and exaltation with its patterns becomes the interpretative key. For the Logos who is one with the Father is encountered also in the earthly Jesus, and the Church's post-Easter proclamation has but one purpose, namely the encounter with the Logos. In the encounter with the earthly Jesus and in the post-Easter proclamation, the object and content of faith remain identical, namely, the revealer who as Logos is one with the Father. The communication of historical facts legitimated through the eye-witness accounts of apostles does not profit at all as such,[25] just as the earthly Jesus himself was met with more unbelief than faith in spite of all his miracles. Likewise, the dogmatic proclamation of the Church profits nothing as such unless it opens the path to Jesus himself. Dogmatic proclamation as such could substantiate merely one religion with specific saving facts among other religions. Conversely, Jesus drew near to us on earth and he also wills to come to us on earth in the Spirit. While on earth, he already cast his message in dogmatic form as the message of his divine Sonship. Thus the Church cannot surrender the dogmatic commitment in its own proclamation, because otherwise the Church would not take up Jesus' proclamation. The encounter on earth and obligation to the dogma belong together, both before and after Easter. They belong together, in so far as both are held together by and subsumed under the concept of 'witness'. Witness in John is a strictly forensic concept, presupposing the situation of legal proceedings.[26] The earthly Jesus himself is no less 'witness' than the Spirit

[25] Contrary to Cullmann, *op. cit.*, p. 48 (ET, pp. 47f.).
[26] So already Heitmüller, *op. cit.*, p. 16; Dahl, *op. cit.*, pp. 139f.; also Bultmann, *passim.*

who speaks in and through the post-Easter Church, or the fathers of the Old Testament who testified before the incarnation and John the Baptist. It is very important to note that Jesus unceasingly opposes the idea of bearing witness merely for himself and thus seeking his own glory. But he also opposes the idea that the voices of the Baptist or of the fathers of the Old Testament are to be regarded as the final court of appeal. As witnesses they point beyond themselves. The dogmatic proclamation of the post-Easter church likewise points beyond itself. Were it not dogmatic, then it would not do justice to Jesus' claim to divine Sonship. If it did not point beyond itself, it would not lead to Jesus himself. If this is so, then the earthly Jesus as witness must also point beyond himself, to the Father. Thus the truth can never be imprisoned and objectified in any earthly object as such, not even in the earthly Jesus, whom, with the intention of objectifying, we call the historical Jesus. His dignity is to be the Logos and his claim is that by means of all Logoi one can come to the Logos himself. In the Son, but also in the message of the fathers or in the Church's tradition, the Father will and must be known. And according to 17.3, only through this knowledge can one gain eternal life.

To summarize the results thus far: the witness of the fathers, the word and work of the earthly Jesus and the dogmatic proclamation of the Church are the historical aspects of the one and unvarying revelation of the Logos who is one with the Father. These aspects each have their own peculiar function. They indicate the dimensions of the revelation in its depth reaching back to creation, in its nearness as salvation and in its world-wide scope. As historical aspects of the revelation, they are also subject to the same danger of misunderstanding, that is, that their earthly appearance blocks the access to the heavenly truth manifesting itself in them. Just as the Old Testament fathers can become the court of appeal against Christ and the Church's proclamation again and again threatens to replace Christ, so likewise the claim of the earthly Jesus based on his incarnation becomes unbelievable to some and to others the occasion for temptation by dreams of earthly materialistic salvation. Even the incarnation stands in the twilight and in conflict which is overcome only by that faith which perceives the glory of Jesus and all glory only in Jesus. The revelation of the Logos is the meaning and the criterion of the incarnation, not *vice versa*, as if the incarnation were the truth, the confines and limits of the Logos. The Logos determines the function of the incarnation just as he determines the function of the witness of the fathers and of the Church's tradition. They all serve his presence, but his presence cannot be detained in any one of them forever. For history is the sphere of revelation and the earthly reality is the shape of the epiphany of revelation, but history and the earthly reality are at the same time the realm of his pilgrimage. They do not and cannot guarantee that he remains, for they do not have power over him whom the Father has sent and who himself sends the Spirit when, where and how it pleases him. In the historical and earthly sphere of this world, his works and signs are erected, but his kingdom is not of this world. When this is understood then the Church's worship and the sacraments also receive their proper place. They also point beyond themselves. Everything depends on remaining with Jesus himself and remaining under his Word. Therefore the sacraments are oriented towards the Word and his epiphany, and are interpreted in the light of the Word. The truth of the sacraments is the lordship of the Word. Apart from this insight the sacraments are not dealt with.

The customary interpretation of John emphasizes the sacraments and their significance for the Fourth Gospel, because the incarnation is understood in the light of the sacrament. The incarnation is then interpreted within the context of the so-called anti-docetic realism of this Gospel.[27] However, the Johannine trend runs in the very opposite direction. Just as John does not regard the Church as the institution of salvation, so he does not give a picture of the so-called historical Jesus. Not even the Synoptics had given one, though historicizing tendencies can be shown to be present in them. Apart from material which was transmitted to John by his tradition, namely the traditional miracle stories and the passion tradition, John's supposed realism can be based only on the statement in 1.14a, as is usually unhesitatingly done by the customary interpretation. The fact that incarnation does not have to mean kenosis (Phil. 2.7), total entering into our humanity, is rarely even considered, and, if so, generally rejected. It then appears insignificant that the Johannine Christ says to his mother, 'Woman, what have I to do with you?', that he confronts all his disciples and all his opponents as the incomparable and unique one. It also appears insignificant, or else it is overlooked, that John understands the sacraments as a possible encounter with the Logos and thus robs them of the kind of 'sacramental'

---

[27] Cullmann, *op. cit.*, pp. 38f., 56f., 112 (ET, pp. 37f., 55f., 115); Hoskyns, *op. cit.*, pp. 17f.; Barrett, *op. cit.*, p. 69; Wilckens, *op. cit.*, pp. 24, 91; quite carefully on the other hand, Brown, *op. cit.*, pp. LXXVIf., CXIff.

quality usually associated with them. Historical realism, in the period after the Enlightenment, has become one of the last bastions of Christianity, which now uses slogans that were originally hostile to Christianity and which understands the incarnation in a modern sense, that is, historically. Of course, John maintains that the encounter with the revealer took place in the earthly sphere and is still taking place there. Otherwise the encounter would become a religious dream and an illusion. But this does not mean that the revealer himself gives up his divinity and becomes as earthly as we are. Judged by the modern concept of reality, our Gospel is more fantastic than any other writing of the New Testament. We render poor service to John, and we can hardly deceive true realists, if we attach the label 'anti-docetic' to John, to guarantee the 'once and for all historical event'.[28] Over against this the opposite slogans 'spiritualistic' and 'mystical' at least had heuristic significance, even though by themselves they are unusable and misleading. We take note that even in his ecclesiology John's naïve docetism which is not thought through nor elevated into dogma and which we had affirmed for his christology is continued.[29] It is for this very reason that neither the incarnation nor tradition, the historical past nor the sacraments possess the significance which modern interpreters assign to them and which we would expect them to exert at the end of the first century. For this reason, the Church is not yet regarded as the institution of salvation and history is viewed only as the place of the inbreaking of the Creator, not the realm in which he can become objectified and limited.

If the two magical formulae, 'historical realism' and 'mystical spiritualism', both fail in the same way, then we are left with that category which is already offered in the prologue, that is, the category of the Word. It is exclusively this category which dominates John's ecclesiology, thus expressing most succinctly that his ecclesiology is unfolded without any qualifications from his christology as the point of departure, namely from the Logos. As the Church is the community under the Word and as all characteristic features of the Church are related to the Word, so likewise the Spirit is related to the Word. In John, the Spirit is nothing else but the continual possibility and reality of the new encounter with Jesus in the post-Easter

[28] Contrary to Köster, *op. cit.*, p. 69 (ET, p. 123).
[29] Our argumentation thus far has not yet conclusively proved this point, as the analysis of Christ's relationship to the world and of the heavenly union will show. But at this earlier point I would like to prepare the way for my later thesis.

situation as the one who is revealing his Word to his own and through them to the world. For the first time in Christian history, the Spirit is bound exclusively to and dependent on the Word of Jesus. Paul had already moved in that direction when he no longer interpreted the Spirit primarily in terms of a miracle-producing and ecstasy-evoking supernatural power. For Paul, the exalted Christ is manifest on earth in the proclamation and this manifestation is mediated by the Spirit. Therefore, antithetically, Paul can argue in I Cor. 12.2 that the idolaters were moved by dumb spirits. But the final step was not taken by Paul. For him, the Word remains the means and effect of the Spirit, but the Spirit itself remains the heavenly power manifesting itself also in miracles and ecstasies. John, however, identified the Spirit with the voice of Jesus which in the form of the Paraclete continues to speak from heaven to the disciples when he himself is no longer with them. Only in his Word is the heavenly Christ still accessible, just as the power of the resurrection and therefore the Spirit bring the Gospel ever anew into the community. The watchword of the earthly Jesus was: 'Abide with me, that is, in my Word', and this continues to be the sole watchword for the Christian and for Christianity after Jesus' death. Discipleship means to remain with him. Since time, space and life incessantly change, therefore discipleship is possible only when the prophetic Word is heard ever anew. Abiding with Jesus is possible only in the pilgrimage on that way which is Jesus himself. The same subject, the prophetic Word, is stated in II Peter 1.19, but there it deals with the prophecy which is enclosed in the Bible, proclaimed by prophets, and interpreted by the Church as the final court of doctrinal decisions. The difference from John is self-evident. In radical reduction John made Jesus and his witness into the sole content and criterion of the true tradition of the Spirit. In so doing he retained the living voice of prophecy at a time when otherwise it had already receded or disappeared, a time when the sound doctrine of a developing orthodoxy and the edifying historicizing report became important. For John, Jesus himself is the continuity of the Christian community in all ages, whose other qualities must be judged from there. In John salvation history is Jesus' history, communicated and sustained by the Word which unites all generations. It is not its tradition as such, not even its love toward Jesus and certainly not its organization which unites the Church, but the Word of Jesus alone, his electing, sanctifying and uniting Word. Therefore hearing, listening, is the outstanding feature

of this community and no other criterion may replace it or over-
shadow it. Those who hear Jesus' Word and follow him, the disciples,
are the beloved, the friends, the elect. Only the Word which is heard
can save and preserve. The confirmation of this interpretation lies in
John's viewpoint of the world as the antagonist of the Church. The
world, for John, is that which desires miracles but closes its ears to the
Word of Jesus. Faith and sin, salvation and condemnation, part
company on Jesus' Word and are also determined by Jesus' Word.
Perhaps for this reason the Jews are regarded as the representatives
of the world. They have not only been the opponents of the earthly
Jesus, as a later Gentile Christian point of view would argue, fore-
shortening and schematizing historical facts at this point also. For
John, the Jews are also the representatives of the religious tradition,
so that the problem of hearing—of being unwilling to hear and
unable to hear—could best be exemplified in them.

This, however, raises an important and difficult problem. Everything said thus far remains meaningless if this Word of Jesus is without definite content. There would be sheer anarchy if Jesus' Word
were controlled only by the prophetic Spirit and the particular
historical situation. The earliest communities soon came to know
that the prophets rarely agree when left to themselves. And, in
general, the ever-changing historical situations are not so unambi-
guous that the commandment to love God and one's neighbour would
suffice, even apart from the consideration that this 'great commandment' itself does not have to be understood within a Christian context. The apocalyptic visionaries are not the only ones who have to
ask, 'What does the Spirit say to the churches?' Does not this
Gospel, too, leave us completely in the lurch?

At first glance it certainly appears that John teaches nothing
'specific or concrete',[30] no particular doctrine.[31] Johannine interpretation has tried to solve this in various ways. Some scholars have
even gone so far as to dissolve the 'word-character' of the Johannine
Logos and to substitute a particular content[32] or else, in opposition to

[30] Bultmann, *Theologie*, p. 414 (ET II, p. 62).
[31] Bultmann, *Theologie*, p. 415 (ET II, p. 63). Bultmann, *Evangelium*, p. 42;
Hirsch, *op. cit.*, p. 269.
[32] Dodd, *Interpretation*, p. 330, speaks of God's self-disclosure in the broadest
possible sense, even in the silent operation within the mind of man; Hirsch, *op.
cit.*, p. 269, speaks of the power of love which . . . changes heart and conscience;
Gaugler, *op. cit.*, pp. 185f., speaks of mystical, and Cullmann, *op. cit.*, p. 109
(ET, p. 113), of eucharistic communion.

this kind of solution, they have simply emphasized the actual utterance of the word as being of sole importance.[33] In Bultmann's formulation the 'that', the fact that there is a word spoken, has displaced the 'what', the content of the word.[34] This alternative is the means by which Bultmann interprets the peculiar phenomenon, that the Johannine Christ always and everywhere proclaims only himself as the divine revealer. At least modern Protestantism is no longer willing to understand the assertions of the Johannine Christ about himself in terms of dogmatic statements, say, within the context of the doctrine of the Trinity. Therefore, Protestants must necessarily make his assertions about himself into an abbreviation, a cipher, of the divine reality and love revealing itself there, or of the encounter with the divine claim taking place ever anew in Christian preaching. In the first case, the Johannine mythology can be understood as the symbolic expression of a metaphysical truth; in the second case, the Johannine mythology is regarded as an ancient form which is meant to express the fact that the demand for decisions is inherent in the divine call which results in life or death.[35] It follows that in the first case faith is described in experiential categories as 'turning toward the *eschaton* through faithful believing'[36] or as a form of vision,[37] while in the second, faith is described from the existentialist viewpoint in formal categories as the ever-new 'overcoming of the offence'.[38] The dilemma of an interpretation which moves in extreme alternatives should already prompt us to ask whether modern premises and assumptions have not been read into the text. Does the Johannine mythology really have only a symbolic significance, so that it indicates either a particular idea of God and a particular understanding of the world resulting from that idea or the importance of the situation of decision? Is this sort of demythologizing really conceivable anywhere in primitive Christianity of the first century? If we answer in the negative, then evidently we have no other possibility except to give up the modern premises, that John or his tradition were incapable of saying what they really wanted to say, or that the Johannine mythology was not meant to be taken literally by them, or that it could not be an early form of dogmatic statements.

[33] Bultmann, *Evangelium*, p. 432; *Theologie*, p. 416 (ET II, p. 63).
[34] Bultmann, *Theologie*, pp. 419f. (ET II, pp. 66f.).
[35] Bultmann, *Theologie*, pp. 414f. (ET II, p. 62).
[36] Faulhaber, *op. cit.*, p. 32.
[37] Dodd, *Interpretation*, p. 186.
[38] Bultmann, *Theologie*, pp. 421ff., 428f. (ET II, pp. 68ff., 75f.)

The christological witness of the Fourth Gospel is meant and formulated in a thoroughly dogmatic manner. The witness of the glory of Jesus, of his unity with the Father, in short, the witness of his divinity, is really the content of the Johannine message. The communication of content and the direct address are inseparable in John as they are in the Synoptics.

But can this observation help us any further? This kind of dogmatic declaration about Jesus' divinity can be continuously repeated and paraphrased with synonyms as is also done in John. But can such a declaration also be unfolded prophetically, can it be actualized in the ever-changing situations through admonition, judgment, comfort and teaching? In short, can such dogmatic declaration be used as *kerygma*? A Protestantism which has ceased to be oriented to dogma will have to ask questions such as these. The alternatives in modern Johannine interpretation did not arise by accident, but resulted from the attempt at translation which produced the two most extreme possibilities. Is there a middle-of-the-road approach which the Gospel itself indicates? We shall have to consider the remarkable feat which distinguishes the Word, in the singular, from the words of Jesus, without wanting to separate the two. For the singular use does not designate the sum total of the individual words, their content or their meaning.[39] Instead, the Johannine parallelism and identification of works and words must be taken into account.[40] The words of Jesus are simply the ever-new proclamation of the one Word, which is Jesus himself, in different ways and circumstances. We could boldly put it in this way: It is the interpretation of the Word having become Spirit, through the Word becoming flesh entering a specific time and space in the Christian proclamation. We do not have this one Word in the multiplicity of different doctrines, nor in a *summa theologica*, even if the one Word should produce these out of itself, though John does not reflect on this. Nor do we have the one Word in a multiplicity of ethical demands.[41] To be sure, the Fourth Gospel does identify the words of Jesus with his commandments. But they in turn are comprehended in the one demand, to remain with Jesus in faith. The commandments make Jesus' claim concrete in specific situations. Later, we shall show that the commandment of

---

[39] Contrary to Dodd, *Interpretation*, p. 266.
[40] Bultmann, *Theologie*, pp. 413f. (ET II, pp. 6of.).
[41] W. Bauer, *Johannesevangelium*, p. 191 on John 15.7ff., speaks of the moral aspect of the relationship to Christ.

love does not negate this observation. The radical reduction of the whole theology to christology is also reflected in the terminological dialectic of Word, words, and commandments. We have the one Word, which is Jesus himself, only in the words of Christian preaching. We have the one Word—since the words of Christian preaching can be merely a witness—only if those words move us to come to Jesus himself and to remain with him in discipleship and under the lordship of the Word. At least we have now gained the insight that John knew the actualization of the witness of Jesus about himself to be both feasible and necessary in continually new situations. He could clothe his doctrine in the form of a Gospel, because in his view his doctrine was not merely the object of assent. Just as he would not separate doctrine from the *kerygma*, so he demanded that it must be kerygmatically developed.

We make some further progress when we recognize another terminological variation in John 17. The participation which Jesus granted his disciples in his glory is described in John 13 and 15 as a participation in his love. This motif is taken up in John 17 in terms of participation in the Word of God or of the revelation of the divine name. Apparently, Jesus' glory, his love, the revelation of the Word of God, of truth and of the divine name belong together and become interchangeable. They designate the same occurrence under different aspects, just as the formulae of Jesus' commission by the Father, the oneness with him and the election express different aspects of the same occurrence. We now must inquire about the reason, the hidden basis and purpose of this multiplicity of expressions. What all these various expressions have in common is that through them the activity of Jesus is described as the activity of God and *vice versa*, the work of God is designated as the work of Jesus. In Jesus, and only in him, we encounter God himself. He alone is the revealer. This is brought out most clearly when John employs the traditional expression of the revelation of the divine name. In antiquity, the name meant the manifestation of a being. Through its manifestation one can know and take hold of that being. The name of God is God himself as he manifests himself within the earthly realm. In his activity, Jesus proclaims, represents and brings God manifesting himself. Jesus is the one who is sent from heaven and as such, according to the rabbinical principle, he is like the sender himself, with the whole divine authority standing behind him.

This compels us to further inquiry. Who, according to our Gospel, is the God who is coming to earth in Jesus? The Johannine figurative discourses and 'I am' sayings give the answer when they refer to light, truth, life, heavenly bread and water, to those figures of speech of which Bultmann is the supreme interpreter—they speak of what enables man to live. In so doing they proclaim exclusiveness and absoluteness, by confronting his gift with the earthly possibilities. Earthly bread, life, water and light are at best the reflection and the sign of such a gift, but usually they become false substitutes for the heavenly possibility and reality. This means that only God is, and gives, life, light and truth, only he can satisfy hunger and thirst always and everywhere. He can do this as the Creator. If the nature and work are manifest in Jesus and if his commission, his authority and his own nature are to make God manifest, then we encounter the Creator in Jesus. He is the way, the truth and the life because he reveals the Father as the Creator and the Creator as the Father. He is God in his turning towards the world, and in this respect he is one with the Father, yet simultaneously our Lord, helper and friend. His glory, love and election are shown in that he brings the world back into the state of creation and that his Word, issuing forth ever again, calls us to remain the creation reborn. We have stated earlier that in our Gospel eschatology has turned into protology. Now we understand the reason and the necessity for this shift, namely, the last creation leads back to the first. The one who is the end also reveals the beginning, God himself who as the Creator is the father of his creature. What is stated in the primitive Christian hymns and confessions about Christ as mediator of creation is extended by John, with the radicalism typical of him, into man's everyday life. Paul had moved in the same direction when he regarded the new creature as the work of Christ and, conversely, John does not permit the eschatological aspect of the Pauline declaration to disappear, since for him the resurrection and eternal life are the gifts of Jesus. However, he does not give the eschatological aspects only a dimension of depth, which comprises world history up to creation. This was still possible for Paul, too, though for him it was more unusual. The real difference from Paul is indicated by the absence of a theology of the cross. For John, the cross is Jesus' victory over the world. Therefore the power of the resurrection is no longer expressed primarily in the fact that the community is willing and able to carry the cross and follow Jesus. The community is not spared temptation and suffering. They are no longer the eschatological birth-pangs through which the new creature is being born, but rather the pressure of a hostile environment. Consequently the future is not anticipated in the present through the preservation of the faith and urgent expectation, whereby the Spirit is the power of hope and the down-payment of glorification. The eschatological future in John only brings the final separation from the world, and with it the confirmation of the freedom now already granted. What is missing is the great Pauline paradox, that the power of the resurrection can be experienced only in the shadow of the cross, and that the reality of the resurrection now implies a position under the cross. The place of this paradox is taken by the dialectical declaration that no one can remain with Jesus unless he continually encounters him anew. One must be with him on the way, otherwise one cannot have him. In distinction from most other New Testament writers, John does not regard the world as an enticing, tempting power against which only the cross can protect. Christian existence is not, as in Paul, endangered by the flesh which signifies man's own worldliness. Accordingly our Gospel has no need of an explicit anthropology. The problem of the disciple's existence is not whether he actually reaches the goal, but rather whether he remains with Jesus. This is not, as so largely in the Synoptics, a question of the disciple's faithfulness, but rather of the preserving love of his Lord. The one who has created him through rebirth to eternal life must also preserve him. It is the glory of the parting Christ that he has lost no one except Judas, who was predestined by Scripture to perdition. As the Good Shepherd, Jesus protects his own, keeps them together and thus exhibits the omnipotence which the Father entrusted to him. No power can tear them out of his hands. He is the victor both in gathering and in preserving his community, whose existence is and remains the manifestation of his sole creative efficacy.

We realize that John, in distinction to the Corinthian enthusiasts, takes quite seriously the danger from the world which threatens the Christian and Christendom. He does not take the easy way and, like them, proclaim that freedom from temptation and inner turmoil is the result of receiving the sacraments. In John the community is exposed to satanic attacks. For this very reason the community is incapable of resisting through its own power and resources. The community remains the flock which the Good Shepherd must defend. Nevertheless John also proclaims the victory won over the community, and the basis for that is Christ's divinity. We shall have to interpret the miracle stories of this Gospel from this perspective, too. Beyond doubt, the miracles in John are primarily meant to be manifestations of the glory of Jesus. This point is brought out not only in the story of the wedding at Cana, but also in the account of the raising of Lazarus who has to lie in the grave for four days before Jesus intervenes. But the recognition of the manifestation of Jesus' glory in miracles should not mislead us into excluding completely the notion of divine help and mercy which is present at least in the healing narratives and in the story of the miraculous feeding. For John, that which is true is not contained in the earthly reality, for the earthly reality is at best the reflection of that which is heavenly. For this reason, all miracles remain signs pointing beyond themselves to the revelation occurring in the Logos himself. Nevertheless, for John the miracles are also 'proofs' of divine power in the sphere of the transitory.[42] They demonstrate the truth of the saying in 10.10, that Jesus came that his own might have life and have it abundantly. Such proofs are naturally ambiguous and, if isolated from the Logos, misleading, as the objections against the pre-Johannine miracle tradition indicate. Anyone who does not recognize and acknowledge the giver in the gifts and does not see the gifts as signs that lead to the giver himself exchanges the heavenly reality for the earthly and in so doing comes to naught. Conversely, the Logos drawing near to man does not designate himself only in terms of heavenly water, bread, light, life, truth and joy which are received through him, so that all depends on assent to this message. He also acts in such a way that even in the realm of the transitory, his Word is being confirmed and signs point and call attention to his true dignity. Even though these signs may confuse the world, in them his own disciples experience the presence of the Good Shepherd and the door to their pasture. The Word is not without signs.

In conclusion, we may summarize: John, with his message of the revealer who has come and who is one with the Father, places the community in the situation of which his first verses speak, in the situation of the beginning when the Word of God came forth and called the world out of darkness into light and life. This beginning is not a past occurrence in saving history, which is lost for ever. It is instead the new reality eschatologically revealed, which in the Christian community is disclosed every day and on earth through the Word and which every day and on earth must be received and

[42] Contrary to Hirsch, *op. cit.*, p. 124 and Haenchen, *op. cit.*, p. 209; in more dialectical terms, F. C. Baur, *op. cit.*, pp. 143f., 183, 309.

laid hold of in faith.[43] The community under the Word lives and exists from the place granted to it in the presence of the Creator and from its ever-new experience of the first day of creation in its own life. This is the meaning of the dogmatic christology in our Gospel. Therefore the perspective of saving history, not only of the cross, Easter, Ascension and the Parousia, but also of the pre-Christian epoch, is decisively foreshortened. Here lies the real difference between him and Paul. For John, the presence of Christ extends over all times because it is the presence of the Creator. Abraham and Moses already saw his day, the day of his presence which began with the creation. What formerly was veiled in heaven has now come near and remains near in the voice of Jesus in the community. The presence of Christ will find its conclusion, just as it has had a past. But the eternal today, in which the light shines, can only with strain and difficulty be arranged into epochs. The fact that God is present and active, and appoints time, space and history, cannot, however, itself be limited by temporal, spatial and historical categories. Consequently the proclamation is no longer in terms of history but in terms of dogma. God's presence has burst open the realm of human history and changes time and world into spheres in which the eternal light shines into the earthly darkness.

John has developed and illustrated this viewpoint with examples. The redactor who in 21.25 fell back upon and interpreted 20.30 has understood him quite correctly. The occurrence which our Gospel reports can never be narrated completely. John's Gospel is and remains an abbreviation, and the same applies to his doctrine. His doctrine provokes interpretation and kerygmatic unfolding instead of freezing and absolutizing it. John employed many means to point this out. He pictured Jesus in Hellenistic categories as miracle worker, as saviour of the world and as pre-existent heavenly being. But in the Hellenistic world there were many miracle-workers, sons of God, and Jesus is something more than they. John also made use of the Jewish categories of prophet, teacher and Messiah, but these do not adequately disclose his cosmic significance. The symbols of water, bread, light, truth, life, shepherd and door are best suited, because every man has need of them and perishes without them. The one who makes alive is at the same time the judge of the world which rejects him. No one can reject him without choosing death by so doing, and falling into delusion and darkness. Salvation and

[43] Compare Bultmann, *Evangelium*, p. 413, Brown, *op. cit.*, p. cxxi.

condemnation belong quite closely together here. The Johannine dualism receives its depth and cutting-edge from the fact that in the presence of the Creator, one can respond only with yes or no, and in so doing in the last analysis deny or affirm one's own existence.

When the community under the Word confesses the divinity of Jesus, then according to 17.3 it has eternal life, but only so long as it recognizes and declares anew what that means. It is never self-evident and never really preserved without being heard again and again and laid hold of repeatedly. We have to be reminded of this by means of polemic, since the world does not understand itself in the light of its Creator, but desires to live from itself, seeking its glory by itself. There are critical consequences even for the Church and in the Church. One can resist the presence of God in the Word by calling upon the fathers and upon former saving occurrences. One can set one's mind against the prophetic grasp of the Spirit by hiding in the fortifications of religiosity; this is what the Jews do, according to John. Then salvation history and the means of salvation become bulwarks of the pious man against the Creator, whom we need daily anew. Jesus is always an offence, too, and becomes a stumbling block even for his disciples. In distinction from Paul's view, the Johannine Christ becomes a stumbling-block, not on account of his cross and lowliness, but because, in the world which finds its self-understanding in itself, he proclaims the rightful sovereign claim of the Creator upon his creation and demands our obedience. As in Paul, so here man loses his own claim, his self-made rights and privileges, when the name of the Father is proclaimed, where man is placed into the state of the creature. The community under the Word is therefore always also the community in which the offence of the world is overcome. The eschatological creation can exist only in separation from the world.

IV

CHRISTIAN UNITY

THE UNITY OF Christianity has always been threatened. Occasionally the threat has been imposed from without, but it is always present from within. Christian unity exists concretely only so long as it remains a task to be fulfilled. Since uniformity cannot be a Christian solution, this task becomes all the more difficult. Neither the use of force nor the category of norm can fulfil the task, for the quest for unity can never consist in levelling off the differences. The multi-structured world can only be penetrated by the multi-structured gifts and ministries which proceed from the fullness of Christ's possibilities. Therefore, unity does not mean uniformity, but solidarity, the tension-filled interconnection between those who differ among themselves. Christian unity implies the freedom of the individual in the exercise of the gift and of the service entrusted to him. Thus it teaches men to tolerate and even to appreciate tensions, to avoid pressing everything into the same mould. This solidarity advocates freedom to the very limits of what would break up the fellowship. If it were otherwise, Christianity would become sterile and unfit for service. Therefore Christian unity must not merely be demanded, but also be rightly understood, rightly substantiated and taught. Every age in the history of the Church has endeavoured to do this. For this reason Paul described the Church as the Body of Christ. The admonition to preserve unity constituted the very core of the eucharistic exhortation which he adopted. Such admonitions gain importance through the growth of the Church in the succeeding generations. Now the horizon expands from the congregation in worship to world-wide Christendom whose coherence in time and space must be clarified. The Letter to the Ephesians has accomplished this in a daring design. John 17 is closely related to it. Here, too, the unity has been made into the dominant criterion of the true

Church and the key words through which the unity is described have become technical terms.

The background, as well as the impelling forces of this new phase of development in primitive Christian history, can be inferred from the carefully stylized tripartite acclamation in Eph. 4.5: 'One Lord, one faith, one baptism'. 'Faith' obviously refers here to the formulated confession. The administration of baptism in which this acclamation may originally have had its setting is now not merely the basis of the individual Christian's life, but rather, according to Eph. 5.26, the act out of which the Church itself grows. In the solemn confession, the Christian Church testifies to the basic factors of its origin and being. Because these basic factors are not subjected to earthly changes, they guarantee the unity of that community which exists under their control. An acclamation like this is meaningful only when imminent dangers are to be warded off through it. When the Church confesses that its unity is realized in heaven and perpetually guaranteed, it is obviously delimiting itself from heretics and their attempts induced by the 'Spirit' to dissolve it into sectarian fellowships. It is significant that we do not find here just an admonition to preserve the unity of the Christian brotherhood. Nor are the divisions and schisms any longer regarded from an apocalyptic viewpoint as signs of the great confusion of the end-times, as we find in I Cor. 11.19. Now factions are considered as a sacrilege against that fellowship which is grounded in heaven and which, according to I Tim. 3.15, is the pillar and bulwark of truth. That fellowship possesses unity essentially and intrinsically, namely as the mark of truth. In Eph. 4.5, a formative orthodoxy asserts itself which considers itself to be constitutively bound to heaven and in this respect to be the institution of salvation and not merely the instrument of grace. The unity of this orthodoxy now becomes identical with the truth of the right doctrine which it must administer as the mystery of divine revelation. Earthly reality may show its nature as dispersion and division. The heavenly reality is of necessity one and indivisible.

These preliminary remarks sketch the context in which John 17 must be seen. We can hardly understand this chapter and its concluding petition for unity unless we take into account the conflict within the Church which was almost universal at the end of the first century. The position of the Gospel is dominated by the fact that church unity here is not only based on heavenly realities but also deduced from the relationship of the Father to the Son and of the

Son to the Father and of both to the disciples. Of course, this can be understood as being a solemn comparison resulting from edifying rhetoric. However, if this is so, we fail to get a difficult theological problem into focus by hiding it behind clouds of pious verbiage. The emphasis then quite necessarily rests upon the demand for unity which the disciples themselves must realize. It is no longer clear that the summons to human effort is unimportant in the text. The Johannine Christ prays to God for unity rather than demanding it from men. Apparently the realization of unity does not lie in the hands of the disciples. If the prayer is also indirectly a summons, it reminds the disciples of their obligation to retain the gift which has been granted, for it can be lost through man's own fault. It is, however, of crucial importance to realize that unity can be testified to as the earthly mark of the Christian community only because unity is already prefigured in the relationship between the Father and the Son and because unity is transferred through the activity of the Father and the Son to the community. We would do well to ponder the strangeness of this mode of thinking. It is not sufficient to take only its theological scope seriously. We are here first of all confronted with a problem which needs to be discussed on the basis of the methodology of comparative religion. Without its solution, important connections and relations within this Gospel remain unclear.

If the disciples are drawn into the unity of the Father and the Son, then it is once again indicated that the ecclesiology is unfolded with the christology as its point of orientation and departure. This was already the case with the Pauline motif of the Church as the Body of Christ. John, however, goes further, in that he brings the Father directly into his ecclesiology and does not merely lay stress on the obedience of the servants and members of Christ. The mark of Christianity is its unity with its Lord and his Father. This implies that the motif of unity is not restricted to christology any more than christology is restricted to soteriology. If John is labelled a mystic as a result,[1] the real problem is being concealed behind a vague catchword. We must rather ask: In what sense can the key word unity embrace the Father, Son and the disciples in theological thought, and in which historical situation is this Johannine concept of unity possible? We must be careful that the differences between them are not blurred. Only arbitrariness could refuse to recognize the difference between the Father and the Son. Just as the Father remains superior

[1] Gaugler, op. cit., p. 37.

to the Son even when the Son's divinity is stressed, so likewise both Father and Son remain superior to the community, even though the community reflects the divine relationship between the Father and the Son. Here, too, unity seems to mean the solidarity of differences. But in what sense is this so?

We usually bypass the question at this point with edifying language by reducing unity to what we call love.[2] The Gospel itself misleads us into doing just that because in 3.35; 10.17; 15.9; 17.23ff., John speaks of the Father's love for the Son; in 14.31 he refers to the Son's love for the Father, and correspondingly also speaks of the love of both for the community. Love and unity are here brought together and identified. Once again we have the appearance of a dialectical play with certain key words which aim to express the same subject-matter from different aspects. But this insight should protect us from indiscriminately connecting what must be kept distinct and oversimplifying the whole problem. What we quite vaguely call love must not rob the Johannine motif of its importance. If love should turn out to be the concrete expression of unity, unity still remains love's origin and basis. Distinctions like these indicate that the concept of love in the Fourth Gospel is not without problems. It is not even universally recognized that John demands love for one's brethren, but not for one's enemies, and correspondingly that Jesus loves his own, but not the world. This fact may not be diminished in importance by explaining it in the context of the situation of the farewell speeches, which are concerned with the existence of the circle of the disciples and with the preservation of Jesus' gift.[3] There is no indication in John that love for one's brother would also include love toward one's neighbour,[4] as demanded in the other books of the New Testament. On the contrary, John here sets forth an unmistakable restriction[5] such as we also know from the Qumran community,[6] and this also indicates the historical situation of our Gospel with unusual clarity.

It should not be overlooked that according to 3.16 God loved the world. But it is more than doubtful whether this statement, which is

[2] Compare H. Odeberg, *The Fourth Gospel* (1929), p. 114; Dodd, *Interpretation*, pp. 194–9; Barrett, *op. cit.*, p. 428; Michel, *op. cit.*, p. 532.

[3] Bultmann, *Evangelium*, p. 405; *Theologie*, p. 435 (ET II, p. 82).

[4] Contrary to Hoskyns, *op. cit.*, p. 451; Barrett, *op. cit.*, pp. 81f.

[5] So W. Bauer, *Johannesevangelium*, p. 248; Gaugler, *op. cit.*, pp. 218f.; Schweizer, *op. cit.*, p. 375 (ET, p. 238).

[6] Brown, *op. cit.*, p. LXIII.

nowhere repeated in John, should give us the right to interpret the whole Johannine proclamation from this perspective. According to the context, we have every reason to consider this verse as a traditional primitive Christian formula which the Evangelist employed.[7] Its sole purpose in John is to stress the glory of Jesus' mission, that is to say the miracle of the incarnation. References to God's love for the world are absent in Jesus' own witness to himself as well as in his commandment given to his disciples. It is just the same with the predication 'saviour of the world', which appears in 4.42 but does not adequately designate the Johannine Christ. To be sure, according to 3.17; 6.33; 12.47 Jesus is sent to save the world and to give it life and, according to 9.5; 12.46, he is the light of the world. But the Gospel shows that his mission results in the judgment of the world. It is not accidental, therefore, that the commandment of brotherly love is part of the esoteric instruction of the disciples and not without reason that we read in I John 2.15, in sharp contrast to John 3.16: 'If anyone loves the world, in him is not the love of the Father.' While the Johannine school is heard in I John 2.15, in this case it does not deviate from the teaching of John's Gospel which just as emphatically uses the hatred of the world as a contrasting background to the love within the community. This becomes even clearer when the concept of love in the Fourth Gospel is analysed without naïvely presupposing straight away that it means nothing more than normal ethical conduct.[8]

In 15.9ff., love is defined as the keeping of the commandments, and this definition of love applies to Jesus as well as to the disciples. According to 15.15, Jesus' love for his disciples is expressed by his communicating to them the word of the Father. Apparently the communication of the word to the disciples is also the essence of the Father's love for the community. Hence, we may infer that the Father's love for the Son from 'before the foundations of the world' which, according to 17.24, made him to be the Son and the revealer, can only mean that God has always spoken to Jesus. Therefore he is the exclusive and unique Word of God for the world. If this is so, then the conclusion seems inevitable: If Jesus sends his own into the world in order to speak the Word there and if in this proclamation the

[7] W. Bauer, *op. cit.*, p. 57; S. Schulz, *Untersuchungen zur Menschensohnschristologie im Johannesevangelium* (1957), p. 140; against this view, Bultmann, *Evangelium*, p. 110, n. 5.

[8] Contrary to Dodd, *Interpretation*, pp. 398f.; correctly, Bultmann, *Evangelium*, pp. 403f.

divine love is revealed, then the disciples' mission in the world, like Christ's own mission, bears the mark of divine love. It is surprising that this obvious and logical conclusion has nowhere explicitly been drawn. We have now reached one of the cruxes of Johannine interpretation. The understanding of the entire Gospel depends on how we now interpret this strange phenomenon and in what direction we move from there. To repeat our last result once more: Love in John is inseparably bound to the event of the Word, to speaking the Word on one hand and to receiving and preserving it on the other. This is just as true for the Father's relation to the Son as it is for the relation of both to the community. We should not be side-tracked from this insight by 10.17f., where the Father's love for the Son is based on the Son's free surrender of his life. John 15.13 takes up this idea again in the form of a proverb and thus emphasizes it. Undoubtedly John cannot conceive of love without selfless service and surrender,[9] and 13.1 shows that Jesus' service and surrender implies death. We may and should add that with this idea our Gospel follows primitive Christian traditions in which love consistently means existence for others. However, this is not the characteristic Johannine manner of speaking of love. As soon as John reflects on the nature of love, he shows that selfless service and surrender are connected with the Word. Even in 15.13, the connection is made between the Word, the commandment of Jesus and love as sacrifice. According to 10.18, Jesus follows the Father's commandment when he lays down his life of his own accord. The Father loves the Son by showing him all that he himself is doing (5.20).

For John, real communication is impossible without words, discussion, dialogue and, conversely, he understands such dialogue as the communication of one's being and therefore as love. If we wanted to pursue this line of thought, we would have to discover that obedience for him is, at the very core, the 'yes' of our response to the Word that is heard, as is intimated already by the derivation of the Greek verb 'to obey' from the verb 'to hear'. At any rate, love in John means something other than an emotion and it transcends even the sphere of ethical decisions. Love does not merely respect the rights or the needs of the other person in personal conduct. Love speaks to the other person and thus communicates itself, or else it preserves what is heard and so accepts the self-disclosure of the other person also through its own deeds of love. Thus in the disciple, faith and love

[9] Faulhaber, *op. cit.*, pp. 37, 41; Haenchen, *op. cit.*, p. 212.

indeed coincide.[10] But it must be carefully considered whether this may be interpreted as constituting a material unity, so that the decision of faith for the Word that has been heard would be identical with the decision of love for the claim of one's brother. Such an interpretation could no longer be deduced from the divine relationship between Father and Son as demanded by the Johannine context. In it, love is not primarily concerned with the claim of the other person, but with the Word. Faith means the acceptance of the Word and love means self-surrender to the Word in service. This corresponds to the conduct of Jesus, who lets himself be guided by his Father's word, not, of course, as a believer, but as the revealer. He did not receive the Word of God in time, nor in conjunction with the alternative of unbelief. This even corresponds to the activity of God himself who, from the beginning, communicated himself in the Word. This Word is his self-disclosure and it is therefore taken up in the Gospel as the self-disclosure of Jesus. Because in Jesus the Word places us before God himself, it is called sanctifying truth. The Word gives eternal life because through Jesus it enables us to recognize the Father who alone can be eternal life. However, what places us before God also separates us from the world. It continues to separate us even when we are not taken out of the world. Thus the disciples are simultaneously the elect, the friends, the loved ones, as well as those who are the object of the world's hatred. The love of God cannot be connected with the love of the world. For love, in John, means the communion which is established through the Word and preserved by the Word. The world, however, does not exist in the communion of this Word, but, as the Gospel describes it, at best under its judgment, because it does not accept it. Consequently, it is not accidental that John never speaks of the new world, and not even of the new creation, even though the Church, which was in his time already engaged in world-wide mission work, could have been given this name. A characteristic trait of our Gospel is the tension between universalism and predestination.[11] Jesus is designated the 'saviour of the world', who has come not to judge but to save the world, yet it is only the believers, the elect, his own, who are in fact saved. May one really argue that the believers represent the world, because God's purpose and goal is directed to the world?[12] Some Johannine texts obviously point this way, as seems

[10] In opposition to Bultmann, *Evangelium*, p. 421.
[11] Barrett, *op. cit.*, p. 428.
[12] Faulhaber, *op. cit.*, p. 29; Bultmann, *Evangelium*, p. 382.

necessary whenever the idea of creation strongly influences the whole proclamation. On the other hand, the Johannine dualism is an insurmountable barrier for the idea that the disciples represent the world. The possibilities inherent in apocalypticism no longer have validity, even if traditional formulae and a few phrases here and there are distant reminders of it. John is a man between the times. He lives in the age of world-wide mission. Yet he is no longer interested in a new world and its proclamation, which may perhaps even appear to him as something fantastic and absurd. He recognizes the new creation only in the form of reborn disciples. They, however, no longer represent the earthly but the heavenly world and therefore they are not the representatives of a restored creation.

Nowhere in the New Testament do we meet a more rigorous dualism than in John. It is one of the odd and almost comical features of the history of Johannine interpretation that this writing should have been connected with the Ephesian presbyter who as a very old man could speak only about love. Not even Paul, with his outbursts of anger and his irony, exhibited the cutting iciness of the so-called apostle of love, shown already in his style. Of course the Johannine dualism has not been driven to its radical conclusions. For the Christian community unceasingly grows out of this world and the disciples are unceasingly being sent into the world. The world is the arena of divine history. It can be that arena because God has created it. On the other hand, one must be saved from the world and one is saved through hearing and receiving the Word. The Johannine dualism is certainly not a metaphysical dualism. Heaven and earth are not on principle and unalterably in opposition. The earth as the creation of God remains the realm of his call. But it would also be inexact to speak of a dualism of decision.[13] That faith and unbelief involve decision cannot be denied. However, it is not man's decision which brings about the great separation of the two realms. The Johannine dualism marks the effect of the Word in that world in which the light has always shone into the darkness. As specific decisions of individual men, faith and unbelief confirm the separation which already exists. The decisions for or against the Word constantly take place on an earth which has already been separated into two hostile spheres through the event of the Word. As in Paul, for instance in I Cor. 1.18ff.; II Cor. 2.15f., so also here the Word of God effects the final separation between life and death, truth and lie,

[13] Bultmann, *Theologie*, pp. 373, 429 (ET II, pp. 21, 76).

light and darkness, Church and world. As the Word of the Creator it unceasingly separates creation from chaos, as on the first day. Therefore, together with creation, the Word also brings about chaos. In this sense the Word effects all things. The Johannine dualism is nothing but the doctrine of the omnipotence of the Word. Nowhere else is the whole salvation and the whole condemnation more radically dependent on the hearing of the Word than in our Gospel. Just as the Word precedes faith, so also it continually brings out anew the quality of darkness, and of unbelief as remaining in darkness. Rebirth is quite impossible for human understanding, and even for Christian insight it remains a mysterious miracle, because the notion of a restored creation is given up. Faith arises only through the power and in the manner of the resurrection of the dead, but this is not effective everywhere. In Judaism as a whole, for instance, the resurrection power bounces off on the insurmountable rule of the power of death. There exists not merely the possibility that a man does not want to believe. There is also the other one, that he cannot believe. To decide in favour of Jesus is a divine gift and possible only for the elect. Conversely, in faith election becomes apparent and the divine gift is offered to everyone.

From this perspective John drew far-reaching consequences. The world-wide commission and mission of the Church and the duty of every individual believer to participate in it are all presupposed. The call to discipleship also includes being sent forth. Not even women are excluded. The obligation to do mission work knows no exceptions. In 17.18 the departing Christ summarizes this task once again as constituting his will, just as his own way on earth as the messenger of the Father stood under the same commandment and served as a heavenly example for his own. Christian life as such is mission. No one can say this more loudly and emphatically than John. This does not yet answer the question of the expectations and intentions that are connected with this task. It is of the utmost importance to recognize that here, too, the arena of the disciples' mission is not its goal, and the limitless scope of the task is not meant to produce or to give form to a new world. The disciples who are being sent into all the world are at the same time reminded that they themselves are not and cannot be of this world. So little are they a part of the world that in 17.15 the departing Christ must express his will, declaring that he does not want them to be taken out of this world. Their task leads them into the world which at its core is an alien realm for the disciples, just as, according to John, Jesus himself has been an alien sojourner in this world below. The paradox of the incarnation finds its extension in the Christian mission and receives its meaning anew there. Incarnation in John does not mean complete, total entry into the earth, into human existence, but rather the encounter between the heavenly and the earthly. For the disciples, as for Jesus, inasmuch as both are representatives of heaven, this world below is the realm of activity through which they must pass without establishing a permanent home in it. Actually the Christian mission according to John does not have validity for the world as such, but only for those who, being in the world, are given to Christ by his Father, in short to the elect who are called to faith. We do not know beforehand who belongs to this group or how many they are. This becomes evident in the reaction to the Word. Thus the world is the object of mission only in so far as it is necessary to gather the elect. John 11.52 expresses this idea unmistakably, transferring a part of the apocalyptic hope of Judaism into a new context. The scattered children of God must be gathered together. If this is the task of the disciples, then we understand why the object of Christian love in John is not one's neighbour as such. In practice, he may be that object, since the message is directed to all and since prior to the reaction of a man to the Word it is not decided whether or not he will be a brother. But what in a practical sense has always yet to be discovered, has, theologically and in principle, already been decided. The object of Christian love for John is only what belongs to the community under the Word, or what is elected to belong to it, that is, the brotherhood of Jesus.

Once again new light is shed on the historical situation of the Evangelist. One can hardly be unaware of a dogmatic hardening and contraction at this point. In the course of church history, it was usually the conventicles that considered the relationship between Church and world from this perspective. The earthly Jesus who went to publicans and sinners and who told the parable of the Good Samaritan is just as remote as the Pauline proclamation of the justification of the ungodly. This does not mean that John could not have pictured Jesus as a Good Samaritan, making him an example for us, nor does it mean that the Johannine community had no room for erstwhile sinners. The proclamation of rebirth outdoes the Pauline preaching of justification rather than falling behind it. The difference is not in regard to morality but instead in a different relation to the earthly reality. The message of the God who walks on the face of the earth finds its correspondence in the community which, being conscious of its mission, is without a feeling of solidarity for the world. The omnipotence of the Word is emphasized most strongly. However, this omnipotence which refers to the Creator's activity is not related to the world. Even when the omnipotence of the Word is regarded as having a world-wide scope, it is still limited to the experience of the individual and of the group. The notion of the liberated community takes the place of the concept of the new world. In John, overcoming no longer means the conquest and transformation of everyday earthly existence, but, in agreement with his christology, separation from an earth which as such no longer belongs to Christ. Individual people, who may be scattered across the face of the world, belong to him and in this sense they constitute a world-wide Church. When the title 'the spiritual Gospel' was attached to the Fourth Gospel it denoted a true insight, though one might argue about the propriety of the label. Even where the Logos, like Sophia, comes to his own and is rejected by his own, the idea does not produce the firm conviction of the Old Testament and the primitive Christian message that: 'The earth is the Lord's and the fullness thereof.' My key word, unreflected docetism, takes its point of orientation from here. John does not consider removing the marks and characteristics of creation from this earth. Nor, however, does he allow the earth really to remain creation nor does he orient it on its new creation, even though Old Testament and Jewish reminiscences still linger in his ear, and God's creative activity is of utmost importance to his theology. The problem of comparative religion which arises here cannot be pursued in this context. Thus we cannot decide how strong Qumran's influence is on John and whether John presupposes the beginnings of a Christian gnosticism or whether he contributes to its formation. The relationship to the world is, at any rate, quite similar in John and in gnosticism. Bousset's interpretation[14] may to a large extent be the product of his age, inadequate or even wrong. But Bousset did correctly point out the atmosphere of a Christian mystery-community which permeates John. Temporally and theologically John is separated from post-Easter apocalypticism and at most he took from it some themes which he then reinterpreted. Spatially, at least, he is remote from the beginnings of early Catholicism and theologically he does not share its trends

[14] *Kyrios Christos* (1921), pp. 154–83.

even though he shares a number of its premises. But he challenges all forms of Christianity which want to build their home on earth, and ironically it can be noted that it was precisely those forms of Christianity which did not comprehend his challenge or else sublimated it to the extreme. The question of the nature of John's 'spirituality' will largely remain an argument of terminology. Yet it can hardly be denied that at all times he gave strength and shelter to spiritualism within and without the Church.

Only now can it be stated what is meant by unity in our Gospel. Unity expresses the solidarity of the heavenly. But here above all we must delineate clearly, since the various emphases of the differing interpretations become quite apparent and at cross purposes with each other. In understandable reaction against earlier interpretations, modern Protestant studies on John, though by no means only Protestant studies, endeavour to ward off or at least to curb an approach to John in terms of metaphysical categories. The category of personality in manifold variations seems to offer itself as an appropriate key to John, though it would be rather difficult to define the nature of the heavenly personality when it is not easy to do so even with regard to the human personality. In theological language, so one might argue, the word love can never be wrong. John himself used it, indicating that love expresses and preserves the unity and conversely that unity is the presupposition as well as the result of love. Therefore interpreters declare that, 'the only kind of personal union . . . with which we are acquainted is love',[15] as if people could not also be united in dialogue or in common action. That love is God's own life and activity may, in view of the biblical proclamation of God as judge and Lord, hardly be regarded as being a general, more or less self-evident truth.[16] Finally, what does it mean to speak of our love for God or for Christ? To speak in terms of a 'real community of being, a sharing of life' with God,[17] remains quite obscure so long as the interpreter does not employ but, in liberalist fashion, dilutes the concept of *gratia infusa*, of infused grace. Others place in opposition or relate positively to each other 'metaphysical' and 'ethical' categories, so that, for instance, the ethical unity is substantiated by a metaphysical foundation.[18] When the trinitarian problem is not

[15] Dodd, *Interpretation*, p. 199.
[16] *Ibid.*, p. 196.
[17] *Ibid.*, p. 197.
[18] Hoskyns, *op. cit.*, pp. 389f.; W. Bauer, *Johannesevangelium*, p. 84.

ignored, the unity of will[19] is often made into the decisive feature and Jesus' obedience, to which our obedience must correspond, is then sharply accentuated.[20] If, on the other hand, the notion of the divine revealer is stressed,[21] there is a deliberate move away from an ethical interpretation in order to set forth the identity of Father and Son. In that case, of course, it is necessary to separate the statement of the unity of the community from the unity of the Father and the Son and to describe the former in terms of an inner unity in the tradition of the Word and of faith, or even as uniformity. But the unity of the community may not be detached from the unity of Father and Son which is its foundation. For John, unity is a mark and a quality of the heavenly realm in the same way in which truth, light and life are the quality and mark of the heavenly reality. Therefore unity cannot be interpreted on the basis of earthly analogies like friendship or covenant, nor may it be reduced to a uniformity of will. Unity in our Gospel exists only as heavenly reality and therefore in antithesis to the earthly, which bears the mark of isolations, differences and antagonisms.[22] If unity exists on earth, then it can only exist as a projection from heaven, that is, as the mark and object of revelation.

John is not content with simply stating unity as a fact. He also sees it rooted in certain relations and the interpretation of those relations is the real problem of our texts. It is typical for these relations that a heavenly gradation, a process through a series of stages, unites the superior with the inferior. We also meet this notion in Ephesians. Thus the controversial passage Eph. 3.15 carries force only if all earthly fatherhood has its prototype in the divine fatherhood and is derived from it. Still more clearly, in Eph. 5.25ff., the relationship between Christ and the Church serves as the model for Christian marriage. This marriage represents the mystery of the perfect union announced in Gen. 2.24. The word 'model' is, of course, too modern, since more than merely an example or a norm is implied here. We are rather dealing with the reflection of the heavenly reality in the earthly counterpart and the participation, arranged in gradations, of the earthly counterpart in the nature of the heavenly prototype. Thus the sequence, given by Paul in I Cor. 11.3ff., of God, Christ, man, woman does not refer by accident to gradations of heavenly glory.

[19] C. Maurer, *Ignatius von Antiochien und das Johannesevangelium* (1949), p. 6of.; Michel, *op. cit.*, p. 532; Barrett, *op. cit.*, p. 428.

[20] Hirsch, *op. cit.*, pp. 377ff.; Haenchen, *op. cit.*, pp. 215f.

[21] Bultmann, *Evangelium*, pp. 187f.; 392f.

[22] Compare the excellent interpretation in Odeberg, *op. cit.*, pp. 113f.

Heaven here is not a realm closed in itself, for the heavenly reality invades the earth with explosive power in order to unfold itself in representations as its earthly counterparts. While those representations no longer possess the full reality of their heavenly origin, they still participate in it in degree. The successions of emanations in later gnosticism are based on the same notions. Yet nowhere else in the New Testament do such ideas have greater significance than in John. His symbolic discourses are determined by them, for they are based on the premise that the earthly things, such as earthly bread, light, etc., have their truth in the heavenly prototype. Therefore, what is earthly becomes a phantom of salvation if it becomes the object of human longing. The earthly counterpart may not be isolated from the full reality of its origin. While it has no lifegiving powers in itself, its significance lies in the fact that it can be a sign pointing to the heavenly reality.

This is the context in which John's view of Christian unity belongs. Unity on earth exists only as a reflection and an extension of heavenly reality. Therefore it can exist only within that realm which can reflect the heavenly reality, namely the realm of the divine Word. The relationship of the Father to the Son and of the Son to the Father is the prototype of true solidarity. There the Word is spoken and received, that Word which is the beginning and the end of salvation, since God reveals himself in it. Out of this solidarity the Word is revealed through Christ to the world so that God himself becomes manifest as Creator. The community under the Word is his creation and remains his creation so long as it remains under the Word that is continually addressed to it anew. The community, like the first creation, cannot live from itself. But in so far as it lives from the Word, it lives from heaven even while on earth, being drawn into the community between Father and Son. Because of this, the community itself is a heavenly reality. This idea is expressed in the most astonishing form in 10.34f. There the statement of Ps. 82.6, 'You are gods', is justified through the reception of the divine Word. To be sure, the verse has a christological slant, but it cannot be limited to christology only, since it already had validity for the community of the old covenant. The accepted Word of God produces an extension of heavenly reality on earth, for the Word participates in the communion of Father and Son. This unity between Father and Son is the quality and mark of the heavenly world. It projects itself to the earth in the Word in order to create the community there which, through rebirth from above, becomes integrated into the unity of Father and Son. This almost frightening understanding of the Johannine community must be called gnosticizing. Here one perceives most clearly John's naïve docetism which extends to his ecclesiology also. His interpretation of the Old Testament is also gnosticizing, and this does not merely apply to the above-quoted text.[23] This kind of approach to the Old Testament has nothing to do with the historical Jesus. In these verses there speaks the one whom John 1.18 calls the exegete of the invisible God, on whose bosom and in unity with whom he remains even while on earth. He is the Logos to whom, according to 1.51, even in his earthly existence the angels of God descend and from whom they ascend, thus demonstrating for the eyes of the believers his unbroken contact with the heavenly world. In his function as the revealer, Jesus is all that the 'I am' words declare him to be. Therefore the earthly community participates in the heavenly world through him as he speaks to it. This is not only true for the whole of Christianity; it is no less true for the individual members and their reciprocal relationship. Brotherly love is all that is needed, for brotherly love means seeing one's brother as existing under the Word of God, receiving him through the Word and giving him the possibility of remaining under the Word. Brotherly love is heavenly solidarity directed towards individual Christians. Finally, Christian mission is solidarity in the process of seeking out brothers through the proclamation of the Word which proceeded from God to Christ and thence to the community. The purpose of missionary proclamation is to gain the outsider as a brother. The assertion of 4.35, that the fields are already ripe for the harvest, applies to this seeking out in missionary work.

John's idea of mission is the reinterpretation of an apocalyptic motif. This insight can serve as a transition for our next affirmation, that the catchword 'realized eschatology' does not fully do justice to John, in spite of the fact that John placed the *praesentia Christi* in the centre of his proclamation. On the basis of his presuppositions, John developed something like a unique futurist eschatology and John 17 indicates that the Evangelist not only focussed his attention upon the past and the present but that he also possessed a future hope. It is no longer the hope held in the period immediately following Easter. John, along with early Catholicism, shares the perspective held by a time which is no longer overshadowed by the imminent *eschaton*.

[23] Compare Dahl, *op. cit.*, pp. 141f.

For him, as well as for early Catholicism, the decisive event had already taken place and was now being developed within Christianity's sphere of influence. For John it was not being developed in the form of a church organization, but rather as the encounter with Jesus and his Word. This difference does not change the Evangelist's understanding of the time and situation in which he found himself. On the other hand, it would be false to argue that his understanding reckoned simply with an endless stretch of time and its inevitable developments. Not even the early Catholic Church held this view, for it never surrendered the idea of the end, however often the idea grew pale and became insignificant. John 17.20ff. shows that John, on the basis of his own theological premises, did hold a futurist eschatological expectation. It represents a modification of the Church's tradition, but his expectation for the future is urgent nevertheless.

The petition for unity is now varied because attention is focussed on those who come to faith in the future through the Christian proclamation of the Word. The formula which in 4.39 referred to the proclamation to the Samaritans is now applied to them. The first generation is united with those still to come under the Word, and each generation has its peculiar advantage and bears its special risk. While the first disciples had the advantage of coming to Jesus in person, they did not know and could not yet see the world-wide witness of the succeeding community in which the glory of Jesus extends itself. And while that world-wide witness opens the door to Jesus more easily for later generations, they in turn are in greater danger of being subjected to a proclamation which, according to 4.43, can become sheer idle talk. Thus Jesus' petition must enclose all, and he prays here for all with the oft-quoted words 'that they may all be one'. This is not edifying rhetoric, as most interpreters suppose. If my previous analysis was correct, then John here speaks of the gathering under the dominion of the Word of what belongs to heaven. The same idea is stated in 10.16 with the formula of the 'one flock and one shepherd'. John 17.23 repeats, slightly modifying the expression, 'that they may be perfected into unity'. Perfection in John means that the perils are past and overcome. The gathering of the community points to a goal, and that goal is free from earthly perils. Once more this idea is restated by the following verse (17.24): It is the will of Jesus that all who are his should be with him in that heavenly place where he is and there behold his eternal glory. This heavenly place is, according to 14.2f., his Father's house with many rooms, which Jesus no longer needs to prepare for his own because the Father has done so already. John 12.32 promised the disciples that the exalted Lord would draw them to himself into his heavenly glory.

We have seen that only a few texts contain the futurist eschatology which is peculiar to John. But these texts gain unusual importance as soon as we compare them with the futurist eschatology of the Synoptics or of Paul. The fact that this futurist hope is simply taken for granted in John, that it is expressed almost incidentally and emphasized only at the end of chapter 17 makes his hope all the more significant. For the disciples of Jesus on earth the goal of the sojourn is the final unification of the community in heaven, where, like its Lord, the community too is removed from earthly persecution.[24] Of course, John 14.2f. does not mean that in the hour of death, Jesus brings his own to himself,[25] or else 17.24 would also have to be understood in this fashion.[26] Nor, however, does the Johannine Jesus refer to a cosmic process in which humanity is called and gathered to unity with God.[27] Rather, John spiritualized old apocalyptic traditions. The point of departure for primitive Christian apocalypticism and especially of the post-Easter ecclesiology was the hope of the gathering of the scattered tribes of Israel or of the rebuilding of Israel on the basis of a remnant. For the present we cannot show how primitive Christian apocalypticism developed into the Johannine reinterpretation. But we can note that the Jewish-Christian hope has been transposed from the earthly realm into the metaphysical dimension.[28] In place of the scattered people of God we find the children of God scattered throughout the world; in place of the earthly kingdom with its eschatological Zion we find unification in heaven. As in II Peter 1.11, the ingathering of the faithful into the eternal kingdom takes the place of Christ's *parousia* for the final judgment. In all such modifications the notion of the gathering of the elect is present. This notion is united in John with the idea found, for

[24] W. Bauer, *Johannesevangelium*, pp. 178f.; Barrett, *op. cit.*, p. 429.

[25] Bultmann, *Evangelium*, p. 465, n. 1.

[26] So Bultmann, *Evangelium*, p. 399.

[27] Faulhaber, *op. cit.*, p. 58; Michel, *op. cit.*, p. 533; Thüsing's interpretation, pp. 23f., of the gathering around the cross is absurd.

[28] This is different in Bultmann, *Theologie*, p. 444 (ET II, p. 92), who speaks of the reality of the Invisible Church in the Visible Church. Gaugler, *op. cit.*, pp. 209f., 216, presents a similar view, though from different presuppositions.

instance, in Ephesians, that in the Church the heavenly unification is already taking place and is growing in a world-wide dimension. Thus the perfection of the unification is but the end and goal of the eschatological process which is already in motion. What is heavenly cannot remain on earth, even though it must be gathered on earth. If we formulate our result in this way, then it becomes apparent that John prepares for the gnostic proclamation or else already stands under its influence. For gnosticism regards the gathering of the souls scattered on earth as the goal of world history. The gnostic problem does not appear just with the original circulation and use of the Fourth Gospel. It is already raised by the whole of Johannine eschatology. The outstanding marks of Johannine eschatology are (1) its transformation into protology; (2) the consistent presentation of Jesus as God walking on the face of the earth; (3) the ecclesiology of the community which consists of individuals who are reborn through the divine call, which lives from the Word, and which represents the heavenly unification on earth; (4) the understanding of the world and of the community's mission; (5) the reduction of Christian exhortation to brotherly love, and (6), finally, the hope of heavenly perfection. These characteristic marks of Johannine eschatology dovetail perfectly with each other and should not be interpreted in isolation from each other. The Johannine problem may not be cut up into a series of minor problems, but must be seen as a whole. Of course, each detail is important, but the whole may not be dissolved into details to the extent that one cannot see the wood for the trees. The Johannine problem as a whole, however, exhibits more than a temporal distance from the post-Easter Church and thus a closeness to the rising early Catholicism.[29] It also exhibits a contrast with early Catholicism shown by a conventicle with gnosticizing tendencies.

[29] Gaugler, *op. cit.*, p. 42, saw this most clearly when he spoke of a forerunner of a naturally 'pure' Catholicism.

V

CONCLUSION

THE RESULT FORMULATED in the previous paragraph differs greatly from traditional church views, as well as from the interpretation of John prevalent today. If one is aware of the almost desperate endeavours during the past century of investigations into the most difficult of all New Testament problems, which have resulted in a constant succession of new approaches and the postulation of endless new theses, one will also retain a critical stance towards one's own proposed solution. We can only say which questions and which possibilities we have recognized. Whether with our viewpoints and the results thus gained we will succeed in finding common approval is not decisive for scholarship. What is important is only that new questions again force us to engage in further reflection and teach us to listen to the texts anew. In order for this to be done rightly, we must be clear about the implication of an interpretation which departs from the customary approach. Some concluding remarks are meant to give some guidance for this.

Hardly any other writing in the New Testament has exercised as much fascination as John both inside and outside the Church throughout the centuries. Those who found Christ's true voice in it and called it, in distinction from the Synoptics, the spiritual Gospel, acknowledged the claim raised by the Gospel itself. Yet its inclusion in the canon is not without irony. The Gospel of John was called the heavenly Gospel because the Church which included it in the canon no longer knew John's earthly, historical situation, and it employed legends of apostolic authorship here as elsewhere in order to cover up its ignorance. Neither apostolic authorship nor apostolic content can be affirmed for it, despite the efforts of apologetics to this very day. The criterion of apostolicity contradicts the Johannine insight that earthly tradition as such is always incapable of legitimating the Christian witness. For John, all earthly tradition has a right to exist only if it serves the voice of Jesus, and it must be examined accordingly. If historically the Gospel reflects that development which led from the enthusiasts of Corinth and of II Tim. 2.18 to Christian gnosticism, then its acceptance into the Church's canon took place through man's error and God's providence. Against all its own intentions, and misled by the picture of Jesus as God walking on the face of the earth, the Church assigned to the apostles the voice of those whom it otherwise ignored and one generation later condemned as heretics.[1] The label 'heavenly' was attached to the Gospel which

---

[1] The above formulation is intentionally open to that kind of criticism which was made on the occasion of the republication of Walter Bauer's book, *Rechtgläubigkeit und Ketzerei im ältesten Christentum*. H. D. Altendorf's criticisms of Bauer and his successors, including myself, in his review in *ThLZ* (see Bibliography) are fundamental, striking and typical. I agree that it is indeed lamentable if by our doing 'the primitive Christian history threatens to dissolve into some sort of wild mish-mash of conflicting and mutually exclusive theological trends'. The criticism by the church historian of my at times disagreeable and always contestable results is well known to me, and I am even more aware of the uneasiness about my exegetical methodology. But are Altendorf and almost all the other opponents of Bauer's basic approach aware of the difficult situation in which the New Testament exegete, in distinction from other exegetes and historians, finds himself? Our work is carried out within a field of 657 pages of Nestle text which represents the fragment of a history of almost one hundred years. Eighteen hundred years of exegesis have investigated each line and each syllable from all possible perspectives, reading it backwards and forwards, turning it upside down, comparing it and raising one question after another. It is easy for outsiders to ridicule us, that we think we can hear the grass grow and the bedbugs cough. But what else should we try to do in the light of the situation with which we are confronted? It is easy to declare that 'a truly historical understanding cannot be gained in this manner'. If only it were clear what is meant by a 'truly historical understanding'! The historian who has a bird's-eye view of two thousand years of history will, even if he analyses individual texts, be able to see other perspectives, in contrast to the historian who crawls on his belly from molehill to molehill investigating the tiniest detail. The former sees as continuous what for the latter dissolves into a 'wild mish-mash'. Furthermore, the historian with the bird's-eye view is also confronted not only by the spirit in history, but also by every-day existence, which is usually more or less confusing and contradictory. Finally, for us who have learned from Bauer and Bultmann to be told by someone within the academic community that earlier exegetes of the New Testament had a closer relationship to the Church than we seem to have is a bit much! We spent half a lifetime in the pastorate and were formed by it. Again, we may be permitted to ask, which Church is actually meant? We ourselves have experienced to our sorrow 'the wild mish-mash' in the Church and we are therefore aware of ecclesiastical mythology and the legends which continue to grow exuberantly even since 1945. On the basis of our experiences within the Church, we as exegetes tend toward criticism of the tradition. Can we not postulate at least as a possible working hypothesis that the every-day life of primitive Christianity was determined by similar realities which also produced a 'wild mish-mash'? We do not operate completely without practical experience, even if some no longer remember and others do not want to know.

could no longer be located in time and space. The Church could no longer localize what had originated apart from or had run against the current of the broad stream which led to early Catholicism. However, the reception of the Fourth Gospel into the canon is but the most lucid and most significant example of the integration of originally opposing ideas and traditions into the ecclesiastical tradition. Pauline terminology and impulses had already taken up catchwords of his opponents. Later Hellenistic enthusiasts furnished material and points of argumentation for the opposing party, as can be concluded from the deutero-Pauline epistles and especially from the Letter of Jude. Early Catholicism as well as the canon did not originate without the influence of those trends which, since the end of the first century, were already considered by many as being heretical and thus were rejected.

With this we encounter the theological problem of the canon of the New Testament. It exists only as a diverse entity with many theological contradictions in which the complicated history of primitive Christianity is reflected. By affirming the canon we also acknowledge its divergent trends and even its contradictions. This cannot, however, imply that everything in it must be regarded as having equal validity or else be harmonized into a normative theology in which the divergencies are levelled off. While we have little right to reduce the canon within the Old or New Testament, because of its inner differences and divergences we are continually compelled to engage in new interpretations, decisions born out of our own hearing of the texts. The authority of the canon is never greater than the authority of the Gospel which should be heard from it.

Which authority, then, does belong to the Gospel of John? The inclusion of this book in the canon does not answer this question once and for all, especially since the Fourth Gospel itself has no conception of closed revelation, but rather advocates, even against itself, the ongoing operation of the Spirit's witness.[2] From the historical viewpoint, the Church committed an error when it declared the Gospel to be orthodox. Was this, from a theological viewpoint, a fortunate error? We cannot give an answer without first knowing what 'Gospel' means. But, on the other hand, the hermeneutical circle does not tell us about that. We rather have to hear the Gospel afresh, again by listening to John. Of course, this does not mean that leaping from one position to another, we could always postpone a decision about

---

[2] Gaugler, *op. cit.*, p. 193.

the meaning of the Gospel and therefore avoid all dogmatic statements. There is not only the threat of dogmatic security, but also the opposite threat, of a theological existence which is delivered up to the impulses and whims of the moment, no longer knowing anything except what can just as well be found outside the canon. *That* someone preaches is meaningful only when he knows to some extent *what* he must preach and what he may not preach. The fear of dogmatism misled modern Protestantism into the tyranny of arbitrary interpretations, and this threat is still greater today, in spite of all attempts at theological repristination, than the threat from the dogma which is not merely the result of blind assent and the sacrifice of the intellect. Many sacrifices are offered to folly today on many altars by those who are in agreement on only one point, namely, that one altar, the altar of dogma, must be abolished at all costs. Certainly faith and interpretation never exist otherwise than in human entanglement and disorder. This is just as true for those who receive the truth from a fixed dogmatic system as for those who are misled into becoming theological vagabonds through the adventure of exegesis. In the first case as well as in the second superstition is celebrating its triumphs. Much would have been won if we became aware of the dilemma and saw ourselves set in a twofold struggle. At least the struggle against two opponents is typical for the majority of New Testament writings, including our Gospel. John looks both backwards and forwards,[3] and he proclaims his message as much in dogmatic polemical form as in prophetic adaption of originally enthusiastic traditions. As an historical phenomenon, the Fourth Gospel also stands in the twilight and is subjected to human entanglement from which theological existence cannot remove itself. Is the naïve docetism into which it slipped more harmless than the sacramental institution from which it disengaged itself? Did our Gospel at least know the way of answering questions such as these, when it demanded that we must continually surrender ourselves anew to the Word of Jesus, when it evaluated every church in the light of the one question, do we know Jesus?

Here our final problem arises. John 17 certainly does not contain the words of the earthly Jesus, who was so thoroughly undocetic. The question arises: What is the relationship between the exalted Christ who is proclaimed here and the earthly Jesus? Can the Johannine claim be defended that here the last, the ultimate testament of Jesus is

[3] Gaugler, *op. cit.*, p. 41.

being heard? The answer to this question depends on who Jesus is for us and whether he and he alone does lead us to the Father. It is precisely John's fascinating and dangerous theology that calls us into our creatureliness through his christological proclamation. In doing so, does he not also actually show us the one final testament of the earthly Jesus and his glory?

BIBLIOGRAPHY

T. ARVEDSON, *Das Mysterium Christ: Eine Studie zu Mt. 11.25–30* (Acta Seminarii Neotestamentici Upsaliensis 7), 1937.

H. D. ALTENDORF, Review in *ThLZ* 91 (1966), cols. 192ff., of Walter Bauer, *Rechtgläubigkeit und Ketzerei im ältesten Christentum*, q.v.

C. K. BARRETT, *The Gospel according to St John: An Introduction with Commentary and Notes on the Greek Text* (London: 1955).

W. BAUER, *Das Johannesevangelium* (HzNT 6), 3rd ed., 1933.
Rechtgläubigkeit und Ketzerei im ältesten Christentum, 2nd ed. with supplement by G. Strecker (Tübingen: 1964); ET, ed. R. Kraft and G. Krodel (Philadelphia: 1969).

F. C. BAUR, *Kritische Untersuchungen über die kanonischen Evangelien, ihr Verhältnis zueinander, ihren Charakter und Ursprung* (Tübingen: 1847).

W. BOUSSET, *Kyrios Christos: Geschichte des Christusglaubens von den Anfängen des Christentums bis Irenaeus* (FRLANT, NF 4, 2nd ed., 1921).

R. E. BROWN, *The Gospel according to St John*, Vol. I (chs. 1–12): Introduction, Translation and Notes (The Anchor Bible 29, New York: 1966).

R. BULTMANN, *Das Evangelium des Johannes* (KeK 2, 10th ed., 1941) (cited as *Evangelium*).
Theologie des Neuen Testaments, 5th ed. (Tübingen: 1965) (cited as *Theologie*); ET of 1st ed. by K. Grobel: *Theology of the New Testament* (New York and London: Vol. I, 1951; Vol. II, 1955).

O. CULLMANN, *Urchristentum und Gottesdienst*, 2nd ed. (Zürich: 1950); ET by A. S. Todd and J. B. Torrance: *Early Christian Worship* (SBT 10, 1953).

N. A. DAHL, 'The Johannine Church and History', *Current Issues in New Testament Interpretation: Essays in Honor of Otto Piper*, ed. W. Klassen and G. F. Snyder (New York and London: 1962), pp. 124–42.

C. H. DODD, *The Interpretation of the Fourth Gospel* (Cambridge: 1955) (cited as *Interpretation*).
Historical Tradition in the Fourth Gospel (Cambridge: 1963) (cited as *Tradition*).

J. DUPONT, *Essais sur la Christologie de Saint Jean* (Bruges: 1951).

D. FAULHABER, *Das Johannesevangelium und die Kirche* (Dissertation, University of Heidelberg: 1935; also Kassel: 1938).

E. GAUGLER, 'Die Bedeutung der Kirche in den johanneischen Schriften', *Internationale kirchliche Zeitschrift* 14 (Bern: 1924), pp. 97–117 and 181–219; ibid., 15 (1925), pp. 27–42.

J. GRILL, *Untersuchungen über die Entstehung des 4. Evangeliums* (Vol. I, Tübingen and Leipzig: 1902; Vol. II, Tübingen: 1923).

E. HAENCHEN, 'Der Vater, der mich gesandt hat', *NTS* 9 (1962–3), pp. 208–16.

80 BIBLIOGRAPHY

H. HEGERMANN, *Die Vorstellung vom Schöpfungsmittler im hellenistischen Judentum und Urchristentum* (TU 82, 1961).

W. HEITMÜLLER, *Das Johannesevangelium* (Die Schriften des Neuen Testaments 4, ed. J. Weiss), 3rd. ed. (Göttingen: 1918).

E. HIRSCH, *Das vierte Evangelium in seiner ursprünglichen Gestalt verdeutscht und erklärt* (Tübingen: 1936).

E. C. HOSKYNS, *The Fourth Gospel*, ed. F. N. Davey, 2nd ed. (London: 1947).

J. JEREMIAS, *Die Abendsmahlworte Jesu*, 3rd ed. (Göttingen: 1960); ET with the author's revisions to 1964 by N. Perrin: *The Eucharistic Words of Jesus* (London and New York: 1966).

E. KÄSEMANN, 'Aufbau und Anliegen des johanneischen Prologs', *Libertas Christiana: Festschrift für F. Delekat* (Munich: 1957), pp. 75–99; reprinted in *Exegetische Versuche und Besinnungen*, Vol. II (Göttingen: 1964), pp. 155–80. References are to the latter.

H. KÖSTER, 'Geschichte und Kultus im Johannesevangelium und bei Ignatius von Antiochen', *ZThK* 54 (1957), pp. 56–69; ET by A. Bellinzoni: 'History and Cult in the Gospel of John and in Ignatius of Antioch', *JThC* I (vol. entitled *The Bultmann School of Biblical Interpretation: New Directions*), ed. R. W. Funk (1965), pp. 111–23.

A. KRAGERUD, *Der Lieblingsjünger im Johannesevangelium: Ein exegetischer Versuch* (Oslo and Hamburg: 1959).

E. LOHSE, 'Wort und Sakrament im Johannesevangelium', *NTS* 7 (1960–1), pp. 110–25.

A. LOISY, *Le quatrième Évangile*, 2nd ed. (Paris: 1921).

T. W. MANSON, *On Paul and John* (SBT 38, 1963).

C. MAURER, *Ignatius und das Johannesevangelium* (Abhandlungen zur Theologie Alten und Neuen Testaments 18, Zürich: 1949).

O. MICHEL, 'Das Gebet des scheidenden Erlösers', *ZsystTh* 18 (1941), pp. 521–34.

F. MUSSNER, 'Die johanneischen Parakletsprüche und die apostolische Tradition', *BZ*, NF 5 (1961), pp. 56–70.

H. ODEBERG, *The Fourth Gospel: Interpreted in its Relation to the Contemporaneous Religious Currents in Palestine and the Hellenistic-Oriental World* (Uppsala: 1929).

F. OVERBECK, *Das Johannesevangelium: Studien zur Kritik seiner Erforschung*, ed. A. Bernoulli (Tübingen: 1911).

A. SCHLATTER, *Der Evangelist Johannes: Wie er spricht, denkt und glaubt. Ein Kommentar zum vierten Evangelium*, 2nd ed. (Stuttgart: 1948).

R. SCHNACKENBURG, *Das Johannesevangelium: I. Teil: Einleitung und Kommentar zu Kap. 1–4* (Herders theologischer Kommentar zum Neuen Testament 4, Freiburg and New York: 1965).
Die Kirche im Neuen Testament: Ihre Wirklichkeit und theologische Deutung, ihr Wesen und Geheimnis (Quaestiones Disputatae 14, Freiburg and New York: 1961); ET by W. J. O'Hara: *The Church in the New Testament* (New York: 1965).
'Der Menschensohn im Johannesevangelium', *NTS* 11 (1964–5), pp. 123–37.

S. Schulz, *Untersuchungen zur Menschensohn-Christologie im Johannesevangelium: Zugleich ein Beitrag zur Methodengeschichte der Auslegung des 4. Evangeliums* (Göttingen: 1957).

E. Schweizer, 'Der Kirchenbegriff im Evangelium und den Briefen des Johannes', *Studia Evangelica: Papers Presented to the International Congress on 'The Four Gospels in 1957' held at Christ Church, Oxford, in 1957* (TU 73, 1959), pp. 363–81; also in: E. Schweizer, *Neotestamentica* (Zürich and Stuttgart: 1963), pp. 254–71; ET in *New Testament Essays: Studies in Memory of T. W. Manson*, ed. A. J. B. Higgins (Manchester: 1959), pp. 230–45.

E. Stauffer, *Die Theologie des Neuen Testaments*, 4th ed. (Stuttgart: 1948); ET by J. Marsh: *New Testament Theology* (London and New York: 1955).

H. Strathmann, *Das Evangelium nach Johannes* (NTD 4), 7th ed.; 2nd ed. of the new revision (1954).

W. Thüsing, *Die Erhöhung und Verherrlichung Jesu im Johannesevangelium* (Neutestamentliche Abhandlungen 21, Münster, 1960).

R. Walker, 'Jüngerwort und Herrenwort', *ZNW* 57 (1966), pp. 49–54.

J. Wellhausen, *Das Evangelium Johannis* (Berlin: 1908).

G. P. Wetter, *Der Sohn Gottes: Eine Untersuchung über den Charakter und die Tendenz des Johannesevangeliums* (FRLANT, NF 9, 1916).

W. Wilckens, *Die Entstehungsgeschichte des vierten Evangeliums* (Zürich: 1958).

INDEX OF SUBJECTS

INDEX OF MODERN AUTHORS

INDEX OF BIBLICAL REFERENCES